SOMETHING WICKED

Books by Lisa Jackson

Stand-Alones

SEE HOW SHE DIES
FINAL SCREAM
RUNNING SCARED
WHISPERS
TWICE KISSED
UNSPOKEN
DEEP FREEZE
FATAL BURN
MOST LIKELY TO DIE
WICKED GAME
WICKED LIES
SOMETHING WICKED
WITHOUT MERCY
YOU DON'T WANT TO KNOW

Anthony Paterno/ Cahill Family Novels

IF SHE ONLY KNEW
ALMOST DEAD

Rick Bentz/Reuben Montoya Novels

HOT BLOODED
COLD BLOODED
SHIVER
ABSOLUTE FEAR
LOST SOULS
MALICE
DEVIOUS

Pierce Reed/Nikki Gillette Novels

THE NIGHT BEFORE
THE MORNING AFTER
TELL ME

Selena Alvarez/Regan Pescoli Novels

LEFT TO DIE
CHOSEN TO DIE
BORN TO DIE
AFRAID TO DIE
READY TO DIE

Books by Nancy Bush

CANDY APPLE RED
ELECTRIC BLUE
ULTRAVIOLET
WICKED GAME
WICKED LIES
SOMETHING WICKED
UNSEEN
BLIND SPOT
HUSH
NOWHERE TO RUN
NOWHERE TO HIDE
NOWHERE SAFE

Published by Kensington Publishing Corporation

LISA JACKSON

Something Wicked

NANCY BUSH

KENSINGTON BOOKS
www.kensingtonbooks.com

KENSINGTON BOOKS are published by

Kensington Publishing Corp.
119 West 40th Street
New York, NY 10018

All Kensington titles, imprints, and distributed lines are available at special quantity discounts for bulk purchases for sales promotion, premiums, fundraising, educational, or institutional use.

Special book excerpts or customized printings can also be created to fit specific needs. For details, write or phone the office of the Kensington Special Sales Manager: Attn. Special Sales Department. Kensington Publishing Corp., 119 West 40th Street, New York, NY 10018. Phone: 1-800-221-2647.

Kensington and the K logo Reg. U.S. Pat. & TM Off.

Library of Congress Card Catalogue Number: 2012954297

ISBN-13: 978-0-7582-8750-2
ISBN-10: 0-7582-8750-X

First Printing: February 2013

10 9 8 7 6 5 4 3 2 1

Printed in the United States of America

SOMETHING WICKED

PROLOGUE

September . . .

She'd made such a horrible mess of things. . . .

Catherine rode in Earl's motorboat to Echo Island, her mouth set in a grim line. With all her good intentions in trying to save her charges from heartache, ridicule, and pain, she had only made things worse. She'd been so relieved after that monster Justice's death that she'd relaxed her hold on the gates of Siren Song, briefly, but when her lack of vigilance had started leading to anarchy, she'd clamped down again. Now, though everything was locked up tight, the work and rules restored, there was a restlessness within the girls that was not to be denied. It simmered below the surface, and Catherine knew the order she had preached, had tried desperately to instill, was forever broken. Ravinia was chomping at the bit to leave; the others would follow.

It was to be expected, she supposed. They'd been sheltered from the real world so long that when they'd realized how their sisters had melded into society—Rebecca with her husband and little girl, and then Lorelei, saved by that reporter Harrison Frost—the remaining sisters behind the gates of Siren Song had been swept away by the fantasy and romance of it all. And that they knew Harrison had risked his life for Lorelei? Well, it was the stuff fairy tales were made of.

As Earl guided the boat to the small dock, here on Mary's island of exile, her "Elba" she'd once called it, Catherine wondered what she would say to her sister, how she would explain her change of heart. After all, her charges weren't even her own issue. Mary had given birth to each and every one of them, though there had been a long line of fathers, studs whom Mary had used and tossed aside. Catherine was their guardian, yes, but still only their aunt.

Could she now admit that she'd been wrong? That perhaps Mary should return to Siren Song and, as far as anyone knew, from the grave? Of course that wouldn't work. There were laws about those kinds of things . . . laws about faking someone's death, she supposed.

She would have to think of something else.

The sound of the sea was louder here, the tides splashing around the rocks and shoals. Mary had always said she'd found it comforting.

Catherine wondered.

But if she was happy, so be it. Of course, Mary had always been delusional. . . . It ran in their family. . . .

"I shouldn't be too long," she told Earl as he cut the engine and tied up. "Half an hour, maybe."

The handyman nodded. "I'll wait. Got my pole."

With his help, she climbed onto the dock and left him opening his cooler of bait. Holding her skirt so that the hem of her dress wouldn't skim the dirt and bird excrement on the old boards, she bustled along the sandy, overgrown path that wound a hundred feet to Mary's home. The cottage was little more than a one-room cabin with a sleeping area, even more austere and cut off from the world than Siren Song. It was no wonder no one had ever found her here. . . . But then Catherine knew from her own experience that even the most bizarre circumstances did exist. . . . How else to explain all the gifts the girls had received?

There were rumors in Deception Bay, of course, of a hermit who lived on the island. An old hag that ran sightseers off, but if anyone had made the connection between the recluse and Mary Rutledge Beeman, Catherine didn't know about it.

She swatted at a fly as she walked, the sun hot against her face, beads of sweat forming on her brow. It was late summer now, going on September, one of the few times of the year you could actually trust to not have your boat dashed against the forbidding rocks that surrounded Echo.

A *fly?* she thought. *Out here?*

Odd.

Then again, what wasn't odd these days? Everything about her sister had been "out of sync," "a little off," or "odd" since her birth. Upon her exile, the cover story was that Mary had fallen to her death on one of her solitary walks, though another version suggested she'd died from a miscarriage, which was somewhat closer to the truth. Neither, however, was accurate, and the solitary figure sometimes seen on Echo Island, according to the rumors Catherine made sure were spread, was believed to be the bereaved, reclusive wife of one of the lighthouse caretakers from nearby Whittier Island who had died from misery after the death of her only child. In truth, no one really paid attention anymore. Everyone today was all caught up in their own lives, too interested in themselves or celebrities or television reality shows to do more than gossip about the weird old lady of Echo Island.

Catherine hurried on. Squinting against a lowering sun, she noticed that Mary's garden, usually so perfect, was untended. Beach grass had taken over, and the tea roses were leggy, the blooms dried and dying. "Mary?" she called as she walked toward the front door and saw the boxes of supplies left on the porch. The cardboard was sun bleached, the fruit and vegetables had gone bad, and the stink of rotting meat was overpowering. And there were more flies.

What the devil?

"Mary!" she called again and pushed on the door. How long had it been since she'd been here?

It was unlatched, and from within the stench was worse. It hit Catherine with the force of a malodorous tidal wave. The buzzing of swarming flies competed with the sound of the surf. They swept outward from the door of the sleeping area like a black tide. Catherine's stomach revolted as she pressed forward, ever more concerned, her eyes growing accustomed to the darkened interior.

Pulse rising, she forced herself to enter the bedroom. On the bed lay a corpse.

What was left of her sister was little more than dried, rotting flesh and exposed bones. Mary's face was unrecognizable, her eyes gone, two dark exposed sockets where those beautiful blue orbs had once been. Her hair was brittle, long tufts jutting from a skull of darkened, dried skin. Her lips had rotted away, exposing her teeth in a ghoulish, wicked grin. Her cheeks were only bone.

"No . . . oh, dear Lord . . ." Revulsion squeezed Catherine's stomach as she tried to process the horrid sight.

The hilt of a knife rose from Mary's chest. The skeletal fingers of her right hand surrounded it, as if she'd tried to yank the blade out and failed. Hanks of old flesh hung from her fingers and arm.

A scream boiled to the heavens. A wild shriek of pure fear.

It took Catherine a moment to realize it came from her own throat.

"Holy mother of God," she whispered, retching, backing away.

But the vision of Mary was burned in her brain as she scrambled backward, nearly tripping over her own skirts. Trying not to vomit, she turned blindly and ran for the door.

What in God's good name had happened to her sister?

This has nothing to do with God!

Running out the door, she half tripped, half fell down the steps and the path toward the boat, another scream churning upward from within her soul. The vision of her sister's rotting corpse blinded her to the ocean and this rocky shelf of an island. *Mary,* she thought on a choked sob. *Mary . . .*

She felt someone reach for her and flailed at them in terror.

"Stop, stop!" she wanted to shriek, but her body shuddered with fear and her cries now were no more than whimpers.

"Miss Catherine . . ."

She peered around herself but couldn't see for her sudden, all-encompassing blindness.

"Miss Catherine . . ."

Earl. Of course, it was Earl . . . who'd rowed her to Echo Island with supplies for Mary. Only, Mary was dead. Stabbed through the heart.

"Earl?" she whispered feebly.

"Right this way," he told her soothingly, and his hands grasped her by the elbows.

She collapsed into Earl's arms and quavered, "Take me back. Please . . . take me back. . . ."

"What did you behold?" he asked as he helped her into the boat.

Death, she thought, a chill as cold as the deep settling into her soul.

*   *   *

Now the memory faded away, and Catherine opened her eyes in the dark to find herself in her own room at Siren Song. Her vision had returned from that momentary blindness, but currently all she could see was a faint strip of light slipping in through the small window above her bed. Lifting her head, she realized she was alone. No Earl . . . no corpse of her sister. The dream was fading. With trembling fingers, she lit the oil lamp on the nightstand beside her bed.

It had been the same each night this week, ever since she'd returned from Echo Island. The memory of what she'd seen and her own reaction to it was caught in a recess of her brain, and her subconscious pulled it out every time she went to bed.

"Earl?" she said now, unable to stop herself, even though she knew there was no one there. She peered anxiously into the dim corners of the room. She had done it each time she'd woken, and had been met with the same response: nothing.

Of course, he was not there. Earl was the only man allowed on the Siren Song grounds by her own decree, and even he would not be on the second floor and certainly not in her bedroom. She was merely reliving those terrible moments after she'd found her sister. Again.

Awake now, she remembered how her blindness had receded in time for her to see Earl's eyes lift from her shivering form and move back toward the cabin as he rowed with strong arms away from the deadly stony shore. She'd looked back, too, toward her sister's cabin, the only building on Echo Island, the place where she'd exiled her sister, whose mind had rotted long before her earthly body.

What did you behold?

Now Catherine climbed from her bed, her bones feeling as old as time, though she was scarcely fifty-one. Earl, truculent at the best of times, had asked her what she'd beheld. She'd been unable to voice the words. It was beyond belief, but she, who had commanded and ruled her family with iron surety and a belief in the rightness of what she'd done, had been reduced to a quivering mound of flesh on that boat ride back to the mainland. She couldn't tell him that she'd left her ailing sister on that island and that someone—*something*—had driven a knife through her chest and left her to turn to dust.

Grabbing up a shawl, she pulled it over her nightgown and cracked open the door to the second-floor hallway. It was dark as pitch, and she relied on the weakening light from her oil lamp and the rail guiding her hand to move along the upper hall and then down the stairway to the first floor, where the generator supplied power and illumination. In the kitchen she snapped on the overhead light, and the shadows were chased back, revealing a black stove— once wood, now electric—and a long pine trestle table with rows of wooden chairs. They had a refrigerator and a deep porcelain sink, but no automatic dishwasher. The lodge had been designed and re-designed and retrofitted and changed, but when Mary's mind had weakened and her lovers, and children, had grown in numbers, Catherine had been forced to take charge. She'd stopped everything.

What did you behold?

Earl had helped her kidnap Mary years before. He'd seen the need, too, though he said nothing, and when Catherine had asked him to ready the abandoned cabin on Echo Island—a small rock jut-ting from the Pacific, not horribly far out to sea, but treacherous and private and left alone by the superstitious locals—he'd silently nod-ded his agreement. The island was owned by the Rutledge sisters and was rarely visited. The last time a couple of drunken teens had tried to put their boat ashore, the craft had smashed against the rocks and they'd died for their efforts, their bodies floating to the lighthouse on a nearby spit of land that was islanded at high tide. Their parents set up a hue and cry, wanting something to be done, trying to blame everyone and anyone other than their foolish chil-dren, who'd stolen someone's boat and rowed out to try to see the old woman on the island. The sheriff's department sent out a boat, which was subsequently ripped from stem to stern on the sub-merged rocks and nearly caused more deaths. After that Catherine merely received a call, as she was the owner of record. She'd lied, saying that she sometimes stayed at the cabin and the overworked county deputies had given up any further attempts to reach the is-land. Earl, an accomplished seaman, would not go to Echo unless the weather could be counted on, and even then the crossing could be dicey. The summer months were the best, but there was really only one place to dock safely and you still had to know how to approach it.

Earl had spent the better part of the year before Mary's incarcera-tion preparing the cabin, getting to the island whenever he could. Both he and Catherine had been much younger then, and when the time came, they merely gave Mary a mixture of narcotic herbs to lull her to sleep. When her latest lover finally roused himself and realized he couldn't wake her, he'd stumbled from Siren Song, blinking in fear. Catherine had locked the gates behind him, the last man. She and Earl had then packed Mary into his truck, and he'd done the rest, while Catherine stayed at the lodge with Mary's children, the girls, who were now women. She'd lied to them, too. Told them Mary had died from a fall and was buried in the graveyard behind Siren Song, their lodge. They were young enough to accept it, and though they'd cried, Mary had always been less of a mother to them than Catherine and they'd accepted Catherine's story without question. They sometimes knelt beside the grave and left flowers for their mother, and every time Catherine's heart gave a little clutch, but no one knew the truth except for Catherine and Earl and, of course, Mary.

But now Mary was dead. Killed. Stabbed through the chest and left lying on her back in her bed, her skeletal hand still around the knife's hilt. Catherine knew the corpse couldn't have remained in that position. Someone had staged her. Had murdered her, then had come back at least once and molded her hand around that knife. Catherine had been too terrified to look closely the day she discovered Mary. She had screamed and thrashed her way outside—her mind trying to shut out the sight—and hadn't been back since. But she knew the staging had been purposely done, and she suspected it was a message meant for her . . . or maybe all of them at Siren Song. A message to Mary's children, the women of Siren Song, the women with the "gifts."

Who? Why?

She shivered, wondering if she knew, but as her thoughts turned in that direction, she forced them back to the furthest recesses of her mind. *No. No . . .*

Sitting at the table, she watched the sun rise through the east window. It had been the better part of a week since she'd found the body. Today she would tell Earl what she'd beheld. And she would ask him to bring Mary back to Siren Song, and they would bury her somewhere in the graveyard behind the lodge, not in the grave with her name on it, unfortunately, as that one was already filled with another's body.

CHAPTER 1

November . . .

M iddle of the day, and it was as gloomy as night. Rain spattered Detective Savannah Dunbar's windshield as her vehicle bumped along the cracked and broken drive, and she worried that the precipitation might turn from a misting swirl to an out-and-out deluge of renowned Oregon rain. She was wearing sneakers with her black pants and blouse. Not exactly regulation, but in her condition she didn't much care.

She had caught the call that had come into the Tillamook County Sheriff's Department, and had said she would check out the abandoned property that was reported to have evidence of squatters. She was driving back from lunch, and Bankruptcy Bluff—well, Bancroft Bluff, though anyone who knew the tale of the doomed homes slowly sliding off the dune into the Pacific referred to the debacle by its nickname—was right on her way.

Now she pulled up cautiously in front of one of the mammoth homes. It sat well back from the cliff, but if Mother Nature had her way, the house might eventually become an abandoned ruin as well. The lawsuits over this construction folly were ongoing and vicious. All that was needed was for some vagrant to either burn the place down or get in some accident where he was injured or killed.

Her cell phone buzzed. She picked it up and glanced down at its face as she was opening her door. Clausen. Her unofficial partner at the moment. Grimacing, knowing what she would hear, she answered cautiously, "Hey, there."

"Savannah, what the goddamn hell? Don't you dare go into that building alone! *You* shouldn't be there."

She found herself irked beyond measure. They all treated her like she was porcelain these days. "Then get your ass down here, Fred," she snapped.

"I'm on my way. Don't go in there!"

"I'll wait," she said, punching the off button on her phone.

Over the past six months she'd changed from the quiet newbie on the force to the impatient, growling pregnant woman with no sense of humor. Well, too damn bad. Yes, pregnancy had transformed her, and yes, everyone in the department wanted to baby and coddle her, and yes, there was a part of her that appreciated it, but damn it all . . . she could still make her own choices. Being knocked up hadn't addled her brain.

Much.

She grimaced as she stepped outside, feeling the cold drops fall on her head. She quickly pulled up the hood of her jacket before the precipitation could flatten her hair to her scalp. The reasons for agreeing to become her sister's surrogate were actually getting a little harder to remember. Kristina had begged, begged, begged her to help her have a baby, as she and her husband, Hale, were unable to conceive. Savannah had reluctantly agreed, even going so far as to volunteer to be a surrogate. In actual fact it was a gestational pregnancy: the embryo created by Kristina's egg and Hale's sperm had been implanted into Savannah's womb. She was merely the vessel to give them their heart's desire, except . . . recently she'd wondered if her sister was really feeling the same all-consuming need to be a mother. She'd been so gung ho, almost desperate, in the beginning, but as her due date approached, Savannah had sensed a weakening in Kristina's ardor to join the ranks of motherhood. Troubling, especially when Hale St. Cloud's enthusiasm had always been a little hard for Savannah to read. But then Hale was part Bancroft, as in Bancroft Bluff, and he was involved in the family real estate business with his grandfather, Declan Bancroft, an irascible entrepreneur who'd begun Bancroft Development decades before. Though Savvy had met Declan only a handful of times, it was clear he was a real piece of work, and she figured that Hale was probably cut from the same cloth.

But their baby boy was on his way, and they both were going to have to step up and *soon*. Savannah kept telling herself that once the baby was here, their maternal and paternal instincts would kick in. They all, herself included, were just feeling the predelivery jitters.

Expelling her breath, she looked toward the largest house in this cul-de-sac cluster. The Donatellas'. Right on the cliff's edge and being eroded underneath. She knew it well, as it had been the scene of a double homicide earlier in the year, which was still under investigation. The case had languished for months with no new information.

Savannah walked a few steps closer to the behemoth of a house, her eyes taking in the red tile roof and the wrought-iron filigree of the Spanish Colonial. It was too dangerous to enter, but she wasn't in need of going inside, as it wasn't the one with the reported vagrants. That house was coming up on her right—a Northwest contemporary—and, though it was still standing on firm ground, given enough time, it looked to be in definite peril of crashing down to the beach far below. She could smell smoke in the damp air. The nut bag inside had built himself or herself a fire.

She hoped to God it was in one of the fireplaces.

Waiting impatiently for Clausen, she let her gaze fall to her own wide stomach, which was already straining her jacket's buttons. Man, she was going to be glad to be herself again. This "looking like a beached whale" thing was highly overrated, no matter what anyone said.

Five minutes later Clausen pulled into the drive in a department-issued black Jeep with TILLAMOOK COUNTY SHERIFF'S DEPARTMENT slashed across it in italicized, bold yellow letters. Someone had dubbed the officers bumblebees, which was maybe better than pigs, but the jury was still out on that.

Clausen, midfifties, with short gray hair and a roundish body, which he was constantly trying to keep from becoming full-on fat, stalked up to her hatless, water coalescing in his hair. "Stay out here," he ordered.

"Bite me," she returned.

"Jesus, Dunbar. Pregnancy has made you unreasonable."

"Cranky, yes, but I'm the voice of reason."

He shot her a look that could have meant anything and then headed to the front door and turned the knob. "Locked," he said.

"Must be a way in."

"Stay here. I'll go around the back."

She bit back what she wanted to say about that and let him commandeer the investigation as he was her senior and felt he was just plain better than she was, anyway. Tamping down her annoyance, she stepped onto the porch and kept her eyes on the front door, flanked by two shuttered windows. The owners of this house had all but abandoned it, as had most of those who owned property here, and she could see the first signs of neglect: blistering paint on the siding, a yard where dandelions and crabgrass were edging out the lawn, a weathered welcome sign that listed to one side.

Her cell phone *blooped*, meaning someone had sent her a text, and she glanced down at her pocket, debating about checking it.

Suddenly the front lock clicked loudly, and the door swung inward. Savannah placed her hand on the butt of her gun, which was sticking up from her hip holster. A man came staggering through, his eyes wild, his breathing rapid. He stopped short upon seeing Savannah. His hair was chin length, matted and separated, and his beard was an uneven mess of brown and gray. If he'd changed his clothes in this decade, she would have been surprised. His denim jeans were more brown than blue, and his shirt was also brown, though she suspected it hadn't started out that color. She hoped to hell it was from dirt.

"Ohhh . . ." he said, his eyes traveling down to her girth. He staggered forward, and she stepped back, her hand yanking out the gun.

"Don't move," she ordered fiercely, but his hands reached out and his palms spread over her belly, even while she held up her gun.

"A baby," he said, his mouth showing a gap-toothed smile.

Her barrel was pointed at his chin, but he didn't seem to notice. She hesitated, her heart pounding, and then Clausen shot through the door behind him, saw he was right in front of her, grabbed the guy by his collar, and yanked him backward, hard.

"Police! Get down on the ground!" he ordered. His own gun had jumped into his hand.

"Wait, wait," Savannah warned.

"Down on the ground!"

"No, no! It's okay. It's okay. Fred!" she yelled as Clausen threw the guy onto the porch face-first. "He didn't do anything. Really. I'm okay. He didn't do anything!"

Clausen quickly zip-tied his hands behind his back, and when the man didn't resist, he helped him to his feet.

There was a red scrape on his cheek, but the man murmured, "Unto us a child is born," smiling beatifically, his eyes closed as he rocked from side to side. "The baby Jesus come to save us all."

"Are you all right?" Clausen demanded of Savannah, never taking his gaze from the man.

"I'm fine. He didn't hurt me. I think he was . . . congratulating me."

Clausen's eyes narrowed on the bedraggled man as he continued to mutter and chant. "He for real?"

"Maybe. I don't know."

"What's your name?" Clausen asked him loudly. The man kept swaying and murmured something that sounded like a song. "You're trespassing. Broke a window in the back. That's breaking and entering, you understand? Sir? What's he saying?" Clausen demanded, throwing a quick glare at Savannah.

"I think it's 'Jesus loves me! This I know.'"

The man suddenly opened his eyes and gasped, his gaze turning to Savannah. "You're having a boy! Is he the savior? Are you Mary?"

"She's not even the mother," Clausen growled, snapping a pair of cuffs on the nut job's thin wrists. "C'mon, pal. Let's get you outta here. Lucky you didn't burn the place down." To Savannah, he said, "He had the fireplace crammed with trash and driftwood. It was spilling over the hearth and onto the carpet."

Clausen marched him to his Jeep, but the guy kept twisting around, trying to see Savannah.

"You are his mother," he said over his shoulder. "You are!"

There was no way she could explain to him that technically, no, she wasn't. She walked back to her Ford Escape, the vehicle she'd traded in her Jeep for earlier in her pregnancy. There were only so many black and yellow department vehicles available, thank God; it was the only good thing about the budget cuts plaguing the state and counties. As she climbed inside, she felt Kristina and Hale's boy kick one insistent foot under her right ribs. He had gone head down early and had been bicycling merrily away for the past few weeks. She laid her hand on the spot and smiled. A moment later she reminded herself that he wasn't hers. Her smile dropped, and she put both hands on the wheel and drove away from Bancroft Bluff.

She arrived at the station a couple of minutes behind Clausen and the vagrant. They both pulled into the back lot and headed toward the rear door.

"His name's Mickey," Clausen told her as she let him lead the suspect in ahead of her.

"Last name?" Savannah asked.

"Haven't got that far yet."

She watched them head down the department's back hall, and as they turned the corner that led to the holding cells beyond, Mickey was in full voice, singing, "Cuz the Bible tells me so!"

There was something eerie about his obsession, and Savannah tried to shake off the feeling as she glanced straight ahead across the wide room, which ran north/south and offered a full-line view from rear door to front. To her left was the back hall where Clausen had just taken Mickey, a deceptively short walk to the warren of offices and holding cells that took up the western side of the building.

"Who was that?" May Johnson, the dour officer who manned the department's front desk, asked from across the room. It was damn near impossible to scare a smile out of the woman, though she liked Savannah well enough.

"Mickey," Savannah said, her eye turning to the puddle of water growing beneath her own feet from the rivulets of water falling off her jacket.

"Getting nasty out there," Johnson observed, frowning as she glanced out the front windows.

"Yep." The misting rain was now starting to come down in buckets. As Savannah unbuttoned her jacket and shrugged out of it, she finally noticed the woman seated on the wooden bench in the waiting area, by the front door. She wore a long blue dress with a high collar trimmed in unbleached white lace, and her hands were folded in her lap. Her blond-gray hair was pulled back in a bun, and she had a way of sitting stiffly that spoke of rigidity in nature. Savannah recognized her immediately.

"Miss Rutledge?" Savannah asked. Catherine Rutledge was the mistress of Siren Song. Savannah had already met her a number of times. Walking toward her with an extended hand, she introduced herself again in case Catherine couldn't remember her name. "Savvy Dunbar."

Catherine shook her outstretched hand, but her gaze traveled to her protruding belly, and Savannah inwardly sighed. It wasn't the pregnancy that she minded as much as the explanations that invariably followed.

"Detective," Catherine said, seemingly distracted by the evidence of her pregnancy. The last time they'd met, Savannah had been just entering her second trimester. Now she was close to delivery.

"Are you here to see Detective Stone?" Savvy asked her. The mistress of Siren Song and Langdon Stone had a history—one of those relationships built on basic mistrust and grudging respect—because Lang had been the detective in charge of several investigations that involved Catherine and her brood at the lodge. Lang was about the only man Catherine trusted within the Tillamook County Sheriff's Department, even though she had known Sheriff Sean O'Halloran for years. But circumstances had turned Lang into her current go-to guy whenever there was some new crisis at Siren Song, which happened more often than one would think.

"Well, yes, I came here to talk to him about something, but . . . I've changed my mind."

"Want to leave him a message?" Savvy knew Siren Song did not have a working telephone, and cell phones were way out of Catherine's experience. The woman ruled the place as if they all lived in a distant century.

"Ms. Dunbar . . . Detective . . . I think I would like to talk to you instead."

"Well, okay, my desk is right down the hall." She gestured with her arm. "If you want to—"

"Would it be possible to meet at some other location?" she asked, then turned to throw a stern glance to Johnson, who was unabashedly listening. Johnson, however, was hard to cow, and she just stared back until it was Savannah's turn to frown at her. With a sniff, Johnson slammed her chair back and stalked down the hall toward the break room.

"Want to tell me what this is about?" Savvy asked.

"Could we meet at Siren Song?" Catherine said. "Maybe this afternoon? I . . . um . . . have some troubles. . . ."

"Some troubles," Savannah repeated, wondering what fresh hell this was.

"I prefer not to talk here."

Savannah inwardly assessed the idea. She'd always wanted to enter the locked gates of the lodge and get her own look at what was going on inside. Some of the locals thought Catherine was running a cult, and they'd dubbed it the Colony. Invitations inside were as rare as a black swan, and Catherine never invited men within Siren Song's sacred walls at all. Lang hadn't made it past the gates. Now, Savannah wanted to go, but she was about to start maternity leave, and she had no earthly idea what Catherine expected of her.

"When are you due?" Catherine asked.

"Three weeks? About."

"Ah . . . would this afternoon be convenient?"

"Not really." Savannah needed to talk to Lang about this, and maybe the sheriff, or something. "Tomorrow? Or maybe this evening?" she proposed, seeing the shadow that crossed the older woman's face.

"What time could you be there?" Catherine asked.

"Um . . . seven?" Savvy was already beginning to feel like she was overcommitting herself, but it was too late. Catherine had risen to her feet and was heading for the door, just as Johnson got within earshot.

"I'll see you then, Detective," Catherine said in that regal tone she unconsciously used. She glanced down at Savannah's belly once more and said, "Boys can be a handful."

Johnson returned to her desk as the door closed behind Catherine. "That woman's got more secrets than a magician. Be careful when you go out there. That place is haunted."

"No, it's not."

"Haunted," Johnson repeated sternly.

"She assumed I was having a boy."

"She knew."

Savannah shook her head, then walked down the hall toward her office, making a stop at the restroom first to relieve her bladder. This endgame of pregnancy was no picnic. Many times over the past few months she'd asked herself why she'd volunteered to carry Kristina's baby. She wasn't really all that selfless by nature, and truthfully,

Kristina could be one helluva pain in the ass. She was surprised her sister hadn't contacted her in the past few hours. The past few weeks she'd called and texted and about driven Savannah crazy.

Texted.

Remembering the earlier *bloop* from her phone, Savannah pulled her cell from her pocket. Sure enough, there was a message from Kristina.

Dinner tonight? I need to see you.

Savannah made a sound of annoyance, grumbling as she entered the squad room and found her desk. She was glad to see she was alone, and she texted back.

Got a 7 pm appt. Will call when I'm done.

Her cell phone rang almost the instant Savannah set it down on her desk. *This must be serious,* she thought when she saw it was Kristina. When her sister moved from texts to actually phoning, it was a red-letter day.

"What's up?" Savannah answered.

"I told you!" Kristina blurted, half angry. "We've got to talk. The baby's almost here, and I just feel . . . out of control."

Savannah tamped down her impatience as Baby St. Cloud started another round of bicycling. "Well, get in control," she said. She could hear male voices down the hall, so she knew she wouldn't be alone much longer. "This baby's on his way, and you need to be ready."

"Ready? My God, Savvy. How do you get ready? I don't know how."

"Well, figure it out."

"I'm—I'm—I'm . . ."

"What?"

"I'm—I'm not sure Hale even wants this child," she said in a rush, as if spitting out poison.

"Too damn bad. It's too late for him to change his mind." Savvy had been half expecting this. Things had just gotten so squirrelly these past few weeks, and Savannah was sick to the back teeth of both her sister and Hale waffling about this child. "Pull yourself together," she muttered through her teeth, "and get the hell ready. You're not the first person to have a baby."

"Come over tonight. Please. Get out of whatever you're doing. I need to talk to you. Really."

"I can't cancel." She felt like throwing something, eyeing the paperweight on Lang's desk, which was butted up against hers. It was a clear glass ball shaped like the earth, with the continents etched in frosted glass. Pulling herself back from the brink, she relented. "If I stop by, it won't be till probably nine o'clock."

"That's fine. That's fine," Kristina said with relief.

"Okay . . . whatever."

She clicked off, annoyed. Kristina's inability to have children with her husband, Hale, had tugged on Savvy's heartstrings in the beginning. One drunken night, when she was out with Kristina shortly after their mother's death from a long battle with cancer, and after hearing Kristina ask—beg—for her "help" for months, Savannah had blithely announced that she would carry the St. Cloud baby. She'd wanted to connect with her sister, her only family member left, as their father had died when they were children. Kristina had shrieked with delight, hugged her fiercely, and sent out a Facebook blast within hours, going on and on about her wonderful, giving, generous, *fabuloso* sister.

When Savannah woke up the next day, slightly hung over and full of trepidation—her stomach felt filled with lead—she'd tried to think of a way to back out. But her sister's joy and excitement were hard to squelch, and when Hale St. Cloud, one of those impossibly handsome dark-haired men, with gray eyes that seemed to pierce through all the layers of protection and burn into your soul, asked her, "Are you certain about this? Especially with your demanding job?" he kinda pissed Savannah off, and she declared, "Never been certainer," which made Kristina jump up and hug her fiercely, and the deal was set.

Savannah had thought that she might still have a chance to get out of it, that maybe the procedure just wouldn't take, but nope, one IVF session and *bam,* she was pregnant. Knocked up. With child. Hale's sperm and Kristina's egg had combined in one tenacious little embryo, and suddenly Savannah was in the midst of a gestational pregnancy—the correct term, as it was not a surrogacy, though she used both indiscriminately when explaining her situation to others—and that was all she wrote, folks. Savannah Dunbar was pregnant with Hale and Kristina St. Cloud's child.

Now all Savannah wanted was to deliver a healthy baby to her sister, and soon, and then get back to being Savvy. Whatever problems, second thoughts, or God knew whatever else her sister might be having, didn't matter. Kristina was going to have a baby with Hale, and Savannah was going to give birth to the little guy and become his aunt. Game over.

Pain in the ass, she thought now, not sure whether she meant her sister, her sister's husband, or the situation as a whole.

And now she had to go to the bathroom. Again. Swear to God, once it started, it just wouldn't give up.

Easing herself from her chair, she headed back to the bathroom, trying to remember what it was like to be able to bend forward and tie her sneakers, her footwear choice du jour. Her feet had swelled just enough to make other shoes feel like instruments of torture. Currently she had to sit down and bend her legs in one by one to bring her feet within reach.

When she returned to the squad room, Detective Langdon Stone was at his desk. He threw her a smile and said, "You look uncomfortable."

"I am uncomfortable."

"What the hell were you doing with that vagrant?"

"Mickey," she said a little more loudly as a phone at a nearby desk began to ring over the hum of conversation and the rumble of the furnace.

"You shouldn't have gone there. Start your maternity leave. Please. You're making us all nervous around here."

"Clausen was with me."

"He came later," he corrected. "This isn't just me who feels this way. Sorry if you think we're all misogynistic pigs, but you worry us."

"I'm going to have this baby before you know it. Just don't treat me like that's all I am—a baby incubator."

Lang gave her an "Oh, really?" look. Like Hale St. Cloud, he was handsome in a lean, hard way and had dark hair and white teeth. "How many weeks are left?"

"About three."

"Okay, fine. I'll try. And we're meeting in the conference room in about ten," he said.

"About what?"

"The Donatella homicides. O'Halloran's got something new apparently."

"Really?"

"That's the word."

"I was just at Bankruptcy Bluff," she said, surprised.

"I know." He shrugged.

Savannah and the rest of the department had been working on the Donatella case for long months and were no closer to an arrest than they'd been when the crime was committed. The double homicide of Marcus and Chandra Donatella had taken place at their home on Bancroft Bluff. It was weird that she'd just come from there today, after rousting out Mickey, and now there was new information? Kind of mind-boggling.

But sometimes cases were like that, she reminded herself. Nothing forever, and then things suddenly broke open and started running hot as a fever.

Maybe they were actually going to solve this damn thing.

CHAPTER 2

"Could you put *that* down for one minute?" Declan Bancroft grumbled irritably from the oversize executive desk chair in his home office. He pointed to the cell phone pressed to his grandson's ear.

"I want to catch Russo before he leaves work." Hale St. Cloud stayed on the line, waiting for the Portland manager to answer. "Vledich said we were red tagged, and I want to know who he talked to at the city and why construction was stopped."

"Who's this Vledich?" the old man demanded.

"The foreman," Hale answered, staring through the window of his grandfather's sprawling Bancroft Development home, the grounds of which meandered over several acres along a rocky tor with a spectacular view of Deception Bay. "You know Clark Russo in the Portland office. Vledich works for him."

"Of course I know Russo," Declan said grumpily.

Russo was one of the newer managers employed by Bancroft Development. He had started in the Seaside office and had recently been transferred to Portland at the recommendation of Sylvie Strahan, Hale's right-hand woman. Their Portland manager had quit after the debacle over Bancroft Bluff, and when the opening in Portland popped up, Sylvie suggested Russo, at least for the interim. It had taken a little talking as Russo had been reluctant to leave the area; he'd grown up on the coast.

"But this Vledich I don't know," Declan said, taking a deep breath, as if he was about to launch into a diatribe about being the last to know, a favorite gripe of his, but Hale held up a hand as he left a mes-

sage for Russo, asking the manager to call him. As soon as he was finished, he clicked off, but Declan snorted and waved at his phone.
"What's happened to the world? Yes, yes, it's good to be able to catch
someone at a job site, but all this texting and e-mail and playing with
the phone . . . *ack*." That was his grandfather's favorite sound of disgust: *ack*.

"If I don't hear back from him, I'll send him a text."

"In my day we answered the phone so as not to lose a customer."

Another favorite diatribe, which Hale ignored. There was no
changing his grandfather's mind about the evils of technology, and
he'd wasted enough breath trying to last him a lifetime. That was
why Hale had built his own home north of Deception Bay, closer to
Seaside and the Bancroft Development offices, on a similar rocky
bluff, a little bit removed from his grandfather.

But Declan had made his home in Deception Bay for most of his
life, preferring the sleepy oceanside hamlet to the joint tourist mecca
of Seaside and Cannon Beach. It was pure irony, therefore, that
through his own real estate development, Declan was helping
change the landscape of the town, and Deception Bay had recently
become the new destination for those with disposable income and
wealth. Bancroft Bluff, built south of the bay that Deception Bay was
named after, was supposed to have been the first jewel in the crown
of successive Bancroft luxury home developments around the area,
but the unstable dune had turned that plan to, well, sand. Declan
had pushed for Hale and Kristina to build on the spot, but Hale had
resisted, and in hindsight it was fortuitous that Hale had decided to
build his home closer to the Seaside Bancroft Development offices.

"What are you doing?" Declan demanded, frowning at Hale as his
fingers pressed buttons on his phone.

"Sending that text. I want to know what the city said about the
Lake Chinook project," Hale added as he pressed the button that
sent the message to Russo and Vledich. Bancroft Development had
purchased a section of lake frontage land—three adjoining lots on
Lake Chinook, the two-mile-long lake ten miles south of Portland—
and the older homes and cabins that had been there had already
been demolished, readying the site for new construction. Now the
City of Lake Chinook had determined there was a sewer easement
that ran under the water, and they'd red tagged the job, stopping

construction of the first of the three boathouses that were being erected before the actual houses.

"We get red tagged when we shouldn't, and we're allowed to build on a goddamn dune. I'd like to kill DeWitt!" Declan bit out furiously for about the millionth time. His blue eyes burned with rage at the thought of the engineer who'd green-lighted the Bancroft Bluff project. Hale had just started with the family company when that project was under way, and though he didn't say it, he still remembered that there was an undercurrent of worry about the dune's stability even then. That fear had proved founded, but it was too late. Only the fact that his grandfather had made a boatload of money over the past decades was saving the company now from the pending lawsuits. Bancroft Development had bought most of the condemned properties back, settling the first lawsuits, though now some of the home owners were suing for mental anguish and suffering. Not that the lawsuits had merit, the settlements had precluded that. But it didn't mean it wasn't more bad publicity, and then, just when things had looked to be settling down, the horror of the Donatella murders had occurred right in their own Bancroft Bluff home.

Hale had seen the words scrawled in red paint on the wall with his own eyes—*blood money*—and even now the memory sent a chill down his spine. Worse yet, the Donatellas had been partners with Bancroft Development in Bancroft Bluff, and with that horrific message, it was generally assumed that their deaths had to do with the debacle of the doomed project. One of the prevailing thoughts was the perpetrator was a home owner or investor who'd lost their property to the dune, but since Declan had purchased, or offered to purchase, all the homes back, that theory didn't make a lot of sense. What was the motive, then?

Hale wanted to take down all the abandoned houses and let the dune go back to nature, but since Bancroft Development still didn't own all the homes, there was myriad red tape to untangle before any demolition could happen. He just wished to high heaven that the Tillamook County Sheriff's Department would figure out who had killed the Donatellas and arrest the bastards.

As if his grandfather's thoughts were traveling down the same path, Declan said, "What about that detective? Your sister-in-law."

"Savannah?"

"Yeah, her. What's she doing? And when's my great-grandson due?"

"Soon," Hale said, holding back his impatience. This was another topic Declan brought up again and again. Along with "What's wrong with that wife of yours that she can't have a baby?" and "You sure this young lady's going to want to give the boy up? I know all about those people who change their minds, say they're theirs and just run off with 'em."

Truth be told, Hale was having some serious problems with the whole surrogacy thing himself. He never should have agreed to let Savannah carry their baby. He never should have let his wife talk him into the child. Things had become strained between him and Kristina, growing worse, rather than better, during the pregnancy. His marriage had never been as solid as he'd hoped, but he'd believed he could make it work, and Kristina had been so desperately eager for a child that he'd said yes to her screwball plan. Now, he wasn't sure she even wanted a baby any longer. He didn't have a clue what was going on with her, but none of it was good.

A few minutes later, with guilty thoughts chasing around in his head, he left his grandfather's house, dodging raindrops as he dashed to his black Chevy TrailBlazer. Kristina drove a Mercedes sedan, which she'd begged him for, and he'd acquiesced more because he didn't care than because the expensive car was so dear to her heart. He'd known for a while that his reasons for marrying her in the first place were both more, and less, complicated than love, which didn't really enter into it at all. He'd been wrapped in grief during his father's death from a slow, lingering sickness—cancer, Preston St. Cloud had told him—though after his death Hale had learned that none of his doctors had given him that diagnosis. Preston's last doctor, more an herbalist than a trained physician, had simply lifted his shoulders and said, "Sometimes the dying just know."

Kristina had been everywhere during that time, helping him, soothing him, running his house, even keeping in contact with Hale's mother in Philadelphia, who wanted to be apprised of his father's condition though she and Preston had ceased even to speak since the divorce. Hale and Kristina had dated casually only a few times before Preston's last bout in the hospital, but Kristina had suddenly charged to the rescue, and when Preston died, Hale had leaned on her.

And shortly thereafter, he'd married her. A case of temporary insanity, apparently, for when he'd woken up from his grief, he'd found himself with a wife who was little more than a stranger to him. Still, she was his wife, he'd told himself, and he'd been determined that he was going to make their union work. He'd balked initially when she'd come to him crying, saying she had just learned she couldn't have a baby, and wanted to use a surrogate. He'd given her a list of reasons why that wouldn't work, leaving out the biggest one: that he wasn't sure about their marriage. And then, when she revealed that her sister would be their surrogate, he'd really put his foot down.

But . . . he did want a child, he'd realized. And though things with Kristina weren't perfect, he was in no hurry to divorce her. She was his wife, for better or worse. So they weren't madly in love. They had made plans together and, with the help of an interior designer, had just put the finishing touches on their new home, a Bancroft Development architectural dream, which had a spectacular view of the Pacific and was set well back on a rocky headland, unlike those built on the shifting sands beneath Bancroft Bluff.

So . . . ? he'd asked himself one long night, when he'd stood on the back deck of their home while it was still being framed. Surrogacy? Was that the answer? He'd been lost in thought for hours, and in the end he'd signed the papers, half expecting nothing to come of the IVF implant. And then the news: the pregnancy had taken. A shock. And he'd shared Kristina's joy, until she said something about the baby being the cement that would keep them together. When he'd questioned her on that, it slowly came out that she'd been afraid he was going to leave her, and she'd wanted to have a baby to keep their marriage together. Not exactly a shocking revelation, but he'd expected her to eventually join more in the joy and anticipation he was feeling with the impending birth. They were going to have a child together, for God's sake. The fact that she clearly hadn't experienced any of that had eaten him up inside throughout the whole pregnancy to the point where now he found himself unable to talk about the baby with her much at all. Worse yet, she seemed to have no interest in talking to him about some very real concerns *she* was having.

It was all just . . . hell.

Now, driving up to his house, seeing its natural shingles and white trim, its sweeping drive, lush yard, and three-car garage, he swallowed back his misgivings. He hit the button on the garage-door opener and had a chest-tightening sensation of playacting. This wasn't right. He needed to get things square between them and fast because he and Kristina were having a baby very soon. *Their* baby.

Her silver Mercedes was in its spot. He exhaled a pent-up breath. *Good.* She was home. He needed to talk to her while he was full of resolve to put things back together between them.

"Kristina?" he called as he walked through the kitchen, all stainless steel appliances and cream granite with silvery veins. There was a sunroom off the back with windows that looked toward the ocean, but she wasn't there. As he walked through the kitchen to the great room, which jutted even farther toward the edge of the headland, and looked through the windows to the deck where he'd spent so many long hours that one night, deciding what to do about his marriage and the surrogacy, he didn't expect her to be outside. The rain was heavy, and it was already growing dark, but there she was, her rich mahogany hair whipping around her face as she hugged her jacket close.

"Hey," he said, cracking open the French door. Even then the rain slapped against his face. "What's going on?"

She half turned, and he could see that her face was pale, her lips pinched. She moved toward him, and he stepped back, closing the door hard behind her as a gust of wind rattled the panes.

"Something wrong?" he asked.

"No, I'm . . ." She trailed off and shook her head.

"You were standing in the rain," he pointed out, trying to get her going again.

She gazed up at him through pale blue eyes that seemed to look right through him. He had a strange moment of recalling her sister, Savannah's, deeper blue ones, and that made him feel uncomfortable.

Kristina's hair was unnaturally darkened by the rain, and she ran her right-hand fingers through it somewhat listlessly. "I was just taking a moment."

"You couldn't have taken your moment inside?"

"Magda came late and just left," she said, referring to the woman who cleaned their house and also the Seaside Bancroft Development office. "She'll be here Monday again to finish up."

"You were outside to avoid her?"

"Leave me alone, Hale."

He was leery of her flat tone. "If there's something going on . . ."

"I'm just tired. I feel like we've been on a treadmill for a long time."

He hardly knew what to do with her in her uncertain mood. "Got any ideas how to slow the treadmill down? The baby is coming."

"You think I've forgotten?" She shot him a fierce glance.

He lifted his hands in surrender. "I'm kinda playing catch-up here. If I'm missing something, let me know."

"You're not missing anything. It's just . . ." She squeezed one fist inside her other hand, looking for all the world like she was hanging on by a thread.

"We need to get ready for the baby," Hale said. "We need to work together. You know we do."

"We're prepared," she said, not looking at him. "We've got everything we need."

It sounded like she was running through an inventory in her mind, and that worried Hale even more. "Do you still want our little boy?" he wanted to ask her. "Do you?" He felt angry and helpless. *Because I do.*

His anger dissipated as he saw how unsettled she really was. "You want a glass of wine?" he asked her as she stared into the middle distance. "I'm going to have one."

"Okay . . ."

Returning to the kitchen, he pulled a bottle of cabernet from the built-in wine rack, which was part of the center island. Yanking open a drawer, he found the corkscrew and quickly twisted out the cork. Kristina moved slowly into the kitchen and out to the sunroom, where rain was running in rivulets down the panes. He poured each of them a glass, brought hers to her, then took a deep swallow of his own, more like a gulp.

"I know I've been distant," she said, as if feeling her way.

This was the first attempt she'd made to reach out to him, so he kept his mouth shut, waiting for her to go on. It was his fault, too, he knew. He'd been buried in work; the lawsuits alone took up more time than he wanted to think about, and Bancroft Development was deep into construction projects both at the coast and around the Portland area.

She suddenly turned her back to the window and faced him, forcing her lips into a smile that just missed the mark. Before she could muster up more words, the smile fell off her face entirely, clearly too difficult to maintain. Sensing that, she buried her nose in her glass and took a long swallow herself.

What does this say about us? Hale wondered as they both drank deep gulps of wine in silence. *Nothing good.*

When she finally took a breath and offered up something, it took him aback.

"Do you believe in sorcery?" she asked tightly.

He half choked on his wine, laughed, then swallowed back the immediate gibe that sprang to his lips. "Well . . . no," he said carefully.

"I knew you'd say that."

He lifted a hand in a "You got me" gesture.

"I know how crazy it sounds, but I feel like something's got ahold of me."

"Bad juju?"

"Hale, please . . ." She brushed past him back into the kitchen and over to the counter, setting the wineglass on the island and then bracing herself. "I'm trying really hard to be honest with you and open and *sharing* . . . and you're just pissing me off."

"I don't know where you're going with this," he said, following after her.

"I've made some bad decisions," she said after a moment.

"Like what?"

"Things I thought I would never do. Nothing . . . criminal," she assured him, though a spasm crossed her face. "Don't look at me like that."

"Like what?"

"Like I'm fucking crazy!"

"I don't think you're crazy," he said, taken aback.

"Some stuff's happened, and it wasn't my fault. I made mistakes, but I honestly don't think I was really in control at the time."

"You gotta be more specific."

"I think . . ." She struggled for a moment, choosing her words. "Well, maybe I am crazy, because it feels like I'm under a spell. Like I have no will . . . like I've been hypnotized."

"At the risk of pissing you off some more, you seem pretty awake to me."

"It just doesn't make sense," she said, on her own track. She made a sound between a laugh and a hiccup. "Maybe I am losing my mind a little. I don't know. What do you think?"

He had no idea in the world how to answer her. "This couldn't be pre-mommy jitters, could it?"

"You're not listening," she declared, looking for all the world as if she were about to cry.

"I'm trying . . . but you're not saying anything that makes sense."

"That's the problem. It *doesn't* make sense, but I'm not making this up. It's like I'm all over the place. Feeling things I shouldn't. And yet, I don't feel them, really. Not in my heart. It's like it's someone else and I'm watching myself from a distance."

Hale regarded her soberly. He hardly knew what to say. "It sounds like fear."

She blinked a couple of times. "I am afraid."

"Of having a baby?"

She didn't answer.

"Have you talked to Savannah about this?" he asked.

"I called her, but she can't come over till later. Work, I guess. It always is." She clenched her teeth, then shook her head and shrugged her shoulders several times. "Oh, let's not talk about it anymore."

"Wait. We need to—"

"What do you want to do about dinner? I'm not hungry."

Hale fought back an angry comeback. He knew better. Whenever she changed her mind like this, further discussion was impossible.

This had become another usual thing for them. Separate meal times by virtue of different schedules. The only problem was Kristina was turning into skin and bones. She was never hungry. "We could go to that Italian restaurant," he suggested, tamping down his frustration, hoping to continue the conversation later.

"Gino's? It'll take too long. I want to be here when Savvy gets here."

"How about if we order and I go pick up?"

"I said I wasn't hungry."

"I'll just get something for me, then."

She didn't respond, and Hale gave up and headed for the phone. Unlike Kristina, he was half starved. It had been a long day even before he got to his grandfather's house, and he'd missed lunch. The wine was going straight to his head, and he needed to counteract the effects.

He ordered chicken and artichoke linguine, a Caesar salad, and garlic bread, enough for two regardless of what she'd said, then drank a glass of water as he waited for the fifteen minutes to pass while the food was being prepared. Kristina poured herself a second glass of wine, but she didn't touch it while he was there.

He drove to the restaurant and noticed she'd left her overnight bag in his car—again. She was forever borrowing the TrailBlazer for a quick trip over the mountains, then forgetting her bag. Then again, she was forgetting a lot these days, like how desperately she had wanted a child.

When he returned from Gino's with the bag, she was nowhere in sight. He filled two plates with the food, set them on the counter, then went in search of his wife. She was sitting on the bed, leaning against the headboard and staring into space. The untouched wine was sitting on the nightstand.

"You're starting to really worry me," he said.

"I don't want you to leave me, Hale. Whatever happens. Promise me you won't leave me."

"What the hell, Kristina?" This was a new tack for her.

"Promise me," she insisted.

"I'm not going to leave you."

"Even if you find out terrible things about me?"

He started to answer automatically, to lie, but stopped himself. "I'm not doing this. I'm going to eat," he said and stalked back down the hall, his heart heavy with doubts and his head full of worries about the future.

CHAPTER 3

The rain slanted against the windshield as Savannah drove north from the TCSD toward Deception Bay and Siren Song. She'd stopped by her house—once her parents', now hers and her sister's—and grabbed a peanut butter and jelly sandwich, her one true craving, before heading out to Siren Song and Catherine Rutledge.

The meeting over the Donatella homicides had run long, mainly because everyone in the conference room had wanted to have their say. Sheriff Sean O'Halloran, white-haired, with bright blue eyes and a growing girth, which worried him mightily, had started by saying, "A woman called in. An employee for Bancroft Development." He glanced down at the notepad in his hand. "Ella Blessert. She works in the Seaside office and does some bookkeeping and general office work. She claims Marcus Donatella was having an affair with his administrative assistant, Hillary Enders, whose boyfriend found out about the affair and killed Marcus and his wife out of jealousy but made it look like payback for the real estate debacle. The boyfriend's name is . . ." He frowned down at his notes. "Kyle Furstenberg."

"Did you talk to Blessert?" Lang asked the sheriff.

"I took the call," Clausen answered. "She didn't want to be overheard, so she just gave us the brief version."

"How does Blessert know this?" Lang asked.

Clausen shook his head. "All I know is she became friendly with Enders. Girlfriends. They'd go to lunch whenever Blessert went to the Donatella trailer at Bancroft Bluff, where Enders worked."

Lang said, remembering, "When that project was finished, Donatella moved the construction trailer to his next project, the restaurant they were building just outside the city limits of Garibaldi. What happened to Enders?"

"She moved with them," Savannah answered. "I interviewed Hillary Enders at the time of the homicides," she reminded them. "The restaurant was only half completed when the Donatellas were killed, so that's when construction stopped. The trailer's still there, but we took all the files from it. The Donatellas were in that project alone, not with the Bancrofts."

"The project's dead, right?" Lang said. "Died with the Donatellas."

Savvy looked to O'Halloran, who nodded and said, "Seems to be. The Donatellas didn't have children, and no one in the family's stepped up."

Everyone thought that over, but nothing had really changed since the last time they'd gone over the particulars, except the information about Marcus's supposed affair with Hillary Enders.

"Clausen, make a date with Blessert and see what else she has to say. If she doesn't want to be overheard, bring her to the station, or at least get her out of the office somehow," the sheriff said.

"Okay," the detective answered. Clausen was in a race with O'Halloran on whose girth could grow the widest, although currently Savannah had them both beat.

"What about Enders and Furstenberg?" Lang asked.

"Go ahead and follow up with them," the sheriff instructed.

"Shouldn't it be me?" Savvy asked. *Since I interviewed Hillary first?*

"Since you're a short timer, let's have Lang do the follow-up," O'Halloran said.

"I'm out for only a month or so. I'm not the baby's parent," she protested.

The sheriff nodded, as if she'd answered her own question, which, actually, she had.

Clausen said, "Enders is living in Seaside now, according to Blessert. No job since she worked for the Donatellas. Just drifting, apparently."

Savannah held her tongue, though she still wanted to jump in. Knowing why she was being overlooked didn't make it any easier.

"What took Blessert so long to come forward?" Lang asked.

"Maybe she didn't want to give up her friend?" O'Halloran hiked his shoulders.

"Blessert made it sound like Enders and Furstenberg had a falling-out after the killings," Clausen added. "Maybe Blessert just decided the time was right."

The three men were looking at each other and subtly edging Savannah out. She tried to hold down her rising blood pressure, but it was a trick. Working to keep the edge out of her voice, she said, "Marcus and Chandra Donatella were tied up and shot in the back of the head execution-style. Is Kyle Furstenberg the kind of guy who would do something like that?"

When Savvy first interviewed Hillary Enders, the girl had been clearly shaken to the core and lost, asking, "Why? Why?" over and over again and squeezing Savannah's hand as if she were afraid to let go. If Hillary's boyfriend was a stone-cold killer, it didn't read right that he would be with someone like Hillary.

"I'll shake down Furstenberg and see what falls out," Lang said. "And I'll try to get Hillary Enders to the station. See what she says while surrounded by 'the law.'"

"What should I do?" Savannah asked.

All three of them turned to her as if they wondered why she was still in the room. She could read their collective expressions: nothing. They didn't want her anywhere near a crime scene in her condition, nor did they want her interviewing witnesses, informants, and the like. They didn't want her around police work of any kind until after she'd given birth.

Well, screw that. The absolute last thing she wanted to do was sit and wait . . . and wait . . . and wait. "I'll check with the Bancrofts again," she offered up. She knew there could possibly be some objection to having her interview her sister's in-laws, but it would just be a follow-up call and in many ways she was the natural person for the job. Kristina would just love being re-questioned, but too damn bad.

"Okay." O'Halloran seemed relieved that that was all she'd asked for.

Now Savannah narrowed her eyes through the gloom outside and tamped down her annoyance. She'd enjoyed working at the sheriff's department until her pregnancy became visible and everyone started treating her like an outsider or, worse yet, like she should be handled with kid gloves. She liked the people she worked with as a rule. But this was no fun.

It's just temporary. Don't let it get to you, she reminded herself sternly.

Shaking her head, she thought back to the case. If Hillary Enders's boyfriend had killed Marcus in a jealous rage, the *blood money* message sure seemed like an elaborate deflection. Also, it was kind of cold, and if it wasn't premeditated, it was certainly opportunistic. Who was this guy?

And why take out the wife? she asked herself, something that had bothered her in the back of her mind. Chandra Donatella wasn't to blame for the affair; she was a victim of it, for crying out loud. Unless she was somehow involved? Or maybe she was just in the way, though killing her, too, didn't really seem like the actions of a spurned lover. Those kinds of murders were born out of passion. But this was cold. Ice cold.

If Savannah were asked to place a bet, she'd make it against the motive being jealousy. It just didn't wash. But they didn't have much else to go on, so she supposed at least it was a direction to move in.

She checked the clock on the dash: 7:15 p.m. She was a little bit late and wondered if Catherine was likely to rap her knuckles. Ha! Then her thoughts turned to her sister. Kristina and Hale's house was in Deception Bay, not all that far from the Siren Song lodge. Maybe she should try to stop by first and find out what was wrong, but then she would really be late for her meeting with Catherine.

And don't you want the time to ask Hale and Kristina about the Bancroft-Donatella connection again? Whether they like it or not, they're connected to Bankruptcy Bluff.

Savannah made a face. Nope. There was no time. She would have to see them after her visit with Catherine.

Keeping her Escape aimed toward the access road that turned off Highway 101 and led to the long Siren Song drive, Savannah stared through the rhythmically slapping window wipers to the darkness beyond. By the time she had angled the Ford onto the rutted lane that led to the lodge, the bumpy drive was filled with overflowing mud puddles and it was almost seven thirty. She parked in front of the wrought-iron gate, letting her headlights wash the enormous shingled building. A few minutes later she cut the engine.

She didn't have to wait long. Catherine herself appeared in a dark hooded cloak, walking carefully toward the gate that secured the property, carrying a flashlight and a sturdy black umbrella, apparently in case the hood failed. She unlocked the gate as Savannah climbed from her car. "Park over there," Catherine ordered, motioning to a wet grassy section, so Savannah got back behind the wheel, nosed the SUV around, and parked where Catherine had indicated. She gingerly skirted the puddles; and once inside the gate, which Catherine pulled shut with a high, keening wail of protest from its rusted hinges, she waited while Catherine relocked it; and they walked together beneath her umbrella to the front door.

Inside the lodge, Savannah let her eyes sweep over the heavy, overstuffed furniture and the Tiffany lamps with their soft light. To her surprise, there was an old, bubble-eyed console television in one corner of the room. Old technology at best, but still unexpected, given Catherine's obsession with keeping the current world outside of her gates.

Inside the large stone fireplace the fire had burned down to glowing embers, the red logs about to break apart. Heavy shades were drawn across the windows, and two young women were in the room, one standing by the hearth and staring at Savannah through sharp eyes, her blond hair several shades darker than that of the one in the wheelchair, whose hands were folded in her lap, her expression eager and expectant.

"Ravinia, Lillibeth." Catherine waved them away.

"Who are you?" the standing girl asked Savannah.

"I told you both to wait in your rooms," Catherine said crisply. "Lillibeth?"

Sighing, the girl in the wheelchair turned her chair around and headed toward a back door.

The dark blond girl stood her ground and repeated, "Who are you?"

"I'm Detective—"

"Ravinia." Catherine's tone was fierce.

"You never have people here this late," she retorted, flipping her long hair over her shoulder with one hand in a gesture of disdain. "Tell me why. I have a right to know. We all have a right to know."

"I'll tell you about this later. For now, I need to speak to Detective Dunbar alone."

There was a moment when Savannah thought Ravinia was going to challenge Catherine some more. Her lips tightened rebelliously. Seeing it, Catherine added, "Isadora, Cassandra, and Ophelia are upstairs, and Lillibeth's gone to her room. Go on now."

Ravinia's eyes, a dark blue, flashed fire, but she turned and headed to the stairs. She hesitated on the bottom step, her hand on the heavy oak newel post, and said through tight teeth, "I'm not like them." Then she gathered her long skirts and bolted up the stairway to a second-floor gallery. From where she stood, Savannah could see Ravinia run along the hallway, until she finally turned a corner and disappeared.

Catherine sighed. "Ravinia's the youngest."

"The youngest of how many?" Savannah asked.

Catherine acted like she didn't hear her as she said, "Let's go to the kitchen."

Savannah followed after her to the east side of the lodge and a large room with an impressive oak plank trestle table big enough to seat twelve. Catherine indicated for her to take a chair at the table, and when Savannah did, she sat down across from her. The scents of onion, tomato, and beef broth still lingered, and she could see a large pot of something cooling on the stove. Beef stew was her guess.

"What is it you wanted to talk about?" Savannah asked when the older woman lapsed into thoughtful silence.

She clasped her hands in front of her and set them on the table, looking down at them. "I've been thinking about this for a while. I need to know about my sister."

"Your sister?"

"Yes. Mary Rutledge . . . Beeman."

Savannah waited, wondering where she was going with this. For a moment she'd thought Catherine meant some other sister, though the only one on record that she knew of was Mary. "She's deceased?"

"Yes."

"Okay." When Catherine still seemed reluctant to proceed, Savannah said, "I don't know a lot about her."

"But you've heard the rumors about Mary."

"Some." You couldn't live in or around Deception Bay without gleaning some information about the Colony whether you wanted to or not.

"Have you read *A Short History of the Colony,* by Herman Smythe?"

"The book at the Deception Bay Historical Society?"

"If you can call it a book," Catherine said and sniffed.

"Not yet."

"Don't bother." Catherine's blue eyes grew chilly. "Most of the genealogy inside it is correct," she admitted grudgingly, "but there are errors and omissions, and what's written about my sister is mostly erroneous." She waved a dismissive hand. "I never cared what Herman wrote. He was more harmless than most of my sister's . . . men. But maybe it's time to set the record straight."

Savannah waited expectantly. She already knew that Mary Rutledge Beeman had been very sexually active during the seventies and eighties and had given birth to a lot of children, almost one a year, during that time, most all of them girls. There was the belief, maybe even proof, that Mary's children possessed extra abilities beyond the normal, abilities that defied explanation. *A Short History of the Colony* explained much of that, apparently, though Savannah had yet to read it herself. Despite Catherine's condemnation of the book, it was something she planned to rectify right away.

"I want to tell you about my sister's death," Catherine said at length.

"Okay."

"I want to set the record straight, and I'm hoping you can help me."

"Unless a crime's been committed, the Tillamook County Sheriff's Department might not be the government body to contact."

"I'm aware of that." Catherine pressed her lips together, then said, "I've explained my sister's death over the years in a number of ways, none of them completely truthful. I've said she died from a miscarriage suffered from the result of a fall . . . or sometimes I just said she just died from a fall. In truth, both were a lie."

Now she had Savannah's attention. "What did she die of?"

"She didn't. Not then. Not back when I said she did." Catherine unclasped and reclasped her hands several times. "She was living on Echo Island."

"Echo Island." Savannah regarded the woman skeptically.

"I know. It's barely more than a rock. It's owned by my family, and I guess that means just me now, until I bequeath it to the girls. But there is a cabin on it, and I assure you that Mary lived there for years."

Savannah couldn't help staring at her. What in God's name was this all about? "But she is dead now."

"Yes."

"You think a crime's been committed? A homicide?" Savannah asked, guessing. What other reason would she have to reach out to the TCSD?

Catherine seemed about to answer, swallowed her reply back, thought hard for a moment, then finally said, "What do you think of us here at the Colony?" There was a sneer in her voice when she said "Colony."

"What do *I* think of you?" Savannah hiked her shoulders. She wondered if she was just wasting her time. Now that she'd seen the inside of the lodge, she was kind of over all the mystique. It was just a rustic, roomy home where people lived a simpler life. No serious woo-woo evident.

"You must have some impression. The locals surely do. Some people think we're Wiccans, or so I've heard."

"I'm not really sure what Wiccans are," Savannah said with a smile. "Witches of some kind, I guess, but I don't believe in any of that."

"I've been careful not to add to the rumors. My sister was promiscuous. That's a documented fact. She had many lovers and many children from those lovers. She was indiscriminate . . . and she was also touched by madness." Catherine looked past Savannah, toward the fire, but her gaze was clearly down some hallway to the past. "At that time when Mary's mind was failing, I took matters into my own hands. I radically changed the way things were handled here. I wasn't about to let Mary turn Siren Song into a brothel. She had young daughters growing up around her, and she didn't even notice."

"What about sons?" Savannah asked.

"Not many." Catherine stopped, and Savannah realized she had interrupted her train of thought. She determined not to speak again unless asked a question, because she wanted to hear everything Catherine had to say about Siren Song and her nieces who lived there.

When Catherine spoke again, however, it was in a completely different direction. "What do you know about genetics, Detective Dunbar?"

Savannah lifted her palms skyward. "Uh . . . well . . . I know we get our traits from our genes and that genes are collected on chromosomes."

"Very good, Detective. To be exact, there are twenty-three pairs of chromosomes in the human body, and each chromosome is packed with genes, and each gene holds myriad genetic information," Catherine explained. "My family has the same genes as everyone else, as far as I know, but there are genes that scientists don't really know the complete functions of. Some appear to be cancer inhibitive, and others can give doctors a clue that a patient has a susceptibility to a disease. I don't know all the particulars, but I've done some reading on the subject."

No kidding, Savvy thought. In her long dress, with its throwback design to another century, Catherine was the last person she would have expected to be in a conversation with about modern science, technology, and genetics. This time she remained quiet, however, waiting for the older woman to make her point.

"Have you ever seen pictures of chromosomes?" Catherine asked.

"Well . . . they kind of look like *X*s. . . ."

"Yes, they come in pairs. Two Xs. Except for the sex chromosome, which can be XY if it's male."

Savannah nodded, not sure what else to do.

"There are twenty-two autosome chromosomes and one sex chromosome. The sex chromosome combines to form XX or XY, a girl or a boy. An ovum has only half of the pair, that is, one X rather than two, and the sperm has the other half, one X or one Y. An X from the mother's ovum and an X from the father's sperm produces a female child, whereas an X from the mother's ovum and a Y from the father's sperm produces a male child. Are you with me so far?"

"I think so."

"If you look through an electron or magnification microscope at the sex chromosome pair for a female, you'll see two Xs. If you look through the microscope at the chromosome for a male, you'll see an X and a Y, because the bottom tail of the X is shortened in the male. That's why it's called Y. Again, you end up with XX for female, XY for male."

"So, that's why they're named XX or XY? Because of the way the chromosome actually looks?"

"Generally speaking. The women of Siren Song have two Xs, as all females do," Catherine said, finally getting to the point she was making with her talk on chromosomes. "Most of us here at Siren Song have something a little extra, part of our own particular genetic brew. One or several of our genes seem to be . . . different. Some of us also have physical anomalies, like an extra rib bone."

"Don't women have extra rib bones, anyway?"

"Yes, but some of the women of our clan, for lack of a better word, have even more. And there are other differences as well. Some not so physically obvious. Mental changes." She stared pensively past Savannah. "The results of our gifts can sometimes be a little dangerous, it seems."

"Gifts?" Savannah questioned, ignoring her earlier advice to herself.

"We're different, Detective. I'm sure you've heard. We do have special abilities, which can be a blessing or a curse, depending on how you look at it. It's not something I care to go into in depth, but be assured those abilities are real."

"Okay."

"Mary possessed a dark gift. A gift that ruined her." Catherine pursed her lips and shifted in her chair. "She entranced men."

Savannah was inclined to believe many women had that same gift, often to their detriment as well, but declined to say so. "Do you have a gift?" she asked cautiously.

"Not that you'd notice. What I have is my sanity, which is cold and hard." Now she did smile, but there was no humor in it. "You knew my 'cousin' of sorts, Madeline Turnbull."

Mad Maddie. Savannah kept the moniker to herself, but she said, "We met." A psychic with a surprisingly accurate track record, Madeline Turnbull had predicted that Savannah would have a boy before

Savvy was certain she was even pregnant. Shortly after that meeting, Savannah was called to the nursing home where Maddie resided, and arrived to learn that she had died. Her death was later confirmed to be a homicide.

"There is madness sometimes," Catherine said. "Sometimes the stronger the gift, the closer you dance to the edge of that madness."

Savannah didn't know if she believed fully in these "gifts," but there had been a number of inexplicable incidents concerning the women of Siren Song, and it was clear that Catherine believed completely, and, well, she didn't want to piss her off. Besides, what did she know, really? The world was full of the unexplained.

Catherine looked down at her clasped hands, which had turned white under the pressure, and she slowly released them. "But it's the Y chromosome, the missing piece, that seems to intensify the effects in the males. They do feel their gifts more strongly. Luckily, there aren't many males born to us. But when they are, it's just . . ." She lifted a hand and let it fall into her lap.

Savannah thought of Justice Turnbull, a distant relative of Catherine's. He'd focused on the women of Siren Song with an unrelenting passion to kill, and his own death some six months earlier had been a blessing for Catherine and her brood. He'd definitely suffered from mental issues; there was no denying that.

Savannah had a sudden really bad feeling about this, and as if in response, the baby inside her started furiously kicking. She laid a light hand under her right ribs and asked, "What happened to them? The males?"

"What do you mean?"

"Well, they're not here, from what I can tell, so where are they?"

Catherine frowned, as if Savvy had asked an unseemly question. "Mary adopted out her sons, except for Nathaniel, who was sweet, but slow. He died when he was young, but he wasn't strong."

"How many were adopted out?"

"Several."

"You're kind of loose on the numbers," Savvy pointed out.

"We just felt it was better if they were raised by others."

"Because being male, their gift would be . . . too much to handle?"

"Mary had a lot of children, and she wasn't capable of taking care of so many of them."

"But the males were more difficult as a rule," Savannah said, pressing. "That's what you're saying."

Catherine wanted to deny it, but in the end she went back to genetics. "I believe that with the female, the two Xs counterbalance each other, but with the males, on that missing part of the X that makes it a Y, there is no counterbalance, and therefore whatever gift you've been given is stronger and can manifest itself in psychotic behavior, which it has."

"You're talking about Justice Turnbull," Savvy said and felt a particular chill when she considered his extreme cruelty and fixation.

"Mary, like Justice, possessed a dark gift, but Justice's was more intense, and he was so *focused*. . . ."

"Are you saying you think he was involved with your sister's death?"

"No, not Justice. But maybe a man . . ."

"A man with your family's 'gift'?" Savvy questioned.

"I don't know. Maybe I'm skittish and overly careful, but Mary couldn't leave men alone. Wait here. . . ."

Savannah hazarded a glance at her watch as Catherine left the room. Catherine *was* skittish and overly careful, but she clearly had something specific on her mind.

She heard the older woman's tread on the stairs, and as her footsteps faded away, she heard the sound of quick approaching feet, and soon another young woman entered the room, one she hadn't met before. She stood at the edge of the kitchen, her shoulder-length hair ashy blond, her eyes a faded blue, her pupils and irises seemingly disproportionately large compared to the whites of her eyes. She was barefoot, and her dress was a blue and yellow calico print that swept her ankles.

"Hello," Savannah said.

"Hello," she answered, her eyes drifting to Savannah's protruding stomach. "I'm Maggie."

"I'm Detective Dunbar. Savannah," she said.

"You're having someone else's child?"

Savannah stared at her. Did she mean what it sounded like she meant? "I'm a surrogate for my sister," she admitted. "How did you guess?"

"I didn't guess. I knew. That's why they call me Cassandra, even though my real name is Margaret."

Like Cassandra, the seer of mythology, Savvy thought.

"Aunt Catherine says my mother thought it was more appropriate. Because of the myth, you know."

Savvy nodded.

"Do you have a name for him yet?"

Savannah ran a protective hand over her large mound, a little boggled by the switch in subjects. "Um . . . no . . . My sister will name him."

"You're from the sheriff's department," Cassandra said, her voice taking on an urgent tone. Footsteps sounded on the stairs again, and Cassandra edged closer. "I told Aunt Catherine about him and about the bones. I knew about Justice, too. But now he's *coming.* He came for Mary, and he's coming for us, too." She gazed hard at Savannah and added meaningfully, "All of us."

"But Justice is dead," Savannah said, feeling more than a little shivery at the girl's intensity.

"Not Justice. There are many heads to the Hydra. You cut one off, and another grows in its place."

"Who's coming? What does he look like?"

Cassandra shook her head, squeezing her eyes closed. "I see only his beauty," she whispered, then darted around the edge of the kitchen counter and into an alcove that led to a back room. "Be careful," she warned.

By the time Catherine appeared, Cassandra was long gone, but Catherine's gaze followed the girl's departure as if she'd left a vapor trail behind. Her mouth tightened, but she said nothing as she set a tooled-leather box on the table. She laid her hands on either side of it, bracing herself, and then she drew up her chin and flipped back the box's lid. From inside she withdrew a plastic bag and held it toward Savannah. Within the plastic lay a knife with a curved blade.

"My sister was killed with this."

Savvy stared at the knife, and Catherine slid the bag across the table to her. "How do you know this?"

"Can you accept that I just know?"

"Not really. If she was killed with that knife, you're talking homicide."

"I think it could be suicide."

Savvy's gaze hardened on Catherine. She had the distinct feeling she was lying.

"Will you do a DNA test on it?" Catherine asked.

"It sounds like you want me to open an investigation into your sister's death. If that's the case—"

"Can we first start with the DNA test?"

"I would have to know more about—"

"I can pay for it. Keep it private," Catherine said, cutting in. "It's just that I needed someone to . . . turn to, Detective. Do you understand?"

"You want a DNA test with no questions asked."

"Yes."

"Ms. Rutledge, there's clearly a lot you're not saying. I'm going on maternity leave soon. I'm not even sure I could do this," Savannah said. "You might need someone else. And then there's the question of the body. We would have to do an exhumation."

As if she hadn't heard her, Catherine asked, "Will you please do me this favor?"

Savvy expelled a breath. "I can send the knife to the DNA lab, but if it's for private purposes, it may take some time before they get to it. There are a lot of requests, most of them more urgent, as they're tied to known crimes."

"That's fine. I just . . . If there's anything on the knife—blood, fingerprints, tissue—I want to know whose it is."

"That sounds a lot like you believe this knife was used in a homicide."

"If I truly believed that, I would ask you to investigate her death."

Not likely, Savannah thought.

"It may well be that the only DNA evidence will be my sister's, and if that's the case, then I'll accept that it was suicide, or even an accident, and that will be enough."

"The ME tends to make the decision on whether a weapon was used in a homicide or a suicide, but, of course, we need a body."

Catherine's lips pressed into a line. "You're going to force this investigation, aren't you?"

Savannah stared at the knife for a long moment, then slowly

picked the plastic bag up. "I'll take this back to Detective Stone, and we'll go from there."

Catherine seemed to want to say something else, but she let it slide. "What did Cassandra say to you?" she asked instead.

"She said her name was Maggie and that she told you *he* was coming. That he came for Mary, and he was coming for you and maybe even me, too."

"She said that?" Catherine whispered.

"Who is this he? Does he have anything to do with the DNA you're looking for on the knife?"

"Cassandra sees things, but they're not always accurate," she said, in complete denial of her own body language, which was reflecting her intense fear.

"She knew I was carrying my baby for someone else."

It was a role reversal. Now Savvy was the one intimating that she believed in the women of the Colony's gifts, and Catherine was the skeptic. The two women stared each other down.

Finally, Catherine declared, "Cassandra has a flair for the dramatic. No one's coming for us. And certainly not for you, Detective."

"That's good to hear." Deciding it was time to stop talking in circles and get on with the Donatella investigation, Savannah got to her feet and said, "I'd better get going."

"You'll test the knife?"

"I . . . yes. I'll bill you." She walked around the table, out of the kitchen, and toward the rough-hewn front door, sensing Catherine behind her. Turning, she saw that Catherine's eyes were following the bag in her hand, as if she was afraid to let it out of her sight. "I'll talk to Detective Stone about it, too."

"Thank you."

"As I said, he may ask to exhume Mary's body if he thinks a crime's been committed."

"There's no reason for that," Catherine stated quickly. "If Detective Stone wants to take things that far, have him get in contact with me."

She opened the door and accompanied Savannah down the flag-stone path to the gate, unlocked it, waited for Savvy to pass through, then relocked the gate before turning back to the lodge. Savannah climbed into her vehicle and looked back at Catherine's stiffly held spine as the older woman reentered the lodge.

Who is he? she wondered again, her gaze sliding toward the knife inside the plastic bag, as she sensed in her bones that there was some real threat out there and tried like hell to shake the eerie feeling that had been with her since she first stepped through the gate of Siren Song.

CHAPTER 4

The bar was crowded with would-be cowboys and girls in skintight dresses, along with a few after-work businessmen, who had ripped off their ties and were knocking back shots, as if trying to prove they were twice as macho as any of the men wearing jeans, boots, hats, and oversize belt buckles. It was a rockin' Thursday night at the Rib-I, a Portland steak and baked potato restaurant and bar, whose logo was spelled out in ropelike orange neon and encircled by a lasso.

Yes, the Rib-I was class all the way, and Charlie—no, that wasn't his real name, but it was the only one he gave out—was pretty sure every fucker in sight would be worth more to the world if he were six feet under. With that thought in mind, Charlie wondered how many he could kill. How long it would take. How much forethought. He didn't plan to ever get caught, and so mass murder or even serial murders were problematic, something to avoid. But recently he'd gotten the killing urge and gotten it bad. It was powerful, almost sexual. Well, actually, it was sexual. He had to beat off almost immediately after every last choking sound. He didn't care how they expired. He just liked staring into their eyes, their damned souls, and watching them suck in those last tortured breaths, and then, man, the hard-on was so huge and uncomfortable that with a few quick strokes he was spewing like a volcano.

Now . . . there was danger in that. DNA danger. He'd learned to carry around ziplock bags, just in case he wasn't somewhere safe.

It was a strange phenomenon, he thought as he sipped his beer. He'd never really understood his own power, but it was always there, always with him, an old friend. In his youth he'd worked his power on animals that he wanted to befriend. It ran through him with the heat of blood in his veins, and the zing of energy down his nerves. It was a power he couldn't explain, though he'd tried to several times, the last time to his adoptive mother, who had looked pained and a little frightened while he struggled to name his power, and then had simply changed the subject. But by then he was sixteen and as horny as he could be.

To hell with befriending animals, he'd decided; he wanted sex. One night he moved up close to his mother and said softly that he wanted her, and he let his own invisible power slide over to her. When she stared at his lips and the look of horror slowly fled from her face, to be replaced by something else, he knew he had her. He moved forward and pushed her unresisting form onto the couch, and he screwed her every which way but loose, and she clasped him to her and howled with her head thrown back and her spine bent in a U, her legs locked around his back, meeting his thrusts with a body that jerked and stiffened and begged for more. The next day she threw herself off a freeway bridge, but he was gone by then, starting his vagabond new life, where he lured women with a wink and a smile, and by the time he was through with them, they'd given him everything they had and more. He stuck with a professor's daughter through three terms of college and then moved on to the professor herself. He could have gotten a degree in business without hardly trying, but he got bored with the whole thing and quit before achieving that goal.

Which was why he was wondering if he should hook up with more of those academic types. *Hmmm.* He took another swallow from his long-necked bottle and saw a redhead checking him out. She was kinda swaying to the twangy country music—a come-on that he ignored for now. There was something desperate about her, and he didn't need desperate.

He knew his looks dragged them in. Of course he knew. But it was his power that really got them going, a power he struggled to keep under leash. Sometimes when he looked at the turn of a woman's calf or the soft curve of her breast or the rounded lushness of her buttocks, he just couldn't help himself, and he just let it out. They couldn't say no to him. Sometimes they didn't want to at first; sometimes he was just too impatient. But they couldn't say no. He'd been trying very hard to put a lid on the whole damn thing, because he didn't want to move anymore; he was still enraged over that last relo. He didn't want to have to keep leaving just because some crazed husband or boyfriend thought it was time to take care of Good Time Charlie, so he'd had to put a lid on his power for a while. It was while he'd been in this state of weird abstinence that he learned what it felt like to kill.

Mother . . . fucker.

As he relived that last fatal encounter, his dick jumped up as if electrified, and he suddenly had the boner of all boners. He looked around for the redhead, but she'd disappeared, so he had to move up next to a chick wearing a short denim jacket and low-cut jeans, whose hair was bleached white with black roots, and he let a little of his power out so she wouldn't object when he pressed himself into her butt and rubbed a little. She jerked away at first, then snapped around to look at him, a snarl on her lips, and he smiled and said, "C'mon, gimme some sugar," and she said, "Fuck you," a little breathlessly, and then she was all over him, twisting and squirming, and he had to put a stop to it right there or get thrown out on the street.

"Hey!"

The guy coming toward him wore a black cowboy hat, nose-picker boots, a bronze buckle with, of course, a buckin' bronco on it, and a scowl dark enough to blacken the western United States.

This power Charlie possessed, unfortunately, did not seem to work on men.

"Garth," she protested as he bore down on them.

He grabbed Charlie by the collar of his black shirt and got in his grill and yelled, "Get your fuckin' hands off Tammie, or I'll break every bone in 'em."

Charlie considered pointing out that it wasn't his hands that had been on Tammie, but decided it probably wasn't the time.

"You touch him, I'll kick your ass," Tammie declared.

"Shut your mouth, slut."

"Call me that again, you'll be short one ball."

"Fuck you."

"Fuck *you!*" she screamed.

She was still under the influence of his power, but her target had shifted, and as Charlie eased back, she practically attacked Garth. He tried to throw her off to get to Charlie, but she was insistent and shrieking and clawing like a cat in heat. For a moment it looked like it was going to happen right there on the plank wood floor, but the bouncer was suddenly on the scene, and then another husky brute showed up. Charlie stepped away from the melee and was out the door and into a shivery November night that threatened rain or snow or maybe both.

He waited around awhile, leaning against a black SUV, wondering how long it would take and if he had the time. He wanted sex and he wanted it now, but even more, he wanted to kill someone. This was a dangerous new twist to his power that had begun a few months back, ever since those days and weeks with Mother Mary.

His lips curled and he was just straightening when Garth finally staggered out with Tammie clinging to him like a burr, and they got into a red truck with monster tires and rocked and rolled for long enough to get the deed done. He watched from a distance—warring with himself—then let his mind travel down delicious paths as he thought of killing them. Maybe he should leave before dangerous things happened. Maybe . . .

But he couldn't stop. Didn't want to.

Slipping on a pair of supple leather gloves, smooth as butter, he crept up to the cab of the big truck and flung open the door. The knife slid across Garth's throat in one smooth stroke while Garth was trying to get his pants buckled up. Fucking bucking bronco buckle. Tammie opened her mouth to scream, and he did the same to her. She let out a strangled gurgle and gazed at him in horror, and he smiled as he watched them both until the last of Garth's breath whistled out and Tammie's eyes went blank. He stayed as long as he dared, and then he was out of the cab and walking quickly around to the back of the restaurant, pulling out his plastic bag. One hard stroke was all he needed, and he pumped like a stallion into the receptacle, holding back a groan of ecstasy that nearly killed him. Then he cleaned up and put the ziplock inside a second one and tucked them inside his jacket pocket and strolled away. He would get rid of this specimen of DNA somewhere safe. Couldn't leave any evidence behind.

Ever since he'd killed the beautiful but aging woman who'd told him she was his mother, his power had grown. She was the woman who'd given him this power, he'd realized when she'd lured him to the island where she lived. He'd damn near lost his life trying to get there, but she'd been impossible to resist. A real temptation—a siren. She had answered many of his questions, had even told him who his father was, but had held back even more, and it had burned him up. Worse yet, he'd been flummoxed to learn that she was resistant to his charms. Impossible! Especially when she'd been able to damn near use him up, so strong was her own power.

"Your gift comes from me, and you owe me," she'd told him with that knowing smile, which, he'd found, gripped him from the inside out. "I need your help to be free of them, one and all."

"Who?" he'd asked, locked in her spell. She hadn't had sex with him, and it was pure torture. He wanted her, his cock throbbing painfully, and he knew she was the one doing it to him, making him sweat with desire. Sending out her pheromones. His own mother. Doing it *on purpose.*

He would have done anything for her. *Anything!*

She whispered their names in his ear. She wanted to be there when it was done. She wanted him with her. Always. He agreed readily. He was her slave. *Just please, please, please fuck me. Fuck me. Fuck me.*

But she wouldn't. Ironically, she held all the power. She didn't feel for him what he was feeling for her. She wouldn't let him have her. Nor would she release him. She just kept him on the island until finally she was ready and he was half mad with sexual desire.

"Tomorrow," she told him, her blue eyes glowing with anticipation. "We'll go together."

But tomorrow came and the winds were up and the rowboat he'd used to get to the island wouldn't hold up. For a long, angry moment she looked upward, her blond hair flying, whipping around her head in wild strands. Her hands were fists, which she shook skyward as she railed against the dark heavens and the gods who held her prisoner.

And that was when she let go. Just a little. He felt it, that special tingle, and he was on her in an instant, wrestling her to the ground and the weeds of her garden. A flash, and he saw the knife that had been hidden in the folds of her dress. She raised it high, intent on taking his life, but he was stronger. Forcefully, he yanked the weapon from her fingers, then slipped the blade between her ribs in one fluid motion, watching her die, watching her eyes, feeling her power shrink down to a tiny dot and die out, feeling it enter him and make him even stronger.

He carried her back inside the cottage and laid her on her bed. Then he went into the bathroom and masturbated, filled with a wondrous sexual power far greater than he'd possessed before. Once he was finished, he returned to the bedroom, and with a rag he wiped the hilt of the knife clean. Then he pressed her right hand around it and held it until rigor mortis set in hours later. Before he left, he took a thin strip of cloth ripped from the bed and wrapped her hand to the hilt. Surveying his handiwork objectively, he decided that maybe she'd given him his mission in life. Find these women, screw the hell out of 'em, and then kill them, one by one. And maybe take some others, too.

After all, she was his mother. It was the least he could do.

Thinking about it now brought on another erection, and he struggled to tamp down his libido, bring the galloping horses under control, turn his thoughts around, but it was no good. He was in his black Range Rover and driving away, thinking of who he could have sex with. He was too jazzed to call it a night just yet, but he knew another kill was too risky.

But that didn't mean he couldn't find some woman ready to spread her legs and moan and thrash like an animal. He didn't have to be quite so careful if he didn't kill 'em. They always came back for more.

There was one in particular who couldn't get enough of Good Time Charlie.

With that thought in mind, he turned the nose of his car west, out of Portland and toward the coast.

CHAPTER 5

By the time Savvy got to Kristina's, it was going on nine o'clock and she could feel her own tail dragging. How long had she been up? Too long for her condition, that was for sure. She needed a bath and a rest, and it would be nice to have a drink, but since that was out, a cold Perrier sounded fantastic.

But first . . . Kristina.

She knocked on the door and peeked through the sidelight windows that ran along each side of the mahogany door. She looked past the entry toward the kitchen and sunroom beyond, but there was no one in sight. She rang the bell again and heard approaching footsteps—Hale's probably, as the sound was heavier than her sister's—and sure enough, Hale St. Cloud came into view and threw open the door.

He'd dressed down from work into a collared gray sweatshirt with a zipper at the throat and a clearly beloved pair of jeans, if the worn-white areas near his knees were any indication. "Hey, Savvy. How are ya?" he asked, giving her a quick hug, the most affection she ever got from him, as he seemed to be one of those guys who was naturally distant, or maybe he was just not interested in knowing anyone from Kristina's family all that well.

"Not bad," she said as she followed him into the kitchen, where a bottle of red wine and a half-empty glass sat on the counter. There was a bag with Gino's name on it, and her mouth watered at the thought of Italian food. Her earlier peanut butter and jelly sandwich wasn't going to cut it till tomorrow's breakfast.

Hale saw her look at the bag and asked, "You had dinner, right?"

"Well . . . yes."

"I've got an untouched plate that Kristina refused. Chicken and artichoke linguine."

"She doesn't want it?"

"Apparently not."

"Then, yes," she said with feeling.

He laughed, and Savannah was taken aback at how attractive he was without that layer of reserve. She'd always sort of felt Kristina had married him for his good looks and, well, money, but now she wondered if she'd been too narrow in her scope. There might be other reasons as well.

"What would you like to drink?" he asked.

"You have any sparkling water?"

"Ummm . . ."

"Or ice water?"

"That I have." He plucked a glass from the cupboard and took it to the refrigerator door, where he first held it under the ice-maker slot and pressed a button, then, after several cubes had clinked inside, slid it under the cold-water dispenser and filled the glass to just below the brim. "Kristina's in bed." He handed the ice water to Savannah.

"She asked me to come by," she said, surprised. "Is something wrong?"

He picked up the glass of wine and took a swallow. "Maybe. I don't know."

"Have any ideas? She sounded urgent earlier." Savannah watched as he pulled out a plate of pasta wrapped tightly with plastic wrap and placed it in the microwave.

"She said . . ." He stopped himself and looked over to his left quickly. Kristina was suddenly standing in the aperture that led down the hall to the bedrooms. Her face was pale, and she wore a peach satin nightgown that accentuated her narrow shoulders and collarbones beneath the fall of her dark reddish hair.

"Go on. Tell her what I said," Kristina stated flatly. "I'd love to hear it."

Hale turned his attention back to the microwave, and they all waited for the *ding* that let them know the food was hot. "She said she didn't feel like herself," Hale added as he slid the plate in front of one of the stools that clustered around the bar, then turned his palm to it in a gesture that meant for Savannah to sit. "She said she did things she didn't want to."

"That's not exactly what I said," Kristina protested half angrily.

"Close enough."

As Savannah seated herself, Hale pulled out flatware and yanked a square of white paper towel from a stainless steel holder on the counter, then handed them to Savannah. Then, with a lift of his hand and a smile of good-bye that was more of a grimace, he strode out of the room and down the hall toward the bedrooms.

Savannah gazed after him, realizing she'd lost her opportunity tonight to interview him about anything to do with Bankruptcy Bluff and the Donatella homicides. At some level she was almost relieved. Given her pregnancy and the fact that he was feeding her dinner, she didn't really want to throw his hospitality in his face by jumping into an investigative interview. *Better to do it in the light of day,* she consoled herself. *Tomorrow.*

"What *did* you say?" Savannah asked her sister when Kristina also continued to stare after Hale, her face a mixture of worry, anger, and what? Maybe fear?

"Oh, I don't know. It's all so crazy. I just told him I feel out of control sometimes, like I'm . . ." She shook her head and made a face. "He really pissed me off. I told him I thought I was losing my mind, and I don't think he gave a shit. Or he didn't believe me. Or both." She perched on the stool at the opposite end of the bar from Savannah and watched her lift the plastic wrap from her linguine. Steam lifted upward.

"I believe this is really your dinner," Savannah said.

"I don't want it. Please. I can't eat anything."

"You look like you could use a good meal."

"Hale tells me I'm skin and bones, but what does he know?"

"I'm looking at you, and I think he might be right."

Kristina shook her head. "When this is all over, then I can eat. It'll all be all right."

"When what's all over? The pregnancy?"

"Well, yeah."

"*Are* you losing your mind?" Savannah asked, smiling to take the sting out of it.

"No, I just have to get rid of . . . some baggage that I've spent way too much time on."

"What baggage?" Forking linguine into her mouth, Savannah had to force herself not to moan aloud. "Damn, but Gino's is good. You really should have some." She tried to push the plate her sister's way, but Kristina was already on her feet, walking away.

"I don't feel hunger . . . for food," she said.

"Meaning?"

She shook her head. "It's just been weird, that's all."

"Weird with Hale?"

"Just weird. Sometimes I feel like I'm having an out-of-body experience, staring at myself from a distance, like I'm a stranger. Ever feel that way?"

"Umm . . ."

"Of course not. You're too squared away, as ever. It's just your wacko older sister who has a problem."

"What's the problem?" Savannah asked. "You and Hale are going to be parents soon, and I want everything to be as good as it can be when that day comes."

"I'm fine, Savvy. For God's sakes, a baby! I mean, we've all been just dying for this day to get here, right? I'm making too much of this. My whole life's going to change soon, and it's good, it's really good, but I am freaking the hell out. I don't mean to be selfish. I mean, look at you. You're huge!"

"Thanks," Savannah said dryly.

"All I'm saying is, it shouldn't be about me right now. You're the one who's pregnant. For me. I should just be eager and excited, and I am. It's just . . ." She pressed her fingers to her eyes and shook her head. "God, can you believe it? I sound like such a bitch."

"You just sound kind of . . . rattled." Savvy ate some more linguine and drank from her glass of water, sending Kristina a sidelong glance when her sister went quiet. After a moment, she asked, "Was there something more specific, or did you just want me to be here with you?"

"I guess I just wanted you to be here."

"Okay."

Savannah finished up her plate, slightly alarmed at how much her food intake had grown. Kristina seemed lost in thought, and when Savannah set her fork down, she swung herself to her feet and took her plate, absentmindedly rinsing it off before putting it in the dishwasher. Then she leaned against the counter and faced her sister.

"I asked Hale earlier if he believed in sorcery," Kristina said. "You can imagine."

"Were you serious?"

"Well, sort of."

She had a slight smile on her face, but even so, Savvy thought she looked worried. "Why did you ask him that?"

She shrugged. "He's just always so together, y'know. I just kinda wanted to get him, I guess. Everything is so rational in Hale's world."

"That's not why you did it."

Kristina's pale blue eyes met hers for the space of two heartbeats, and then she looked away. "I've just been feeling so off."

"What happened?"

"Nothing happened . . . .nothing specific, anyway."

"Well, how did this start? This off feeling?"

"It just . . ." She pushed away from the counter and paced to the sunroom door. "Maybe it's just fear of the future. I mean, when this little guy gets here, everything's going to be different. Up all night. Diapers. Formula. Total upheaval. Panic time, you know?"

"You're having second thoughts?"

"No, no, no." Kristina shot back to the kitchen again and said earnestly, "I can't wait for this baby. I just can't wait! Once he's here, everything's going to be okay. Maybe there is some panic in there, sure, but I so want this baby. I've just never been as good as you are about keeping a lid on my own craziness."

"I don't know about that."

"You know how put together you are. You've got a great governor on your emotions. You always have. Me? Not so much." She ran her hands through her hair. "Never mind. I'm just tired and acting nutty. Forget everything I said."

Nope, this was definitely not the time to reinterview Kristina about the Donatellas, either. And contrary to all her protestations, Kristina *was* having second thoughts. Something sure as hell was going on. Savvy was really getting worried that Kristina and Hale's marriage might be in serious trouble, and this little baby inside her, the one she was beginning to feel very protective of, wasn't going to save it.

She tried to draw more out of her sister, hoping to deduce exactly what was bothering her, what the "baggage" was, but it was as if Kristina had expended all her energy and had just kinda shut down, seating herself on one of the bar stools, not really offering up much more in conversation. Half an hour later Savannah was out the door and driving south to her home, no wiser to Kristina's issues. Her sister was an enigma, plain and simple.

The rain had turned to a fine mist, and it was dark as midnight. Savannah drove carefully as winds buffeted the SUV, making it shudder and feel loose on the road, and she let out a pent-up breath when she finally pulled into the driveway of the little gray ranch perched on the east side of 101, with a surprisingly spectacular view north to the Pacific. Tonight, however, the ocean was a black expanse, and as she hit the garage-door button, she was glad for the automatic light that came on as the door slid upward. Driving inside the garage, she shut the door with another push of the button, eased her shape out of the driver's door and around the car, then trudged up the two wooden steps that led into the kitchen. Dropping her coat on a chair, she saw the plate that held traces of her earlier peanut butter and jelly sandwich. For one moment she debated about having another one, even though she'd just eaten Gino's linguine.

Better not, she decided regretfully and headed through the living room to her second bedroom, which functioned as a den. Her laptop lay open on the desktop, plugged in, its green light on. She woke it from hibernation and waited to connect to the Internet, annoyed that her mind was still on the peanut butter and jelly sandwich.

She sat for a moment, shrugging off her unsettling meeting with Kristina with an effort, concentrating instead on her earlier interview with Catherine. Thinking of Catherine sent her thoughts to Maggie/Cassandra, and she Googled "Cassandra" and "seer" and found scads of links to information about the mythical princess who could predict the future. She also learned that when Cassandra rejected the advances of the god Apollo, she was cursed to never have anyone believe her.

Cassandra sees things, but they're not always accurate. . . .

Was that the truth? Catherine's body language had belied her words, but did that mean Maggie/Cassandra Rutledge . . . Beeman—or whatever the hell her name was—*could* actually see the future?

"Bullshit."

Savannah decided to put thoughts of Catherine and Maggie/Cassandra aside as well, but first she checked out the story of the Hydra, a mythical beast whose heads grew back every time they were cut off. The Hydra was one of Hercules's seven labors and was finally defeated after Hercules cut off one of its heads, then burned the neck right afterward, cauterizing the wound and thereby making the head unable to regrow.

Burning. Fire. Had Maggie/Cassandra told that story because fire was all that would stop the man who was coming for them?

She laid her hands on her stomach and said aloud, "Now, you're just getting freaky."

Shutting down her computer, she considered the women of Siren Song with their gifts, some of them dark gifts. Hearing a floorboard squeak, she jerked around, her eyes searching the dark corners of the room.

Nothing there.

"Creepy," she said, mad at herself for her attack of nerves. A moment later she decided she needed that peanut butter and jelly sandwich, after all.

The following morning Savannah stopped off for a vanilla yogurt, a banana, and a cup of decaf coffee at the Sands of Thyme Bakery, where she collected her breakfast items, then grabbed a white mug from the pyramid stack next to the "serve yourself" thermoses. She poured her mug full, added a dash of cream, and picked up a spoon before finding a table at the far end of the room.

Sipping her decaf, she peeled the banana and slowly ate it. She wasn't that big of a banana fan, but it was loaded with potassium, and she'd been told it would be a good thing for her to eat as many as possible. So be it. She was a short timer, and she didn't want to do anything to screw things up at this late date. Still, it was downright amazing how much food she could put away and how much she thought about eating.

Her mind drifted back to Catherine and her bizarre lesson on genetics. She was still trying to figure out where the mistress of Siren Song's head had been when she'd gone into her impromptu genetics lesson, what she'd really been thinking about and trying to tell Savvy. Clearly, she was pointing a finger at the Colony males. When Savvy had asked about them, however, Catherine had dismissed them, saying they'd been adopted out, as if that were the only course of action given their condensed power. But there was something more there as well.

The Colony. Savannah couldn't get the vision of a bee colony out of her head. She'd seen many documentaries that said bee colonies kicked out the males—the drones—in the fall, after the summer season was over and before hibernation. The worker bees were all female, and apparently, once the males had serviced the queen, they were persona non grata and were left to die outside the hive.

Was that what had happened at Siren Song? Had the women, the worker bees, kicked out the males? Savvy rubbed her eyes, feeling like she was getting fanciful. Whatever the case, it kinda sucked for the boy children, being pushed out, though, unless you considered that maybe staying under Catherine's roof and abiding by her rules wasn't the greatest answer, either.

Making a mental note to herself to follow up on the Colony's male children, Savvy finished her banana and started in on her yogurt. What she really needed to do was get on the Donatella homicides before she herself was kicked out of the nest of the Tillamook County Sheriff's Department. She chafed at the idea that they would be continuing without her, and she had a somewhat irrational fear that once she was gone, they wouldn't really want her back.

Twenty minutes later she was dashing through a light rain, then hurrying up the short flight of stairs that led to the department's rear entrance. Shedding her coat, she was glad to see she was leaving fewer puddles on the tile floor today. May Johnson was at her desk, and she looked across the room and lifted a hand in greeting. Savannah nodded, then carried her coat over one arm as she turned toward the hallway that led to the working offices in the back of the department. She went to the break room and hung her coat on a rack, then opened a cupboard and pulled out some instant decaf crystals and heated her second cup of coffee in the microwave. By the time she got to her desk, she was one minute late, but there was no one else in sight. Locking her messenger bag in a bottom drawer, she then stared into space a moment, thinking about her sister. What the hell was going on there? Did she even want to know? Kristina had always been flightier than Savannah, but she was really walking the edge right now, which sorta pissed Savannah off.

"Try really being pregnant," she muttered aloud as Lang cruised in, crossed to the desk butting up to Savannah's, and flopped himself into his chair.

"You're still here," he said, smiling.

"Pregnancy isn't a disease."

"Uncalled for," he said, his smile widening.

Savannah nodded, half embarrassed. She thought about blaming her snippiness on her pregnancy, but then she would just be making his point. "I'm going to the Bancroft offices today to reinterview Hale St. Cloud—"

"Your brother-in-law."

"And Declan Bancroft, his grandfather, among others."

Lang nodded. "I'm still chasing down Kyle Furstenberg. I think he may be purposely unavailable."

"Think that's an admission of guilt?" Savannah asked.

"It's an admission of being scared. Maybe an admission of being an asshole. Either way, he's not returning my calls, and everybody around his apartment acts like they've never heard of him."

"Who's around his apartment?"

"Roommates in varying states of slacker-dom. A lot of blank stares, empty pizza boxes, beer cans, and Bic lighters. No cigarettes, though, so I'm guessing they are thinking about their overall health and might be smoking a little something else."

"That's gotta be it," she agreed.

They shared a smile. "I am going to miss you, y'know. When you leave," he said.

"It's only a temporary leave."

"Of course." He inclined his head. "You'll be back in time for the wedding."

"Long before. Long, *long* before," she stressed. Lang and his fiancée, Claire Norris, were tying the knot sometime next spring, and it made Savannah's heart clutch to even think he might believe she would still be gone.

"Kidding," he said, and Savannah narrowed her eyes at him, which turned the smile threatening his lips into a full-grown grin.

"How are things going with Baby Bea?" she asked now, determined to get the spotlight off herself.

"They're going. Catherine didn't say anything about it, huh?"

Claire and Lang had been fighting to become adoptive parents to a little girl who had ties to the Colony and Catherine. Though Catherine seemed to approve of Lang and Claire as parents as a whole, she'd made noise about trying to adopt the baby herself. So far Beatrice was in Claire and Lang's care, but it was anyone's guess what Catherine would try to do, though at present, Savvy knew, she was wrapped up in some other mystery, which seemed to be absorbing her.

She thought about the plastic bag inside her purse but wasn't quite ready to pull it out yet. "What happened with Hillary Enders, the girlfriend?"

"She's coming in after work today, unless she chickens out. She was pretty anxious on the phone."

Savannah checked the time on the wall clock, then unlocked her desk drawer and pulled out her messenger bag, plucking her cell phone from its side pocket. "Better let Hale know I'm coming."

"Hale, yes."

"Funny," she said, then decided to place the call after first speaking with Lang about the knife. She slipped her hand inside her bag, pulled out the plastic square, and laid it on her desk.

Lang's brows lifted as he registered the knife inside.

"It's from Catherine Rutledge," Savvy said. "She wants it tested for DNA evidence."

"Why?" he asked carefully.

"She said it has to do with her sister, Mary. She believes Mary used it to commit suicide, or at least that's what she wanted me to think."

"I thought Mary fell or something. I think that's what it said in *A Short History of the Colony*."

"I've got to read that thing, no doubt about it. Apparently, Catherine told different stories about how Mary died. She said she fell to her death or she died from complications of a miscarriage, but now, by her own admission, those are lies. Mary had been living on Echo Island until fairly recently, I guess. Catherine says I'll likely find Mary's DNA on the knife."

"Echo Island?"

"I know. But there was supposed to be an old harridan living there. That's one of the rumors, anyway."

Lang slowly pulled the plastic bag nearer to get a closer look at the knife inside. "Catherine isn't the type to let out her secrets. Ever. What the hell is she doing?"

"Trying to skirt a full-on homicide investigation and still get some answers from the knife. She asked for a private DNA test and said she wanted to be billed for it, but I'm thinking I'd like to press this myself. Something weird there."

"You're gonna go ahead and process the knife as if it's evidence in a homicide."

"I'm not going to tell Catherine that just yet. I'll wait for the results. But I'm not putting it through as any private request. I want the results back as soon as I can get 'em."

"That woman . . ." Lang shook his head.

"I know. Oh, and I said you might ask for an exhumation of Mary's body."

"Is that what I want to do?"

"Catherine says Mary's dead and the knife had something to do with it. Maybe Gilmore should take a look at her body."

"Maybe," he said glumly.

"What?" Savvy asked.

"You're going to ride off into the sunset, have a baby, and leave me dealing with Catherine and the Colony again."

"I'm coming back. Jesus, Lang. How many times do I have to say it?"

"Lots more."

"I'm coming back," she said again. Then she punched in the digits to Hale St. Cloud's cell phone.

CHAPTER 6

The Seaside office of Bancroft Development was on the top floor of a two-story commercial office building overlooking the Necanicum River. The company used to sprawl throughout the entire building, but with a sluggish economy and the lawsuit looming over Bancroft Bluff, Hale had rented out the lower floor and had condensed the office staff and assigned it to the top floor. Their Portland office, on the other hand, was expanding, as not only did they have the Lake Chinook development, but there were also several apartment projects around Portland nearing completion. With the current sizzling rental market, those buildings already had several offers from would-be investors to buy them outright before they were even finished. And an investment group with a solid reputation had already put in an offer for a high-rise on the east side that was barely in the planning phase. Business, as they say, was booming.

But not at the coast. At least not for Bancroft Development. Currently, they had only three projects under construction, two small commercial buildings and one residential house right on the Promenade, where they were in the process of demolishing the existing house and starting from the bottom up. Of the two commercial buildings, one was a four-unit office condo complex north of the city, near the town of Gearhart; the other was an apartment building with six units, three upper and three lower, tucked along the Necanicum to the south of their offices. To date, they'd poured the foundation for the office complex, and the apartments were being framed. None of the coast projects were even close to completion, and with their limited staff, Hale was wearing a lot of hats these days. He could trust the people in Portland to apprise him of what was going on, but the Seaside projects required daily supervision.

He checked the time on his desk clock. Nine forty-five a.m. Declan hadn't come into the office yet, but as he'd aged, his time of arrival had grown later and later. Sometimes he didn't get in till noon, but since he was more of a figurehead now than ever before, it really mattered only to Declan whether he even showed or not.

Glancing out the window at the now driving rain, he strode out of his office and grabbed his jacket from the wooden tree in the entryway. As he passed by the open door to Sylvie Strahan's office, she glanced up and said in a stage whisper, "Ella's going to give you hell again."

Ella Blessert was their receptionist and bookkeeper. She'd been an assistant bookkeeper before the economic downtown, but after their full-time bookkeeper, Nadine, made the move to Portland with Clark Russo, Ella had taken over all the office bookkeeping duties. She had also, unfortunately, adopted a proprietary attitude about Hale and his well-being, and she was constantly mother henning him. For someone in her midtwenties, Ella was a fussbudget like he'd never seen. Hale wondered if he could sneak out without her seeing him. He didn't really want to be reminded that he never dressed for the weather, or anything else.

But from her reception desk angled in a corner of the upper gallery, Ella saw him before he'd taken the first step down the curving staircase to the first floor.

"You can't go out in this weather without a hat, Mr. St. Cloud. Here, take my umbrella."

"I'm fine, Ella."

Sylvie strolled out of her office with a smile threatening her lips, ostensibly to turn toward the butler's pantry–type coffee room, but she hesitated at the upper stairway rail. Hale gave her a "Don't go there" look, which she ignored, and then she had to cut off some laughter when she saw the lavender umbrella Ella was holding out to Hale.

"We can't afford to have the boss come down with the flu or worse," Ella told him. "You're the engine around here, Mr. St. Cloud."

"It's Hale," he told her for about the thousandth time. Her mannerisms and rigid office protocol tickled Declan, who flirted outrageously with her, but they just made Hale feel tired and impatient.

He glared again at Sylvie, who simply lifted her hands and turned away, her shoulders shaking with suppressed laughter. Though Hale had no interest in Sylvie other than as his right-hand woman, he sometimes wondered why he couldn't have chosen someone more like her as a mate than Kristina. She seemed, at least as well as he could ascertain, to have a strong sense of herself and what she wanted and where she was going. Kristina, on the other hand, was losing confidence daily, and he didn't know what, if anything, he could do about it.

It was all he could do to circumvent the lavender umbrella as he headed downstairs. He was just about to push through the glass double doors to the outside and dash across the parking lot to his SUV when his cell phone started singing the default ring he'd chosen for his sister-in-law. Grabbing it from his pocket, he glanced at the caller: Savannah.

"Hey, Savvy," he answered as he gauged the strength of the rain. A deluge. Maybe he'd been too hasty in ignoring Ella's umbrella.

"Hi, Hale. I need to talk to you some more about the Donatella homicides. Go over some Bancroft Bluff records again. Sometime today convenient for you?"

That caught him up. He'd been expecting to hear something about the baby. "Something happen?"

"We're going over the case again, and I volunteered to talk to you and your grandfather again, in fact everyone from your side of the partnership associated with the Bancroft Bluff project."

"Ahh . . ."

"Would you rather have someone else?" she asked, misinterpreting his reluctance.

"No. Hell." He made a face. It was just that the last thing he wanted to do was rake all that up again. Not that he didn't want to find the killer. It was enough to freeze the blood the way the Donatellas had been executed, and it filled him with rage whenever he thought of the person who'd taken the lives of his friends. If going over all their testimony and files again would help, fine. "My grandfather should be in this afternoon. How does one o'clock sound?"

"Can we make it two?" she suggested. "At your offices."

"That'll work," he said.

With that he ran out to his TrailBlazer, hitting the remote several times and reaping the reward of flashing lights, which let him know the doors would be open. He slammed himself inside, then switched on the ignition as beaded water broke and ran down the sleeves of his jacket, and drips slid down his neck and under his collar.

He drove first to the residential demolition site on the Promenade, the walkway that ran in front of Seaside's oceanfront houses. Finding a parking spot across the street, he waited a few moments, looking at the house they were about to tear down, with its once proud, now tired and worn wooden siding and porch. It had been a very nice home once, but years of pounding wind and rain and sand had beaten it down. The new owners wanted something modern and gleaming, and though Hale was a fervent believer in giving the customer what they wanted, in this case he'd tried to talk them into saving something of the original beach cottage architecture to keep with the surroundings. His advice had fallen on deaf ears.

Seeing the new owners, the Carmichaels, he climbed from his car and jogged across the street, meeting them on the front porch. They were young and wealthy, and Ian's grandfather was friends with Declan. Hale shook hands with both Ian and Astrid, who was six months pregnant. He could hardly talk about the house at all for all the questions Astrid asked him about his "own" pregnancy. How was Savannah feeling? How was Kristina doing? Were they excited? Had they picked out any names? Did they think Savannah would go past the due date? How late did they plan to go before asking about being induced?

"I don't really know," Hale admitted when confronted with this last question.

"I bet you're just so excited," she declared. "Oh, my God. If I was as close as you are . . ." She made a squealing sound and looked delightedly to her husband.

Ian put an arm around her and asked Hale, "So, when's the demolition?"

"Should be next week, barring unforeseen circumstances." This was old news, and Ian was clearly just trying to turn the conversation away from babies and to something else.

But Astrid would have none of it. "As soon as my little girl comes along, we'll have to get together. If you move closer to Seaside, they could go to the same schools together. You should really consider it."

"Leave him alone," Ian said good-naturedly. "Now, about that outdoor planking. You don't think it should be wood?"

"Not if you want it to last," Hale said, leading them through the house, up the stairs, and out to the deck that overlooked the ocean. They discussed the merits of some of the new products on the market. Then Astrid brought the conversation back to babies, and by the time Hale left, he had a mountainous headache. No breakfast this morning, and he needed food.

He left them and drove into Seaside, heading down Broadway and crossing the bridge to stop at the Bridgeport Bistro to pick up a Dungeness crab and Havarti sandwich on an onion bun and a Coke to go. He took them back to his office and ate at his desk. Ella had clucked at him when he'd returned, his dark hair slick with rain, and for half a second he'd seriously thought about acting like he was shivering and hacking up a lung just to see what she would do. Instead, he'd shut his office door and settled at his desk, and that was where Declan found him when he knocked lightly on the panels, then stuck his head inside.

"Did you pick me up a sandwich, too?" he asked, seeing the remnants of the waxed paper that had been wrapped around the sandwich and pinned with a toothpick.

"You need to call me and let me know."

"Cell phones," Declan said with a snort.

"They work," Hale pointed out.

"I'm not hungry, anyway. Just had breakfast."

Hale slid a glance to the clock. Twelve forty-five. "I met with the Carmichaels earlier."

"Who?"

"The people who bought the house on the Promenade." It was worrisome the way his grandfather seemed sometimes to lose track. He didn't want to borrow trouble, but there was definitely some short-term memory loss going on. Was it age or something else?

"Oh, yes, yes." Declan looked slightly embarrassed.

Hale brought his grandfather up to date on what had transpired with the plans for the Carmichaels' house and then moved on to some of the other projects. "We're still red tagged on the Lake Chinook project," he noted at the end, "but I talked to Russo, and he thinks he and Vledich can get it going again without too much more delay."

"You think he's right?" Declan was skeptical of the abilities of Clark Russo, and, for that matter, anyone else who worked for them.

"I don't want to have to go to Lake Chinook if I don't have to," Hale admitted.

"Bad time of year to cross the mountains. Storms are coming," Declan said.

Hale nodded, but he'd been thinking more of the time it would take, two hours plus each way in good weather. "Let's see what Clark can pull off."

Declan harrumphed and let it go. "How's Kristina?" he asked, which was his roundabout way of really asking, "How's Savannah?" which, distilled down, actually meant, "How's the baby?"

"Savannah's coming by today," Hale said.

"Here? To the office?"

"She wants to reinterview us about Bancroft Bluff."

"*Ack.* When in God's name is she going to quit that job with the sheriff's department?"

"As soon as she goes into labor."

"Not before? I don't like thinking about her chasing after criminal scum in her condition. It's not right."

"Well, today she's chasing after us." Hale smiled.

"What are you going to tell her?"

"What do you mean?"

"How many times do we have to rake up DeWitt's incompetence? Our lawyers are handling the whole goddamn mess. We don't need to be talking to the police."

"They have a double murder to solve," Hale reminded, seeking to deflect Declan from another diatribe about their onetime geological engineer.

"Well, it's not our fault. Shoulda never gotten involved in that whole mess with Marcus. It's a shame. A goddamn shame about what happened to him and Chandra. I'm not sayin' different. But it's not our fault, for God sakes. We built in good faith, and if DeWitt had had half a brain, we wouldn't be in this shit storm!"

"She's going to be here at two," Hale said.

"Well, fine." He turned toward the door. "I'll be in my office."

CHAPTER 7

Savannah picked up a chicken Caesar salad at the Drift In Market and ate it at one of the picnic tables crowned with red-and-white-checked plastic tablecloths and bunched into a corner by the west windows. She gazed through the panes, but her view of the Pacific was blocked by other buildings in the small town of Deception Bay, plus there were dense low clouds turning everything fuzzy and indistinct. She had headed north from Tillamook on her way to Seaside and had purposely stopped to eat, but her main reason for choosing the locale was that she wanted to go to the Deception Bay Historical Society and read *A Short History of the Colony,* by Herman Smythe. Lang had told her that the powers that be at the historical society would not allow it to be checked out, but that it was only a few pages long and she could easily read it on-site.

Finishing her salad and the hunk of baguette that came with it, she eyed the cheesecake in the deli case and then left before she was caught in the tractor beam of the desire for sweets. Man, but her resistance was down.

"You're killing me," she said to the mound of her stomach, lightly placing a palm just beneath her right ribs. Baby St. Cloud gave her a kick, and she chuckled as she climbed into the Escape and drove the few blocks to the historical society.

She didn't know all the particulars about the romance between Lang and Dr. Claire Norris, but it was during the time when they were getting together that he'd had his first run-ins with Catherine Rutledge. In the course of that particular investigation, which also delved into the women of the Colony, Lang had learned of Herman

Smythe's small book. It was this compilation that Savannah wanted to see.

The historical society resided in a clapboard building at the edge of town, a building that had once been an old-fashioned one-room church. It still even had its steeple, and Savvy gazed at it as she crossed the parking lot and went up the short flight of wooden steps to the front door. A sign in hand-painted blue letters read DECEPTION BAY HISTORICAL SOCIETY, and when she pulled open one side of the double doors, a little bell tinkled overhead, heralding her arrival.

Glass cases extended in rows, with aisles between them that led toward a counter that ran across the back wall. Behind the counter stood a woman, who'd risen to her feet at the sound of the bell. Currently, Savvy was the only visitor.

"May I be of help?" the woman asked. She was the epitome of an old-time librarian with her gray-streaked brown hair pulled into a bun and a pair of pince-nez glasses perched on her nose, the glasses attached to a thin silver chain looped around the back of the woman's neck. A brooch with a large amber stone was pinned to a dark brown cardigan sweater, which she wore over a white blouse that topped a tan, ankle-length skirt.

"I'm looking for the book *A Short History of the Colony*, by Herman Smythe."

The woman examined Savannah's appearance. Savvy had on black slacks and a tan T-shirt, with folds of material to give her belly room to grow, and over it all she wore a black jacket. Her Glock lay at her right hip.

"You're with the sheriff's department?" the woman asked, staring at her gun.

"Yes, I'm—"

"You'll need a court to requisition the book. It is a one of a kind and does not leave the property." She met Savvy's eyes, a challenge in hers.

"I'm not trying to requisition it. I just want to read it."

She narrowed her eyes at her, plainly trying to decipher whether Savvy was telling the truth.

"Would that be possible?"

For an answer, the woman walked over to a bookcase and unerringly pulled out a thin volume. She held it a moment in her hands, as if loath to relinquish it even for a moment to Savvy's care. Then she shook her head and held it out. "You can sit at the table over there."

"Thank you."

Settling herself down, Savvy opened the book and read.

A SHORT HISTORY OF THE COLONY
by Herman Smythe

Introduction by Joyce Powell-Pritchett, Director,

Deception Bay Historical Society

Let me introduce myself first. My name is Joyce Powell-Pritchett, and I've been the director of the Deception Bay Historical Society for the last twelve years. A Short History of the Colony was given to the historical society by the estate of Dr. Parnell Loman. Though it was originally believed that the account was written by Dr. Loman, subsequent discovery showed that it was really Mr. Herman Smythe, a contemporary of Dr. Loman, who compiled and wrote the narrative.

"The Colony" is a loose term for the group of women who live together at Siren Song Lodge in Deception Bay, and who are the descendants of Nathaniel and Abigail Abernathy. Mr. Smythe is honest about the fact that his account was taken from word of mouth, mostly from a colony member, Mary Rutledge Beeman, who is one of the two last descendants listed in the book. Mr. Smythe personally knew Mary Beeman before her death, as well as her sister, Catherine Rutledge, who still resides at the lodge with some of Mary's children, who are unnamed in the account.

Mr. Smythe is still living, and when I told him I was going to write an introduction for him, he smiled at me, his eyes twinkled, and he said, "People keep acting like the book is all lore, but believe me, I was there during the seventies and eighties, and I'll stand by my words as fact!"

Whether truth, or truth mixed with fiction, I'm sure
you'll agree, A Short History of the Colony is a fascinat-
ing read.
Enjoy!
Joyce Powell-Pritchett

Savvy looked at the woman, who was staring back at her.

"Yes, I'm Joyce Powell-Pritchett," she said, as if Savvy had asked the question.

Nodding to her, Savvy dropped her gaze back to the narrative.

FROM THE ANNALS OF HERMAN SMYTHE:
The locals around Deception Bay call them the
Colony. Why? Because in the late 1800s they built a lodge,
which was named Siren Song somewhere over the years,
and they've lived there together in a commune-like tra-
dition ever since. Who are they? Well, let me tell you
what I learned from Mary Rutledge Beeman, my friend
and one of the most colorful characters from the
Colony's already colorful past!
It all started when Nathaniel Abernathy married his
young bride, Abigail, and moved from the East Coast to
the West Coast, about as far as humanly possible across
North America. Both Nathaniel's family and Abigail's
were rumored to be descendants of the women who
were condemned to die during the Salem,
Massachusetts, witch trials of the 1600s. Incidentally, the
capital of Oregon is Salem, and it was named after
Salem, Massachusetts.
Nathaniel and Abigail must have gotten a big
surprise when they realized their union spawned chil-
dren with extraordinary abilities. No one knows how,
but it's a proven fact that Colony members—usually
women—can do amazing things. How? It's been specu-
lated that it's in the genetic code for this tribe, the result
of a mutated gene, maybe. Whatever its cause, it has
played havoc with Colony members and locals alike
throughout the years.

When Nathaniel and Abigail Abernathy reached the Pacific Ocean, they decided that's where they wanted to live, and set about buying up as much real estate as they could. They purchased a stretch of property along the Oregon coast and therefore amassed vast acreage that included mountain forests with old-growth timber, a large rock quarry, and a hunk of coastline. In a very short period of time their holdings stretched from the foothills of the Coast Range on the eastern edge, across the land on both sides of what is now Highway 101, to the Pacific Ocean itself (though, because of a later Oregon law, the beaches that were their property were ceded back to the state, as all Oregon beaches are now publicly owned).

The Abernathys cleared smaller tracts of land, too, and Siren Song was erected in a spot that was clear cut of timber. Stands of forest still abut the south section of the lodge and grounds, framing the lodge and a makeshift unincorporated "town," which is inhabited mostly by Foothillers. (More about them later.) Southwest of the lodge is the small town of Deception Bay, which spills across Highway 101 in both directions toward the timberland to the east and the Pacific to the west.

From the onset Nathaniel and Abigail bartered and bought even more adjacent lands to expand their isolated retreat. Though their descendants no longer own that stretch of beach or Serpent's Eye, the small jut of rocky coastline directly across from the lodge, where a now-unused lighthouse still stands (an area that's islanded when the tide comes in), they do own a larger island, Echo Island, which is about one square mile and is located in the treacherous waters of the mouth of Deception Bay itself—the bay the town was named after, which in itself was named for the deceptive and deadly currents and waves that swallow fishing boats almost every season.

Nathaniel and Abigail got busy right away starting a family, but of their children, only two survived: Sarah and Beth (Elizabeth). All the boys died in infancy or were stillborn, as were several other girls. Abigail was late in her life by the time Sarah and Beth arrived, and though she lived into her late eighties, long past her husband, she wasn't much of a parent to her daughters, so they mostly raised themselves. Beth, plagued by visions or sounds or sensations she couldn't handle, apparently went mad when she was in her early thirties. She had one son out of wedlock, Harold Abernathy, who was scorned by the townspeople both for being born a bastard and for always acting decidedly odd. A hermit, Harold lived in sin with his young wife, an Indian shaman's daughter, who died giving birth to Harold's only child, Madeline "Mad Maddie" Abernathy, who lives in Deception Bay to this day.

Savannah stopped reading again, though she didn't lift her eyes from the page. She was remembering her own meeting with Madeline Abernathy Turnbull and the woman's predictions that she would have a boy—before Savvy even knew she was pregnant. Though Madeline had never lived at Siren Song, and had mostly been shunned by Catherine and Mary, she'd certainly seemed to have received the "gift" of precognition.

The further Savvy delved into the history of the Abernathys, Rutledges, Beemans, et al., the more she felt as if she were being sucked into a mire that, although interesting, wasn't going to help her discover the truth about Mary's death or anything else. Still, she was determined to finish *A Short History of the Colony,* if for no other reason than to be as informed as everyone else.

She turned back to the page.

Beth either fell or threw herself off a cliff into the sea. She was presumed dead, though her body was never retrieved from the cold waters of the Pacific. Some people think she was pushed to her death, possibly by her sister Sarah, who got rid of Beth in order to become sole heir to the vast property amassed by their parents, Nathaniel and Abigail.

Sarah Abernathy, the surviving daughter, married James Fitzhugh in 1909, but James died in a hunting accident on their tenth wedding anniversary. In 1920, a full year after her husband's death, Sarah gave birth to a baby girl, Grace. It's been theorized that Sarah had an affair with an Indian shaman, whom she seemed to fall under the spell of sometime before her husband's death. Rumors have it that Sarah and the shaman plotted to kill James, but no one knows for certain, and his "accident/murder" has never been solved. Sarah has been much vilified by the Deception Bay townies over the years, and even her descendants are suspicious of what her intentions were.

But everyone agrees that Sarah was remarkably bright and learned about the value of land ownership from her father, Nathaniel. She managed to increase the family's amount of acres of timber and farmland and their coastal holdings during her lifetime. Sarah raised Grace alone and modernized the original homestead, transforming it into the imposing lodge it is today, although electricity and indoor plumbing run only on the main floor. The upper floors are much as they were when the place was first erected.

During Sarah's time, there was a bunkhouse on the property, left over from her parents' days of ranching and farming. Some say she enticed local men to do the work by offering up sexual favors. Others fervently believe Sarah possessed strange powers and that she used those powers to persuade the neighboring farmers, millwrights, and lumbermen to build onto the lodge and improve the grounds. Whatever the case, men seemed to come from far and wide to help out, while their wives and sweethearts stewed and gossiped about Sarah, only adding to the rumors of witchcraft that continually plagued the Colony and their supposed demon-possessed ancestors.

Members of the local community, Deception Bay, have long regarded the growing "cult" with suspicion.

Fueled by gossip and the strange heritage of the Colony, the townspeople felt Sarah believed she was some kind of high priestess. It's not clear who dubbed the lodge Siren's Song, whether it was the locals or someone associated with the Colony itself, but Sarah's actions seemed to be the reason, and the name stuck. Sarah's shaman lover never acknowledged that he was a) her lover or b) Grace's father, but his friendship and relationship with Sarah continued until her death in 1956, shortly after her daughter Grace's marriage to Thomas Durant, a hard-drinking, good-looking, and hotheaded lumberjack who grew up in and around the Colony. Thomas was the son of one of the male workers who seemed completely under Sarah's spell. (Thomas Durant's mother, who was known by the single name of Storm, was a member of the same Indian tribe as Sarah's shaman lover. Some say that Storm was the shaman's sister and that Thomas was really Grace's first cousin. This is the same tribe from which the sole member of the other branch of the Abernathy family tree— Harold Abernathy—took his young Indian bride.)

At the time of Grace and Thomas's marriage, Grace was already pregnant with Mary, who was born June 21, 1958, the summer solstice, and the town gossip is that Thomas raped Grace in a night of drunken debauchery. From the get-go, Mary was a fussy, unhappy baby—the result of "nature" or "nurture," or possibly both, as the fights between Grace and Thomas were legendary. He was a womanizer; she a fiery, angry woman who could give as good as she got. (Baby Mary seemed to absorb the fury, wrath, and passion between her parents, Grace and Thomas, and was herself an unstable brew of mystical, inexplicable genetic material. She grew psychologically twisted herself. A dark personality at best, a deranged one at worst, Mary's strange behavior became legendary.)

After Mary's birth, Grace and Thomas's relationship, always tumultuous, grew even more strained. They both recognized something strange and dangerous in their daughter, though neither really addressed the issue head-on. They always spoke of it in the abstract, though even when she was a baby, Mary's precognitive skills were obvious.

When Thomas inexplicably disappeared bare months after Mary was born, the locals breathed a sigh of relief, as he was a notorious drinker and brawler. But then more rumors swirled. What happened to him? Where did he go? Was foul play involved? No one, however, was really interested in asking a lot of questions, not even the local sheriff, as Thomas Durant was in and out of the local jail more often than not, always causing problems. People were kind of glad he was gone. Maybe he was killed; maybe he wasn't. A number of people said they'd spotted Thomas in the days after his disappearance, and everyone allowed that he'd probably just taken off. It was the safest assumption. Still, like Grace's aunt Beth's body a generation earlier, he never resurfaced in Deception Bay.

Grace, free of Thomas, married John Rutledge in 1959, regardless of the question of the marriage's legality (since no one knew whether Thomas was missing or dead). From the moment of the marriage Grace maintained that Mary was a Rutledge and never used the name Durant again. Within the year, Grace and John had one child together, a girl, whom they named Catherine.

In 1975 Grace and John were killed in a freak automobile accident: their car missed a turn and plummeted into the Pacific Ocean at the sharp corner known as Devil's Point, a spot where the storms that rage across the Pacific hit the shore with incredible force. The funneling waters at that cove have become the graveyard for many a boater or surfer. Grace's daughters, Mary and Catherine, were seventeen and fifteen, respectively, at the time of the accident. Though Grace and John had always planned to write a will in which

*they named Catherine as the primary beneficiary—
therefore leaving her in control of Siren Song and all the
other property—Catherine was too young at the time of
their death and they never fully formed their plans.
Their eldest daughter, Mary, took over, and that's when
the fun really began.*

*Mary treated her new position much as her maternal
grandmother, Sarah, had: as if she were a high priestess
and the only rules that mattered were the ones she made
herself. But Mary wasn't as innately intelligent as Sarah,
and her hot anger wasn't tempered by cold calculation,
like her father, Thomas's could be. Mary was a very sexual being and took lovers indiscriminately. This is a fact
I'm personally aware of, as I spent time at Siren Song
myself, one of Mary's many willing conquests.*

But this story is of the Colony, not me.

*Another of Mary's lovers was one Richard Beeman,
who, Mary claimed, was her husband. There is no
record of this union, though Catherine insists the marriage was real. If Richard Beeman were truly Mary's
husband, he certainly slipped in and out of Deception
Bay and Siren Song without much more than a "How do
you do?" I'm inclined to believe he is a fabrication.*

*At the time of her parents' death, Mary, wealthy
enough to do as she pleased, was beyond a narcissistic
megalomaniac. Her mind was fractured, however, and
self-satisfaction and even cruelty were her way of life. As
far as relationships went, Mary slept with whomever she
wanted, and damn the consequences. She left behind a
string of lovers and a number of children whose paternity has never been fully established.*

*Mary's sister, Catherine, never married. She became a
midwife to Mary, who delivered children like a mother
cat, indiscriminately and without much interest in the
newborns once they were a couple of months old, and
she was also called occasionally by the townies, if a midwife's help was needed. They feared her less than they
did Mary.*

The Colony had a feel of a commune after Mary took over, during the last half of the late seventies and into the eighties, with Mary still as sexually active as ever and Catherine managing the care of the growing brood of Mary's offspring.

Beyond Catherine and Mary, there were a number of men who lived in the bunkhouse, which burned down in the mid-1980s. These men were there to service Mary, and there are tales of Catherine shooing them out time and again, and rumors that she actually struck the match that finally burned the bunkhouse down. There were also a number of cottages built along the eastern rim of land, which leads toward the Coast Range, and a smattering of families still live there. These Foothillers— whom I mentioned before—formed their own "town," which has never been really named or incorporated. Most Foothillers are Native American, but some were shirttail Colony members, never fully recognized, but bound by some ill-defined relationship. Some of them ex-hibited extra abilities. Some of them pretended to be special. Some of them claimed to be Mary's past lovers. Mary paid scant attention to them, as she did the men who later cruised through the bunkhouse, while she de-scended into a darker interior world. Eventually, those Foothillers who were tied to the Colony all but disappeared.

The core of the Colony has always been women. As a rule, they possess the strongest extra abilities and seem to be the hardiest. Mary almost seemed tuned to some inner radar when it came to picking her lovers, the fa-thers of her children. With surprising success, she bore mostly girls, and those girls possess extraordinary abili-ties, which seem to reach their zenith around puberty. Of the boys born during this time—if there were any—little is known.

The Colony has tried to live in relative isolation. Peo-ple in Deception Bay are wary of them. They seem to be from some other place and time, especially after Cather-

*ine took total control, somehow wresting it from Mary.
When that happened, Catherine changed everything,
right down to her own and Mary's daughters' daily ap-
parel. Per Catherine's decree, they all dress as if they
were from a previous century, wearing long skirts and
calico prints, with their hair mostly in buns. The townies
live in uneasy coexistence with Catherine and watch her
closely on the rare times she deigns to go into town for
supplies, mostly food and gasoline/fuel. The enlightened
locals of Deception Bay consider those of the Colony
merely benign oddballs, out of step with reality and the
world, young women who live with their "clan." Still,
there are the dissenters, who consider them beyond
weird, even evil, based on the lingering rumors of witchcraft, all the missing people, and the unexplained deaths.*

*The absence of men—other than the "studs," who
moved through the commune either from the bunkhouse
or the Foothillers community, or were random lovers like
myself—hasn't gone unnoticed, either. There is definitely
a townie element that is resentful, mistrusting, and envi-
ous of the women of Siren Song and their dark gifts.*

*Mary started her brood of children in 1976, when she
was eighteen. They are:*

1. 1976 – Isad

*This is where the account ends, I'm afraid. We know
the eldest daughter's name is Isadora, but the rest of Herman Smythe's book has been lost. Older members of the
historical society remember there being a leather book
with notes and letters, into which this smaller, laminated
volume was tucked, but it, like many things associated
with the women who live at Siren Song, has gone missing.*

*If you have further questions, please drop by the De-
ception Bay Historical Society next time you're in town.
I would be happy to discuss the history of the Colony
with you personally.*

Joyce Powell-Pritchett

Savannah closed the book and looked across the room at Joyce, who was standing behind the desk, still watching her.

"May I ask what your interest is in the Colony?" Joyce asked.

"I'm just educating myself."

"Has something happened that's involved the sheriff's department?"

Savannah assumed it was normal curiosity on the part of Joyce, but she wasn't about to satisfy it. "Only that I'm the newest hire at the department and have the least information."

"Ah."

"So, no one knows what happened to the larger book that this smaller one was inside?"

Joyce sighed. "There's even a question of its existence. The members of the historical society I referred to in my comments have not been . . . as reliable as I'd first believed. It may be that it exists, or it may be that they have it confused with Mary Beeman's journal."

"There's a journal?"

"Several of Mary's acquaintances have said so." She stressed the word *acquaintances* ever so slightly.

"Thank you," Savvy said, handing the book back and heading toward the door. She could see that she needed to put an interview with Herman Smythe on her to-do list.

"Looks like you'll be taking a leave soon," Joyce remarked to Savannah's back as she pushed open the door.

"How right you are." It was like having a neon sign that read PREGNANT flashing above her head all the time.

A few more weeks, she told herself. *Only a few more weeks.*

CHAPTER 8

The garden and graveyard behind Siren Song held many secrets. Catherine's ancestors had had a very checkered existence, and sometimes when she reviewed their decisions, she wondered how she'd ever been born to such a wild and infamous crowd, and then other times she believed her very survival was because she was so clinical and cool and able to make the hard choices—the ones required after whatever newest and latest debacle occurred.

The wind was up, and she could barely hang on to her hood and cloak. She hurried along the garden pathways, then stepped gingerly into the small graveyard, bypassing slapping wet bare branches from the maples and shivering birches, which were starting to overgrow on the grounds. First, she walked to Mary's grave, with its headstone that read MARY DURANT RUTLEDGE BEEMAN, BORN JUNE 21, 1958, DIED APRIL 13, 1995. More than one lie was mixed into that information. After staring down solemnly a moment or two, she moved down the path, glancing back toward the lodge, where the downstairs lights gleamed through the windows, piercing the afternoon's gloom.

Mary's real grave was toward the back of the graveyard and had been covered by several transplanted Mrs. G. W. Leak rhododendrons, which would bloom in April or May, depending on when they got their first good weather and the lush pink flowers unfurled, tiny stamens and pistils waving from their red-throated trumpets. Catherine knew Mary must have died this past spring, and after Earl had brought her body back to Siren Song, she'd planted the rhododendrons above her for a dual purpose: to honor her sister and to hide the fact that the ground in the back of the graveyard had been recently disturbed.

Currently, the rhododendrons were thick green bushes with flat, wet leaves. Catherine glanced their way but walked past them, not wanting anyone from the lodge to see her and wonder what she was doing. She knelt down at Nathaniel's grave, kissed her fingers, and placed them to the flat headstone. He'd been a good boy. Slow, but sweet, and the victim of another's evil intent, or so she'd always suspected. He, of the boy children born to her sister, was the only one who had been allowed to stay.

She waited another few moments, glanced back once more toward the rhododendrons, then retraced her steps to the lodge. She couldn't give Mary's real grave any attention without inviting a lot of questions, and she didn't give Mary's believed grave much attention, either, as she knew the prevailing thought among Mary's children was that she and Mary had suffered a parting of the ways, one that had never been resolved, one that Catherine couldn't forgive. In truth, though, yes, she and her sister had definitely suffered a falling-out, she ignored her sister's "grave" mainly because of who lay inside the coffin.

Entering the lodge by the back door, she passed through the length of a long, narrow storeroom, and she hung her cloak upon a peg near the alcove that led to the kitchen. Row upon row of home-canned goods lined the walls: peaches, pears, green beans, tomatoes, corn. Opening the door, she entered the alcove, an anteroom that held their sewing machine and was where she and Ophelia and Isadora made their clothes. The alcove led directly to the kitchen, and when she passed through it, she found Cassandra sitting at one end of the oak trestle table, her hands folded on its smooth lacquered top.

"Where is everyone?" Catherine asked.

"Upstairs. Lillibeth is in her room. Ravinia is planning to leave sometime soon, you know."

Catherine sighed. "I was hoping she'd be over that by now."

They stared at each other. Catherine had her problems with Ravinia, but Cassandra was the one she could fathom the least. Catherine herself had a bit of Cassandra's precognition, but she could not see into Cassandra's mind the way she could sometimes see into the minds of others, and she was always amazed, grateful, and a tiny bit frightened at the strength of the girl's ability.

"You're mad at me for talking to her," Cassandra said. "The detective."

"No."

"Yes, you are."

"I'm concerned. There's a difference. I gave Detective Dunbar something that, unfortunately, may shine a light on us here. A light I would prefer not to shine, but I need her to get me some information."

"What kind of information?"

Catherine smiled faintly. If Cassandra didn't know, she wasn't about to tell her. "What did you tell Detective Dunbar?"

"I told her he was coming."

"Ah, yes. He's coming." Catherine closed her eyes and pressed a finger to her temple, fighting a headache.

"It really is like the Cassandra of mythology, isn't it?" the girl said suddenly, with some bitterness. "You don't believe me."

"Oh, I believe you, all right. That's not it. I just wish you hadn't said anything to Detective Dunbar."

Cassandra shook her head angrily. "You can talk to her, but I can't?"

"You know it's wiser to keep your predictions inside these walls."

"I think I'd like to be Margaret again," she stated flatly. "Call me Maggie from now on."

"Cassandra." Catherine was deeply shocked.

"Rebecca and Lorelei have lives outside of these gates. Happy lives. Normal lives. And after Justice died, I thought things would change. *You* said they would change."

"You said 'He's coming,' and you didn't mean Justice," Catherine countered. "That should be reason enough to keep things as they are."

"No, I don't mean Justice. . . ." Cassandra darted a glance to the back window suddenly, toward the graveyard. "The bones," she whispered.

"The bones?"

They both stared silently for a moment, and then Cassandra drew in an unsteady breath. "You don't see them?" she asked her.

"Them?" Catherine slowly wagged her head, even while her nerves jangled. Sometimes Catherine could see a trace of Cassandra's vision. Not often, but sometimes.

"He came from bones."

"We all have bones," Catherine said, seeking to deflect Cassandra from this line of thought.

"You don't need to treat us like children, Aunt Catherine. You've got to let go of us. You do know that."

"I made a vow to myself to keep you all safe."

"It's not going to work this time. Our world is about to fall apart."

Catherine's heart seized. "What do you mean?"

"This isn't working. You know it's not working, but you won't change. And you're keeping secrets that are dangerous to us," she accused.

"I'm not keeping secrets," Catherine replied, surprised.

Cassandra's blue eyes looked toward Catherine, but they weren't seeing anything in the room. "There's something about Lillibeth. . . ."

Catherine shut her brain down, focusing on a black wall inside her head. She didn't want to go there. Not now. Not ever. And she couldn't have Cassandra seeing things she shouldn't. This was new and unsettling.

"You blame Mary for what happened to her. . . ."

"Who is he? Who's coming?" Catherine demanded. "The one from the bones?" Then, "What did you tell Detective Dunbar?"

Cassandra stared at her but didn't answer.

"Cassandra, I need to know."

"Call me Maggie," she said, suddenly standing erect. With a cold look that Catherine had never seen before on her expressive face, she stalked out of the room and away.

For a moment Catherine just stood there. She didn't know how much of what Cassandra had predicted was the truth and how much was what she simply wanted Catherine to believe. Hearing the squeak of Lillibeth's wheelchair, she turned her head, and moments later the girl appeared in the aperture between the kitchen and the great room.

In a dark blue dress, her hair in a golden plait down her back, her blue eyes full of questions, Lillibeth asked, "What's wrong?"

Cassandra's words echoed in Catherine's mind. *You blame Mary for what happened to her. . . .* "Nothing's wrong."

"What did Cassandra see?"

"She said that Ravinia wants to leave."

Lillibeth gave her a look. "Everybody knows that. What else did she see?"

"Nothing specific."

Feeling a rising despair, Catherine fled upstairs to her room, but once inside she turned around and reversed her steps, heading down the gallery and past the girls' rooms to the steep, narrow stairs that led to the third floor. She held her skirts in one hand and the rail with the other, climbing the full flight and feeling a little out of breath at the upper hallway. At the far end of that hallway was a set of double doors that led to a suite that was never opened. Mary's suite, directly over Catherine's head. No one ever went inside; Catherine hadn't allowed it since Mary's last lover staggered out after learning of Mary's death and half fell, half ran down the stairs and outside and Catherine had locked the gates after him.

Now, however, she pulled a ring of keys from her dress pocket, unlocked the right-side door, and pushed it open. The shriek from its rusted hinges made Catherine jump in spite of herself. Quickly, she closed the door behind her and turned the lock from the inside. Then she faced the musty unused room, leaning against the door she'd just locked for support.

A shag area rug in bright orange lay on the fir plank floor. A four-poster bed with a gold lamé bedspread stood in the center of the room, while wisps of silvery netting feathered from the canopy, waving in the breeze that Catherine's entrance had created. It all looked fragile and weak; it would probably go poof and disintegrate if she touched it. She could count the times she'd entered this room since she and Earl had drugged Mary and taken her to Echo Island. She never liked entering it even when her sister was alive, especially during the heyday of Mary's sexual activity, though there had been that time she'd sneaked in and rolled like a cat in heat upon the bed with the only man she'd ever loved.

Pressing her hands to her cheeks at the memory, Catherine walked quickly to the mirrored bureau, opening every drawer, searching inside and behind and beneath. Nothing. She then moved on to the vanity, with no success, and finally reached under armchairs and peered beneath the rug, though there was clearly nothing there. On her hands and knees she fumbled around under the bed, but all she disturbed were spiderwebs and dust bunnies, which made her sneeze six times in a row.

On her feet again, she walked to the closet, which was fairly small given the dimensions of the oversize room. She dug through shelves and folded clothes and hatboxes and kicked through the shoes lying haphazardly on the floor. She knew what she was looking for. A box. The matching one to the tooled-leather one where she'd kept the knife. She and Mary had each been given a keepsake box by their mother, and Catherine had kept hers in pride of place on her bedroom vanity while she was growing up. But Mary had squirreled hers away, and Catherine knew there were secrets inside, secrets that she now wanted to know more than anything. All these years . . . *all these years!* . . . and it suddenly felt imperative that she find the box and learn as much about Mary as she could. Both she and her sister had kept journals, though most of Catherine's were full of the mundane moments in her life, the dreams of an adolescent girl who was shy around boys; while Mary, whose gift had driven her down a different path, had kept her journal secret and hidden away, and long after Catherine had given up on hers, Mary had kept writing. Once Catherine had come upon her, and Mary had screamed at her to get out, but not before Catherine had seen the words *sexual power,* and she'd known her sister was writing about her own dark desires.

For the first time ever Catherine wanted that journal. She was no longer afraid to see what it contained and felt with certainty—as if Cassandra had told her herself—that there would be something inside that would lead her to find out who had come to Mary at Echo Island. One of her lovers? One of her sons? One of her *daughters . . . ?* No, the only daughters Mary had given birth to were part of Siren Song, and none of them were capable of taking a boat through the treacherous waters to Echo Island.

Some stranger, then? Someone who knew how to navigate about the island? It truly wasn't all that hard if you knew what to do and you had the strength to do it. Both were a necessity to avoid having your craft thrown against the rocks. At least that was Earl's contention, and Catherine believed it. The foolish who set off for Echo ended up in real trouble, their boats smashed to smithereens, their lives at risk. There had been enough deaths to keep most people from bothering with the island, but there were always a few who took a gamble. The last attempt had been made by young men fueled by alcohol and the desire to prove something to their friends—a bad combination. All of them had failed spectacularly.

But *someone* had made it ashore. Despite what she'd told young Detective Dunbar, Catherine knew Mary had not committed suicide. Her narcissistic sister would never take her own life. It was just a question of who had.

He came from bones.

Shivering, she pushed that thought aside, even while she determined she was going to have to go through the adoption pages, which were undoubtedly with Mary's journal, and find out what had happened to the boys.

CHAPTER 9

The rain slashed against his office window as the wind rattled the panes and whooshed around the corners of the building. Hale looked up and checked the clock. He'd done the same thing every minute for the last ten. It was almost two o'clock.

As if she'd heard the thoughts crossing his mind, he heard voices in the outside mezzanine and knew Savannah had arrived. Pushing back from his desk, he rose to his feet and smoothed an imaginary tie, as he wore an open-throated gray shirt and darker gray Dockers, decent enough for the office but sturdy enough when he went to the construction sites.

He opened his office door and saw Ella just finishing with his sister-in-law. Savvy was saying, "I'd like to talk to you later, if that's all right."

Ella's face was ashen; her eyes were huge. "All right."

"You're scaring my employees," Hale told her.

Savvy sent him a faint smile as she came his way. She wore black pants and a tan shirt, and he saw that she'd hung her black jacket on an empty peg. "I'm dripping water all over your floor," she said.

"You and everybody else. It's unavoidable. Come on in."

As a detective, she wasn't required to wear the regulation uniform that the deputies sported, which, she'd told him, suited her just fine, because interviewees in the course of her work found it less intimidating—at least until she said something that gave her job away, as she apparently had with Ella.

He held the door and watched her walk across the expanse of his office floor and ease herself into one of the two visitor's chairs. Circling the desk, he retook his chair. He knew she was here to ask more questions about the Donatella murders, but he couldn't help just staring at her. It boggled the mind that she was carrying his child. His and Kristina's.

"How's it going?" he asked her.

"Good. Dinner last night was just what the doctor ordered. Wonderful stuff. Thank you."

He waved that away. "What did you and Kristina talk about?" Then he heard himself and said, "Never mind. That's not why you're here."

"No, it's fine. We talked about the baby a little. It's getting close now. Could be any time, really, and I think Kristina's feeling . . ." She hesitated a moment, then said, "Scared. A little."

Scared a lot, he thought but said, "What about you?"

"Oh, I'm fine." A shadow crossed her eyes.

"What?"

"I'm being treated like a leper at work. No, that's not quite right. More like an alien. It's difficult."

That faint smile again. Hale examined her smooth cheeks, blue eyes, the auburn hair pulled upward into a messy bun of sorts that looked, well, sexy. *A woman in a uniform, so to speak. Who knew?*

"What?" she asked, noticing his expression, which he realized had grown a bit wistful.

"I was just thinking about Kristina." Wishing, once again, that she was more certain of herself, more in control, he thought.

"You're going to make great parents," she said, and he wondered if the words sounded as hollow to her ears as they did to his. With that she flipped open the small notepad, which he hadn't noticed she was carrying, and detached the pen she'd clipped on to it.

She started asking him the same questions as another member of the Tillamook County Sheriff's Department had asked him months earlier, at the time of the murders. Then, he'd been so stunned by the Donatellas' deaths that he couldn't recall his answers as soon as they were uttered; he didn't know what he'd said. He'd felt like a blathering idiot.

But he sure recognized the same questions now: Where were you at the time of their deaths? What was the tenor of your working relationship? Were you aware of any enemies they might have had?

He answered that he'd been home the night the murders took

place. The lawsuits had been at full boil at the time, and there were people mad at both the Bancrofts and the Donatellas, but he did not believe they were mad enough to actually *execute* Marcus and Chandra. Personally, he and Kristina had been good friends with them.

"When was the last time you saw them?" Savvy asked.

"I saw Marcus that day . . . the day they were killed," he said soberly. "Chandra the Saturday before. The four of us had gotten together for dinner at our house to bond, I guess you could say. Not just because of the lawsuits, but seeing all those properties condemned . . . We were going through hell. Our engineer, Owen DeWitt, was practically drinking himself to death, and Marcus and I were trying to figure out what to do next. Kristina didn't even want to talk about it. She was sick about the Donatellas' house in particular. She loved it."

"I remember her mentioning it," Savvy said.

"Chandra felt the same. We were all . . . glum."

"On that last day, the next Friday, when you saw Marcus?" she prompted.

"We all met at their house. It wasn't in immediate danger of structural problems. It still isn't, actually. But the owners had abandoned the surrounding houses, which we hadn't purchased from them yet, so it was a ghost town."

"Who's 'we'?"

"Declan and I met with Marcus. We tried to come up with a plan, but nothing concrete was decided upon. When Declan and I left, Marcus was still at the house."

Hale wasn't telling Savannah anything new, but she was writing notes to herself, and he supposed it always helped to have a fresh look.

"He didn't mention anything about meeting his wife there later that night?"

"No." He gazed at her directly. "I understand you rousted a vagrant out of one of the homes yesterday."

She seemed surprised by his information. "Did Detective Clausen call you?"

"Stone. He wanted to know if we had any information on what happened to Marcus's office girl, Hillary, and he told me that you and

Clausen got some guy out of the Pemberton house before he could start a fire."

"Do the Pembertons still own the house?"

"It reverted to Bancroft Development. The Pembertons sold it to us, and they stayed out of the lawsuit. The dune's been temporarily stabilized, and we're looking for a long-term solution for the houses that remain." He lifted his shoulders. "We'll see."

"You think that's a serious possibility?"

"Maybe. Hopefully." He hesitated, then admitted, "It's a long shot."

"Do you have an updated list of home owners that are suing you?" She moved around in her seat a bit and said, "Braxton Hicks contractions," to Hale's questioning look. "They're going away now."

He turned to the filing cabinets that lined the east wall. "There's a ton of paperwork here. You want a copy of something, Ella will get it for you. What did you say to her that shook her up, by the way?"

"I asked her about Hillary Enders after Detective Stone already had. She and Hillary are apparently friends, and Detective Stone is following up on that angle, but when I saw the name Blessert on her desk nameplate, I mentioned Hillary and said I wanted to talk to her after our meeting. I think she feels double-teamed."

"Maybe it'll give her something else to think about and get her to stop overcaring," he said dryly. He told her the story of the lavender umbrella, and Savvy, who'd seemed awfully tense, relaxed a bit. "Shouldn't you be giving this up soon?" he asked, nodding toward her protruding belly.

"That's the song everyone's singing," she said, expelling a breath.

"Don't like being the alien?"

"I just want to make some progress on this investigation before I go on maternity leave."

She was being so formal with him. So official. A far cry from the Savvy of last night, even. "What's going to happen after the baby's here?" he asked her. "Have you and Kristina talked about it? Because I haven't got a clue. Are you . . . just turning the baby over at the hospital? Or are you . . . breast-feeding?" he asked, feeling uncomfortable even asking, but hell, Kristina wasn't telling him anything and he had a right to know.

"We haven't talked about it," she admitted, dropping eye contact. "I'm not sure what Kristina wants."

"What do you want?"

"I'm not sure about that, either." She looked up briefly, then back down at her notes. "What do you want?"

"I guess none of us have a clue."

A long silence passed; neither of them seemed to know what to say. Eventually, Savvy drew a breath and said, "I think I'll look through those files now. . . ."

Hale showed her which drawers held the files that pertained to Bancroft Bluff, and then he left the office, feeling slightly disturbed. He was going to have to pin Kristina down and soon. She clearly wasn't going to come to him, so he was going to have to go to her.

He returned a few moments later with two bottles of water. Savvy had several files spread out on the small conference table in the corner and was examining the newest papers on the lawsuit. Technically, without a court order, the company didn't have to show her anything more than what they'd already given, but Bancroft Development had nothing to hide, and Hale wanted to find Marcus and Chandra's killer as much as anyone, and, well, Savvy was his sister-in-law and was pregnant with his baby.

"Thanks," she said when he handed her the water.

"Think any of this is going to really help?" he asked, gesturing to the spread-out papers.

"I hope so."

"You want those photocopies?"

"That would be great, actually."

He walked to the door and called, "Sylvie?"

"She's on a break," Ella said.

"I actually wanted you, anyway. Can you start on some photocopies for me?"

"Sure, Mr. St. Cloud."

"Hale." He gestured for her to enter the office, and when she spied Savannah, she stopped in the doorway. "It's the Bancroft Bluff files."

"All of them?" She looked taken aback.

"Just these last few months' worth," Savvy told her.

"Okay . . . ," Ella replied.

"I understand you talked to Detective Stone today," Savvy added.

"He wanted information on Hillary, too," Ella said quickly. "I gave him her address." Ella grabbed up the files that Savannah handed to her and scurried out.

"I am really scary," Savannah said.

"You are," Hale agreed lazily.

She suddenly smiled at him. Really smiled. His breath caught for a moment, and then there was a rap on his door. Hale opened it to find his grandfather standing just outside, leaning on an ebony-handled cane.

"What's going on?" he asked, stepping into the office. His white hair had lifted in tufts, and he looked surprisingly disheveled, not his usual immaculate self.

"Savannah's here, working the Donatella murders. I told you."

Declan's bushy gray eyebrows slammed together. "You're about to have my great-grandson, miss. What in God's name are you doing investigating Hale?"

"I'm not really investigating Hale—" she started to say, but he cut her off.

"You should be making plans to have this baby. That's what you should be doing." Declan shuffled around and looked out the door, asking querulously, "Where's Sylvie?" Then, "Oh ho!"

Hale took two steps to the door. He peered out to see what had captured his grandfather's attention just as his wife's voice demanded, "Where is everybody?"

Kristina was just cresting the top step and was in the process of folding up an umbrella and shrugging out of her coat. She added them to the clothes tree by the reception area and gazed expectantly at Hale.

"Ella's in the copy room, and Sylvie's on break. Savvy's here," Hale said.

Kristina was marching toward his door, but his words caused her to stop short. "Here?"

"I told her she should quit this nonsense," Declan declared. "Time to start thinking about the baby."

Kristina headed forward again. As she entered the office and moved past Declan, who stood just inside the door, she demanded, "What nonsense?"

"My job," Savannah said.

Hale waited until everyone was inside before closing the door. Declan worked his way to one of the visitor's chairs, and Kristina moved to the table where Savannah was closing the files that Ella hadn't taken to the copy room.

Hale was wondering what in the hell had brought his wife to Bancroft Development. Once upon a time Kristina might have been interested in what he did for a living, but those days were long gone. Now he had no idea what she did with her time, and he almost didn't want to ask.

Do you believe in sorcery?

"Your job?" Kristina repeated.

"Working the Donatella homicides," Savvy said. "Getting some background."

"Didn't you already do that? Has something happened?" Kristina quizzed.

"We've been through this already." Declan waved a dismissive hand.

"And yet the killer hasn't been found," Hale said mildly. "We want to do everything we can to help the Tillamook County Sheriff's Department catch them," he said for his grandfather's benefit.

"I don't even want to talk about it," Kristina said with a shudder. "We're having a baby. That's what we should concentrate on."

"You are right, honey," Declan agreed. "That's what's important. My great-grandson and my grandsons. That's what matters. That's what counts."

"Grandson," Hale reminded. "I'm your only one."

"What did I say?" Declan asked.

"Leave him alone, Hale," Kristina admonished, turning to Savannah, who was heading toward the door. "Are you finished?"

"When Ella brings me the photocopies," Savvy responded.

Hale beat Savannah to the door and pulled it open again. Ella was just returning from the copy room, and Sylvie, back from her break, had reached the top step.

"Here you go," Ella said as she handed Savvy the files with a challenging lift of her chin, clearly feeling Savvy's investigation was a heinous and traitorous act.

"Wha'd I miss?" Sylvie asked.

"A Bancroft family reunion," Hale said dryly.

"Your mother isn't here," Declan said.

"Janet lives in Philadelphia and probably wouldn't show, anyway," Kristina answered for him.

Hale didn't feel like talking about his mother, who had divorced his father when Hale was eighteen, and had moved away. Preston St. Cloud's health had failed following the divorce, and he'd slowly declined until his death. End of story.

At the mezzanine Savannah suddenly stiffened and leaned forward a bit, dropping a hand to her belly.

"What is it?" Hale demanded.

"More Braxton Hicks. I've been having them on and off for weeks," she said.

"False labor," Kristina called from inside the office.

"Yes . . ." After a moment, Savannah collected herself and said, "I'm heading to Portland next to check with your office there. I understand some of your employees used to work here in Seaside."

"A number of them," Hale agreed.

"You can't go to Portland," Kristina declared, coming to stand in the office doorway. "You're . . ."

"Pregnant. I know." Savannah nodded. "It'll just be a day trip. Can you give me a list of the people who were working in Seaside at the time of the homicides?"

"Sure." Hale didn't like the idea of Savannah heading to Portland, either, though there was no real reason to feel that way. Yes, the weather wasn't great, but a lot of storms swept through the mountains in the winter, and everyone who lived at the coast and had business in the valley learned to deal with it. "Clark Russo is the manager of the Portland office. Everything got kind of shaken up when the lawsuits started, and he moved over. Then, after the Donatellas were killed, we all kind of . . . made changes."

Sylvie said, "I suggested Clark for Portland."

"It was a good choice," Hale added. "We needed someone who could really take the reins, and that was Clark. Besides, he wanted to go."

"He got spooked," Declan said, his tone disparaging.

"Anyone else?" Savannah asked.

Hale nodded. "The project manager. Neil Vledich. Russo's in the office, while Vledich is our on-site manager." He thought about things and said, "Our bookkeeper quit and moved to Portland, Nadine Gretz. Ella took over her job here. Nadine's no longer with us, but she was integral to the company."

Ella piped up. "We have some construction guys who move back and forth. They're like temporary employees."

"I'd like their names, too," Savvy said.

"And there's Sean Ingles. He's our architect," Sylvie said. "He works out of his home, and he's not exclusive to Bancroft Development, but he designed most of the houses at the bluff."

"Can you alert Mr. Russo that I'm coming tomorrow?" Savannah asked.

Kristina sighed. "Can't you put it off? Or let someone else go?"

Savvy met Hale's eyes, and though she was careful not to reveal her thoughts, he was pretty sure she was silently thinking, *See what I mean?*

"You might as well talk to DeWitt, too," Declan said with a snort. "He's the nincompoop who okayed building on the bluff in the first place. Cost us a fortune! Should be criminal charges against him."

"DeWitt lives in the Portland area," Hale allowed. "As I said, he was the project engineer. We let him go after the problems with Bancroft Bluff surfaced."

"Fired his ass," Declan said. Then his neck turned red with embarrassment. Hale knew his grandfather was old school enough not to want to swear in front of the women. Which just went to show you how deep-down furious he was with DeWitt. Not that Hale was happy with the man, but it was all water under the bridge now.

"Are we good here, then?" Hale asked Savannah, who nodded and thanked him again. Sylvie returned to her office, and Ella to her desk, and Declan, after a moment, said he was going to get his things from his office before heading toward the elevator.

When Savannah had gathered her jacket and was saying good-bye to Kristina, Hale retraced his steps to his office, lost in thought, and it was only when Kristina suddenly appeared in his office doorway again that he thought to ask her why she'd come.

"Can't I stop by and just visit my husband?" she asked, moving inside.

"You never have before."

"Well, maybe I'm turning over a new leaf. We need to be together more now, Hale. You know?"

She gazed at him somewhat anxiously, and Hale shook his head. "Because of the baby?"

"Well, of course, because of the baby. And for us, too." She actually came around his desk and sat herself on his lap. It was so unusual that Hale just stared at her in disbelief. "Don't look at me that way. Don't you want to get closer?"

"Can we talk about this at home?" He glanced at the pile of papers on his desk, though his mind was still on the meeting with Savannah.

"Kiss me," she demanded.

"Kristina . . ."

"You just don't know how to be romantic!" she declared, jumping up from his lap and stalking across the room. "I want you to sweep me off my feet. Make my knees go weak. Just *undo* me."

He lifted his hands, palms up, at a complete loss. "Since when?"

"Fuck you, Hale," she snapped, and to his shock, there were tears standing in her eyes. "I need help. We need help, and all you do is stand there and stare at me like I'm completely mad!"

"This isn't who we are, Kristina."

"And whose fault is that?"

"If you want something different in our relationship, I'll sure as hell give it the old college try, but I can't go from zero to sixty that fast."

She shot across the room, back to him, leaning over his desk urgently. "I can. I can get hot so fast, it's like . . . record breaking."

"Since when?" he wanted to ask, but said instead, "Okay . . ."

"Could you try to meet me halfway? Just try?"

"Well, tonight I've got a meeting with—"

"Break it. Come home. Make love to me, and let's put some heat back in this marriage."

Hale slowly nodded. It was the last thing he wanted, he realized, and that made him feel guilty as hell.

"I need to have sex with my husband," she said, as if she could read his thoughts.

The elevator bell dinged, and Hale heard the doors whisper open. A moment later Declan stood in the office doorway, looking a bit confused. "Can't find my damn keys."

Hale got up from his desk and hurried to help him. Anything to get away from Kristina and her strangely desperate need to put things "right" in their marriage.

A few moments later Declan declared, "In my pocket! I swear, I searched there."

Hale said, "I'll head down with you," and waited while Declan worked his way into the elevator car again. As the doors closed, he saw Kristina throw him a look as she grabbed her coat, and he couldn't decipher what was on her face. The closest emotion he could come up with was fear.

CHAPTER 10

Savannah drove away from Bancroft Development, shifting in her seat, as her Braxton Hicks contractions kept right on coming. She had lied about them going away and had done her best to ignore them through the rest of the interview. But maybe these contractions were something more, although every other time she'd felt that way, the contractions had disappeared, so she wasn't about to make that prediction yet. It was almost as if her eagerness to think they were real scared them away. Screw that. She wasn't going to think about them too hard unless they settled down into rhythmic waves.

She sighed. On her way to Hale's offices her mind had been full of thoughts of the women of Siren Song and what she'd learned from Herman Smythe's account, *A Short History of the Colony*. Mostly she'd focused on the "gifts" that had apparently been bestowed upon the young women who still resided there, the fact that they'd been passed down from generation to generation. She'd also gotten a further insight into Mary Rutledge Beeman's days of uninhibited sex and why Catherine Rutledge had drawn a halt to all of them. Savvy had concluded that she should learn more about the offspring—the girls and the boys—whom Mary had given birth to, find out their names at the very least. Since Catherine wasn't eager to pass out that information, she would contact Herman Smythe, and even though he'd been much younger when he'd written the account of the Colony, there was nothing like going to the source.

But after meeting with Hale and running up against Kristina, Declan, and everyone else at Bancroft Development—that was what it had felt like, a battle more than an interview—she'd dropped thoughts of Catherine and the Colony in favor of the department's ongoing investigation into the Donatellas' deaths.

The good thing about that meeting was that Hale St. Cloud had been easy to get along with and more than helpful. In fact, the whole staff had followed his lead and had bent over backward to give her anything she needed. In her experience, everyone—*everyone*—resented the police looking into their business, no matter if they had something to hide or not, so it was a pleasure being treated with respect and an eagerness to help. She'd never seen that side of Hale before. Was it because she was carrying Baby St. Cloud? Undoubtedly, that was a factor, but was there something else there, too? Maybe he thought he could dissuade her from delving deeper into his company books if he was extra nice?

"Cynical," she said aloud, driving along the curving cliff-side highway.

Still, it seemed like he'd handed over everything she could have asked for. Was it really that he had nothing to hide, or was he merely killing her with kindness?

Her abdominal muscles suddenly seized, and she sucked air between her teeth. *That* was a particularly hard contraction. Could this be it? Could it? Nope . . . nope . . . she wasn't going to be fooled this time. She would just wait.

Fleetingly she wondered if she should change her plans about driving to Portland in the morning. Maybe it was a foolish decision to go, but could she just stand by, waiting and waiting and waiting, while Stone and Clausen and everyone else kept moving forward on the case? Was her interest in being involved less about results and more about her just being obsessive, anxious, and competitive?

She growled in her throat, annoyed at herself. She should probably stay on this side of the mountains and make some phone calls. It wasn't the same as in person, but it was still just follow-up information. On the other hand, it was all she had.

Her cell phone rang, and she recognized the ring tone she'd assigned to her sister. She answered through Bluetooth. "Hey, there."

"Savvy, what the hell? Don't go all 'Just the facts, ma'am' on us. You don't know Hale as well as you think you do. He's really, really volatile, and the Donatellas' murders have nothing to do with the Bancrofts, anyway."

"Hale was nothing but nice."

"I'm telling you, that's an act. Don't mix up the Bancrofts with the Donatellas. I don't know what the hell that was about, but you're all wrong."

"I'm looking for the killer of your friends."

"Of course. And I want you to find the sick bastard, but just . . . give it up. Go on maternity leave. Please, please, please. For me. Take a break until after the baby gets here."

Savannah stared through the windshield at the driving rain. Maybe Kristina was right. She gritted her teeth, unable to explain to her sister all the reasons why she wanted to keep going.

"And it sounds like it was a lovers' quarrel that went bad, anyway. It has nothing to do with us," Kristina noted.

"What did you say? How'd you know that?"

"I heard on the news that Marcus was having an affair with Hillary Enders and her boyfriend was the one who shot them. It was on at noon. Channel Seven, with that Kirby bitch."

"Pauline Kirby *said* that they were killed by Kyle Furstenberg?" Savannah asked as she braked for a hairpin curve, the SUV sliding a bit before straightening out.

"That sounds like the name. She said it was the prevailing theory," Kristina added, "but then he got on and said he didn't shoot them, but, of course, they all say that."

"You mean *Furstenberg* was actually interviewed on television?"

"That's what I said." Kristina was getting perturbed. "But did *you* hear *me?* About giving up the investigation?"

"Pauline Kirby asked Kyle Furstenberg whether he shot Marcus and Chandra Donatella on the Channel Seven noon news," Savannah said, clarifying everything.

"Yes. That's right," her sister said with barely controlled patience.

"And he denied the crime."

"Again. Yes."

"Was Hillary Enders part of the interview?"

"God, Savannah! I already told you everything I know. You've gotta stop this."

"Was there anyone else in the interview besides Furstenberg?"

"*No.*"

"I'll call you later." Savannah was terse.

"No, no! God damn it. Don't get further involved, if that's what you're trying to do. Let it go."

Savvy clicked off without another word, then put a call in to Lang's cell, wondering if he'd gone home already.

He picked up on the second ring. "Hey, Savvy."

"Did you know Kyle Furstenberg gave an interview with Channel Seven today?"

"I heard." He sounded disgusted.

"What's the deal with Hillary Enders? I saw Ella Blessert at Bancroft and asked for Hillary's address, but you'd already talked to her, and she thought you'd probably already talked to Hillary, too."

"Hillary Enders is here."

"Here? You mean at TCSD? Now?"

"In the interview room. She wanted to meet with us, and so I said, 'Come on down.'"

"What about Furstenberg?"

"He *doesn't* want to meet with us. I got through to him, but when I said I was with the sheriff's department, he got off fast."

"So, he talks to the media but not to us." She was disgusted as well.

"Par for the course. I'm hoping Hillary can shed some light on her relationship with Marcus Donatella, and we'll go from there. I've gotta go. We're all set up."

"Wait! I'm on my way."

"Look, Savvy. Hillary's ready to talk. She *wants* to talk. I'm not going to put this off and have her get cold feet," he responded. "She's one scared chicken, although I'm not sure she really knows anything, anyway."

"I'm twenty minutes out."

"I'm not waiting," he said, exasperated. "You don't even have to come."

"Don't piss me off, Lang. Really. Don't piss me off."

"Jesus H—" He cut himself off. "O'Halloran wants to talk to *you,*" he said meaningfully after a pause, "and you know what that's about."

"Yeah. He wants me to start my maternity leave. Well, stand in line. If he wants me to quit early, then he can tell me in person. I'm almost there, so save me a seat."

He muttered a few words under his breath.

"What's that?" she demanded. "Got something to say?"

"Just hurry up," he ordered, then clicked off.

Savvy wasn't near as bold as she'd been on the phone by the time she wheeled into the back parking lot of the TCSD. The rain had turned to a blowing wind, which shivered and bent the firs and caused the overhead wires to swing to and fro. The mud puddles were full of cold water, and Savvy skirted them as she made her way to the rear entry, hurrying up the few steps and then stalking down the hallway to the interview room without bothering to drop her jacket on one of the pegs by the door. As predicted, her Braxton Hicks contractions had disappeared, and she entered the room feeling more in control of her body than she had all day.

Hillary Enders sat at a table, a Styrofoam cup of coffee cradled in her hands, her head bent, long dark hair falling forward, screening her face. She was thin, almost waiflike, shivering and pale.

Lang was seated opposite her and was saying quietly, "I believe you. I don't want you to feel interrogated. If you say there's no truth to what we heard, I believe you."

She nodded jerkily, her whole body rocking.

"It's just that we really need to talk to Kyle, too, and he's avoiding us," Lang went on after shooting Savannah a look that warned her not to disturb him. Message received, Savvy stayed back by the wall, trying to blend into the surroundings.

"Kyle wouldn't hurt anybody," Hillary said.

"He told a reporter that you were having an affair with Marcus Donatella. Now, he may have been lying, or he may have really believed it."

"He knows I would never." She gulped at the coffee, spilling a little.

"So he was lying, then?"

"I don't know. I didn't see the interview."

"We can sure get you a copy of it, but in the meantime, let me tell you what he said." He looked down at the file in front of him. "'She dumped me for her boss, but I didn't kill him, and anybody who says I did is a lying piece of . . .' The last word was bleeped out for all the viewers' delicate ears."

She shot him an upward glance to see if he was joking. "Sounds like him."

"Well, it is like him. He said those things."

"I wasn't cheating on him. We broke up after what happened to Marcus and Chandra. . . . I was a mess. It was just awful." She slowly shook her head, staring into the middle distance. "But Kyle . . . he didn't get it."

"Didn't get . . . ?"

"Why I was so upset. I mean . . . really? He couldn't understand?" She took a hand from the Styrofoam cup and placed trembling fingers to her temple. "It didn't affect him like it did me, so he was just the same. It didn't work between us anymore. Maybe he did think I was seeing Marcus. I don't know. I haven't talked to him in months."

Lang considered. "Let's assume he did believe you were in a relationship with Marcus Donatella, since that's what he said on the news."

She didn't respond.

"Maybe he killed Marcus and Chandra Donatella as a means to get back at you."

"No. Oh, no." She was positive. "He's not like that."

"Was he over you? The relationship?" Lang asked.

She shook her head, whether in answer to his questions or just because she didn't even want to consider them, Savvy couldn't tell. "Where did Channel Seven get the idea that he killed the Donatellas?" she demanded. "It's ludicrous. You don't understand what Kyle's like."

"Maybe you could fill us in."

"He's a big doofus," she declared. "We've known each other for years. Were we dating? Yeah. But it wasn't going anywhere. He's not marriage material, if you know what I mean."

"Is that what you're looking for?"

She turned her gaze from Lang to Savvy and then over to O'Halloran and Deputy Burghsmith, who were sitting at a back table, listening. Hillary had clearly allowed them to be there, but now she looked like she was changing her mind.

"You think I had designs on Marcus Donatella? That's what Ella told you, isn't it? Ella Blessert. Because I told her I thought he was good-looking and successful. *Marriage material.* Except, well, he was *already* married, and in my book, that counts for something. Ella's a doofus, too." She pressed her lips together and scowled at Lang. "I wasn't having an affair with Marcus Donatella, and I'm not in love with Kyle and never have been. Maybe Kyle thought I wanted Marcus, but he never said so when Marcus was alive, so I don't see how you people even got his name." A moment later she said, "Ella. This all comes back to Ella, doesn't it?"

"Kyle's the one who said you dumped him for your boss," Lang reminded, though in truth, Hillary was right on in her assessment.

"I've got to see this TV interview," Hillary declared. "If Kyle said that, somebody must've put the idea in his head and he just repeated it."

She was one smart cookie, Savvy thought with admiration. The reason she'd come to the station was that she knew there was no truth to the accusations and she wanted to nip this story in the bud. Lang sensed it, too, because he leaned back in his chair and regarded the woman thoughtfully.

"You think you could get Kyle to talk to us?" he asked. "If he doesn't want to come to the station, I could go to him."

"Do you believe me?"

"Can you help me with Kyle?"

"I don't see him anymore, but I could call him, I suppose," she said reluctantly.

Lang nodded, pointed to her purse, and Hillary, catching his drift, grabbed up the purse, dug around inside it, then pulled out her cell and placed the call. After a moment, she said, "Voice mail," in a stage whisper. Then a few more moments passed, and she launched into, "Hey, Kyle. It's me. The police want to talk to you. Just try to tell them the truth, okay? I don't appreciate your lies. You know I wasn't with Marcus Donatella. Don't be such a dick." Clicking off, she looked up at them half angrily, a flush creeping up her face.

"Thanks," Lang said, closing the file.

"Are we done here?" she asked.

"For now. We appreciate you coming in."

For the first time she relaxed a little. "I was afraid you were all going to be so eager to close the case that I would have to get a lawyer and time would go by, and the real killer would be still out there. I want you to find him and lock him away forever. I liked both of them, Marcus and Chandra. . . ." She trailed off, and her eyes became slightly moist. "String the bastard up."

Fifteen minutes later Hillary Enders was on her way back to Seaside, and Lang, Savvy, O'Halloran, and Burghsmith were looking at each other.

"Back to square one," Lang said.

"You think she was telling the truth?" Burghsmith asked.

"Uh-huh," Savvy said, and they all nodded in agreement. "Where's Clausen?" she asked.

"Had to cut your friend Mickey loose on the trespassing violation, so he followed him to make sure he wasn't heading right back up to Bankruptcy Bluff," Lang revealed.

"He will go back there," Burghsmith said knowingly. "They always do."

"What about Toonie?" Savannah asked. Toonie was Althea Tunewell, who ran a shelter on the south side of Tillamook. She was often contacted by the department when there was a homeless situation.

"We called her, and she came by," Lang said. "She offered him space, but he didn't sound ready to go. There was a lot of Jesus talk between them, but Toonie's for real, whereas your friend Mickey just spouts off stuff randomly, so I'm not sure it's gonna take."

"Why is he my friend Mickey?" Savannah asked.

"You found him," Lang pointed out.

The sheriff, who'd been standing by, listening, cleared his throat and asked, "Dunbar, can I see you in my office?"

Savvy shot a look toward Lang, who just raised his brows in that "Didn't I warn you?" way. She followed O'Halloran into his office and waited as he took a seat, his chair squeaking in protest under his weight.

"When are you due?" he asked without preliminaries.

"Sean, I know you want me to quit now," Savvy responded. "I don't want to, but I will soon. I just have a couple things I want to finish first. Tomorrow I'm driving to Portland to interview the Bancroft Development employees in that office. I saw Hale St. Cloud today, and he's let them know I'm coming. On Monday I'll come in and file a report on those interviews, and then . . . okay . . ." She felt slightly depressed, but it was sort of a relief, too. She was pissed off and tired of fighting, and there was only so much she could do, anyway.

"We'll talk about this on Monday. It's just the fieldwork we need to cut out," O'Halloran said.

"Okay."

"You sure you want to go to Portland? Could be bad weather. Somebody said something about a cold front coming."

"I'll stay in Portland if the weather gets bad."

He held up his hands in surrender, and Savvy left the room, feeling like she'd won a major battle, even if she'd lost the war.

Hale entered the house through the garage door and tossed his keys on the kitchen counter, by the phone. He pulled out his cell phone and snapped on the charger, which was already plugged into the electrical outlet. Then he went back into the garage and took off his jacket, leaving it on the coatrack that hung next to the row of cabinets that held lawn and gardening tools.

They'd lived in the house for about two years. It was Sean Ingles's architectural design, the last of his work for Bancroft Development and Hale personally before he'd left for Portland. Everyone said how beautiful the house was, how the rock and wood beams and shingled siding were a work of art, depicting the beauty of the Northwest to perfection. Hale supposed it was true, but somehow it had never felt like a home. Maybe it was too staged for him. Maybe it was too perfect. All he wanted when he came home was an easy chair in front of a television and a glass of wine or a beer and a good meal, which constituted anything from take-out pizza to soup and/or sandwiches to something gourmet and elegant. His tastes ran from pedestrian to exotic. He wasn't picky, and he'd even cook himself, although his repertoire was somewhat limited.

He didn't, as a rule, think he was hard to live with. Yet somehow Kristina made him feel like he was. Was he kidding himself?

Well, he'd moved the meeting over the office condo project per his wife's instructions, and now he was trying to work up some enthusiasm for the romantic evening she had planned. Since he hadn't seen her, he wondered if she was already in the bedroom. Uncomfortably, he recalled the conversation he'd had with his grandfather when he'd walked him to his car.

"Woman troubles?" the old man had asked after complaining loud and long about not needing a babysitter to get to his vehicle. Hale had accepted the verbal scolding in silence until Declan's last comment.

"Kristina and I have a lot of stuff going on right now."

"That's a lot of bullshit, son. Pardon my French."

Hale wasn't about to go into it further and said simply, "Maybe Kristina and I can straighten some stuff out tonight."

Now he walked down the hall to the bedroom, carefully pushing open the door. The nightstand lamps were on, set to the lowest setting of the three-way lightbulb, giving the room a soft ambiance. There was no sign of Kristina, however, and Hale stepped into the room and then ducked his head into the en suite bathroom. The room gleamed in chrome and Carrara marble with white towels. No Kristina.

"Where are you?" he asked aloud, wondering if she was playing some game. His gaze swept over the room, and he realized there was a note wedged between the quilted tan pillow shams. Apparently, it had fallen between the two pillows. He crossed the room in two quick strides and grabbed it.

Changed my mind. I'm not mad. I just need a little space. Kristina.

It was such an about-face, he might have wondered about its authenticity, except it was written in her distinctive handwriting.

He strode back to the kitchen and opened the refrigerator, grabbing a Corona. There wasn't much of anything in the realm of leftovers, so after a moment he picked up the phone and called Gino's for the second time in two nights. This time he ordered a calzone stuffed with pepperoni, provolone cheese, mushrooms, and olives. For a strange moment he thought about ordering two, though he knew that Kristina wouldn't touch it. But then he wasn't thinking about her. He was thinking about Savannah.

"Is that all?" the voice on the other end of the line asked.

"Yeah." Hale hung up and went back out to the garage, grabbing up his cell phone and jacket on his way to pick up the meal.

Kristina wasn't a religious person in any way, shape, or form, but if there was such a thing as hell, she was surely living it.

She drove north and tried to calm her mind and her body. She'd been so susceptible, so hungry, and the things she'd done. . . . It made her blush to think of them. But even worse were the memories of other things. The sheer horror and depravity and the knowledge she possessed that could get her in serious trouble with the authorities or worse. And when she thought of Marcus and Chandra . . .

A small cry escaped her lips, and she pushed those horrific memories aside, seeking to bury them, as she had for months. She hated herself, and she was embarrassed, too, at how she'd appealed to Hale. Yes, she'd meant all those things, but even if he'd thrown her down on his desk and slid hard and deep inside her, driving to her core, though she might have had sexual fulfillment, she still wouldn't be free.

Free.

She said it aloud, "Free," tasting it on her tongue to see what it felt like, aware her voice had a hollow and fearful quality to it.

She'd made a pact with the devil, and it had ruined nearly everything good in her life. She had to stop it before it consumed her and all the people she loved. She had to stop it tonight.

The rain had abated, and an icy wind had taken its place, the harbinger of a cold front that was moving in from the north. She realized she was shivering uncontrollably by the time she reached the house, and she worried briefly about her tires—would she pick up a nail?—as she drove into the gravel drive, with its fine layer of sawdust, the last traces of which were evident in the blowing wind as it scrubbed the area almost clean.

Clean. Another word she wanted to apply to herself. In her mind's eye she envisioned a huge eraser that was inside her brain, exorcizing the terrible thoughts and desires that had taken root there.

All because of *him.*

Her jaw tightened. Well, she was through with him. Through with all his persuasions and lies, his cold eyes and even colder smile. He was a monster, and she'd been so weak. But now . . . now . . . she was feeling stronger. She and Hale were about to have a baby, and maybe it was latent motherhood—God, she hoped so—but all the nearly incoherent fretting and babbling she'd done for weeks no longer felt necessary. She was going to *do* something, by God. Tonight. Now. And he could just go fuck himself.

Picking up her flashlight from inside the pocket on the driver's door, she tested the beam. *Strong,* she thought with a flutter of assurance. Just like she was. She climbed out of the Mercedes and looked at the old house. She'd chosen the venue for once—the Carmichaels' house, which Hale was reconstructing. She wanted to feel Hale's strength running through her. This was his project. A home base of sorts for her.

Exhaling on a sigh, she mounted the steps to the porch and tried the door, not surprised to find it locked. But the house was scheduled for demolition, and she knew it wouldn't be tightly secured. The windows were either painted shut or wouldn't close. Hale had said as much to her in passing once.

She was early. She'd planned it that way. She needed to catch him unaware to have any hope of coming out of this alive and well. Nervously she walked around the porch, which ran along every side of the house. In the dark, the old, decrepit building seemed sinister and almost anticipatory, like it was waiting for her. She shivered and shook that off. *Ridiculous.* Turning a corner to the beach side, she was hit with a slap of wet wind. She tucked in her chin and groped with her fingers for the window, tugging to open it. No luck. It took her until the third window and a growing desperation before she could get her fingers into the gap beneath it. With all her strength, she shoved it upward. It gave with a wrenching cry, and cradling her purse, she could finally shoulder her way in.

When she climbed through to the living room, she was accompanied by another gust of water-soaked wind, the water dragged off the ocean, as the rain had stopped. There was a puddle inside—the gap in the window had allowed its entry—and she felt dread settle into her heart. What she had planned was unnerving, and yet she intended to go through with it.

She stepped gingerly, still in the peep-toed shoes and outfit she'd worn to Hale's office, hoping against hope to entice him with how desirable and luscious she looked. Her mind shied away from the humiliation of that failure.

Switching on her flashlight, she shone its beam upon the wooden rafters and the balusters of the narrow balcony above. She had been through this house with Hale and hadn't liked its cottage style, though its ocean frontage was fabulous. But the house she and Hale had built was even more fabulous, and the ocean was right there, too. Maybe not at ground level, like this, but accessible via a stairway that hugged and curved down the headland.

Inside she was cold. A quiver had set up residence in her gut. She had told him she would meet him at seven, and then had burned up the road to be here by six thirty. It was her turn to lie in wait. She'd played enough sexual games with him to know his MO, and though she had been a slave to his game—and had admittedly been sick with desire—she'd learned a thing or two along the way. Oh, yes, he had power and a way of setting her senses on fire, but after what had happened, she'd slowly been released from his grip. At first she'd thought it was his doing, that he'd let her go. But she'd come to realize over time that no, this was her own pleasure-drugged conscience slowly awakening, and though she'd panicked with Hale today, begging him to give her the same burning sexual thrill that the devil stirred in her, that same panic had given her a cold-eyed view of what she must do: confront him and kill what was between them forever, no matter what that took.

In fact, if she . . .

Something caught her attention. A noise? A smell? Something was definitely out of place.

Don't be silly, she scolded herself, but her nerves tightened in spite of herself.

She took another step.

"Hey, lover."

His voice shot a thrill of fear through her. She glanced up again, to the balcony. He was already here!

"I'm not here to play games," she said, but her damn voice quaked as if she were terrified.

Then she felt it come at her, like a snake, like a rope, his overwhelming sexual power. Closing her eyes and gritting her teeth, she fought it back. She seized on the idea that if she were a block of ice, he couldn't penetrate her, and it seemed to work, for she was not swamped by a desire so strong that it left her slack and panting and jelly-limbed. After a few moments, she dared to open an eye and glance upward.

He was holding a short, thick beam, his arms straining from the weight though he was strong. She registered this the same moment the beam hurtled toward her.

She opened her mouth to scream, turning.

Crash!

Pain blasted through her head as the beam smashed into her. Jarred and broken, she crumpled into a loose heap. She couldn't move . . . couldn't draw a breath. For a moment she lay awake, her eyes staring upward. Vaguely, she heard running footsteps, and then he was beside her, his face swimming like a mirage, until she focused and saw the intent look in his eyes. Her last thought was, *He's watching me die. . . .*

And then she was gone.

CHAPTER 11

Savannah got out of bed while it was still dark, took a shower, then dried herself off, standing in profile at the mirror to get a good, hard look at her body. Yep. Pregnant. Really, really pregnant.

She towel dried her hair, then let it land lank against the bare skin of her shoulders as she searched for what to wear. As her shape had grown larger, her wardrobe had shrunk down to a tan shirt, a blue one, and a black one, and two pairs of black slacks. Today she went with the blue blouse and a gray pullover sweater, which she would team with the black pants and the black raincoat that hung, waiting, in the closet by the front door.

She'd never been much for high heels, either, which was a bonus in the career field she'd chosen, but occasionally, right now being one of those occasions, she longed to dress up and look attractive. A short skirt, a body-hugging top, a pair of three-inch heels . . . yeah, that would be great. Except she would look ludicrous given her third-trimester shape. Maybe after Baby St. Cloud arrived, and she went through a fitness program to lose the extra pounds . . . maybe then she would treat herself to a shopping spree in Portland. Go to one of those fancy boutiques downtown or up on Twenty-Third. And if she was back at fighting weight, maybe hit Papa Haydn or Voodoo Doughnut for dessert.

She was smiling as she blow-dried her hair and snapped it into a ponytail. She added a bit of blush, then called it good. She spent the next fifteen minutes packing an overnight bag and eating some peanut butter toast. Then she looped the strap of her messenger bag over her neck and shoulder, slipped on a pair of black flats, grabbed her raincoat and her overnight bag, and headed out the door. She was in the garage, climbing into the Escape, when she hesitated, feeling the chill in the air. *Cold front. Hmmm.*

Back inside the house, she rummaged through her closet for a heavier coat. Finding a dark blue ski jacket, she eyed it skeptically. Sliding her arms through the sleeves, she realized it was not going to make it around her middle. She needed something bulkier, but she didn't own such a thing.

I can buy a coat in Portland.

Tossing the ski jacket over her arm, she headed back outside, re-locked the door, then climbed into the SUV, threw the jacket into the back footwell, and placed her messenger bag next to her on the passenger seat. She didn't damn well care what the weather was going to do at this point. If bad weather hit, she would stay overnight in Portland. No harm, no foul.

She gave one more thought to the Braxton Hicks contractions, but they hadn't started again since they'd quit the afternoon before. From everything she'd heard, first labors took a long, long time, so any way around it, she would make it back to the coast in time to have this baby. And, if by some outside chance that didn't happen, well, Portland had some of the best hospitals in the state, most of them, actually. Sure, Kristina and Hale wouldn't be there, but in some ways, that was okay with her. She wasn't sure she even wanted either of them around while she was going through labor. She didn't know if she could stand the ultra-solicitousness. A few nurses, a doctor . . . perfect.

But if all went as planned, she'd be turning and burning and back in Tillamook before it got dark, anyway.

She glanced at the clock on her dash. Six a.m.

She'd be in Portland by eight.

Dawn was still a long way off, but Catherine was seated at the table in the kitchen, staring out the back windows that looked upon the garden—more bare ground than plants this month—and, beyond it, the graveyard. She hadn't found the leather box with Mary's journal, and the only thing a trip to her sister's bedroom had accomplished was to leave Catherine in a state of melancholia that threatened to zap her of all her energy.

She was sitting in the dark. She didn't need a light, as she kept her gaze trained out the window and watched as the blackness seemed to be slowly lifting, the depth of hue leaching to gray as morning arrived. Seagulls were cawing loudly, and she envisioned a wildly flapping flock fluttering above the sand and slapping lightly through the receding waves, searching for a meal.

She used to love the beach. As young girls, she and Mary would race across the flattened sand and into water cold enough to numb your feet in minutes. At that time there was no worrying about "gifts," even though there were signs of what was to come, because, although their special prowesses came into bloom when they were passing through puberty, there were tendrils that took root even early on: Catherine's faint moments of precognition, when she would see something she didn't understand, like sudden pouring rain behind her eyelids, which would disappear instantly when she lifted them and stared into a cloudless sky; or Mary's laser vision as she watched boys flying kites and using skimboards.

But she and Mary had ignored the signs. Hadn't really understood what they were. Until that time Catherine had watched two lovers kissing, the man's hand slowly sliding down his partner's back and over the rounded curve of her bottom, and Mary had said in a knowing tone, "I'm going to take him from her."

Catherine hadn't known what to make of that. Mary was eight years old. But sure enough, she stood there in the sand and stared and stared and stared, and the man stopped touching his friend, as if he'd been burned, and he looked around, searching for something, his gaze dropping briefly on Mary but then moving on when he saw she was just a little girl.

Well. That had been just the start. Catherine had seen things that both awed and horrified her in the years since. And when she thought back to her own ill-fated affair, the way Mary had handled it, the memory left a burning cinder inside her chest that even now flamed hot with injustice. If she . . .

Movement outside the window.

Catherine froze, stayed perfectly still, her eyes straining. Someone was creeping along, trying to duck beneath the windows, heading toward the back door. Her pulse jumped, but she waited until she was certain they were past the point of seeing her, then silently got to her feet. She grabbed a small cast-iron pan that always sat on the back burner—a weapon wielded more than once before—and moved to the nearest light switch and waited. If they came in through the storeroom and alcove . . .

She heard them moving cautiously, carefully, and her heart rate increased. Had someone gotten over the fence? She knew there were places where the foliage grew close to it, and with the right amount of brush and rocks and boards, it would be possible to climb over the fence. Hadn't Ravinia done just that the night Justice tried to scale the fence? And many times since, she was sure, though the girl wouldn't admit to it.

A woman's form suddenly filled the room.

Catherine switched on the light.

"Ravinia," she said into the sudden glare as Ravinia took a large step backward, her breath sweeping in on a gasp.

"What are you doing here?" Ravinia demanded.

"Thinking," Catherine answered shortly. "Something you spend too little time doing."

Underneath Ravinia's cloak Catherine saw the legs of a pair of dark brown pants. At the lodge she wore dresses, but on her evening forays it was the pants that Ophelia had made for her at Ravinia's behest.

"I'm over eighteen," Ravinia answered hotly. "I can leave anytime I want."

"It hasn't been that long since you fought with Justice." Ravinia had been trying to escape at the time, but she'd been wounded by Justice's knife, and it had cooled her ardor for a time.

Automatically Ravinia reached up and touched the shoulder where the knife had penetrated. The blade had hit her collarbone, which saved her from a deeper cut. "Justice is dead."

"If you want to go, I won't stop you," Catherine said.

Ravinia narrowed her eyes on her aunt. "But you'll try."

"What I don't want is to have you climbing the fence and coming and going as you please. If you want out, go. But don't come back."

Her eyes flickered. "Is this some kind of trick?"

"No, Ravinia," Catherine said tiredly. "I don't know where you've been all night, and I don't have the energy to care. I'm going to make the lodge more secure. I guess I should thank you for showing me there are still ways to get in and out. I'll find them and secure them, and then if you ever want to contact us, you can come to the front gate."

Ravinia's face was flushed. "Next time I leave, it's forever!"

"Then we understand each other."

Catherine climbed to her feet and forcibly collected herself, feeling both despair and relief over this final decision. She headed upstairs again, aware Ravinia was staring after her, as if she'd lost her mind, and glanced down the length of the gallery to the steps that led to Mary's room. A faint slip of light showed. Catherine frowned. Daylight was creeping in, but this was lamplight, and the only way there could be lamplight was if the door to Mary's bedroom had been left open.

She walked to the stairs and looked upward, seeing more light. Carefully, she climbed the steps, and when she crested the last one, she gazed down at the locked door. Only it wasn't locked. It was ajar.

Catherine wished she'd hung on to the frying pan, and was debating whether to go in search of a weapon or just boldly walk into the bedroom when she saw a figure come out of the room and softly close the door behind her. Catherine didn't move a muscle as the figure walked from the gloom at the end of the hall across the gallery, toward her, stopping short upon seeing her standing at the top step.

"Ophelia," Catherine said.

She was holding a leather box in her hands. Mary's or her own, Catherine couldn't tell.

Ophelia didn't say a word as she held out the box to Catherine. Catherine took it silently, a thousand questions racing through her brain as she gazed at her niece. Ophelia was in her late twenties, and her hair was the blondest of Mary's girls. She was the one who'd wielded the cast-iron pan against Justice, driving him away from Ravinia, saving her sister's life. Of all of them, Ophelia had the tendency to stay silent and observe, and sometimes Catherine felt she was the niece she knew the least.

"Is this mine?" Catherine asked as she took it.

"It's the one you were looking for."

"Mary's? Where was it?"

"In her room. Behind a panel in the wall." Catherine stared at her, and Ophelia added, "I used to play in her room. She was nice to me. As soon as I saw you looking for it, I remembered where it was."

"You knew I was looking for it?"

Ophelia nodded. "You told me you wanted it."

"No. I didn't tell anyone."

"Didn't you?"

Catherine wagged her head slowly from side to side, and Ophelia seemed suddenly embarrassed. "You read minds," Catherine said.

"Only some," Ophelia said, disabusing Catherine of that notion. "Only when you're desperate."

Catherine absorbed that, wondering how many thoughts of hers Ophelia had read over the years. Until this moment, she'd had no inkling of Ophelia's particular gift; the girl had hidden her abilities well.

Lifting the box, Catherine asked, "Do you know what's in it?"

"Her special things . . . There was a pin . . . and some coins . . . and a book."

In her mind's eye Catherine saw the pearl brooch and the coins from another century, gifts from their ancestors. They were extremely valuable, but it was the book she wanted. Mary's journal.

"Are you afraid to open the book in front of me?" Ophelia asked.

"You haven't looked in it?"

She shook her head.

"Were there any . . . papers with the journal?" Catherine asked diffidently.

"No. Should there have been?"

Catherine had believed the boys' adoption papers were tucked inside the journal, but before she could respond, quick footsteps sounded below them, coming up the first flight of stairs. Ravinia's. "Can we talk about this later?" Catherine asked.

Ophelia nodded, and Catherine moved quickly down the third floor steps, tucking the box under her arm as she passed Ravinia and headed to her own room, where she shut her door behind her and threw the bolt. Then she pulled up the curtains and let the sunlight stream in.

She sat the leather box on her nightstand and carefully opened the lid. The brooch gleamed lustrously, and the coins were scattered along the faded velvet lining on the bottom of the box. There was a hairpin with a line of emeralds, as well, and some earrings that were not heirlooms, just Mary's favorites. But it was the journal that she wanted. A small booklet with a spiral binder, it was tucked beneath another book, a copy of *A Short History of the Colony,* a gift to Mary from that lovesick dope Herman Smythe.

Now she slid the journal from beneath Smythe's chronicle. Gingerly, she opened it to the first page, and a loose folded paper fluttered to the floor. She picked it up, unfolded it, and a chill slid down her spine.

C. If you've gotten this far, you must really be worried, but the secret's still safe. If you let him go, I'll never tell. He's mine. For now and for always. But if you try to keep him, you know I'll make him suffer. M.

Her mouth went dry. She had a momentary vision of Mary writhing atop the one man Catherine had ever cared about, and she forcibly stamped it out. It wasn't the truth. It was only her fear. Mary hadn't been with him.

But Mary had been pregnant shortly thereafter, and the gleam in her eye had begged Catherine to ask her, just ask her, but Catherine hadn't had the nerve.

Then.

Now, however, she was beginning to realize she must.

The Portland offices of Bancroft Development were on the east side of the Willamette River, near the Lloyd Center mall. Savannah nosed her Escape into a spot in the underground parking structure and took an elevator to the lobby, then a different elevator to the eleventh floor. Since it was Saturday, the building was generally deserted, except for the street-level establishments, which were on all four sides of the building and included two restaurants, a Starbucks, a women's clothing store called Lacey's, and a shop that sold all manner of kitchen items.

She glanced down at the list of names Hale and his employees had compiled for her:

Clark Russo
Sean Ingles
Neil Vledich

There were other names below those top three, as well. Nadine Gretz, the ex-bookkeeper. Owen DeWitt, the much-maligned ex–geological engineer. Bridget Townsend, the office receptionist. And then the temporary workmen Ella Blessert had mentioned.

Savvy concentrated on Clark Russo, the Portland project manager, whom Hale had said he would call. She had his number, as well, and debated about whether she should phone him directly with a reminder or just walk through the door. She opted for the latter, testing the glass doors to see if they were locked. They weren't, and she pushed into a vacant reception area with several green chenille armchairs and a small sofa grouped near the west window, while a large reception desk took center stage. An anemic ficus tree stood in the corner behind the desk, and toward the other corner was a door that clearly led to further offices.

Since no one was at the desk, Savvy pulled out her cell phone and punched in the number she had for Clark Russo. It rang six times before going to voice mail. *Oh, joy.* She left a message, then wondered if the number might be to a cell phone and decided to try texting.

Mr. Russo, Hale St. Cloud said he would alert you that I was coming to see you. I'm Detective Savannah Dunbar, and I'm waiting in the reception area of your offices.

If he was anywhere around, that ought to do it. In the meantime she checked out the black-and-white photos lining the walls, which were of buildings in varying stages of completion, the last picture being of the fifteen-story edifice she was currently standing in. So, this building had been one of Bancroft Development's projects. She realized then that one of the names listed at the bottom of the photographs was someone she was hoping to see: Sean Ingles, the architect.

Her cell phone *blooped,* and she knew she had a text.

I'm delayed at a job site. I'll be there as soon as I can. Russo.

Savannah made a face and eased herself into one of the chairs, re-lieved to find they were comfortable and supported her lower back. She felt tired, and for once, the peanut butter wasn't doing it for her. There was a nagging little indigestion going on.

With time on her hands, her mind drifted back to Herman Smythe's *A Short History of the Colony.* A lot of information about Catherine and Mary's ancestors, but not much concerning the pres-ent. The girls' names weren't even listed, although she knew the first one was Isadora, and she'd met Cassandra/Margaret, Ravinia, and Lillibeth. She also knew of Lorelei, who, along with reporter Harri-son Frost, had been instrumental in helping the TCSD track down Justice Turnbull after he'd escaped from Halo Valley Security Hospi-tal. Lorelei was a nurse who'd lived outside of the Colony complex, and Savannah had heard she'd moved with Frost when he took a job in Portland. Lastly, there was another woman who lived in the Port-land area, she thought, who was somehow connected to the Colony, but Savvy didn't have any definitive information on her.

Lang was the one in the department who knew the most about the current clan, but he'd never mentioned anything about any sons of Mary's, though Catherine had alluded to them. More than alluded. She'd intimated that they had stronger gifts that were harder to con-trol and so they'd been shunted outside the gates. Savannah wasn't sure exactly what Catherine had been trying to tell her, but she cer-tainly wanted the knife tested, and with her talk about the boys who'd been adopted out and their "superpowers," it stood to reason there must be some connection between the two. When she got the DNA off the knife, she'd be able to move forward.

Maybe she should try to interview Herman Smythe in person. It was worth a try, although after she was deskbound on Monday, she wasn't sure how much legwork she would be allowed to do. She knew he was at Seagull Pointe, a combined assisted living facility and nursing home. She could stop by this evening, maybe, when she got back to the coast.

Her cell phone rang its new default tone, the one Lang had cho-sen for her one day when he'd commandeered her phone for a while: "Dragnet." Funny. Pulling the cell from her messenger bag, she examined the name. Hale St. Cloud.

"Savannah," she answered.

"Hey, Savvy. How're you doing? You on your way to Portland?"

"Already here, waiting to see Clark Russo."

"He's making you wait?"

"He's on a job site, but on his way back. What's up?"

He hesitated a moment, before saying, "I missed talking to Kristina this morning, and I wondered if she'd contacted you."

"Not today. Why? Something wrong?"

"We've just been missing each other," he said, but something in his tone caught Savvy's attention.

"Did you see each other last night?" she asked.

"No, she had something to do, and I went to bed early."

"She was up before you? Like, what? At dawn? Doesn't sound like her." Kristina had never been a morning person. "Did she have an early appointment?"

"No clue," he said, then changed the subject. "You know, if you don't want to wait, I know Clark's in Lake Chinook, at our job site there. I can give you the address. I'm pretty sure he's with Neil Vledich, our foreman. The property was red tagged by the city, so there's no construction going on. They're just meeting there. You could kill two birds with one stone if you stopped by."

"Okay."

"I'll call Clark and tell him to stay put, then. Tell him you're on your way."

"Thanks, Hale."

"Any records you need, Clark'll help you." Another hesitation, and then he said, "Just don't spend too much time on that side of the mountains. The weather's changing for the worse."

"I'll keep an eye on it."

"I don't mean to be a broken record, but any documentation you need, I can get for you. You don't have to hang around there."

"Message received," she said, half amused, half exasperated.

"All right. Have a safe trip."

"Would you tell Kristina to call me when she shows up?" she asked, trying not to sound worried, even though she was. Her sister was just acting strange right now.

"Will do."

He said good-bye, and Savannah clicked off. Maybe he was right.

Maybe this trip wasn't worth it. She would meet Russo and Vledich and see how she felt about staying or going.

She'd worn her raincoat, so now she slipped the strap of the messenger bag over her head, and as she was in the process, the front door opened and a man stood on the threshold, his expression tense. He stopped short upon seeing her.

"The door's open," he said, as if he had to explain himself. "Where's Bridget?" He looked to the imposing desk.

"Not here. I was waiting for Mr. Russo."

"He isn't here, either?" he asked. He was still standing in the doorway, as if reluctant to enter.

"No." Savvy headed toward him but slowed to a stop when he didn't immediately move out of the way.

"I'm Sean Ingles," he said, introducing himself, and stuck out his hand. "I designed this building, and I do work for Bancroft Development."

Ingles was a slight man with sandy-colored hair, wire-rimmed glasses, and a slight hunch, almost as if he were preparing for a blow. He didn't seem to be in any hurry to move, so Savannah shook his hand and said, "Detective Dunbar with the Tillamook County Sheriff's Department."

His eyebrows shot up, and his gaze skittered down her front.

Yes, Mr. Ingles, police officers get pregnant, too.

He didn't say anything about her condition, however. He was clearly processing her words, and it didn't appear to be a particularly pleasant train of thought. After a long few moments, he said, "Ummm . . . we have a Seaside office."

"I've been there. I spoke to Hale St. Cloud and told him I was coming here." *He's my brother-in-law, and I'm carrying his baby.*

"Oh. Okay." And then, "Oh, does this have to do with Bancroft Bluff and the . . . ?"

"Donatella homicides. Yes."

He met her gaze, his brown eyes owlish behind the lenses. "I hope you get whoever did it," he stated fervently. "If I can help in any way, let me know."

"Did you design the homes at Bancroft Bluff?"

He physically recoiled, as if she'd struck him. "Well . . . yes . . .

most of them. There were a few lots sold to other builders, and sometimes they used their own architects or house designers." He clenched his teeth and moved his lips, as if he was working himself up to say something. Finally, he asked, "Have you talked to DeWitt? Owen DeWitt? He's the brilliant geological engineer who okayed that project." Ingles's voice was full of repressed venom.

"I've put in a call to Mr. DeWitt, but he hasn't responded."

"Figures," he breathed. "He cost the company a lot of money, and I don't have to tell you that's a real black mark on my reputation as well as Hale's." His lips tightened with repressed fury. "DeWitt's an incompetent ass who really sold Declan Bancroft a bill of goods."

Savannah could have told him Declan Bancroft would agree with him 100 percent, but she said instead, "Do you know where I could find Mr. DeWitt?"

"You mean besides in a bottle at the Rib-I?"

"What's the Rib-I?"

"A steak house and bar. The one that had the double murder the other night. DeWitt was probably there when it happened. You should ask him. It's not too far up on Sandy." He waved an arm in a general direction east, toward Sandy Boulevard, a major artery on the eastside of Portland.

Double murder? Like at Bancroft Bluff? Savannah hadn't seen the news in the past twenty-four hours or so and realized she was behind the times. "It's not even nine yet."

"They serve steak burritos and make-your-own Bloody Marys on the weekends. He's there."

"Okay."

She gave him her card, and he returned the favor. She left the office, wondering if she should stop by the steak house on the way to the job site but deciding against it. Russo was expecting her, if Hale had called him, like he'd said he would, and she didn't want to miss the opportunity to talk to him, anyway. By the sounds of it, DeWitt might still be at the Rib-I later today, anyway.

She put in a call to Lang and got his voice mail. It was Saturday, she reminded herself. At the beep, she said, "Hey, I just heard about a double homicide at the Rib-I restaurant in Portland. It's a place DeWitt, the engineer who okayed building on the dune, frequents. Have you talked to Curtis about it? I'm in Portland and thought about going over there to see if I can find DeWitt." Detective Trey Curtis of the Portland Police Department was a longtime friend of Lang's, their relationship having started when Lang was with the PPD, before he joined the Tillamook County Sheriff's Department.

Ten minutes later Lang texted her back. A man and a woman killed Thursday night in parking lot. Throats slit. Looks like they were having sex in his truck when he got them. That's DeWitt's bar?

Savannah grimaced at the thought of the new homicides. She texted: Yep. I'll try to see him before I head back.

Lang answered: I'll let Curtis know.

With a glance out the window to the sky, which was high and gray, she turned south toward the bedroom community of Lake Chinook.

CHAPTER 12

The Lake Chinook job site was at the end of a broken asphalt drive, the result of too many construction vehicles breaking the pavement down with heavy loads. The road opened onto a headland with a spectacular view of the green lake far below. Concrete footings for three separate residences had been poured and were still surrounded by their plywood forms. The house farthest west was the furthest along; it was framed, sided, and rough plumbed, and looked to be in the process of rough electrical, but there was a red work-stoppage notice flapping in the wind. Construction had been red tagged, and the group of men standing just inside the framed house's open doorway seemed to be discussing the situation with barely concealed ire.

The rain had stopped, and the temperature was dropping. Savvy had traded in her raincoat for the dark blue ski jacket, and now she stepped carefully over chunks of two-by-fours and crumbling asphalt as she made her way to their group. An attractive silver-haired man saw her first and stopped talking mid-sentence. The taller, lankier man looked over at her. His long dark hair was pulled into a ponytail, and his eyes seemed penetrating, even from this distance. The third man, who she guessed was the building inspector, barely glanced at her as he said, "You're over a couple of inches, and until you fix it, I can't sign off." Unlike the first two, he was heavyset, his features were close set, and his face pinched. He looked like the epitome of a government employee with a chip on his shoulder.

"I'll take care of it," the silver-haired man said tersely. He was lean and hard, and his eyes were as dark as midnight. As the inspector walked toward his truck, he stood in the doorway with his hands planted on his hips and waited for Savannah to approach. "Clark Russo," he said, holding out a hand.

"Detective Dunbar," she greeted him.

"Ah, yes. You decided to brave the elements and stray from your jurisdiction. This is Neil Vledich, our foreman." Savannah shook hands with Vledich, whose ponytail was a dark sable brown and whose eyes were a brilliant blue. Russo said, as if Savvy had asked a question, "The upper deck on this house is outside the twenty-five percent footprint, all that we're allowed to build on a lot in this damn town. We're going to have to cut it back to make it fit in."

"First, it was the trees," Vledich said as Savvy pulled out her notebook.

"We cut more trees down than the neighbors wanted," Russo explained. "It was within city code, but there was a lot of noise, and they started complaining. Just been one delay after another. Give me Portland any day." He shook his head and seemed to mentally dust off his hands. "What can I do for you?"

"I'm doing a follow-up on the Donatella homicides at Bancroft Bluff. . . ." She trailed off at his rapid nodding.

"Right. Hale said as much. I worked that project. Neil didn't. He was here. What do you want to know?"

Before she could answer, Vledich put in, "A lot of people said they shouldn't build there, but he ignored them."

"He?" Savannah asked.

"DeWitt," Russo answered. "If that guy were on the *Titanic*, he'd swear they hadn't hit an iceberg rather than admit he was wrong. He still stands by his original assessment. Meanwhile, the whole damn dune's falling into the sea."

"I ran into Sean Ingles in your office, and he said that Mr. DeWitt could be found at a local bar," Savannah said.

"Oh, he's a big drinker, all right," Russo answered. "Since the Bancroft Bluff debacle, he's an even bigger drinker." He motioned Savannah inside the framed house, to a hearth that was just the concrete blocks at the moment; the tile or granite or whatever medium they'd chosen to cover the blocks wasn't there yet. Vledich went outside, and through the open doorway Savvy could see him break out a pack of cigarettes and light up.

Russo went on, "Everybody wanted Bancroft Bluff to be a success, so Owen ignored everything he knew, and anything anybody said, and went ahead and green-lighted the project. It was lame-assed, but we all kinda kept our fingers crossed. I mean, nobody wanted a failure. When the dune started failing, we scrambled to put riprap down, trying to stop the erosion."

"Riprap?"

"Big chunks of rock, mostly. Stuff to stabilize the slide and build up a wall, stop the erosion. We put it at the foot of the dune and piled high, but the bluff's right on the ocean. Duh. That's why people want to build there, and the elements don't give a shit, if you know what I mean. The ocean eroded the dune behind the riprap, anyway. Big waste of time."

"Do you think the motive for the Donatella homicides had to do with the development failure?" Savvy asked.

"Seems likely, doesn't it? Isn't that why you're reinterviewing us?"

"One of the reasons," she acknowledged. "'Blood money' was written on the Donatellas' wall with red spray paint."

"Yeah, I know. Somebody was really pissed off. Doesn't make a lot of sense, does it?" Russo mused. "Although . . ."

"Although?"

"Blood money sounds so . . . I don't know . . . like revenge or something, and yet Donatella's house is gonna go, too. Sure, it's still standing now, but the whole area's shut down and basically condemned. Donatella was hurting as much as the next guy."

Savannah nodded. Her own feeling was that logic wasn't the overriding factor in the whole scenario. Why write "blood money"? Everyone knew about Bankruptcy Bluff and the fact that the Donatellas and the Bancrofts were taking it in the shorts, all the while trying to make good on the properties.

It seemed more like misdirection the more she interviewed people close to the real estate debacle.

She asked Russo a few more questions, reexamining where he'd been the night of the murders—to dinner in Seaside with two friends, who'd vouched for him then and would again. Then, as Vledich came back in, she posed a couple more questions to him for good measure. Vledich told her he was in Portland at the time of the homicides and had the word of his live-in girlfriend to back him up.

Savannah asked him his thoughts about motive, and he said, "The can of red paint was just there. Available. Whoever killed 'em just used what was handy."

Vledich was echoing Russo's thoughts and Savannah's, as well.

She checked her watch. Two p.m. "I would like to get in touch with Nadine Gretz and Owen DeWitt before I go, if at all possible."

"Nadine's working at the eastside apartments," Vledich said.

"I thought she quit," Savannah said, surprised.

"She did." Russo shrugged. "But she couldn't find work in this economy, so we're using her as a temp. Mostly she just wants to hang with Henry, though. He's the number two guy after Neil here. If Neil's busy on a project, Henry's the man."

Vledich made a sound of disgust.

Russo said mildly, "Henry would like Neil's job."

"Henry Woodworth is an asshole." Vledich's brows were a sharp, dark line.

Russo told her the address of the eastside apartment complex, and Savannah committed it to memory. "RiverEast Apartments. It's on the sign," he told her.

"And DeWitt?" she asked.

"Should be at the Rib-I. Place used to be a great steak house, but it's kinda gone downhill. Did you hear? They found two dead bodies in an SUV there yesterday. Doesn't do well with the clientele, I'd imagine." Russo smirked.

"Do you know of any theories on that?"

Her cell phoned *blooped,* and she saw it was another message from Lang. As if he'd heard her last question, he'd texted that Curtis wouldn't be able to meet with her, because he was involved in a double homicide. Bound to be the same one.

"We keeping you from something?" Russo asked.

"No." She tucked her phone away and waited, and Russo seemed to run their last few words around in his head and realize she was still waiting for an answer.

"Love triangle, somebody said. The jilted lover killed 'em." He shrugged.

"Nah." Vledich waved that away. "It was executed like a hit."

Like the Donatellas, Savvy thought.

"All right," she said, closing up her notebook and tucking it away. She started to walk toward her car, then stopped, turned back, and said to Russo, "Sylvie Strahan said she recommended you for the Portland job."

For the first time he looked cautious. "Yeah?"

"Who was manager here before you?"

Vledich snorted again, and Russo said, "Paulie Williamson. He's the one who awarded the engineering job to DeWitt."

"I don't have him on my list," Savannah admitted.

"Paulie folded up tent and moved to Tucson. Working on his tan and drinking mojitos now," Russo said. "He ran like a rabbit after the Donatellas were killed. Told you guys he didn't have anything to do with the project, which was technically true, other than being friends with DeWitt, and then took off. I think he was scared he'd be sued along with Bancroft Development."

"Asshole." Vledich sniffed.

"Do you have a number for him?" she asked.

"Got a cell." Russo pulled out his phone, scrolled through some numbers, then rattled off Paul Williamson's number, which Savvy put into her phone list.

She left them a few moments later and headed north and then east across the Willamette again, toward the RiverEast Apartments construction site, driving through a Taco Bell on the way and ordering two chicken gorditas and a water. She ate both gorditas while driving and was sipping the water when she saw the sign COMING SOON RIVEREAST APARTMENTS—which featured a schematic of the ten-story modern glass and steel building in the midst of a parklike setting—coming up on her right. The parklike setting was a dream for the future, apparently, as currently the site sported bare steel rafters and cranes, and men in hard hats walked around purposefully. It was a big project that would probably take years to complete. Savannah parked the Escape well away from the construction zone and walked back slowly.

A good-looking man with dark blond hair and a full-wattage smile approached her, hard hat on his head, his walk a swinging strut, which she'd found common among the more handsome of the male species—or at least the ones who felt they were. He wore jeans and a gray work shirt, and he pointed his finger at her, then made a circling motion with it to encompass her belly. "What are you doing here, Mama?" he asked.

"Are you Henry Woodworth?"

He blinked in surprise. "Why, yes, I am. And who might you be?"

"I'm Detective Savannah Dunbar with the Tillamook County Sheriff's Department." She showed him her badge, then held out a hand, but Henry didn't take it.

"How did you know me, Detective?" he asked cautiously, and she explained about her meeting with Russo and Vledich.

"Vledich," he muttered. "Bet he didn't have nice things to say."

"I was actually hoping to find Nadine Gretz. I was told you and she are friends."

"What do you want to see Nadine for?"

"I'm doing a follow-up investigation on the Donatella homicides in Deception Bay last spring. Nadine worked for Bancroft Development then, and I understand she's working for them again."

"Well, yeah, but just part-time. This isn't . . . Nadine left because she didn't want to work with Bancroft and St. Cloud. She—" He cut himself off.

"She what?" Savannah asked, pressing.

"She didn't think they played fair. She's not here, anyway."

"Do you have a way I can reach her?"

"Well, yeah," he said, but he didn't offer up her number.

"I've already met with Mr. Russo, Mr. Ingles, and Mr. Vledich."

"What a powerhouse. And you, ready to pop." His smile didn't quite reach his eyes.

"I can find her another way," Savvy said evenly, "but it would save me some time if you could help."

"Just hold your horses, Detective." He pulled out a cell phone, checked his call list, then told her Nadine's number, which she inserted into her own list, just as she had Paulie Williamson's.

"Were you working at the coast during the Donatella homicides?" Savannah asked him.

"Nah . . . not that day. We'd just finished a remodel on their house," he admitted, waving a hand back to include the rest of the construction team. One of the men in hard hats had stopped what he was doing and was watching them. "The Donatellas moved out for a while, but they were planning to move back in. They wanted everybody to think that everything was A-OK, you know?"

"But the dune was failing by then."

"Oh, yeah. That's why they were killed, right?"

She was debating interviewing some of the other workers, but the one that had stopped and looked over at her was already back at work, and she knew she would be interrupting a project that hummed with energy like a hive of bees.

Henry's cell phone rang, and he drew it cautiously from his pocket. "Hey, babe," he answered, his eyes on Savannah. They were clear and blue and had warmed at the sound of the caller's voice. She realized he was talking to Nadine when he said, "There's a cop here to see you. A detective from Tillamook County." There was a tinny, fast answer, which had him comically pull the phone from his ear for a moment, before bringing it back and saying, "No big deal. She's just doing a follow-up, and your name's on the list." More tinny screeching, and he suddenly held the phone out to Savannah. "Here she is."

Savvy was a little taken by surprise. Gingerly, she put her fingers around the cell phone and said, "Ms. Gretz?"

"I never had anything to do with anything at Bancroft Bluff! I thought Owen was a dipshit from the start. Everybody did. It's just a disaster, but the Donatellas . . . they were nice people. All we did was try to make a nice community, and look what happened. If you want to go after somebody, go after Hale St. Cloud and that old lech, Declan. They might not've killed Marcus and Chandra, but they pushed through that project when they knew better. And Hale's wife, too. You should look into what she had going on. She was hot as lava and slavering over Marcus."

Savannah could feel her face heat at the accusation.

"Whoa," Henry said. He could hear what was being said because Savvy had pulled the phone about an inch from her ear.

"You're talking about Kristina St. Cloud," Savvy said, pressing the phone close again and holding the emotion out of her voice with an effort.

"I sure am. She was all over him."

Henry stuck out his hand and wiggled his fingers, mutely asking for the phone back.

"You don't believe me?" Nadine demanded into Savvy's silence. "Ask Henry. She came on to him, too."

"Could I meet with you?" Savannah asked.

"I just can't. I'm running errands, and I don't know when I'll be done."

Truthfully, Savannah was somewhat relieved. The last thing she wanted to hear was a decimation of her sister's character, and, anyway, she was starting to believe that no one at Bancroft Development knew anything more than what had already been gleaned earlier. She was also growing sick to the back teeth of listening to gossip and innuendo about people close to her. Nadine's remarks about Kristina dug deep into her soul, far more than they should.

"Can I call you again?" she asked, and Nadine said, "Okay," somewhat reluctantly. She handed the phone back to Henry and thanked him.

He nodded, then pressed the phone to his ear and said, "You're not making the best impression in front of the law here, y'know," as he took a few steps away. Savannah couldn't hear her response aside from the same rapid-fire, tinny voice.

She checked her watch. Five o'clock. The day had shot by, and she still wanted to stop by the Rib-I and see if she could connect with the much-maligned Owen DeWitt, if he was there.

For a moment she was undecided. Truth be told, she felt the urge to head back to the beach and stop off at the Seagull Pointe care facility to see Herman Smythe. Though her priority was the Donatella homicides, and she was on her last few hours before her forced maternity leave, she hadn't forgotten about Catherine Rutledge's request to find DNA on the knife that had allegedly killed her sister, and she certainly hadn't forgotten about the other strange piece: Catherine's genetics lesson, in which she'd intimated that the males of their clan possessed even more potent "gifts." She also still wanted to follow up and learn the names of all the women living at Siren Song, and Herman Smythe was that connection.

Throwing another glance at the sky, she scowled at the dark, forbidding clouds moving in from the west. The prediction of snow in the Coast Range later tonight wasn't a good omen. Though she had chains, she didn't want to risk having to use them; it didn't sound like a winning proposition.

With a wave at Henry, who apparently was still trying to soothe Nadine's ruffled feathers, she headed back to her SUV, checking the GPS for nearby restaurants and finding the Rib-I was only about six blocks away. Owen DeWitt's home away from home.

"Where the hell is she?" Hale said aloud to the empty room.

He was at his desk, and he'd been on the phone with his subs, seeing who was working on Saturday and who was planning to show up Monday morning, checking on material deliveries from Portland and beyond, wondering if he needed to bring Russo back to Seaside when Kristina had the baby or if he would be freer than he currently expected. Apart from his call to Savvy, he'd pushed thoughts of Kristina's disappearance to the back of his mind. She'd done this kind of vanishing act before. There was, in fact, a period the previous spring when he'd wondered if the fact that her sister was pregnant had scared her so badly that Kristina had her own personal break-down. She would disappear for hours, once all night long, only to show up weary and miserable and to admit that she'd checked into a motel to try to meditate away her anxieties. Hale had called the motel surreptitiously, checking her story, and had learned that yes, his wife had stayed there. He felt bad about it, but her behavior had worried him sick. They were having a baby, for God's sake; he needed to know where she was at all times. But then things had seemed to straighten out, and until the past few days he'd thought— hoped—it was all going to be okay.

Now he picked up his cell phone and punched in her number. Again. He had done the same thing three times already but had hung up before she answered. She would come back when she was ready, and then he would have to have a talk with her and tell her that no, this wasn't the way things were going to be. She was going to have to be more responsible. When they had a child to take care of, she wasn't going to be able to just up and *leave*.

Her voicemail answered: "Hi. You've reached Kristina. Leave a message."

Holding on to his temper, Hale waited until the beep, then said, "Okay, I need you to pick up, Kristina. We've got to talk about a few things. This isn't . . ." He wanted to scream at her, but it wasn't going to help. Whatever she was going through was real to her, even if he couldn't understand it.

Do you believe in sorcery?

He shook his head and continued, "We've got to make some plans for this baby, and I mean beyond the crib and car seat. Call me. Please." He tried to sound serious but nonthreatening, but all he wanted to do was swear or throw something or bang his head against a wall.

"God damn it," he said softly into the empty room, looking out his window to the mass of dark clouds that had gathered. It had been dry all day for a change, but it looked like some serious precipitation was on the way. His mind flew to Savvy. Had she left Portland yet? He sure as hell hoped so.

The Rib-I was alive with tiny white lights twinkling around its eaves and windows, but it was still late afternoon, so apart from a few desultory trucks, an SUV, and three sedans, the parking lot was empty. The sun was long gone, and the gloom was pervasive, the sense of the heavens pressing down enough to make Savvy decide to find a motel as soon as she'd seen if DeWitt was here.

Stepping into the bar, she saw one man sitting at a table with an empty glass, a blank expression, and a cell phone lying in front of him. His hands were flat on the tabletop, as if he were getting ready to make a quick draw, but when he saw her, he reached for the cell phone, as if he expected her to take it.

There were other figures farther into the dim recesses beyond, but there was something about him—a self-imposed wall that said, "Back the hell off"—that suggested he might be her man.

"Mr. DeWitt?" she asked, approaching him.

"Who wants to know?" He stared at her belly.

"I'm Detective Dunbar with the Tillamook County Sheriff's Department." She pulled her wallet from her messenger bag, flipped it open, and displayed her badge, not that he seemed to care.

His eyes slowly lifted to hers. They were as red and bleary as she would have expected, given what she knew about his habits. "Yeah?" He lurched forward in his chair. "Lemme see if I can guess why you're here."

"You know why, Mr. DeWitt."

"Bankruptcy Bluff. Oh, sure. I know." He waved the cell phone at her. "I just gotta make a call. My ride. Don't wanna drive drunk."

"Do you mind if I sit down?"

"Suit yourself." He pressed the keys on his phone with serious concentration, then put it to his ear. It rang for long moments, and then Savannah heard the faint sound of someone's voice, but DeWitt snapped the phone shut. He looked despondent and on the verge of surliness. "Fucking voicemail," he muttered.

"You signed off on the stability of the dune. Said it was safe to build on. There have been reports—"

"Reports," he sneered. "Oh, yeah. Reports."

"From professional people who said the ground's always been unstable, and they would have never green-lighted the area."

"Monday morning quarterbacking." He picked up his empty glass, then set it down again, looking around for the bartender. "They're liars. Old man Bancroft wanted that development, and I gave it to him, sure. But they woulda done the same. It was within the parameters."

Savannah had only a basic idea of the whole process, but his growing belligerence and defensive tone suggested he knew more than he was saying. Maybe he cut corners, or maybe those "parameters" were just a little too close to the edge.

"You're saying Declan Bancroft pushed for the development."

"He sure as hell did. And now that old bastard blames me for everything. And Hale," he went on. "He wanted it, too."

"Hale gave you the go-ahead?"

"They all wanted it," he said, waving his arms expansively. "Whad do I gotta do to get a drink around here?" he yelled.

"Sober up," was the bartender's laconic reply.

"Well, fuck that."

"Mr. DeWitt, I'm mainly investigating the Donatella homicides, and it may well be that the construction problems are the reason they were killed," Savvy said.

"Nah . . . It was something else."

A waitress strolled up to them, eyeing DeWitt cautiously, as if she expected him to jump up and grab her. "Would you like anything?" she asked Savannah.

"Get the rib eye," DeWitt said before she could answer.

"Well . . ." Savannah debated.

The waitress made a face, as if she didn't want to agree with DeWitt, but she admitted, "It's what we're known for."

"All right. Medium-rare to rare."

"She likes it bloody," DeWitt said, nodding, as if he'd delivered seriously sage advice.

Ignoring him, the waitress asked, "What kinda dressing on your salad?"

"You have a vinaigrette?"

"Yep." She scribbled that down, then asked, "Baked potato, mashed, or fries? Comes with it." Her eyes slid toward DeWitt. "He might want to share some fries," she suggested meaningfully.

Clearly, the waitress wanted him to eat something, so Savvy said, "Okay, fries."

"Anything to drink?"

"Another scotch," DeWitt answered, jumping in at the same time Savvy said, "Just water, thanks."

The waitress's pencil was poised.

"Just water," Savannah repeated.

"And a scotch," DeWitt insisted.

The waitress put in the order, and she and the bartender conferred for a while. In the end DeWitt got his drink, and he swallowed half his glass in one take.

Savvy dispensed with the salad in record time, feeling ravenous, as ever, and when her main dish arrived, she turned the plate so the french fries were closest to DeWitt. He ignored them, merely sitting back in his chair and waiting, chin down on his chest, as if he were about to nod off.

The steak was good, much better than she'd expected it would be, and she wanted to moan about the way it practically melted on her tongue. It felt like she hadn't eaten in a week, and she would have really enjoyed herself if it weren't for DeWitt's eyes watching her every move.

Finally, she slid her plate away and took a long drink of water. DeWitt finished his drink and studied her, and for a moment she thought he was asleep, until she saw him blink several times. He seemed to be staring at the floor, but Savannah thought he was calculating something. Even though it seemed as if he'd had a lot to drink, and the bar staff certainly thought so, he was fairly lucid. She opened her mouth to ask him another question, but he got there first and blew her thoughts to smithereens.

"He fired me. The old man. But it was Hale who wanted me gone, because I knew, y'see. I knew about his wife. I saw her at the house, and I knew."

More about Kristina. Savannah felt cold inside. "What house?"

"The Donatellas. What we're talking about," he said, as if she were dense. "And she wasn't with St. Cloud. Uh-uh."

"But she was with someone," Savvy said, picking up on his tone. If he said *Marcus Donatella . . .*

He wagged a finger in front of her nose. "You think I don't know who you are? You're the sister. Carrying the next little St. Cloud. Bet Declan'd like to piss himself, he's so excited to have a great-grandson on the way."

The sex of her child was the worst-kept secret on the planet. "You say you saw Kristina with someone?"

But DeWitt wasn't ready to switch back to the original topic. "A boy. That's what she said." He gave her a sly look. "She was talking all about it to him."

"Who? Kristina?" Savvy asked. No wonder he was the goat around the office. Criminal incompetency *and* just being an all-around asshole.

"You figure it out, Miss Cop." He lurched up from the table and headed for the door. "I need a cab," he threw over his shoulder to the bartender.

"I can give you a ride," Savvy said. She didn't want to be in his company any longer than she had to, but she wanted to know what the hell he was alluding to.

"You as hot as your sister?" He leered at her. "I've never made it with a pregnant woman before."

"Not that kind of ride," she said levelly.

He grinned and staggered back a step.

"I'll get that cab," the bartender put in, saving Savvy from wanting to blast the worm.

DeWitt staggered outside and shivered, pulling the collar of his coat closer to his neck. "Gonna snow."

Savannah wanted to pepper him with questions but knew he would just keep playing games. DeWitt was all innuendo and bluster. Except he did know about the baby.

"What do you think you know about my sister?" she asked quietly.

"A helluva lot more than you do, or her husband does. I saw her there a coupla times. With *him.*"

"Does he have a name?"

"Calls himself Charlie when he's trolling for a hot piece of ass," he said. "A real rat bastard. She knew him, all right, and I do mean that in the biblical sense. I was there one night, looking around, feeling sick about the whole goddamn thing. Looking for the goddamn proof that they're all wrong."

"You were at Bancroft Bluff, checking out the integrity of the dune?" she asked, trying to keep up with his rambling talk.

"Didn't I just say so? Hell. It's all political, anyway. Somebody gets pissed at somebody, and they condemn the whole area just because they can." He waved an arm. "It's not my fault."

She wasn't going to point out the obvious, that, well, yes, it was his fault for ignoring the signs that the dune was sloughing into the sea. It was, in fact, his job. "You saw my sister there," she said, prodding him.

"Sure did. He had her up against the wall. Banging her like crazy, and she was . . . man . . . in ecstasy. Head thrown back and first making these little kittenlike sounds and then screamin'! She was riding him and lovin' it." His smile was a leer.

Savvy fought back the urge to do him physical harm. She wanted to slap him silly, and he knew it, the bastard. "You saw my sister with someone in the Donatella house," she reiterated.

"That's what I'm telling you. Doing the dirty right against that same wall. The one that was painted with 'blood money.' You know."

"Who is this Charlie?"

"I told ya. Good Time Charlie. You got questions, ask your sister. She knows him pretty good."

A brisk wind ripped at Savvy's jacket, and she pulled it tighter around her. "You saw Charlie and Kristina St. Cloud together at the Donatella house."

"Why don't you write it down, *Detective?*"

"Could you have been mistaken?"

"Look, I know you probably don't want to believe that your sister's screwing around on her husband, but I know what I saw. They were taking advantage of the fact that the Donatellas had skedaddled. Chickenshits. After they left the dune, everybody went. Oh, sure, they would pretend to be livin' there, just to get people to stay, but it was a lie and everybody knew it. Fuckin' scared they were gonna fall into the goddamn ocean."

"Is Charlie connected to Bancroft Bluff?"

"He was fuckin' the boss's wife. Jesus, woman. How many ways I gotta say it? That's as connected as you get!"

"Kristina picked the venue for this alleged rendezvous?"

"How would I know?" He glanced around. "Christ, it's cold."

Savvy looked up toward the darkening skies. She was going to have to get that room ASAP. "Where can I find this Charlie?"

DeWitt closed his eyes and lost his balance, taking a step backward before catching himself. "Stay away from him. That's my advice to you, pregnant lady. Far, far way . . ."

"Where have you seen him around?"

He waved an expansive arm to encompass the whole world as a cab pulled up in front of the restaurant and he staggered forward to get the door. "Don't charge me too much, man," he whined to the cabbie as he climbed inside.

"What's Charlie's real name?" Savvy asked, raising her voice.

"Beelzebub," he muttered, slamming the door behind him.

Savvy stared after the departing cab for a moment, fighting down a shiver. She thought DeWitt's brain might be alcohol soaked, but he'd definitely put a chill in her soul, and the weather wasn't helping. Walking back to her car, she placed a call to Kristina, whose phone went straight to voicemail again. *Damn it all to hell. Where are you?* Savvy hung up without leaving a message. Kristina would see she'd called from her missed-call list and maybe call her back.

Beelzebub, she thought. *Ridiculous.* If anyone was a devil, it was more likely Owen DeWitt himself.

CHAPTER 13

Mary's journal lay unopened on Catherine's nightstand, next to the oil lamp with its soft, shimmering flame. Knowing she would be drawn into Mary's world as soon as she opened its leather cover, Catherine walked into her bedroom but refused to look at it, just as she had refused to look at it every other time she'd entered the room. Yes, she needed to read it. Yes, she believed it held some of the keys to what had happened to her sister. And yes, there were bound to be clues to the past, the pieces that Catherine did not know herself, the ones Mary had deliberately hidden from her.

But there were also bound to be references to the things Catherine did know about . . . things she would sooner forget.

Still, she was only putting off the inevitable. She'd asked Detective Dunbar for a DNA test on the knife, hoping there would be some sign of the killer.

Yet she thought she might know who he was.

Her jaw clenched, and she forcibly relaxed it. *He* was like Justice. Determined and driven and filled with genetic anomalies that as often as not turned him into an evil monster incapable of living within social boundaries.

She needed to find the adoption records.

"Aunt Catherine?"

She nearly jumped out of her skin as she turned swiftly to the open door of her bedroom. Cassandra stood there, her eyes glimmering in the faint light.

"You scared me!" Catherine exclaimed, one hand over her chest. Her heart was thudding erratically.

"I think he's done something really bad."

"Who?" she asked automatically.

"The man from the bones."

"Cassandra . . ."

"He went to her," Cassandra whispered urgently.

Catherine walked over and put her arms around Cassandra, holding her tightly, knowing how much her visions scared her. "What did he do?"

"Can you see it?"

"No, I—" Catherine paused, momentarily seeing a heavy block of wood.

"He killed her." Cassandra hesitated a moment, her body quivering, and then she added in a voice so soft Catherine could scarcely hear it, even though her lips weren't far from her ear, "And then he watched her die, and . . . he liked the way it felt. He says it's . . . better than sex."

Nothing is better than sex, Mary said, eyeing her sister with that cat-and-cream smile.

"Who did he kill, Cassandra?" Catherine made herself ask, her throat tight.

The girl slowly pulled away from her, and she came back to herself, as if waking from a dream. She looked slightly confused. "Our mother?" she asked, as if Catherine held the answer. Then, "No, it was a different woman." As if suddenly alarmed at being too near to Mary, she added, "And it's Maggie. My name is Maggie."

She left the room in a rush, legs flying beneath her long skirts, as if she wanted nothing more to do with either Catherine or the visions that had plagued her—her gift—since she was young.

Catherine thought about Cassandra's vision. About the man from the bones. Forcing herself to the nightstand, she picked up the small volume and started at the beginning, but Mary's young girl ramblings held little interest for her. Thus she opened the book and held it flat, letting the pages fall to their natural breaking point.

With dread she read the passage.

Cathy thinks she's in love with a prince, but he's just like the rest of them. It's so easy to have any of them, it's

laughable. I lean in and envelop them, and they're
mine. I thought she was going to cry when she asked me,
"Is it a scent?" She kept pestering me, and I told her, "It's
just something you don't have. Sorryyy . . ." Should I let
her have him, or put him in the trophy case?

Catherine slammed the book shut, only to open it again to a later page, a well-thumbed section, one that Mary had apparently gone back to time and again.

I saved Cathy from that rapist, but I wouldn't let her
have happiness. That's what she says to me all the time.
"You won't let me be happy." There is no happiness.
There's only conquest. I took him from her, and I'm not
sorry. It's for her own good. She wasn't meant to have
him.
They're all mine. From Parnell to Seamus to the devil
who gave me D. The rapist. Back from the dead, but
dead again.
Right, Cath? You're reading this, aren't you? You know
who I'm talking about. Is it still a secret? Have you man-
aged to keep your mouth shut? Or have you pointed
your finger at him, like you always point it at me?

Catherine clamped the book shut this time with a soft *whump.* She thought about Mary out on Echo Island and all the years her sister had lived there in obscurity. Mary hadn't wanted to be taken. She'd gone there against her will. But once ensconced, she'd scarcely protested. In fact she'd changed from railing at Catherine whenever she brought supplies to showing her the herb garden she'd begun in the hardscrabble terraced backyard. She'd even asked for different seeds and plants to add to it. This had surprised Catherine greatly because up till then, Mary's single-minded, obsessive nature had seemed to have to do only with men.

Men . . .

They're all mine. From Parnell to Seamus to the devil who gave
me D.

Catherine's eyes traveled to the closed book, and her jaw grew hard. She'd known Parnell well, how his taste for women had grown ever younger. She hadn't mourned his death one iota. And she'd known Seamus, who'd hung around Mary like a dog who smelled a bitch in heat, until he'd finally gotten his chance to mount her. He had been married, of course, and had gone back to his wife, who'd died of a heart attack not long after. Seamus himself had died a few years later, another one Catherine hadn't mourned. He, like so many of Mary's conquests, never knew he'd fathered one of her children. Maybe he'd suspected. Maybe they all had, but no one had stepped up and asked.

Bastards.

Catherine wasn't completely certain just which man had sired which child, though Mary had known. That information might be inside Mary's journal, and it might not. She suspected the key to whoever had killed her sister was related to one of them, however: the man from the bones. And she thought she could maybe narrow it down.

Still, the words her sister had written seemed to leap off the page. Powerful. Evoking memories of those long-ago days before Catherine exiled her sister and slammed shut the gates to Siren Song.

The devil who gave me D. She certainly knew who that was.

Swallowing, she stared into the dark corners of the room while her mind's eye vividly recalled the devil Mary referred to: the only one of her sister's lovers that Mary had been unable to control. The sick bastard who'd forced Catherine into a closet and pressed himself upon her, stripping off her clothes and holding her down while she screamed behind his hand. A man twice her age who'd turned his laser blue eyes on her. Catherine had felt something grip her, something sexual, which she'd mentally fought, even while she was physically frozen. He would have had her, but suddenly Mary was there, slamming the butt of the shotgun from the gun closet downstairs into his skull. He went down hard, his cranium dented, his eyes fixed, and the spell broken. Catherine had been shaking uncontrollably. She'd still been in a daze when Mary said, "Help me," and she'd obeyed, joining her sister in carrying his body from the closet downstairs and out to the graveyard, where he still lay inside the grave now marked with Mary's headstone.

"Who is he?" Catherine had asked her as that late summer's wind blew around them, and they had both cast anxious glances back to the lodge, worried one of the children would see them.

"Richard Beeman," Mary had answered after a long moment. "My husband."

"He's not your husband," Catherine had whispered.

Her sister had smiled coldly. "And his name isn't Richard Beeman."

And then she slammed the sharp end of the blade into the dirt fiercely until it hit something . . . his body . . . and Catherine gasped and turned away.

"Die, devil," Mary spat through her teeth. Then she yanked out the shovel, the tip of the blade dark with the blood, and added conversationally, "We'll get a coffin made. Maybe we can ask Earl. . . ."

CHAPTER 14

Hale pressed a finger to the end call button on his cell and tried to tamp down his concern. *Where the hell is she?* He'd been half annoyed most of the day, but now, as night fell, he crossed the threshold into low-grade alarm. For all her flightiness, Kristina had never walked out for this many hours with no contact whatsoever. He didn't know how many times he'd called her already, but he would be reaching serious "stalker" limits were he some stranger trying to make contact.

"Want another?" the bartender asked him, pointing at his empty beer glass. She was young, with long dark hair and a name tag that read MINNIE.

Hale was seated at the bar end of the Bridgeport Bistro in downtown Seaside. He'd left the office and thought about heading home, but he had a gut feeling Kristina wasn't there waiting for him and he didn't want his worries to escalate just yet. And if she did happen to be there, she could damn well wonder where the hell he was.

"No, thanks," he said. Then, as she turned away, he said, "Maybe a scotch on the rocks."

"Any particular one?"

"Surprise me."

"Dewar's?"

He nodded. He was almost sorry he'd asked for another drink now that she was pouring it for him. He wanted to *do* something. This sitting at the bar and wondering was making him crazy. As Minnie slid him his drink, the door blew open, sending in a swirl of frigid air, which made everyone in the place look up and frown.

"Brrr," the newcomer said. "Sorry about that."

"Well, get on in here, Jimbo, and keep the cold out," Minnie said to him, playfully snapping a towel at him.

Jimbo was a big man in a plaid shirt with a thick beard and a thicker neck. He grinned at Minnie, and Hale caught a spark of romance between them. It left a dark sorrow in his heart in a way that made him angry at himself. *Damn it, Kristina. Where the hell are you?*

Downing his scotch, he rethought his plan to stay away from the house, deciding he was just being immature. As he climbed into the TrailBlazer, the skies suddenly opened and a deluge of cold rain mixed with snow shot down, sending icy fingers slipping beneath his collar. He shivered as he slammed the door shut, fired the ignition, and switched on the wipers.

His house was about ten minutes south of Seaside, depending on traffic and weather. Hale had just passed Cannon Beach on the way south when his cell phone began ringing through his car's speakers as Bluetooth picked up.

"Finally," he muttered, flipping up his cell phone to view the number, but it wasn't Kristina's. The number was his client Ian Carmichael's. Disappointed, he waited till the phone connected and then said, "Hello, Ian?"

"Oh, Godddd !" came a woman's shriek, booming through his speakers.

The sound jolted Hale's heart. "Astrid?" he asked.

"She's . . . dead . . . dead. . . . She's dead! Oh, God. Oh, my God! She's dead!"

"Who? Astrid? Who's dead?" Hale asked as he slowed and pulled over to the side of the road, but in some dark region of his mind he jumped to only one conclusion, and just as quickly pushed that thought aside. This wasn't about him.

There was a sound of scrambling on the phone, as if someone had dropped it and then caught it, and a moment later Ian's voice came on the line. "Hale?" he asked in a strained voice. "Is that you?"

"Yes, Ian. I'm driving home, and—"

"She's not dead. Astrid grabbed the phone before I could call. We phoned nine-one-one when we found her. She was in the living room. There was blood on the wood, a heavy chunk like a beam. Must've fallen from above. I think she was hit with it."

"Where are you?" he demanded, but he knew.

"We're outside the house. She came in through a window. We found her inside."

Hale was already turning the TrailBlazer around, aiming for Seaside and the Carmichaels' house. His pulse was like a surf in his ears. "You found an injured woman inside your house?"

"You said they were going to demo soon and we stopped by and there she was." He gulped audibly. "I think you should come. It might be . . ."

"I'm on my way. It might be what? Ian?" Hale demanded. Then, when Ian wouldn't or couldn't respond, he added, "You're saying a woman climbed through the window."

"'Cause it was locked, I guess. The Seaside police should be here soon," Ian answered distractedly. "Umm . . . we're just outside the front. We saw her and just . . . didn't go in. There was a window open, maybe."

One window. The one that wouldn't close properly. Had some vagrant found it?

He experienced a horrifying, crystal-clear memory of standing with Kristina at their own house and watching rain race down the panes, and him saying, "This weather's hell on wooden window frames. Good thing we're redoing the Carmichaels' house, because it's a sieve."

And then Kristina answering, "My parents' house has wood frames. They either swell shut or just won't latch."

And him nodding, glad for once that they were having an actual conversation about something besides their relationship, and saying, "These windows are in the 'just won't latch' category."

Hale had a sudden vision of Kristina on the Carmichaels' living room floor, the back of her head a mass of blood.

"Ian," he said, forcing the words past his lips. *It couldn't be. Couldn't! And yet . . .* "Do you think the woman is my wife?"

"I don't know, man. Just get here."

Fear seized his chest like a vise, and he pressed his toes to the accelerator as he tore back through the dark night to the job site on the Promenade.

Savannah drove across the Willamette River, through the tunnel, then west on the Sunset Highway. The beams of headlights heading east shimmered on the pavement, and ahead of her pulsed a scarlet trail of taillights. Deception Bay lay over two hours west over the mountains. Her police band sputtered, and she was instantly tired. Damned pregnancy.

There was a Motel 6 coming up on her right, and it seemed as good a choice as any. She took the ramp off the Sunset and pulled into the lot. Zipping up her jacket and holding the collar close, she bent her head to the wind. Tiny flakes of snow swirled around her as she walked into the reception area, which smelled slightly of burned coffee.

She tried Kristina again as she waited for her key at the desk, but her cell phone went straight to voicemail for the dozenth time. She thought about calling Hale, but first Nadine's and then Owen DeWitt's condemnation of her sister was in the forefront of her mind, and she just didn't feel like talking to Kristina's husband right now.

Not that she believed a word of it. Kristina wanted Hale, and she was too determined that they should have a life together for her to blow it on an affair. Gretz and DeWitt were either lying or mistaken. Kristina wasn't a liar or a cheat. That just wasn't the way her sister was made.

"Where are you?" she muttered under her breath.

Her sister's supposed sexual encounters reminded her of Catherine and what she'd said about her own sister, Mary's "gift," as well as her ability to draw men to her. *Weird.* Then there was Catherine's strange lesson in genetics and the boys, now men, who'd been born at Siren Song. Where were they? Did they exist? Had they ever? All questions that were going to have to wait until after she finished her part of the Donatella investigation and had her baby.

She rubbed her stomach, and Baby St. Cloud gave her hand a kick. Not as powerful as before. She was getting too big, and there wasn't the same amount of room for the little guy to move.

"Not much longer," she told him softly.

Key in hand, she picked up her overnight bag and stepped carefully along the walkway, which was growing slippery, then up the exterior stairs to the second floor. Two-twelve was halfway down the balcony, and she let herself into a clean but cold room with a queen bed that, when she switched on the overhead, looked like it sagged a bit in the center.

She found the thermostat and turned up the heat, then, shivering, propped herself on the bed. Her brain was full of the events of the past few days. There were so many things to think about, she felt slightly ADD, her mind jumping from Catherine and the questions surrounding her sister's death to Bancroft Bluff and the Donatella murders, and how they impacted Hale St. Cloud and his family, to the growing worry she felt about Kristina and the allegations that she'd been having an affair with someone named Charlie, to the fact that she, Savannah, was about to go into childbirth and give her sister and husband a child.

And come Monday, she would be relegated to desk duty, which, although it wasn't a bad thing, made her feel cast aside and useless, and she supposed that was all just the baby-growing hormones at work, but she still felt it. Keenly.

She'd stuffed the pages of Bancroft Development's financials that Ella Blessert had copied for her into her messenger bag, and now she pulled out the thick pile and laid it on the bed, starting from the furthest date back and going forward. She'd barely started reading, however, when her eyes began watering from weariness and she began to yawn.

A brief nap. That was all she needed.

Lying back on the bed, she thought she should take her shoes off, but she was too tired to care. She tried to focus instead on only one aspect of the investigation, but for reasons unclear to her, all she could think about was Kristina and her joy when she'd learned Savannah was pregnant.

Call me, she mentally ordered her sister as she drifted off.

As fast as he drove to the Carmichael house, the Seaside police and EMTs beat Hale to the site. Ian and Astrid were huddled on one side of the building as snow swirled around them and fluttered in the flashlight beams and squares of light from the windows. Hale slammed the TrailBlazer into park and leapt onto the ground, slipping a little in the dusting of snow. He rushed forward but was blocked by an officer, who told him they had a crime scene and he couldn't enter, and at that moment a gurney with a body on it was carried through the front door.

One look and he knew. Kristina.

"Oh, God. My God." His legs threatened to buckle.

"Sir?"

He swam back to the present with an effort. A young officer wearing a Seaside police uniform and a name tag that read MILLS was standing in front of him. Hale blinked. "Where are they taking her?"

"I don't know, sir. You recognize the victim?"

"My wife. Kristina . . . St. Cloud."

He brushed past the officer and asked the EMTs, "Where are you going?"

"Ocean Park Hospital."

He turned to leave, but Officer Mills was in front of him again. "An officer will meet you at the hospital, Mr. St. Cloud."

Hale barely heard him as he ran full bore and skidded to his vehicle. A thousand images swirled through his brain in an instant: meeting her at the coffee shop, sharing their first Christmas, a midnight kiss, making love to her . . . and then her sudden disinterest.

"Hale?"

It was Astrid Carmichael. Her voice a wavering plea in the cold night air. To both Astrid and Ian, he said tersely, "It's Kristina. I'm going to the hospital."

Ian Carmichael nodded once, and his wife buried her face in her husband's chest.

The ambulance pulled out with full lights and siren, the wailing *woo-woo-woo-woo* screaming into the night, with Hale right on the emergency vehicle's bumper. He drove somewhat carefully, because of the worsening weather, though he wanted to rip down the highway. Nevertheless, he was only minutes behind the ambulance as they reached Ocean Park Hospital.

Slamming his car into park, he half ran, half jogged through the carpet of snow to the ER, where sliding glass doors shifted backward as he burst through. Kristina's gurney was just being pushed past double swinging doors controlled by a push button. Hale followed right after it, slipping inside before the automatic doors shut him out. Kristina's eyes were closed, and her face was white.

"Kristina," he said.

"Excuse me, sir. Are you a relative?" A woman was suddenly standing in front of him—a nurse—blocking his view.

"That's my wife," he said, holding on tightly to his control with everything he possessed. Dear, Jesus, was she going to make it? What happened? *What happened?*

"If you could wait over here . . ." She gestured toward a chair in a curtained bay that was empty.

"Where's she going?"

"They're doing tests and prepping her for possible surgery."

"Surgery?"

"She has head trauma. Please, sir . . ."

Hale sat down reluctantly, and as soon as he was seated, he felt the blood rush from his head. What the hell was Kristina doing at the Carmichael house? How did she get in? Through the *window?* Why?

"Crime scene," Officer Mills had said.

Hale shook his head, trying to clear it. *Crime scene. No accident?*

"We need you to fill out some forms," another woman said, and a clipboard with papers and a pen were shoved into his hands. Hale stared at the documents a moment, then began filling them in, his mind racing ahead, his hand shaking as he wrote.

Ian Carmichael's words came back to him. *Blood on the wood . . . a heavy chunk like a beam . . .*

Hale drew a careful breath. He'd thought Ian had meant she was hit by a board in an accident. There had been some demolition inside the house already. Sheetrock ripped off, framing hammered out of the walls. He'd initially assumed her injury was accidental. That was what he'd wanted to believe, anyway. What he still wanted to believe.

He pulled his wallet from his pocket, slid out the insurance card, then wrote the information on the form. Out of the corner of his eye he saw an officer enter through the electronically activated swinging doors, a law enforcement man wearing the tan uniform of the sheriff's department.

Hale straightened in his chair as the man introduced himself. "I'm Deputy Warren Burghsmith of the Tillamook County Sheriff's Department."

He blinked, his mind splintered in all directions. "My wife was found in Clatsop County."

"The hospital's in Tillamook County, and I'm first available, Mr. . . . ?"

"St. Cloud. Hale St. Cloud."

"And it's your wife who was brought in."

He nodded. "Kristina St. Cloud."

"Can you tell me what happened?"

"At the job site? No. I wasn't there." He found himself feeling overwhelmed. "I came later."

"Job site?"

"I own Bancroft Development with my grandfather, Declan Bancroft, and the Carmichaels' house is scheduled to be demoed and rebuilt. Kristina went there for some reason."

"Do you know what your wife was doing at the site?"

"Not a clue."

"Could she have been meeting someone?"

Hale just stared at the deputy, who looked to be somewhere in his late forties. "I don't know who that would be."

"Excuse me . . ." The nurse who had given him the admissions documents had returned. "Have you filled out the forms?"

"Um . . . yeah . . . mostly." Hale handed her the clipboard, and she took it away.

"What are the names of the people who own the house?" Burghsmith asked after she disappeared.

"Ian and Astrid Carmichael."

"Did your wife know them?"

"Only by sight. But she knew of the project."

A doctor crossed the area behind Deputy Burghsmith, and Hale jumped up and caught up with him. "Excuse me. My wife is . . . having tests . . . ?"

"Dr. Mellon will be out to talk to you," he said brusquely, moving on by.

The deputy was still standing near Hale's chair, and Hale didn't want to talk to anyone but the medical staff. When he didn't return to his chair, Burghsmith went to him. Before he could ask another question, Hale preempted with, "Am I going to have to go through this with the Seaside police, too?"

"One of their detectives will want to talk to you."

Which made him think of Savannah. Off in Portland. "Excuse me," Hale said and then walked away from Burghsmith, sliding his thumb across the screen of his phone to unlock it.

Then another doctor came into the room, his gaze searching the occupants and falling on Hale. Hale immediately locked the phone again, put it in his pocket, and stalked quickly toward the doctor, who extended his hand as he drew near.

"I'm Dr. Mellon," he said, introducing himself.

"Hale St. Cloud. My wife, Kristina . . . Are you her doctor?"

"Dr. Oberon will be doing the surgery, Mr. St. Cloud. We need to relieve the pressure on her brain. She has a subdural hematoma and—"

"Subdural hematoma?"

"She's bleeding into her brain."

Hale stared at the man, cottony with shock. "Will she be all right?"

"We're taking her into surgery."

"That's no answer."

"We won't know anything until after surgery," the doctor said firmly.

"Tell me *something*, goddamnit!"

"Mr. St. Cloud, if you could just be a little patient. We're doing everything we can—"

"How severe is it?" he interrupted.

"Severe enough to require surgery," Mellon answered after a moment, his expression neutral. Then he was called away.

Hale stared after him. He guessed the doctor hadn't given him anything because the injury was bad. Bad enough that loved ones had to be kept in the dark.

God, Kristina. What were you doing there? he thought.

*　*　*

Charlie expelled air through his teeth, frustrated as hell. The bitch wouldn't die. Just wouldn't die. She had lain there, staring into space, and had just gone on breathing and breathing and *wouldn't die!* He'd tried to wait her out, but she'd won in the end. He had to leave her before he was discovered, and it really pissed him off.

It had been nearly a day and still no report. At least he'd gotten back to his apartment and seen the news before he went to bed. It was all about the murders in the truck at the steak house. Ha, ha, ha. That, at least, had made him feel good. They could speculate all they wanted, but none of them knew his power. He recalled staring at Tammie and Garth as they each died, and that made him feel even better about Mrs. Kristina St. Cloud, who just *wouldn't* die.

He went to the refrigerator and pulled out a Guinness, popping the top and drinking it down in long, thirsty gulps.

He needed to see that last look in their eyes before the light seemed to get pulled back inside them and they were gone. Blink, blink. Gone.

But that was all yesterday, and today some things had happened that made him forget his disappointment with Kristina and remember the highlights with her instead. Man, could that St. Cloud bitch shriek. She would buck and wail and damn near climax before he hardly did anything. She was that susceptible to his power. Made him want to masturbate right now just thinking about it, but alas, he had a date that just couldn't wait.

But then she was kind of a shrieker, too, he thought with a slow grin.

He wondered briefly, foolishly, if he could kill her while they were having sex and watch the light blink out. In his mind's eye he saw the arch of her throat and himself drawing a knife across it, a thin scarlet line of blood rising against her white flesh.

Man, oh, man.

With an effort, he tamped down his thoughts. He had to wait. Had to wait for the perfect time. Then he would slice her lovely throat. He would kill her . . . and like he'd told his mother, he would kill them all.

*   *   *

"They're taking her into the OR," a voice said, and Hale stopped staring into the middle distance to look up and see that the same nurse was talking to him. "There's a waiting room through here."

He followed after her, feeling helpless and lost. As soon as he was seated in the smaller room with the blue and gray molded plastic chairs, he pulled out his cell again. He stared at it a moment before punching in Savannah's cell number.

CHAPTER 15

She knew she was dreaming, but she couldn't wake up.
Kristina was there, dressed in white, beckoning her silently toward a building covered by dense shrubbery. Savannah tried to talk to her, but she couldn't form the words. They were stuck in her throat, and every effort to speak failed her. "I'm not going," she tried to tell the wraithlike Kristina. "I'm not going!"

But it was useless and the screen of bushes seemed to fall away and there was the lodge, Siren Song, only bigger and darker. And there was a light in the third-floor window that shouldn't have been there, Savvy was pretty sure. The gates were open, and she followed Kristina, only it wasn't Kristina anymore. It was someone else. Someone older and old-fashioned, with a cameo brooch at her neck depicting an even older woman, a relative, she knew. Mary? No, someone older. Sarah? That was a name from the book. One of the women from the past who had powers . . . no, *a gift*. That was what they all had, all the women, but it was the men . . . the boys . . . whose gifts were more intense, more deadly.

In front of her eyes floated Xs and Ys, and she heard Catherine's voice saying, "It goes deeper and darker with them. Can you feel it? Can you feel it?"

And Savvy was suddenly drenched with a desire so hot and angry that she felt her body shudder and explode into a climax that had her arching upward. A man was crooning to her, telling her she was his, and she saw that it was Hale St. Cloud.

I'm dreaming. Stop, she told herself. *Stop! Wake up!*

Kristina's eyes were staring into Savvy's accusingly. "I wasn't with

Hale. I wasn't!" she wanted to scream, but Kristina couldn't seem to hear her.

And then Joyce Powell-Pritchett was there, peering at Savannah through her narrow-lensed glasses, saying in her schoolteacher's voice, "It's all in the history. If you would just look deeper, you would see."

"Who's the older lady?" Savvy struggled to ask, and she must have been heard, because Catherine turned slowly to see where she was looking and said in her crisp tones, "That's no lady. Look. *Look.*"

Before Savvy's eyes the woman with the cameo turned into a man wearing a fedora dipped over one eye and a brown suit. He lifted the brim of his hat with one finger, and his eyes burned like hot coals.

Savannah screamed loud enough to wake the dead, and she sat bolt upright in bed.

She was awake, quivering all over, still propped up on the motel room bed. She could feel the faint remnants of her climax and was slightly embarrassed. *What the hell?*

And then Baby St. Cloud rolled over once, and Savvy clutched the covers, seized by a stronger Braxton Hicks as her cell phone shattered the stillness and caused her to gasp, her heart lurching.

"God," she muttered, annoyed at herself, feeling cold sweat on her skin. She searched around for her phone and found it tangled in the covers of the bed. "Hello?" she answered. "Hello?"

"Savvy? It's Hale."

Her sex dream about him momentarily came back, and she pushed it aside with revulsion. She realized she was breathing hard and swallowed once, trying to shake the remnants of the dream. "Hey, there," she said. Then, "Have you talked to Kristina?"

"That's why I'm calling you. There's been an accident."

Savvy sat up straighter, the hairs on the back of her neck lifting. "What kind of accident?"

"At one of our construction sites. She was hit with a beam, it looks like it fell on her, and she's at the hospital, in surgery."

Savannah was on her feet. "What?" When he hesitated, Savannah felt like screaming. "Damn it, Hale. *What?*"

"They're saying subdural hematoma." Another profound hesitation. "She's bleeding into her brain."

"Oh, *God* . . . How? How did this happen?" Her eyes were searching for her shoes, sturdy black slip-ons, but she needed something else. She'd packed her sneakers. Boots with traction would have been better, but sneakers would work. She had her ski jacket. She hadn't unpacked.

"I don't know."

He sounded tired, but Savannah felt wide awake now with every nerve fiber singing. She took two steps to the window and pulled back the curtain. Snow was falling fast and hard. The rail outside her window had an inch on it already.

"I'm coming back," she said.

"No," he said. "The pass is going to be a mess."

"I have four-wheel drive. I have chains in the back. I'm coming back, Hale."

"No, Savannah. I'm here with her! How are you going to put those chains on?"

"If it gets really bad, I'll figure it out."

"You're . . . too . . . pregnant," he stated flatly.

"They're the snap-on kind. I can do it," she flared. "My sister's hurt. What did you think I would do? Sit and wait in a motel room?"

"I've got this handled. No matter what you think, you're not bulletproof, Savannah. And you're—"

Savannah cut him off with one click. To hell with Hale St. Cloud. She grabbed her sneakers, smashed them on her feet, and tied them with the effort of bending over. Snatching up her overnight bag, her messenger bag, and her gun, which she'd laid on the nightstand, she headed outside.

The snow made everything unnaturally light, and its beauty as it fell would have been magical at another time. Now Savvy felt a clock ticking in her head. The same clock that reset and marked off the seconds every time she was in a dangerous situation.

Getting down the stairs and into the Escape took longer than she wanted, but there was no way in hell she was going to slip.

"Hang in there," she said, placing a hand on her belly, though she meant both the baby and her sister. The two-hour trip would be three hours or longer in this weather, but she'd be damned if she'd stay in Portland.

Her mind touched on the dream, and an uneasy feeling spread through her.

She didn't believe in dreams, but then she didn't believe in people with otherworldly gifts, either, or at least she hadn't.

Gritting her teeth, she put a call in to Lang's cell, which, like every call today, went straight to voicemail. She told him she was on her way; then she pulled out of the parking lot and began the long journey back.

"Aunt Catherine?"

Catherine awoke with a start. She'd drifted off in the living room chair, while reading by a strong electric light. Now she glanced quickly down at the journal, which was still open in her lap, and she closed it as Lillibeth wheeled through the doorway from her short hallway and bedroom.

"Someone's here," Lillibeth said, heading toward the door.

"At the gate?" Catherine stirred herself and got to her feet. The fire had died down, and there was a distinct chill in the room, or maybe it was her soul.

"It's Earl."

Catherine gave her a long look. Lillibeth didn't possess Cassandra's gift of seeing the future, but she did have a trace of precognition, as did Catherine, as did, maybe, all of them. "How do you know?"

Lillibeth shrugged. "He told me."

Her head squeezed. "He who?" Catherine demanded. "Don't talk in riddles."

"I think it was Earl."

Catherine found that mildly alarming. She looked around as she headed for the back door to fetch her cloak before returning to the front of the house, where Lillibeth still waited. "Where's everyone else? Still upstairs?" The girls had been quiet at dinner, almost plotting, Catherine thought, and then had all returned to the second floor and their rooms.

"I think so."

"Stay inside," Catherine ordered, then pulled her hood over her head, tightened the cloak at her neck, and stepped into a swirl of dancing snow and rain. The mixed precipitation landed on her face and melted and ran cold.

She trudged carefully along the flagstone path, which was nearly buried in snow, toward the gate, where, sure enough, Earl stood in the dark beyond, outlined by the growing field of white surrounding him.

"What is it?" Catherine asked, approaching him.

"There's a fire on Echo," he said, to which Catherine whipped around, but from the spot where she stood she couldn't see over the bushes to the island beyond.

"A fire! There can't be. No one could be out there in this weather."

"Someone is."

"No one knows the island like you do, and you wouldn't go out there in this."

"Younger men, younger women, they could get there," he argued.

"The last time that happened, the fools were killed!" Catherine reminded him.

"They were drunk."

"I'm not going to stand here in this weather and argue with you," she said with asperity. "I don't believe someone's there."

"It's not as secure as you want to believe," he told her. He'd said it before, but Catherine hadn't wanted to hear it then, and she certainly didn't want to hear it now.

"What kind of fire? How big?"

"Big enough to see."

"The house? The cottage?"

Earl slowly shook his head.

"I'm going back inside. Maybe you just imagined it."

Earl stood stolidly silent. Catherine waited him out, refusing to give in to his theory, even though she believed it.

He turned back to his truck, and Catherine watched him leave.

The terrible part was, she was pretty sure she knew who was out there, who'd caused the fire. But why? What was he doing there? What did he hope to find?

As Earl backed down the drive and then drove away, Catherine stepped to the edge of the gate, craning her neck to try and glimpse the fire. Unless she went back for the key to unlock the gates her view was limited as it was impossible to see anything from inside the Siren Song grounds.

Was he *burning* something?

Shivering, she turned back toward the house, sinking with her first step deep into the snow above the flagstone path and slipping . . . slipping. . . .

Savvy drove coolly and carefully, fighting the urge to press her foot to the accelerator. The roads were snow covered, but with her four-wheel drive she felt secure. If there was enough buildup across the Coast Range, she would have to put on her chains, but in the city the snow had been patchy, with stretches of bare pavement where the snow melted as fast as it came down.

She was hungry. Again. Even with the worry gnawing at her insides, she needed to eat. Carefully, she snapped open her glove box and pulled out an energy bar. She had a bottle of water handy and several more behind her seat, but she wasn't going to drink more than a few swallows at a time. There was the issue of her bladder.

She exhaled, calming her nerves. She'd banished thoughts of Kristina and what had happened to her to a very distant corner of her mind, the only way she could make this drive safely.

Behind her, to the east, the Cascade Range was getting buried in snow, but she was heading west onto the Coast Range, where the highest point was still lower in altitude than most of the peaks in the Cascades. She was nearing the halfway point, but that didn't mean this was going to be a picnic. In fact . . .

She swept in a harsh breath, her hands involuntarily squeezing the steering wheel, as a contraction took her over, and for a moment she felt suspended in pain.

So hard! Labor? No.

That wasn't right . . . was it?

She checked her watch. Eight thirty.

No. She was not in labor. Not yet. Not *now.*

She waited, half convinced her own anxiety had brought on the contraction. Her mind was just beginning to move away from that fear, her attention back on the road, when another wave rolled through her, hard, wrenching, producing sweat, and she found herself holding her breath, waiting desperately for it to pass. Then her brain clicked in, and she quickly started panting like she'd seen in those natural birth videos and every movie where some woman was having a baby.

"God . . ."

It wasn't true. It wasn't true.

Her hands were slick with sweat on the wheel. Timing. Life was all about timing, and this . . . this . . . bad timing couldn't be happening. No . . . way.

Five minutes later the clench was stronger, her uterus blithely unaware that she *could not have a baby now!* She knew it for what it was. True labor. Yup. The real thing. This wasn't like the damn Braxton Hicks contractions. They'd told her and told her that she'd know when it was real, and she'd listened with half an ear. Kind of like she'd treated the whole damn pregnancy: *It's not mine, so it doesn't really count.*

But it counted.

It counted.

Gritting her teeth, she guided her four-wheel-drive vehicle steadily through a thickening carpet of snow. *You can do this, Savannah. You can.* There was nowhere she could stop, no turning back. Sweating, fighting each contraction, she managed to keep her tires in the two tracks that were quickly disappearing after the passing of the last car, which was far enough ahead of her Escape that she could no longer see its taillights. Lining the road, rows of Douglas firs were heavy with snow, their branches blanketed in white.

She wondered how many miles she had to drive until she could risk pulling off and making a call. Or was it too late already? Another pain ripped through her, and she held steady hands clamped over the wheel.

Hold on, Kristina, she thought, jaw clenched, eyes straight forward and steady. She sent up a silent prayer for her sister.

After a moment, she sent one up for herself, as well.

Over an hour since Savannah had hung up on him. Forty-five minutes into Kristina's surgery. Hale sat in the plastic chair and kept glancing at his watch, wondering how minutes had become so long. Eternities.

He tried calling Savvy back, but her phone went straight to voice mail. Because she wasn't answering, or because she was out of range, heading into the storm.

Probably a little of both.

Feeling strangled for air, he left the OR waiting room and headed toward Emergency and the glass doors and hallway windows that offered a view outside. He was shocked at the amount of snow on the ground when he caught his first glimpse of the parking lot. Two inches of accumulation? Three? If there was this much snow at sea level, what must the pass be like?

Worried, he thought about calling the sheriff's department and maybe talking to Savannah's partner of sorts, Detective Stone. Or was it Clausen? He didn't really know. He'd heard her speak of Stone more often. He placed the call and asked for Stone, but the brusque way he was put off by the woman in dispatch told him more about the state of the department before she even brought up the weather.

"Detective Stone is not available. Would you like to leave a message?"

"No. I'm good. Thanks." He clicked off with the lie. He was far from "good," and he half thought about calling 9-1-1, but what would he say? "I'm worried about a pregnant woman driving over the pass." And the probable answer given the condition of the weather: "Yeah, aren't we all, buddy?"

He wished from the bottom of his gut that Savannah had stayed in Portland. Better yet, he wished she'd never left the coast at all.

Snow. Thick crystalline pellets. Everywhere.

Savannah stared through the windshield, her attention laserlike on the white road, her ears tuned to the radio. After a sketchy broadcast that had started warning everyone to just stay inside with a hot toddy or cocoa, and flashlights and blankets at the ready, she was now getting mostly fuzz.

Her police band was sputtering, but she could get no clear signal through the storm. She'd tried calling 9-1-1, but her cell wasn't connecting, either, and when she'd phoned Lang, it had been with the same result. In fact, the last time she'd fumbled with her cell, she'd lost her concentration, and the SUV's back end had swung outward, causing her heart to jolt, before she straightened out the vehicle and eased it back onto the white road ahead of her.

Beads of sweat stood on her forehead, and she felt like she was burning up, like after a hard workout, rather than driving through a frigid landscape where the temperature was dropping by the minute. The predicted storm wasn't supposed to be this severe; she'd heard the surprise in the weather reporter's voice before her radio went to white noise.

"Accident . . . don't go . . . icy conditions until . . ."

Tantalizing snippets were fighting their way through. Savvy kept herself attuned to the radio with the intense concentration of a tightrope walker. It was better than thinking about her sister, better than thinking about the next contraction, which she suspected was about two minutes away.

She could make it. Labor was intense; she'd known it would be. But it took a long time. She could do it. She was halfway through the mountains already, although this second half of the drive was bound to be a lot slower, as she'd gotten down to ten miles an hour or less. At this rate . . .

The radio fuzzed, and she caught a brief snippet of a scratchy voice: "Roads closures . . . all mountain passes . . . Cascade . . . Siskiyou . . . Coast Range . . ."

"What?" she asked aloud, peering into the darkness ahead while white, swirling flakes caught in her headlights.

The finicky radio signal disappeared and gave her back that infuriating, fuzzing nothingness. It was time for the chains. Past time, really. She hadn't been kidding when she'd told Hale they were the snap-on kind. She'd put them on half a dozen times going over the Coast Range in the winter, and though, no, she hadn't been extremely pregnant those times, she wasn't all that worried about it now. She just had to be careful about slipping, and that was the one area where she was lacking: good footwear for snow.

It was too dark to see too far ahead, but she knew this road backward and forward. She passed the last rest stop, which had been closed up and was buried in snow. There was a turnout not far ahead. A blocked-off road on forestry land. She could pull over there and put the chains on.

A contraction seized her, and she slowed the vehicle to a crawl, fighting through the pain. *God. Damn. It.* She could hear Hale and Kristina and Lang in her head, telling her what an idiot she was. But Kristina . . .

A sob escaped her lips. Immediately, she fought it back. No. No falling apart. Not now.

The SUV was barely moving by the time the contraction released her. Surfacing, she saw that the snow had covered the tracks she'd been following. *Roads closed.* That was the last report, followed by something about the Coast Range. She still had confidence her vehicle could get through, but if they were closing roads, this storm appeared to be a helluva lot worse than anyone had dreamed.

Her wipers were having difficulty getting rid of the accumulation of snow on her windshield. She peered through the small peephole each swipe granted her, squinting ahead into darkness. There were actually three passes along Highway 26, a climb and a partial drop, another climb and a partial drop, and then a final climb and a long drop toward the Pacific Ocean. She was near the final summit. Should she try Lang again? Nine-one-one? She was almost afraid to pick up the phone.

Her headlight beams barely seemed to make a difference—twin jet streams of diminishing illumination that seemed only to find snow, snow, and more snow. Finally, she spied the edge of the dirt road—now snowed over—a road that would avail her a shoulder to pull onto, away from the massive ditches on either side. Carefully, she turned the steering wheel, touching the brakes lightly, avoiding any chance of skidding.

"C'mon," she whispered.

The beginning of another contraction. Savvy desperately tried to turn off first. Her rear end fishtailed. Her Escape swung around to the right too quickly. Suddenly she was spinning 360 degrees, agonizingly slowly. She clenched the wheel, took her foot off the brake, bore down on the contraction, and screamed for all she was worth, the sound deafening in the car. Her headlights swung over the ground, but she didn't stop. The Escape kept on turning and turning, out of control. She realized there was a sheet of ice beneath the snow, laid down from the rain that had spit from the sky first.

Swearing in short, staccato monosyllables, she gently tried to reverse the spin. Her heart thundered in her ears. No studs. No grip. "Come on. . . . Come on. . . ." But it was no use. In a slow-motion glide the Escape slid off the road, missed the turnout, and slipped into the ditch, nose first, clattering and banging onto its side.

Savvy sat sideways in the vehicle, hung in place by her seat belt.

Unhurt, but little tremors of fear were running through her. Okay. Okay. She was okay. She was okay. The slide had happened slowly enough that the air bags weren't triggered.

Then she felt the gush of warmth between her legs.

"Oh . . . shit."

Panic wasn't far off now. With an effort, she tamped down her fears. She'd been trained to keep a cool head, but she was playing a losing game with so many strikes against her.

She would try the cell phone again. Maybe there was reception. Maybe. Hopefully. God, hopefully . . .

She'd put the cell back in her messenger bag, which had been on the passenger seat. Now the bag was lying against the passenger door. She tried to reach for it, but her arms weren't long enough, and she could only wave at it like a trapped animal due to her seat belt restraints. She immediately tried to find the release mechanism for the seat belt, but the pressure of her own weight made it difficult to release. "Damn!" She wanted to shriek and flail and cry.

Her fingers pressed hard on the release. She gritted her teeth. She pressed and pressed and pressed, then yanked on the belt itself, then shifted and pressed again. Suddenly, her seat belt snapped open, and she half fell downward into the passenger seat, her legs tangled in the driver's footwell.

Her fingers found her messenger bag. Hallelujah! Her breath came in trembling gasps. Her pulse slammed in her ears. *Relax. Relax. Relax.* Fingers scrabbling beneath the bag's front flap, she searched blindly for her cell.

Please . . . oh, God, please . . .

She could just touch the case, couldn't get a grip. Sweat slipped down the side of her nose.

"Goddamnit!" she yelled.

A fingernail slid across the molded plastic. She tried to scooch closer, and she felt the beginnings of the wave. *How many minutes in between? How many? Three? Two? One?*

No.

Calm. Calm. Stay calm. The contraction overcame her, sending her into the fetal position, as much as she could manage. She counted in her head. *One Mississippi. Two Mississippi. Three Missi . . .*

"Oh, for God's sake!" she yelped.

Slowly, slowly, the contraction ebbed, and as she lay sprawled across the front seats, she listened to her own breathing for several seconds before reaching forward again. She probed with her index finger and worked it around the phone. Her middle finger came next, carefully, and when two fingers surrounded the casing, her thumb came in for the grab. Precarious but caught. She momentarily reveled in victory.

With the patience of a saint, she worked the cell out and let out a sob when it was fully in her hand. Yanking it to her, she quickly pressed the power-on button, slid to unlock, and called up the keypad. Nine-one-one. Then the TCSD. Yes, they would give her hell for her predicament, but that was the least of her worries. She'd be lucky to . . . The phone starting singing, and she nearly dropped it.

"Damn! Son of a . . . Hello?"

"Savannah! Where are you? Tell me you're over the summit. They're closing roads, and I don't know what the hell that means, but nothing good." Hale sounded half frantic. "God. Where are you?"

"I'm . . . over the summit."

"Good. How far? What the hell are the roads like?" He drew a breath.

"What about Kristina?" she demanded.

"She's in surgery."

"Okay. Good. That's good?"

"Yeah, yeah. It's good, as far as I know. They're doing everything they can. When will you be here?"

"Not sure. I'm, um, having some difficulties. I hit some ice and the Escape . . ."

"What?"

"I'm off the road, in a ditch."

"Savannah!"

"I'm fine. Perfectly fine."

"Damn it. You—" He cut himself off.

"I know. I know. I just need a tow." She wasn't going to tell him that her water broke. Not yet. Not until she absolutely had to.

"Okay . . . okay . . . I don't know when that'll be. I just saw on the news, there are accidents everywhere."

"Okay."

"But I'll get someone out there. You're sure you're all right?"

"Yes." She nodded, as if he could see her, but underneath she was beginning to feel panic. "Call nine-one-one."

"You *are* hurt!"

"No, Hale. No. I'm just trapped, and I've been having some contractions."

"Contractions? You're kidding! Say you're kidding."

"Sorry, no." She closed her eyes. "They've gotten stronger."

"Savvy?"

"I'm just going to settle in and wait for the ambulance."

"Savvy? You there? Savvy!"

"I'm here, Hale. Can you hear me?"

"Are you there?"

"My water broke, and I—"

"Savvy?"

"Oh, shit," she muttered, filled with rising panic. He couldn't hear her! "Hale?"

"Damn it. Savannah? Can you hear me?"

"Yes, yes! Can you hear me?"

Silence.

"Hale?" A moment. "Hale?"

She looked down at the screen. CONNECTION FAILED.

She went cold inside. Colder than the world outside. Her teeth started chattering as a whistle of wind rattled the Escape. Swallowing hard, she struggled to make a call, but whatever service she'd had was gone. With mounting anxiety she realized not one single car had passed her since she'd slid off the road.

She was alone in a cold white world.

CHAPTER 16

"Nine-one-one. What is the nature of your emergency?"

"There's a woman in a Ford Escape who's gone off the road just over the summit on Highway Twenty-Six. Toward us, the ocean side, west side, of the summit." Hale felt a pulse in his head beating out a tattoo of fear. "She needs help."

"Sir, what is your name?"

"Hale St. Cloud. Her name . . . the woman in the car is Savannah Dunbar, and she's pregnant. Very pregnant."

"Is she in labor?"

"Yes, she's having contractions! She's unable to move! She's *stuck!*" He thought of Savannah trapped in her car and the cold and the contractions. He thought of his unborn son. . . . What if there were complications? Trauma?

"You're saying you can't pinpoint the location. Does she have a cell phone?"

"Yes, but it just went dead. Can you just send someone out that way?" he demanded impatiently.

"The roads have been closed—"

"I know, damn it. What the hell does that mean?"

"Mr. St. Cloud, we have many emergencies. I'm sending the message, and they'll get to her as soon as they can. But if she could call and we could get a better idea as to where she is? You understand that would help?"

"Yeah. Yeah."

"We'll send EMTs as soon as we can."

The dubiousness of the operator's voice made Hale want to slam his fist into a wall. He assured the operator, who asked him more questions, that he would keep trying to reach Savannah, and then he hung up, feeling utterly useless and frustrated.

Wanting to jump from his skin, he stalked back to the waiting room outside the operating rooms. He thought of his wife fighting for her life, but as safe as she could be, in a doctor's care. But Savannah and the baby . . . He lasted exactly six minutes. Then he strode to the nearest nurses' hub and said loudly, "I need to give someone my cell number. I've got to go. My wife's in surgery, but I've got another emergency."

One of the nurses got up from the chair she'd been sitting in and eyed him thoughtfully. Reaching under the counter, she pulled out a notepad on a clipboard. "Write it down here. Which surgeon is she with?"

"Dr. Oberon." Hale scratched down his cell. He had the prickling feeling that they didn't believe him. That his actions somehow made him seem guilty. Or was that just because Mills had mentioned the words *crime scene?*

He was gone before they could ask more questions. He couldn't do anything more for Kristina other than wring his hands.

But he could help Savvy. She needed help. Definitely needed help, and he didn't trust that dispatched EMTs were on the way, no matter what the 9-1-1 operator had said. *Bullshit.*

For a moment he stared through the window, hands balled by his sides. He could do nothing for Kristina. She was in surgery; she was in the best hands she could be. And his unborn son and his sister-in-law were in immediate danger. There was no contest.

He strode through the doors into a blistering, screaming wind. Ducking his head, he pulled out his cell and looked at it, certain he was going to see NO SERVICE. But there was a signal. Feeble at best. Immediately he tried Savannah again, but the call went to voicemail. He started to put the cell back in his pocket, picking up his pace to a jog, cold fingers of wind slipping under his collar and down his back, when the thing rang in his hand.

He glanced down in relief, but it wasn't Savannah. Punching the button, he said tersely, "Hi, Declan." His feet nearly slid out from under him, and he caught himself and slowed his step.

"Son, where are ya?" His grandfather's voice sounded high and reedy.

"I'm heading home," Hale lied without a qualm. He didn't need his grandfather involved in his problems. "You okay?"

"Yes . . . yes . . . I just thought I saw someone."

"At the house?" Hale glanced around at the stinging ice crystals swirling in the sodium vapor lights outside the hospital.

"Musta dreamed it. Sorry." He sounded embarrassed. "Call me when you're home."

"Want me to get someone to come to your place?" Who, he had no idea.

"No, no. Just an old man's silliness. Call me."

"Will do."

He was relieved he didn't have to attend to his grandfather, who, though his mind shied from the idea, seemed to be slipping a little mentally these days. Or maybe he was just overly tired. No sense borrowing trouble. Hale had enough of that as it was.

His black TrailBlazer was white, covered in an inch of snow. He opened the back and pulled out his chains and a small rolled-up rug. Flipping down the rug, he knelt on it and then wrapped the chain around the first rear tire and snapped it together. Snap-on. Like Savannah's. He did the same to the other rear tire, shook out the wet rug, and tossed it in the back. He was backing out of his parking spot and heading down the long entrance lane to the hospital within a minute. The normally gnarled, wind-blasted trees that lined it were now covered in snow, their mangled limbs softened by the white powder, strangely serene in this frantic night.

He drove intently, forcing himself to stay under control, feeling anxiety buzzing beneath his skin. By his reckoning he was at least forty minutes out. Maybe more. Probably more. But he was going to get there.

Savvy worked herself around, fighting for the driver's door handle. Tightening her fingers around the handle, she pressed it down and tried to shove the door upward. Were she her old limber self, she would pull out a leg and push it open, but in her current state she had to push with her hand. The door opened easily enough, but she couldn't get enough power to push it straight up. It snapped back down twice before she gave up.

And the wind was shrieking and shoving snow inside so fast, she was damp by just opening the door a crack. But at least the door would open; the SUV wasn't torqued too badly. Thank God for small favors.

She was still sprawled across the two front bucket seats. She wondered if she should try to resecure herself with the seat belt. Would that be better or worse? Worse probably. If . . .

The next contraction hit harder, pain ripping through her abdomen. Savannah closed her eyes and panted, counting, waiting it out. It didn't seem to be longer, but it sure as hell seemed stronger.

When it was over, she thought about the baby and about Hale and her sister. Kristina. But again she pushed thoughts of her aside, almost furiously. Couldn't think about Kristina. Not now. Later. After the EMTs got to her. The ones Hale had called through 9-1-1. He said he was going to call. He would. And they would get here.

The Escape's engine was still on, two dim yellow lines that illuminated the snow-laden fir boughs beyond. Savvy switched it off but left the lights on. She would turn the engine over after a bit. Didn't want to lose the battery. She lay still, and then another contraction took her over, squeezing her, leaving her breathless and shaking. Too close after the last one. Too close.

Sucking air between her teeth, Savvy lay still, listening to her own galloping heart.

There was no denying it. This baby was coming.

Soon.

Outside the window, the snow was coming down as hard as Charlie had ever seen it. He watched pensively, his thoughts running along twisting pathways. He'd made mistakes, several that needed immediate attention. The loose ends were unraveling faster and faster, and inside he was starting to feel that same old anxious feeling that meant it was time to take care of business and move on.

He'd seen that woman, that *detective,* today. Something had to be done about her. A pleasurable something, no doubt, but if he did something soon, his cover would be blown and they would start searching for him. He wasn't ready for that yet. There was too much to do. Those women at Siren Song . . .

And what the fuck had he been thinking, talking to that ass DeWitt? *Dimwit! Damn! Fuck!* He wanted to kick something, he was so angry at himself. He'd been bragging to the dense moron, that's what. Letting the bastard know that he, Charlie, could score with anyone he chose. *Anyone!* Women *wanted* him . . . practically spun themselves into a sexual frenzy if he so much as *looked* at them. Could Dimwit even conceive of that? No. He just sat night after night at one bar or another and drank himself stupid.

Now Charlie tamped down his growing anxiety and rage with an effort. This was not the time to drop his mask and let anyone see what was underneath. Too dangerous.

But Dimwit . . . God . . .

Charlie ground his teeth together in remembrance. He'd made some serious mistakes, which had to be corrected once and for all. He'd foolishly told Dimwit all those things because the fucker had seen him banging Kristina up against a wall at the Donatellas' Spanish Colonial. Charlie had caught a glimpse of the man's vehicle as he was tearing away from Bankruptcy Bluff, and he'd known he would have to do something.

A couple of nights later he'd followed him to a bar just down the road from Deception Bay, a local dive called Davy Jones's Locker. He should have killed him right then and there. But did he do that? *Did he?* Hell, no. Instead he'd *crowed* to the stupid ass about all his sexual conquests. Not just about Kristina! About *all* of them, including Chandra Donatella, who was the reason he'd chosen the Bankruptcy Bluff venue in the first place.

He'd even told the miserable little shit about his alter ego: Good Time Charlie.

Fuck.

Well, now he was going to have to do something about Dimwit tout de suite. And there were more developing problems: that fucker had been way too eager to talk to the sweet female detective. And then, of course, that sweet detective herself.

All three of them had to die.

He realized how close he was to being discovered, and a part of him was both angry and appalled that he'd been so careless. But another part looked forward to the killing that was to come. . . . He could get a hard-on just thinking about it.

"Hey," the woman called from the bed, miffed that he wasn't paying attention to her. His date. The one he'd been so eager to be with just hours earlier. The one he wanted to escape from now.

He'd been standing by the window, naked, lost in thought, watching the snow. Now, as he turned toward her, she patted the sheets, inviting him back in.

But he didn't want to have sex with her again. He damn well never wanted to see her again. After he had a woman, he didn't want to go back for seconds unless there was a way to up the ante. Before his first kill, he'd tried anything that was a little more dangerous. Sex in a public place. Sex somewhere precarious, like that time at the construction site. All those Bancroft Development employees around . . . and he'd just silently laughed at them while he was screwing Kristina behind their backs. He knew them all and what they were about. Kristina had helped him know them, and though she didn't understand his obsessive interest in any and all things Bancroft, whenever she'd asked too many questions, he'd distracted her with sex. She was so *easy* to control. He just waggled his finger and she was practically writhing on the ground for him. Some of the women were more of a challenge even with his sexual power, but not Kristina. She was always hot and wet and throbbing like a goddamn pulse, although afterward she cried about not being herself, not wanting him, acting like he'd put her under some kind of spell. Jesus. She was just weak, that was all.

Why hadn't she *just died?*

"Hey," she called again from the bed, her voice more strident.

Charlie put a smile on his face. It wouldn't do to let her see his real self. But he'd made a mistake in choosing her. He'd thought she might satisfy him in all the ways he loved, but she'd been a cheap distraction at best. Tonight she hadn't even shrieked, and the way she looked at him sometimes made him wonder if her earlier enthusiasm had all been a fake. Yes, he could get her to respond, but it wasn't with the same energy as Kristina.

Kristina. It was a fucking shame she'd chosen a coma instead of death: hanging on, thwarting him, laughing at him, making certain he couldn't watch her die.

"Hey!" his date called again, truly irked.

Charlie boiled up with sudden rage. He wanted to slit her throat and watch her gurgle and flail while the light died out of her eyes, but he couldn't yet. Too dangerous. Too many people might remember seeing them together. She didn't have as much to lose as Kristina, so she'd met him at public places. For now he had to play it safe. He would take care of her later, when she was way, way back in his rearview mirror.

He rejoined her in bed, though he didn't want to. All part of the act. But when she kittenishly reached over and grabbed his dick, he felt a wave of revulsion. Too much of this kittenish shit. He wanted a woman who'd go the distance.

Closing his eyes, he strolled back through his memory, searching for a kill that could get him humming, settling on those last moments with his mother, his real mother. He recalled the sensual feel of the knife sinking into her flesh. She'd fought him good, but he'd won easily, overpowering her with his physical strength. His dick stirred at the memory, and his date giggled and thought it was her doing.

Giggling. God, he wanted to squeeze the life from her. Maybe . . . maybe . . .

No.

Just need to get through this. Make it fun.

With an effort, he went back to his memories. The hot, liquid warmth of Kristina St. Cloud surrounded him, and he could hear her in his mind, moaning and screaming and begging. He climbed atop the bitch in his bed and screwed her hard.

Unfortunately, afterward, he felt more anxious than he had before he started, and as she stretched and regarded him languidly, as if she thought she'd been amazing in the sack, Charlie turned away and picked up the remote, clicking on the late news.

"What are you doing?" she demanded.

He didn't answer, just channel surfed around. There should be something on Kristina's condition by now, he figured.

Catching sight of the shingled siding of the Rib-I, Charlie stopped his surfing. *Good.* At least there was more on his first kills of the week. A male reporter was describing the scene from outside the restaurant two nights earlier. Two people murdered. *Garth and Tammie.* Charlie watched with a distant fascination as the reporter stood in the driving snow and urged anyone who'd seen anything to come forward. For a heart-stopping moment he thought of DeWitt, sitting in the Rib-I like a spider in his web, a drunken spider, but nonetheless ready to spin a web of words as he talk, talk, talked. . . .

"Damn you," she suddenly snarled, throwing back the covers and stomping naked to the bathroom.

Charlie barely noticed. His mind was now traveling back to Tammie and Garth, reliving those moments when he'd looked in their eyes, watching the light disappear into nothingness. He felt himself stir to life again, and even with the sex he'd just had, he suddenly wanted to masturbate. Now he wanted her, and of course, the bitch was locked in the bathroom.

But he could be so persuasive.

Rapping on the door panels, he said lightly, "Come outta there. Mr. Happy wants to see you."

"Fuck you."

"Ah, c'mon, baby." He was suddenly hot all over. This was what it was supposed to feel like. This was what Kristina had done for him, what Chandra had almost managed, though she'd been a bit of a cold fish.

Chandra Donatella . . .

He'd called her first that night, told her to meet him at their house. He liked the idea that it was edging toward the rim of the bluff. The vision of it being sucked into the sea got him going sexually. But Chandra had taken her sweet time in getting there. Growing impatient, he'd then sent a hot, seductive message to Kristina, who could pick up his radar like she was standing next him. He sent her the image of a gun. Her handgun, the one she'd told him she'd bought for protection. Protection, ha. He'd understood, even if she hadn't, that she'd bought it because of him, because of the fear he churned inside her, which she was powerless to fight. He'd thought the gun might be an interesting sex toy.

Kristina had shown up with it in her purse, and he'd pulled it out and waggled it in front of her eyes. They were role-playing, and

things were just getting interesting, with Kristina precariously bal-
anced on a couple of kitchen chairs and him on top of her, when
there was the scrape of a key in the front lock and Chandra suddenly
burst in, practically panting with desire. Charlie had the gun in his
hand, and for a split second he thought maybe he could talk them
both into a threesome, when Chandra's husband, Marcus, came in
behind her like a charging bull.

He stopped at the sight of the gun leveled at his chest.

Naked, Charlie had calmly told Marcus to take the chairs and set
them in the living room. Then he had Chandra and Marcus sit on
them. Marcus tried to argue with him, but Charlie had the weapon. A
gun wasn't as intimate as a knife, but it sure as hell commanded respect, and no amount of double-talk from the goddamned high-and-
mighty Marcus Donatella was going to convince Charlie to stop. In
fact . . .

His date suddenly threw open the bathroom door, knocking into
him. "Shit!" he snapped, good and pissed.

"Get out," she ordered.

"Ah . . . no . . . let's make up." Suddenly Charlie was feeling really
horny. The more they fought his power, the better it was. He reached
for her arm, and when she yanked it back, he laughed, grabbed her
around the waist, and tossed her back on the bed.

She quickly scrambled up to a sitting position, folding her arms
over her bare breasts. "Don't you dare touch me!"

"You don't mean that. . . ."

"You can just watch your goddamn TV and leave me the fuck
alone."

He chuckled. "Now you're gonna get it," he singsonged, and she
glared at him.

"I'm really mad," she said.

"Are you?"

"Yes!"

A challenge. Charlie quickly worked his magic, sending out his
sexual pheromones. She tried to resist; she really did. But it didn't
take long for her to crumble, and he sent his mind back to the Donatellas again to increase his enjoyment as he mounted her. The terror on Chandra's face . . . Marcus begging for his wife's life . . .
Kristina in the background, crying and wringing her hands and say-

ing he couldn't do it, he couldn't, it was all a game, and then *blast, blast,* shooting them both in the back of the head and Kristina screaming and screaming and screaming until he grabbed her by the hair and screwed her hard against the wall again while she clawed at him like a wild woman. She lost it a little after that, went into this weird state of denial where she would not admit to herself that she'd watched him execute her friends. She simply would not believe it, and though every time they had sex, he would press his lips to her ear and croon to her that she was his, that she was part of it now, that she had helped kill them, too, she would say it was sorcery. Nothing had happened.

Her denial worked like an aphrodisiac on Charlie. When he thought about her burning, liquid warmth . . . and that cool refusal to accept the truth . . . he felt like he could burst!

He came back to the present with a bang. Realized he was jamming hard and fast into his date, and she was in the throes of a mega-climax and was screaming like she was going to die of pleasure. *Well, all right! Finally. A real response.* He gave a couple of last, good thrusts and then came himself, filled with expanding pleasure, distantly thinking that it was good, but maybe not quite good enough. . . .

Another reason to wait to kill her. Had to make sure his semen wasn't anywhere near her when she met her maker.

He propped himself above her on his elbows and stared down at her. "Good?"

"I hate you," she said peevishly, her chest still heaving, her eyes glistening.

He smiled and sent her his swirling sexual thoughts. Then he put his hands lightly around her neck. "I'm gonna kill you," he whispered in her ear, "with love. . . ."

He was still inside her, and he hardened again, moving more tenderly. She tried to resist, she really did, but she couldn't, of course. Soon enough her hands were clawing his arms and she was moaning.

"Oh, yeah," he said, watching the conflicting messages on her face as she futilely fought his magic love potion. She came again, and with both regret and relief he pulled away from her, staring at the ceiling, wondering how soon he could leave.

He wished he could have had sex with his mother before he killed her. And he wished he'd actually killed that other mother, the one who'd been so sorry she'd adopted him, but she'd beat him to it.

He felt anger lick through him again, just thinking about that bitch. He'd seen the look on her face. How *sorry* she'd been that she'd ever let him in her house. And he'd heard her on the phone to her friends, talking about him, about how he wasn't right. Saying she should have known better. "After all, he's from that strange cult," she'd said softly into the receiver, but he'd been able to read lips from an early age. He could read *her*. He'd pulled her in with his power and screwed her sideways, and she'd looked up at him through glazed, horror-struck eyes, and then . . . and then she'd run off and *killed* herself! *Bitch!* Damn, but it pissed him off.

Afterward, her husband hadn't known what to do with him, the adopted son he didn't want. He kinda thought maybe he should put him in foster care, but Charlie wasn't having any of that. He left three days after her suicide. He'd always known he had a special power, but now he knew what to do with it. There were other women, lots and lots of other women, just aching for what he could give 'em. And he gave it to them—the best they'd ever had in their miserable lives—and for a few years he moved back and forth across the country, doing just enough work to get by, stealing from the parade of women he serviced whenever he needed to, sensing there was some purpose out there that he hadn't yet discovered.

And then he'd felt the irresistible pull—deep in his organs—from Mother Mary. She'd called to him from Echo Island, and he'd had one helluva time negotiating his way to her, all the while hearing her laughing in his head, but also her begging: *Come to me. Save me. I'm here. Waiting for you.*

He'd gone to the island—he damn well could hardly do anything else—and she'd started spinning her spell, wrapping him in it. She wanted off the island. There was work to be done. She needed him to help her. But Charlie wasn't really interested in helping her. All he wanted to do was screw her and maybe learn something about where he came from, but she wouldn't touch him, and she wouldn't give him much beyond his father's name. Good old Pops, the bastard. He would take care of him in time, too.

Charlie had boldly told his mother that he was the only one who counted, and she'd cackled her amusement and said he was an ignorant ass, just like his father. "There are more," she'd then warned him with a thin, cold smile. "More?" he'd asked. "More of us that are stronger than you," she'd assured him. "The ones we need to conquer."

He didn't believe in the "we" part of her plan, but he let her go on because he still thought he could get past her defenses and give her a heaping dose of Good Time Charlie, but it didn't happen. And then he caught her writing things down, things about him and them and what needed to be done. She was sly, hiding her words away, but he knew about them, and he also knew he had to find them. He didn't want anything written down that somebody else could find, so he started searching through her things the moment the light died in her eyes and she was staring through blank, glassy orbs toward the ceiling. He found nothing but her herbs, which she'd dried and put in jars. He was getting really pissed at her—*what did you write, bitch?*—when warning bells went off in his head. Someone out there. One of them, the ones she'd talked about. He could feel the prickle of *her* search for *him* as if it were tangible against his skin.

Who? A lover who hadn't yet revealed herself to him? He tried to send her a mental message, but she didn't respond. He'd tried off and on ever since, but whoever it was was biding their time. Playing coy.

Choking sounds woke him from his reverie, and he saw that his date's eyes were bugging, her hands plucking frantically at his taut fingers circling her neck. He had somehow grabbed her neck in his reverie and was squeezing and squeezing, and squeezing a little more. Immediately, he released her.

She gasped and spit and shrieked, "You goddamn maniac! Get the fuck out!"

"I didn't mean to do that," he admitted honestly.

She slapped at his hand when he tried to smooth her hair. Then she slapped at his arms and head, until he had to pin her arms down before she did some real damage. It was time to move on. Loose ends needed to be taken care of. Twisting away from her, he grabbed up his clothes, dragging them on.

"What are you doing? Where are you going?" she demanded.

"Getting the fuck out, like you asked me so nicely."

When he walked out the door, he heard something slam against it from the other side. Her shoe probably. For all their protestations, they never could get enough.

Sometimes it was almost a hardship.

Snow was falling fast, covering everything. He stood for a moment on her front step, his expression hardening as Good Time Charlie disappeared beneath another persona, the one he loved best, the one closest to his real self.

Time to take care of business.

Closing his eyes, he stood on the sidewalk in front of her building in the falling snow and whipping wind and went inside himself, drawing on his power. He sent a message to Pops, just because he could, the fucker, and then he reached out for the one again. The lover who'd contacted him on Echo Island. The one who'd scared him into leaving before he could find Mary's writings. He could practically feel her slide away from him, eely and just out of reach.

I'm coming for you. He sent the message with all the strength of his sexual power. He knew it was one of them. One of the ones Mary wanted him to destroy. *I'm coming for you.*

And then suddenly a message came back, filling his brain so fast and hot that he jerked physically, as if struck: *I'm way ahead of you.*

Charlie looked around wildly at the snow-covered streets. A game? Way ahead of him? *No way!*

Who the fuck are you? he sent back.

But though he listened with every fiber, muscle, and cell of his being, waiting in the darkness as snow melted on his hair and skin, there was no answer. All he could hear and feel was the moaning rise and fall of the wind.

With fury burning through his veins, he stomped toward his snow-covered truck, ready for the next chapter. He was going to kill them all.

CHAPTER 17

Highway 26 through the mountains was blocked off at the base of the four-lane climb up the farthest west pass. The two eastbound lanes had a line of flashing barriers, the yellow light sputtering in uneven flickers, warning unwary travelers that there was danger ahead.

The two westbound lanes had no such barriers, and there was no one manning the eastbound ones. Emergency workers were needed elsewhere.

Without a qualm Hale turned into the oncoming lanes and drove around the barriers, going a whopping twenty miles per hour. Anything more and he'd be fishtailing up the hill, and that was a best-case scenario. He returned to the eastbound lanes as soon as he was around the flashing obstructions, his TrailBlazer churning through the thick snow, the engine whining a bit in four-wheel drive. His hands were tight on the steering wheel; his jaw was set; his fear mounting.

He hoped he ran into a rescue crew, but if he didn't, he was sure as hell going to find Savannah. She'd asked for 9-1-1, not a tow truck. She was a cop who wouldn't overstate the need, and she'd admitted the baby was coming. He didn't care that she'd said she was fine. She needed help beyond the fact that her vehicle was out of commission, someone to aid her with the birth of his son. If he, or someone, could get to her in time.

Hang in there, Savvy, he thought grimly.

* * *

"Where's Aunt Catherine?" Ravinia demanded. She was covered in snow, her blond hair unnaturally dark from the dampening flakes.

Isadora and Ophelia were in the main room, the room Catherine sometimes called the great hall, which just about summed up her grandiose and formal way of acting, being, and generally annoying Ravinia. Isadora and Ophelia looked over at her blankly, and Isadora lifted a shoulder. She obviously didn't know and certainly didn't care.

"Where's Cassandra?" Ravinia demanded.

"In bed," Isadora said. "Like Lillibeth."

Her schoolteacher tone grated on Ravinia's nerves. Isadora was the oldest of the lodge sisters, and she'd patterned herself after Catherine in about every way Ravinia knew. If there was to be a succession of strict dictators, Isadora had her hand up to be first choice and was waving it.

"You went over the wall again," Isadora said, disapproving, one eyebrow arching.

"It's snowing like a beast out there." Ravinia didn't owe Isadora, or any of them, for that matter, any explanation. Besides which, Catherine had laid down the law, and if she found out Ravinia had left, she might actually kick her out of Siren Song like she'd threatened. And Ravinia wasn't ready for that yet.

"Catherine's probably in bed, too," Ophelia said. She was more of a peacemaker. She'd certainly helped save Ravinia from Justice, and she'd been sewing Ravinia pants and shirts for years, her own way of rebelling against Catherine's strictness, but recently she'd been leaning toward the Isadora camp, and Ravinia just didn't need it.

"Nope. I went to her room," Ravinia declared. "I even lit the oil lamp, and there's no one there." She had done a little bit of snooping while she was inside her aunt's room. Had found something of interest, which she'd taken and slipped inside the back waistband of her pants.

"The door wasn't locked?" Isadora's brows drew into a deep furrow.

Well, of course it was locked, but Ravinia wasn't about to explain more about her special skills. They all talked about their "gifts," but Ravinia's gift was ingenuity and resourcefulness. She knew how to pick a lock with wire and slim pieces of metal, although Catherine's dead bolt was so old, she could just kinda work it back with a pair of needle-nose pliers slipped through the crack. Her true gift, however, was the ability to look into a person's heart and know their secrets, but she kept that one to herself. She'd pretended for years that she had no extra ability, that she was like Catherine and seemed merely to possess a clear head with emotions tightly under control. Okay, hers weren't so tightly controlled, but she had managed over the years to appear that way—at least she hoped she had.

But what she could see was whether a person was good or evil. She had to get close to them, physical contact was best, and then it took only a few words or a sideways glance or sometimes maybe a bit more, if they interested her in some way, before she had them pegged. It was crazy how many real sickos there were out there. Still, she'd rather be walking among them than stuck in this frigid prison. She had her GED—they all did—after years of stultifying home schooling by Catherine. Good God, her aunt was a woman of a billion facts and figures and nothing else. A hollow core. Consumed with rules and regulations, and there was simply no *fire*.

With her last thought, Ravinia turned toward the blaze that was currently crackling and spitting inside the cavernous mouth of the stone fireplace. The only heat this drafty lodge put out. Sure, the generator allowed for lights on the first floor, but that was it. Even now, standing near the hot flames, Ravinia felt cold to the bone, her hair still damp. She rubbed her arms as Isadora, as always, was going on and on, saying, "If she finds out you were in there alone, she's not going to like it. And I don't believe the door was unlocked. You had to have found a way—"

"Where the hell is she?" Ravinia cut her off. "Did she *leave?*"

"Lillibeth said she met with Earl earlier," Ophelia put in hurriedly to avoid a further fight.

"Uncle Earl," Ravinia said, baiting her sister, and was rewarded with Isadora's tightened lips. No, he and Catherine weren't lovers. Catherine was too shut down, and Earl was about as talkative as a corpse. Ravinia couldn't picture them in bed together. Ugh. However, she had managed to learn that Earl actually had some family. He was a Foothiller, a member of one of the Native American tribes who had mixed with the locals and formed a community, which was up the road from Siren Song, in the foothills of the Coast Range. One of Earl's relatives had gotten involved with someone from Ravinia's own screwed-up family, and supposedly there were any number of "gifted" people among the Foothillers, as well.

As long as they weren't as screwed up as Justice, it was fine with Ravinia. She just wanted to leave the lot of them behind with their whole stinking woo-woo nonsense. Was there any truth to it? Sure. Some. Had any good come from it? Not that she could tell.

"Did she leave with him?" Ravinia asked.

"In this weather?" Isadora shook her head. "She's around here somewhere."

"The attic?" Ravinia had done a pretty thorough search of the lodge, apart from the attic and her mother's old bedroom, which was too creepy to go into. It was like walking inside a diorama of a 1960s bedroom, and though very little scared her, Ravinia had felt the echoes of something sick and noxious the few times she'd gone into her mother's room.

"I'll go find her," Ophelia said, gathering her skirts and heading up the stairs.

That left Ravinia with Isadora. Never really a great plan.

Isadora seemed to think the same, so she tilted back her head, with its blond bun so much like Catherine's, then folded her hands over her stomach, tucking each up the opposite sleeve of her dress as she walked toward the kitchen. Again, like Catherine.

"Puke," Ravinia said loudly when she was alone.

Three-quarters of an hour later, Ophelia returned with a cobweb fluttering off the side of her hair. "She's not in the attic."

"How is it you have the keys?" Ravinia asked.

Ophelia eyed her steadily. "Ravinia, if you want Aunt Catherine to trust you, you need to stop going over the wall and doing God knows what."

"I call it living."

"Yes, well . . ."

"Did you go inside our mother's bedroom?"

Ophelia gave a slight shake to her head. "No."

"Well, you better do it. Here comes Isadora, and she looks . . . worried."

Isadora hurried from the kitchen area. A bright flush tinged her cheeks, and her lips were a little blue from the cold. "I went in the backyard. She's not there." She was shaking her head, her tight bun threatening to unravel.

Ravinia immediately turned toward the downstairs hall.

"Where are you going?" Isadora demanded.

"To check with Lillibeth."

"She's sleeping!"

"BFD," Ravinia muttered and kept on going. She gave a sharp rap on the door, then pushed it open. Lillibeth's room was not locked. She had her own bathroom, which had been retro equipped with lowered counters and a handicapped toilet and a shower that was flush with the floor so she could roll in and move herself to a fixed chair that was in reach of the handheld showerhead.

Trying to adjust her eyes to the dim light, Ravinia saw Lillibeth was in her bed. She turned over to face the doorway. "Ravinia?" Lillibeth whispered, sounding confused.

Ravinia hit the light switch and flooded the room with illumination. Lillibeth shot bolt upright, pulling herself to a sitting position with the two bars screwed into the wall on either side of the headboard of her twin bed. Her blond hair was down and tousled, and her beautiful heart-shaped face was turned toward Ravinia in horror.

"What're you doing? I was asleep!"

"I'm looking for Catherine. You saw her last with Earl."

"Aunt Catherine?" Lillibeth repeated, blinking. "Yes . . . she went out to meet him."

"Did you see her come back?" Ravinia asked with forced patience.

"No . . . I went to my room. It was getting late." She eyed her younger sister. "You weren't around."

"No, I wasn't," Ravinia said tightly. "We can't find Catherine anywhere. Did she say anything to you?"

"I knew Earl was at the gate. . . ." She glanced past Ravinia. "He wanted to talk to her."

"How did you know it was Earl? You saw him?"

Lillibeth shrugged. "I just knew."

Ravinia wasn't sure what to make of that. Lillibeth didn't have Cassandra's ability to see things. Lillibeth didn't have any gift as far as Ravinia could tell. She'd had a difficult birth that had done something to her spine, according to Catherine, and had left her crippled.

It had always been assumed that the injury had also stripped her of whatever gift she might have had. Or maybe she just didn't have one. Lillibeth was still very much a little girl. Whatever had happened to her had stunted her emotionally—or so said Catherine—and Lillibeth's slow maturation seemed to bear that out.

"She went out to meet Earl at the gate," Ravinia said, hoping for more information.

Lillibeth bobbed her head, worry beginning to crowd her expression.

"How long was she out there? Did she leave with him?"

"I don't knnnooowww," Lillibeth wailed.

"We need a phone," Ravinia said aloud, more to the room at large or the heavens or the fates than to Lillibeth. She'd said it and said it and said it for years, but no one ever listened. She wondered if Earl had a phone or if he was as antiquated in his thinking as her aunt.

Suddenly anxious, Ravinia left Lillibeth's room, snapping off the light switch and shutting her door on the way out. Sometimes her sister annoyed her, and she felt guilty about it, but Lillibeth was just so immature. It was hard to believe she was older than Ravinia.

She stood in the main room for long moments, thinking hard. Had Catherine left? What had transpired between Catherine and Earl? Something that had sent her away? Because she sure wasn't at the house, as far as Ravinia could tell.

Briefly, she thought back to her latest foray beyond the walls of the lodge. She'd met someone. A boy. A man, actually. And she'd looked into his heart and found, to her surprise, the way had been blocked. That was unsettling. She'd always been able to see to a being's core, except with people who knew how to block her, like Catherine, sometimes, although it wasn't hard to see what she was really like—ice and fortitude—and then Lillibeth was a mystery she couldn't quite penetrate, probably because her mind was full of childlike things.

Ravinia was even able to see into the hearts of animals sometimes. Once she'd met a wolf down from the hills, and its core had been full of instinct: bonding and a fierce connection to the pack. It looked at her through yellow eyes, and she sensed that it was including her, so as much as she knew how, she filled her own center with a responding "I'm with you" kind of message, which might or might not have gotten through. The wolf turned and left, padding away softly, its gray fur fluttering in the breeze. She couldn't tell anyone of the encounter other than to say she'd seen a wolf, and even that was resoundingly pooh-poohed. There were no true wolves in these mountains, she was told by one of the Foothillers, who all thought they knew everything about everything. Ravinia's answer was that maybe it was a fake one, then, but it was a wolf.

But the man . . . his eyes were gray and his hair was dark and he reminded her of the wolf, sort of. He was the first actual human being she'd wanted to spend any time with, and she'd gone looking for him tonight, but she couldn't find him anywhere around Deception Bay or the beach, where she'd first seen him. In the back of her mind she found herself wanting to leave with him, wherever he would go. She'd come back to the lodge tonight, intending to tell Catherine that she would be leaving soon. Forever. Just like Catherine had ordained.

Only now she wasn't sure she wanted to go.

"She's not in the house," Ophelia declared. Ravinia looked up to see Ophelia now hastening down the stairs again. "I went into our mother's bedroom," she said, in answer to Ravinia's unspoken question. "Aunt Catherine's not there. She's nowhere. As if she just vanished."

"Maybe she left with Earl," Ravinia suggested.

"Without telling us?"

Ravinia frowned. That wasn't like Catherine at all. Floorboards creaked, and a door opened. Startled, Ravinia and Ophelia both looked over to see Lillibeth, in her nightgown, rolling out of her room toward them, looking scared. Her skin was ashen, and she worried her lip with her teeth. "I . . . I couldn't sleep."

"You woke her," Ophelia accused Ravinia, as Isadora, who'd gone back upstairs for another check of the second-floor bedrooms, returned to the main floor, where they were now all congregated in front of the fire, shadows flickering across their faces from the leaping flames. Despite the heat and growing embers, the large room felt chilly and without warmth.

"Ask Cassandra," Lillibeth implored.

"We're not waking her up, too, unless we have to," Isadora said.

"We have to!" Lillibeth cried.

"Cassandra doesn't operate that way," Isadora reminded her tersely. "You can't just ask her. She has to tell you."

Lillibeth was knotting her fingers. "But she might knooowww. She might knoowww."

"Maybe Aunt Catherine took the car," Ophelia suggested.

"No." Ravinia shook her head. They were grasping at straws. Yes, Catherine would drive the car, an ancient Buick, from time to time, but not in this weather, not this late, not without telling them.

"Get Cassandra!" Lillibeth's voice was rising, and it wouldn't be long before Cassandra heard them, anyway, so Ophelia turned back to the stairs, pressing her lips together and lifting her skirts once more as she headed to the second level.

All this fret and worry was getting them nowhere fast. "I'm going to the gate," Ravinia said, charging toward the front door.

"Where's your cloak?" Isadora asked automatically.

Cloak. Jesus. Ravinia almost missed a step. Why couldn't they just have coats like everyone else? "It's by the back door." Ravinia pulled open the heavy front door and swung it inward. A swirl of snow and wind and cold swept inside. She pulled the door shut behind her, and instantly realized she should have waited for the *cloak*.

Head down, she plunged into the frigid night, trudging along the buried flagstone path toward the gate. Six steps from the house she saw the large, irregular mound of snow. A body? *Oh, Jesus! Catherine!*

"No!" Heart racing, she ran forward, trampling awkwardly, shot with fear as her aunt's body became more and more defined in her vision. Catherine lay on the ground, nearly covered with white powder, her eyes closed, her mouth half open, and only because her face was turned sideways did air enter her trachea. Ravinia scraped snow away frantically, pressed her ear to Catherine's chest. Her aunt was breathing. Barely. Her heart beating.

"Help!" she screamed.

They needed 9-1-1.

"I found her! Isadora! Ophelia! Help!"

They needed a phone.

"This is the problem, you stubborn old woman!" Ravinia yelled at her aunt. She glanced over to the old shed that was used as a garage. The Buick was inside, but she knew it would be undrivable in these conditions. She didn't know how to drive, anyway, and it was all such a clusterfuck.

The door to the lodge flew open. Yellow light spilled out, and Isadora stood in the aperture.

"She's here!" Ravinia screamed at the top of her lungs. "We need help! Get blankets. Your goddamn *cloak*. For the love of God, get *help!*"

Hale was driving ten miles an hour, and the snow just kept building and building on the road. Ten miles an hour. Too damned slow. His forty-minute estimate was for shit. He was already an hour in, and he had a ways to go.

I'm coming, Savannah. His mind raced to images of her in her car, her Ford, laboring alone in the dark . . . in the freezing night. *I'm coming.*

He was counting the seconds, feeling precious time passing. He stepped on the accelerator, and his rig immediately slid a bit, so he eased off. He would be of no help if he didn't make it to her side. God. Was it going to take forever?

His thoughts kept touching back on Kristina, too, but as soon as they did, they quickly jumped back to the situation at hand. He needed to get to Savvy. Soon. At least he could help her. There was nothing more he could do for his wife but pray.

Rounding a corner, he nearly ran into the back of a tow truck, which was winching up the rear end of a badly smashed Toyota wagon. Silhouetted in the truck's headlights, a man was standing in five inches of snow, staring around himself blankly. Blood was dripping from the end of his hand to the frozen ground.

Hale rolled down his window and eased to a stop. "You need help?" he asked, when all he wanted to do was keep going.

"Nah." The man lifted the arm. "I scraped it, s'all."

"Looks like more than a scrape."

"Isaac'll take me where I need to go," he answered, nodding toward the tow truck driver. Hale could just make out ISAAC'S TOWING stenciled on the side of the snow-crusted truck. "You're going the wrong way, man," the injured man added, pointing with his good arm in the direction Hale was heading. "There's nothing there for miles but a ton of snow. I'm the last one through."

"Gotta find somebody."

"Let the sheriff's department do it," he advised, but Hale just sketched a good-bye with his hand. He couldn't count on the sheriff's department, because he didn't have much faith that Savvy's plight was, despite her connections, next up on the 9-1-1 rotation.

He squinted through the falling snow. If the injured man was the last one through, then his vehicle had crossed all lanes to land in the ditch on the far side of the road.

Clamping down hard on his fears, determined to find her, to help his newborn son, he touched a toe to the accelerator.

Ravinia was over the wall. One moment her gloved hand was scrambling for a handhold; the next she was hauling herself up the last couple of feet and throwing herself to the other side. Normally, this maneuver was a careful climb over the top and a controlled drop to the fir needle carpet outside the walls of Siren Song, but tonight she simply hurled herself into the snow.

Still, she landed with an *ooof.* The air escaped her lungs in a rush. She lay still for two heartbeats. Then, fairly certain she hadn't injured herself, she struggled to her feet and began trudging down the hill through snow-laden trees and brush toward the highway, far below. Past that road and a rambling quarter-mile descent of land to the beach lay the endless blackness that marked the Pacific Ocean. She'd made this trek several dozen times, more and more frequently, as the ludicrousness of her "captivity" had made it impossible for her to stay, and she knew where she was going.

Even so, a ribbon of fear had wound itself around her heart. Catherine was an old biddy—far older than her years on earth—but she was their aunt, and even though she was completely screwed up, she did want only to keep her nieces safe and secure. Ravinia couldn't imagine what would happen if she actually wasn't around.

She kept us safe from Justice, she thought.

Ravinia's jaw locked. It wasn't all Catherine, she reminded herself. She and Ophelia had helped rid the earth of that whack job as well.

At the edge of Highway 101, Ravinia stepped onto the shoulder of the road and slipped right down to her knees. Snow wasn't the norm around here, but she could remember how it was in '08, when it buried everything and everybody lost power for days on end, well, except for Siren Song, with its generator.

Carefully, her nerves thrumming with urgency, she found her footing and started south down the road, toward Deception Bay. There wasn't a car to be seen. Nobody wanted to trust the slickness of the roads, and Ravinia, with an eye toward the western edge of Highway 101, with its limited guardrails, could understand. No, she'd never driven a car, but she'd ridden with "friends" she met on her nightly vigils, and she sure as hell got a thrill when they went around some of these snakelike corners a little too fast. There was a slow decline in the road that wound into Deception Bay, but that descent was still a few miles ahead, and Ravinia was worried. How long was it going to take to find help? Would she be in time?

She and her sisters had carried Catherine into the lodge and stripped her of her clothes. Carefully, they'd wrapped her in blankets and laid her in front of the fire, but with Lillibeth's wailing, and Isadora's fretting thoughts of trying to find Earl, and Cassandra's wide-eyed stares when she'd joined them, as if she were looking into the bowels of hell, well . . . nothing positive had happened. Ophelia's sudden disappearance hadn't helped, and then Cassandra had whispered, "It's because Aunt Catherine knows . . . ," and Ravinia had asked, "Knows what?" and when no one said anything, Ravinia had had enough. They needed action. They needed emergency help. They didn't need to huddle together like scared mice, shivering inside the lodge.

No more, she'd thought then, and now she thought it again. *No more.*

She was fifteen minutes into her hike when a car with chains *chinging* through the snow caught her in the beams of its headlights. The sedan slowed. Cautiously, Ravinia glanced at the driver as he rolled down his window.

"Need a lift?" he asked.

He was old. And there was a woman with him on the passenger side who looked about the same age, his wife, maybe. "We got caught in this mess, but we're almost home," she said.

"Do you have a cell phone?" Ravinia asked.

"Sorry, honey. We don't own one. What are you doing out alone on a night like this?" she asked.

"Are you going to Deception Bay?" Ravinia cut through her concern. No time for explanations.

"We're going through it," the man said. "Heading to Tillamook."

"If we make it," his partner said with asperity.

"You can drop me in Deception Bay," Ravinia decided and opened the back door when he gestured for her to help herself. She could find a phone once she was in the small seaside town, she decided, not realizing she'd crossed her fingers for good luck until she happened to look down at her gloved hands.

CHAPTER 18

Visibility had dropped to the square of snow directly in front of his headlights. Hale found he was saying the same thing over and over again in his head: *Just a little bit farther. Not much more. Just a little bit farther. Not much more.*

He wasn't far from the summit. She'd said she was on this side of it. He couldn't have missed her. Couldn't have. Her lights would be on. Her battery would still be working, or maybe she still had the engine running. God, he hoped so. It was damn cold. Damn cold . . .

He had a blanket in the backseat. And in the cargo area he had the carpet he'd used to put on the chains, although some snow had clung to it and melted, so it was a bit wet. But if Savvy was cold, really cold, he could give her his coat and wrap her in the blanket and carpet, if need be.

Jesus.

His chest felt as if it were in a vise.

A sound came from behind him, and he looked in the rearview mirror to see a sheriff's car following after him, light bar flashing red and blue, but no siren. At the same moment his peripheral vision caught sight of car tires, covered already with an inch of snow, but sticking out of the ditch and spinning slowly like rubber plates on two sticks. The rest of the Escape was in the ditch, on its side.

Savvy! Finally!

Hale yanked his steering wheel a little too energetically, and he immediately went into a slide, which he corrected with a slow turn into the slide as he yanked his foot from the accelerator. His Trail-Blazer took a couple of 360s, but it finally stopped, facing west. The

Clatsop County sheriff's car that had been behind him tried to stop, couldn't, then fishtailed on past him for a bit before the driver got it under control.

Hale didn't have time to look. He was stopped about ten feet east of the Escape and climbed out of the TrailBlazer into sideways snow, only to immediately lose his footing. The road was like glass beneath the snow—a sheet of ice. He wished he had studs. Far better than chains, but the thought flew into his head and out. Scrambling to his feet, he half crab-walked, half slipped and slid through the blinding precipitation to Savvy's car.

"Savannah!" he yelled. "Savannah!"

His gut clenched. What if she wasn't alive? What if she was seriously injured? Having problems with the labor? The birth?

He was almost to the car when he saw the driver's door jiggle and pop open a little bit, only to close again. His heart leapt. She was alive and *aware*. When he got to the ditch, he swiped snow off his face and took a step down into snow-covered weeds, grabbing the back wheel to steady himself before sliding sharply downward. Damn it all. Straining, he had to climb back up a bit to reach the car.

"Savannah!" he yelled.

The Escape was solidly wedged into the ditch, on its side. With an effort, he actually climbed onto the car and knelt on the back door, bending to open the driver's door and yank it upward. It came with a wrench, its hinges torqued.

"Savannah!"

With snow now falling into the car, he looked inside. She was there, struggling to turn herself around so her head could pop out the door. "Thank God. Oh, thank God. . . . Are you okay?"

"Hale," she whispered tremulously.

He reached in for her, wanting to scoop her into his arms and squeeze her hard.

"Hey!" The voice came from behind him.

He turned to see the sheriff's deputy marching toward him through a veil of snow, wearing golf shoes, or a facsimile thereof. "The road's closed," he called, but his attention had turned to Savannah, who was half standing in the car, her head and shoulders outside the door. Her messenger bag was in one hand, and she flung it into the ditch.

"I'm in labor," Savannah said quietly, for Hale's ears only.

"I know. Are you . . . ?"

"Can you help me out?" she asked, her voice calm but slightly quavering. "I need to get out."

He saw then that she might be holding it together, but she was quietly panicking inside. "Don't worry. We'll—"

"You the one who called nine-one-one?" the deputy yelled from behind him.

"Yes," Hale answered tersely. "We need to get her out of the car. ASAP."

"She's pregnant?"

"Yes," he repeated.

"Maybe we should wait for the EMTs."

"No," Savannah said firmly. "No time."

The deputy yelled, "Ma'am, you're probably better off staying inside the vehicle and letting the experts—"

For an answer she placed her arms on the side of the car and started pulling herself upward. Hale didn't like it. He was in too precarious a position to offer much support.

The deputy finally got that he wasn't being listened to and slid down the embankment next to the car. "Lady, listen—"

"I'm a goddamn detective, Deputy!" she spit out furiously and practically pulled herself out with her anger. Hale grabbed her hands as she struggled upward. With all his strength he hauled her up and onto the car so that she was lying on her side.

"If you'd just wait a minute," the deputy sniped.

"She's not going to," Hale said, stating the obvious. "Help her off the car."

While Hale held her arms and slowly inched Savannah over the side, the deputy grabbed her from his position in the ditch and eased her down until her feet touched the ground. Hale released her only when he was certain she was safe, and then he slid off the back of the car to help Savannah climb up from the ditch to the road.

"You're really pregnant, ma'am . . . Detective," the deputy observed, a master of grasping the situation.

As Savannah crawled up to the edge of the road, she suddenly folded herself forward and into a squat.

"Oh . . . God . . ." The deputy's eyes were wide, his mouth hanging open.

"Hale . . . Hale . . . ," she huffed.

"I'm here." He scrambled up to be beside her.

"I need to get to . . . your . . . car and lie down. I need to . . . lie down."

"She gonna have that baby now?" the deputy asked, aghast.

Hale turned on him. "Call somebody. Find out where they are." *Do something!*

The deputy headed for his car as if he'd been released from the gate, staggering and slipping, half falling and fighting his way back up, just generally getting *away.*

Savannah had moved onto her side and was lying on the ground, panting.

"Give me your arm," Hale said.

She lifted one arm limply. "Can you get my bag? My messenger bag?"

"My car's over there. You see it?" he asked as the wind whistled through the gorge. "I don't want you to walk and fall," he said, thinking hard.

"I can crawl."

"Are you sure?"

She started laughing, a hitching sound that said she was fighting tears. "Yes. Remember . . . my bag? In the ditch?"

"I'm getting it."

He leaned into the ditch and hooked the strap of the bag on the third try. Straightening, squinting through the falling snow, he saw she was on her hands and knees and was edging her way to the TrailBlazer. Hale struggled to his feet, looking around. The deputy was at his vehicle and was trying to make contact; Hale could see the walkie at his lips. Beyond his car and Hale's, there wasn't another vehicle on the road.

Slipping and sliding, as quickly as he could, he made his way to her and helped her reach his TrailBlazer. "Can you get in the passenger seat?"

"I—I need to get in the backseat," she panted.

"The backseat?" he repeated.

"Yes!" She suddenly stopped moving and pulled herself into a ball on her side, breathing loudly in and out as another contraction overtook her.

"How close are you?" Hale asked carefully, knowing the baby was coming soon and wishing to high heaven that he could do something, *anything,* to help.

She didn't answer immediately, not until she began to relax from the grip of the contraction. Then she took several deep breaths and said shakily, "The contractions are about two minutes apart. I've been counting in my head."

"That's . . . close." *Real close.*

"Yes, it is. That's why I need to get in the backseat," she said determinedly, rolling to her hands and knees and moving forward again. "Kristina?" she asked after a moment, stopping to glance back at him.

"She was still in surgery when I left."

"It's bad?"

"I don't know." Hale watched her helplessly. Frustrated by the fact that he could do so little to help her, or his wife, for that matter, he glanced toward the deputy once more. The man seemed to be even more boondoggled than he was.

"Can't get through," the deputy said, and Hale nodded.

This was on him and Savannah. He looked back at her, struck by how capable she was. It got him in the gut. Tightening his own resolve, he skated the few steps past her toward the TrailBlazer, thinking about the carpet and the blanket and the toolbox with its box cutter if he needed to cut the umbilical cord himself.

Deception Bay was a white world illuminated by windows of light. Through the windshield Ravinia saw there was a gathering place still open—the Drift In Market.

The man slowed the car and remarked, "They musta stayed open to help people in the storm."

Thank God.

"Thank you," Ravinia said to the couple, then practically bolted from the car when it slid to a stop. Quickly, she half walked, half ran over the powder, snow crunching beneath her boots as she reached the steps of the market. She had been here before a few times and knew the owners normally closed at ten. She didn't care why they were still open this night. She was just glad she might be able to get help.

Stepping inside, she noticed a small crowd hanging out not far from the cash register. Several tables with red-checkered cloths were situated off to one side, near a deli counter. A number of people were seated at them, drinking coffee or tea, and the smells of cinnamon and other spices wafted through the warm interior. Ravinia's mouth watered as she wound her way through the tables to the counter, dripping a trail of wet snow and water like most of the others before her, if the wetness of the wood floor was any indication. There was a woman at the cash register, and Ravinia recognized her and thought she was one of the store's owners.

"I need a phone. It's an emergency."

"Ravinia?" a voice called from behind her.

She whipped around and was blindsided to see Earl's familiar, slightly stooped form. "Earl! What are you doing here?" She was so relieved to see someone she knew, she could have cried.

"Came to get groceries for you all, but there was some need for my truck. People stuck."

A young man with jet-black hair that fell over his forehead and a suspicious look in his blue eyes sidled up next to him and studied Ravinia. She ignored him, had no time for strangers.

"I . . . we need help," she said tautly. "It's Aunt Catherine. She's unconscious. Something happened after she was talking to you. I found her in the snow outside, and we took her into the lodge, but she was out cold. I need to call nine-one-one."

"Catherine?" Earl blinked. "She's okay, though?"

"I don't know!"

"You don't have a phone?" the suspicious man with Earl asked in disbelief.

"We use public phones," Ravinia snapped back. It was Catherine who gathered phone numbers and made calls whenever she went into town. The rest of them didn't have any reason to use a phone, according to Catherine, and now the worst had happened.

The man pulled a cell phone from his pocket, handed it to Earl, and said, "Hit the green phone button and then nine-one-one."

Earl didn't hesitate. He did as he was instructed and began talking to the 9-1-1 operator. The task out of her hands, Ravinia felt her legs tremble, and she grabbed one of the chairs and sat down hard at a table with a middle-aged couple who were bundled in ski jackets and holding gloved hands.

"Our car broke down," the man said to her, though she hadn't asked. "Earl, there . . ." He nodded toward the groundskeeper. "He helped us."

Ravinia nodded. Earl helped everybody. That was apparently what he did, though she knew little about him as a person. She'd rarely spoken to him herself. He and Catherine were thick as thieves, and it generally kind of pissed Ravinia off, though she couldn't say why.

"What's your story?" the man at the table asked her.

Ravinia hesitated from years of training and secrecy, then realized all the solitude and rules of Siren Song were about to change and she didn't need them anymore, anyway. "My aunt is unconscious and was lying in the snow for a long time. I came for help."

The woman placed a hand to her chest, empathizing. "Oh, no. Is she all right?"

Ravinia was saved from engaging in further explanations by Earl's approach. "They already sent someone," he said gruffly. His gray hair, once black, was shaved beneath the hat on his head, and he frowned, looking around the room.

"What? What do you mean?" Ravinia demanded. "To the lodge?"

"Someone called in before I did."

"Who? How? To nine-one-one?" Ravinia asked in disbelief.

Earl turned away, handed the younger man back the phone, and said, "The truck's all loaded. We should go."

"Go?" Ravinia was on her feet, hands balled at her sides. "Where?"

"Back to the lodge," he told her. "Climb in beside Rand, if you're coming."

Ravinia followed them outside and toward the truck. The truck's bed was covered by a bright blue tarp, which was now almost obliterated by snow. "What the hell?" she demanded as Earl got behind the wheel and Rand yanked open the passenger-side door, which screeched in protest.

"We're going to see that Catherine's okay. You can come or not." Earl clearly didn't care what she did. She turned from him to the younger man, who was holding the door open for her. Too relieved that help had come for her aunt to object, she simply climbed into the cab and Rand squeezed in beside her.

For a moment she narrowed her eyes at Rand as they sat there nose to nose, and then he said, "Ravinia. You should have black hair with that name."

"Yeah, well, we're all blond. Mine's the darkest."

Earl pulled onto the highway, his chains *ching-ching-chinging* as the truck lumbered down the road.

"You're the one that escapes all the time," the younger man said.

"Rand," Earl admonished as he fiddled with the truck's heater and stared through the windshield to where the wipers were fighting with the ever-falling snow.

"Who the hell are you?" Ravinia demanded.

"I'm Earl's son. We're related, you and I. Somebody in the past that—"

"Rand," Earl barked with more heat, and the younger man desisted.

But Ravinia was having none of it. Her mother's journal—the treasure she'd stolen from Catherine's room—felt hard against the small of her back. "Somebody in the past that what?"

"One of your kind that fooled around with mine." Rand stared past her at Earl. A challenge.

She'd heard the tales, of course, but now maybe this man had some real information. "Who?" Ravinia asked as Earl turned onto the main highway. The old truck shuddered, its wheels catching.

"Your mom," Rand said, with a "Duh, stupid" hiding in his words.

Earl growled low in his throat, whether from frustration or anger, she couldn't tell. But Ravinia was through asking Rand questions, anyway. She found she didn't like talking to someone who obviously knew so much more about her ancestry than she did.

But Rand's comments made her all the more determined to learn some home truths about her family.

"You okay there?" Hale asked Savannah, staring down at her in the backseat.

"Just drive," she gritted. Despite the cold, her hair was damp, her face warm. "Fast as you dare." The contractions were coming more rapidly and hard—so hard she could barely breathe.

He nodded, then climbed behind the wheel. She waited impatiently for him to get the engine going and hit the accelerator. She wanted to *go*.

But the deputy was standing outside the TrailBlazer, and Savannah chafed at the delay. "The ambulance should get here soon," he said as Hale cracked his window.

"No time!" Savannah yelled again. "Let's go!"

"Drive ahead of us, and make sure we can get through," Hale ordered him. The sheriff's man was so damn dense, Savvy wanted to scream.

"I don't know. The roads are worse and—"

"If you won't do it, get out of the way!" she yelled, just managing not to scream at him.

He stepped back, unsure. But when Hale switched on the engine, he turned and raced, sliding mostly, as fast as he dared back to his Jeep. Once in his vehicle, he hit the lights, eased the Jeep around, and started west. Hale touched his accelerator, and they began to move, following after him.

Pain ripped through Savannah, and she bit down hard so as not to groan. She was in trouble. "Wait . . . wait. . . . We have to stop!" Then another, deeper spasm dug into her, and she let out a low cry.

"Savannah?" Hale glanced over his shoulder, his face white with concern, then stared forward again, his jaw taut. Braking slowly, he threw the SUV in park and slip-slid out the door, opening the backseat driver's door and looking in on her. Outside, the deputy's car had gone around a corner, its red taillights winking out.

The contraction was harder. Took her breath away. She lay her cheek on the window and felt the weight in the small of her back and her limbs, like something shifting, a gravitational pull that made her lower half feel twice as heavy.

"We're not going to make it to the hospital."

Hale's breath was near her, warming her ear. "Okay."

And then another gush of something warm down her leg. Blood. Fluid. Delivery time.

"Help me get my pants off," she said as she lay down.

Earl's truck tried to stall out on the hill up to Siren Song, and Ravinia had tensed, ready to jump out. But the old pickup's wheels caught and inched forward again, and Ravinia clenched her teeth and waited. The drive seemed to take forever. Finally, they reached the lane to the lodge, and through the darkness and snow she caught sight of the ambulance's white and red lights. As they pulled to a stop behind the emergency vehicle, she heard the *bang, bang* as the EMTs slammed the rear doors shut. Two figures walked toward their respective doors.

"Back up, Earl," she urged. "Quick. They're taking her to the hospital."

Earl said, "We need to tell Isadora."

"We need to go!"

But Earl wasn't about to be bullied. He moved his truck to one side and then climbed out, heading toward the gates of Siren Song. Ravinia scrambled out after him, as did Rand, and they all ended up hurrying through the gate into the lodge grounds, a place where men, apart from Earl, were rarely allowed. *Five minutes,* Ravinia told herself. Then she was going to get Earl to follow after the ambulance, or she was going to try to drive his damn truck herself.

Savannah bore down with all her strength. Pinpoints of light exploded behind her eyelids from the effort. She was drenched in sweat. She'd wrestled out of her jacket, but her shirt and bra were almost too much. Hale hovered somewhere in her nether regions, blocking the weather with his body as he stood in the open back door. Her entire body seemed intent on turning itself inside out. She couldn't believe this was happening to her. Could. Not. Believe. It.

Still . . . she was excited. She was having a baby. A baby. And her body was doing everything it should, even though conditions weren't ideal. Very much less than ideal, actually. It was just . . .

Another contraction started, like a grip of huge, monster hands squeezing and forcing her insides down, down, down. She was holding her breath and forced herself to breathe, to pant.

Hale said in a tight voice, "I see the head."

"Is he okay? It's all right?"

"Yeah."

She barked out a laugh and stared at the ceiling of the vehicle. "I'm going to push," she said, feeling the desire come like a hard wave. "I'm gonna push. I'm gonna push. I'm pushing! *Aaaahhhhhh.*"

"Okay, okay, okay."

"Okay?" she gasped.

"Yes, okay."

"Hale, can you do this?"

"He's coming. Yes."

"Okay . . . okay . . ."

A moment later. Tersely. "Push again."

Savvy wanted to argue. What the hell did he know? But she wanted to push. It was coming on her again.

And then she was pushing and there was sharp pain and yet she couldn't stop and he was saying, "Wait, wait, wait!" but she couldn't, and she yelled, "No, no! I can't!"

"It's okay. It's all okay. He's here. He's here!"

"Have you got him? You've got him?"

"I've got him. He's . . . It's okay. . . . It's all just fine. . . ."

And then the wail. The beautiful spiraling wail of the newborn in the cold night, and Savvy laid her head back while tears ran down her temples toward her ears.

CHAPTER 19

Hale came upon the deputy's vehicle stalled out in a pile of snow about a mile and a half ahead of them. He slowed his already slowly moving SUV down to a crawl, seeing the man had tried to turn the Jeep around when he'd realized Hale and Savannah weren't directly behind him. But now Hale wasn't going to stop if he didn't have to, unsure he would get moving again. He rolled his window down, ready to yell that message to the deputy, but as soon as the window was down, he heard in the stillness of the night a grinding engine coming toward them from the west.

"Snowplow," the deputy yelled.

Relieved, Hale gave the man a thumbs-up of understanding. All he had to do was reach the plow and the roads behind it should be clear of drifts. Glancing in the rearview, he saw Savannah sitting with a seat belt strapped across her, swaddled beneath her coat and his; she was wearing her own, and his was the blanket covering her legs. Her eyes were closed, and his son, held to her chest, was invisible from this angle. Was it the safest means of travel? Not by a long shot. Did he see any way around it? No.

He drove with extreme caution, however. Steady and slow. Sweat beaded on his forehead.

My God, he thought. *My God . . . my God.*

Kristina crossed his thoughts, as she had off and on all night. The baby was her son, too.

The baby . . .

His last conversation with Kristina over the baby's name hadn't gone well. "What do you think about Declan?" Hale had suggested, half in jest, half seriously. He wasn't really sure what Kristina's feelings were about his grandfather and thought she might object.

Her reply had offered more questions than answers. "Names are just a way to hide your real identity, so it doesn't really matter."

"What the hell does that mean?" he'd demanded, but she'd simply shrugged and said, "Declan it is."

They'd never had another conversation on the subject.

"Declan it is," he said aloud now, his attention zeroed in on the road ahead of him.

The snowplow came chugging uphill, shooting snow in either direction from its front blade. An ambulance was caught behind it, its lights flashing. Hale tried to flag it down, but the ambulance driver rolled down his window and yelled at him, "Accident just over the summit. Several cars. Trying to get there. There's a pregnant woman on the—"

"She's with me. I'm the one who called."

He stopped himself and asked, "She okay?"

"Yes. I'm taking her to the hospital," Hale yelled back.

The man lifted a hand as they drove past them. Too many other emergencies still out there to help those who could help themselves. Hale eased onto the packed snow the plow had left in its wake, even though now he was essentially driving on the wrong side of the road. But his window was cracked, and he could hear if there was an approaching engine. If he needed to shift over to the deep snow of the westbound lane, so be it. He would have time.

Listening carefully, all he heard were the sounds of his own vehicle and the rapid beating of his heart inside his ears. He stayed close to the centerline, which was buried beneath the snowpack, ready to drive into the deeper snow at the sound of an approaching engine.

"How're we doing?" Savannah asked.

"I'm taking you and Declan straight to the hospital."

"Declan?"

"Yeah."

"Kristina's hospital?" She said it quietly, but he knew it was a request.

Ocean Park might be a little farther than Seaside Hospital from where they were, but not by much. "Yeah," he agreed, and they drove in silence for several more miles. His thoughts random, he said into the quiet, "We need a car seat."

She made a hiccuping sound that could have been a laugh. "We need a lot of things."

"You okay?" he asked, suddenly worried she meant something specific.

"I'm fine." A pause. "We're both okay."

Their eyes met briefly in the rearview mirror. "You warm enough?" he asked.

"More than enough."

"It won't be long."

Savvy nodded and closed her eyes again. Hale returned his concentration solely to the road ahead, pushing aside all the clamoring thoughts of his son's birth, his critically injured wife, and the fact that he was a new father driving along a road made helllishly treacherous by snow and ice.

As soon as she entered Ocean Park Hospital, Ravinia wrinkled her nose at the smell of some tangy disinfectant with a sweeter scent beneath it that she couldn't quite identify but thought could be something gross. She'd never been inside a hospital before, and she didn't like it much. And tonight it was full of people who'd been cold and stranded and injured. The staff seemed a bit overwhelmed. The emergency room was filled not only with people waiting to be attended to, but also with others, like herself, who were just waiting. A wet puddle of melting snow near the doors grew larger every time someone tromped in from outside.

She sucked at her lower lip, half wishing Earl and Rand would just evaporate and leave her to her own devices, half wishing she could lean on one or the other or both of them for support. She paced around the room like a caged lion, irritated that Earl and Rand had seated themselves and seemed to be ready for the long haul. She asked about Catherine and was assured by the staff that someone would be out to give her a report very soon. She was starting to believe they were all a bunch of liars, and she'd come to the conclusion that nurses were trained to be impatient, rude, and dismissive.

After long minutes of pacing with no success, she took a seat across from Earl and Rand, one with a view of the exterior emergency room sliding glass doors and the portico beyond. Her sister Lorelei, one of the few who had escaped Siren Song before Catherine closed the gates, had worked at Ocean Park Hospital as a nurse, and Ravinia had liked her, so maybe they all weren't entirely bad. She wished Lorelei were here now, but she'd quit the spring before, when she'd met the love of her life, a reporter, Harrison Frost, who'd been following after Justice once he escaped from Halo Valley Security Hospital. Lorelei had fallen hard for the reporter, and after Justice's death, with nothing keeping them apart, they'd moved together to Portland when Frost was offered a job there. Again, so said Catherine, although her reports were sketchy at best.

Catherine had added that Lorelei was working at a Portland area hospital now, peacefully and happily, which had prompted Lillibeth to ask her breathlessly, "Are they getting married?" Catherine had muttered something disparaging under her breath, which none of them had caught, but it served to remind Ravinia that, for all her rigidity, her belief in protocol—her decision for all of them to live life in a simpler time—Aunt Catherine sure didn't think much of the institution of marriage. Maybe because she'd never been married herself? Maybe something else? Whatever the case, in this one area, Ravinia actually agreed with her: True love was a myth. It didn't exist, no matter how many books her sisters read on the subject, no matter how many old romantic movies they caught on their dinosaur of a television set.

"Miss Beeman?"

Ravinia looked up. "Yes?"

A doctor was walking toward her. Finally. She flicked a glance toward Earl, who half stood, as well. He'd wanted to bring Isadora, of course, but Lillibeth and Cassandra had both gone into conniptions at the thought of Isadora abandoning them, so Isadora was forced to stay. Ophelia had been Earl's second choice, but she'd said it was Ravinia who should go, for reasons yet to be determined. Whatever the case, she was here, and though she wasn't Catherine's favorite and vice versa, she was currently the chosen decision maker.

"Your aunt is in stable condition," the doctor told her brusquely. He was delivering the information but looking past her; his mind was elsewhere. "We've moved her to a room and are continuing to monitor her."

"Is she awake?"

"She's unconscious, but her signs are good and—"

"What's wrong with her? Did she have some kind of seizure? What is it?"

The doctor, an older man with a close-cropped gray beard, finally turned his attention fully on her. "She has a contusion near her temple. It appears she fell, possibly slipped, and struck her head from the fall."

"She fell?"

"The nurse can get you the number of her room. Phyllis?" he called to a harried-looking young woman, who ignored him as she hurried across the room to a set of double doors, which opened with a soft hiss. "Well, when she's back," he said. "Excuse me."

Ravinia stared after him. Could it really be that simple? When she'd run past the ambulance into the lodge, she'd been certain from Lillibeth's wailing, Cassandra's dire predictions, and Isadora's and Ophelia's frozen attentiveness that Aunt Catherine was practically done for. Ophelia was the one who'd called 9-1-1. She had a disposable cell phone, apparently, a piece of information that would have helped had Ravinia but known it. It really pissed her off the way her sisters kept secrets, but then they'd learned from the best: Catherine.

Ravinia hadn't waited around. She'd wanted to know how Catherine was for herself, so she'd taken off with Earl and Rand and ended up at the hospital shortly after the ambulance. They had already pulled Aunt Catherine's gurney out of the ambulance and taken her past those double doors by the time Earl had parked and Ravinia had hurried inside. They'd been waiting ever since.

Now she looked through the exterior clear-glass sliding doors as a vehicle approached and pulled to a halt directly in front. A man jumped out and hurriedly opened the back door of his SUV.

Suddenly Earl was blocking her vision. "I'm going back for Isadora."

"I can take care of things here," Ravinia said, irked. "My sisters need her at Siren Song."

Earl hadn't wanted to bring Ravinia even though she was the chosen one, but Rand had muscled past his objections, and Ravinia had simply jumped in the car. But now Earl was apparently having second thoughts. He headed toward the door and shot a look at Rand, who was still slouched in his chair.

"I'll stay," Rand said.

"You don't have to," Ravinia told him quickly. She didn't want him expecting something for the favor of helping to convince Earl to bring her here.

He simply shrugged.

Ravinia went to find the nurse who'd ignored the doctor—Phyllis—and found her scurrying toward the group outside. A woman had been helped from the backseat of the SUV to a wheelchair. She was wrapped in coats and was hugging herself closely. The man from the car was talking to the EMT who was pushing the woman inside. The woman wore socks but no shoes, and Ravinia realized with a start that she sure looked a helluva lot like that detective from the sheriff's department. Detective . . . Dunbar. What had happened to her?

She was holding something inside that coat. A baby? *Her baby?* She'd had her baby *in the snow?*

The hissing double doors opened, and Phyllis ushered the detective and her entourage through.

"Excuse me, Phyllis?" Ravinia said.

"I'll be with you in a minute." She was abrupt.

Ravinia wasn't waiting. "I need the number to Catherine Rutledge's room."

"I'll get it for you in a minute."

But she followed the group through the doors. Ravinia sent a look to Rand, then followed after them. As the doors started to close behind her, Ravinia looked around for someone to help her who wasn't busy. There was no such person. Finally, a nurse—her name tag read BARANSKY—appeared, and Ravinia asked her for Catherine's room number, explaining she was her niece. She, too, was hurrying to meet up with the detective, but she hailed another young woman in medical scrubs, who deigned to look up the information.

"Three thirteen," she said. "Just go back through the double doors and turn right. The elevators will be on your right. Your aunt will be there in about twenty minutes."

Ravinia headed back toward the double doors, hearing the wail of the new baby behind her. She looked back and saw Nurse Baransky taking the baby into her arms around the edge of the cubicle's half-closed curtain.

Hitting the large square button on the wall, she watched the doors hiss open and then close behind her. Rand was scooched down in the brown, squarish chair he'd chosen, dozing. She walked over to him and kicked his boot. His eyes opened, but he didn't lift his head.

"Yeah?" he asked.

"I want to know how you're related to me."

"I don't know exactly."

"Who does?"

Rand straightened up. "My great-uncle, I guess. He's the shaman."

"Shaman?" she repeated dubiously.

"Well, not officially." He shrugged. "You know."

"No. I don't know," Ravinia snapped back.

"Your family's got the same thing. The ones that are more spiritual and guide the tribe."

"You don't know what you're talking about," Ravinia muttered.

"You asked," he pointed out with a shrug.

"I'm going to go find my aunt," she said and then left him there. "More spiritual," she repeated with disdain. Maybe his family was. Hers was just messed up.

Savannah felt jazzed inside. Like she'd been hit with an electric current. Anxiety. Nerves. Underlaid with pain and exhaustion and wonder. It was like living inside someone else's body.

A baby. Her baby.

"My sister's in surgery here," she told the EMT who'd wheeled her into the curtained room. "Kristina St. Cloud." She glanced past him to where Hale was giving an account of the birth to a resident as a nurse strode toward them determinedly.

"The baby?" she said to Savannah. Her smile must have been meant to be reassuring, but there was tension, too.

Loath to hand him over, Savannah nevertheless did so without a complaint. "You're going to make sure he's all right?" she said, hearing her own tension.

"I sure am."

"He's Baby St. Cloud," Savannah told her. "I think they're going to call him Declan."

"They?"

"The parents. I'm the surrogate."

The nurse nodded. "I'll make sure he's tagged," she said.

As soon as Declan was out of her arms, he started crying, and Savvy started shaking uncontrollably. They swaddled him up quickly and whisked him into an examining room, and then another nurse—her name tag read Baranksy—wrapped Savvy in new blankets and said something about taking her to a room . . . as soon as one was free. There were numerous victims of the storm at the hospital, and there was a shortage of space. Savvy looked around, but Hale was nowhere to be seen.

"Excuse me," she said through chattering lips. "My sister had surgery. Kristina St. Cloud? Can someone get me some information?"

"I'll check it out as soon as we get you to your room," Baransky said.

"Where's Declan?" Savvy asked.

"The doctor's checking him out. He looks fine. Come on. I've got a place for you. . . ."

She was taken to a room with a shower that had a stool inside. Savvy didn't wait for an invitation. She dropped the jackets and stripped off her blouse and bra with numb fingers, turned on the shower spray, then collapsed onto the stool and let the hot water pour down on her. She hadn't even taken off her socks and was trying to do just that when a different nurse appeared and helped her finish the task. She thought about the blood, the fluids, and the placenta that had ended up in Hale's car and felt herself shudder a little in shock and embarrassment.

But they'd made it. They'd made it.

And Declan was doing fine.

It felt like forever before she stopped shaking, but as soon as she did, she wanted out of the shower and in more than just a damn hospital gown and a diaper of sorts. Savannah had no idea what had happened to her underwear and pants. Probably also still in Hale's TrailBlazer. The nurse insisted she get in bed.

"I'll bring your husband," she said once Savvy was under the covers.

She opened her mouth to deny Hale was her husband but decided that wasn't the hot issue. A deep languor was overcoming her. Pure exhaustion. Maybe she would lie here just a moment or two before she found out about the baby, Hale, and most of all, Kristina.

Kristina.

Her eyes popped open. Had she fallen asleep? She had a sense of very little time passing. Swinging her legs over the side of the bed, she was about to go find somebody to help when Hale appeared in the doorway.

"I had to move my car," he explained.

"Any news on Kristina?"

"She's out of surgery and in recovery. Don't know anything yet."

"The nurse said the baby's okay."

"Yep, he's great." He almost smiled. "I just saw him."

Savannah felt her bones melt in relief. "And how about you?" she asked, looking into his tired gray eyes.

"How about you?" he countered. "That was . . . something."

"Yeah." Savannah laughed faintly. "I told them his name was Declan."

"Good."

"I think I'll just lie down a minute," she said after they fell into silence.

"I'll get you some clothes."

She would have said, "Don't bother," because she was pretty sure there wasn't anything in his car she would ever put on again, but he was already gone.

Ravinia stood beside Catherine's bed, staring down at her. The EMTs and the nurse who'd brought her in had expected the room to be empty and had given Ravinia questioning looks, to which Ravinia had said, "I'm her niece," half expecting them to make something of that, but they hadn't. They'd left, dimming the lights to a soft glow. As soon as they were gone, Ravinia had swept to Catherine's side.

"Aunt Catherine," she said quietly. "Aunt Catherine?"

Never in her life had she seen her aunt asleep. Catherine had the ears of a hunted animal and was ever on alert. This was a first, and it made her feel both powerful and slightly scared at the same time.

"I've got the journal," she told her. "I stole it from your room."

Catherine didn't move. Her breathing was steady and deep.

"It's Mary's journal." Ravinia had determined that when she'd taken it, recognizing that the handwriting wasn't Catherine's distinctive and precise penmanship. This journal had been hastily printed or scrawled, and everything looked haphazard and thrown down quickly.

And then she'd randomly turned to a page and read:

> *C.,*
> *Janet deserves what she gets. You know she took him on purpose. It's a game with her, but I'm the better player. He's mine now, and I can feel the baby already.*

That clearly wasn't written by Catherine. Even if it hadn't been addressed to C., Ravinia would have guessed that was her mother's journal entry. Yep. Dear old Mom was crazy as a loon.

She wondered, with a sudden bad feeling, if the man that her mother took from this Janet was even her own father. . . . It was all a matter of dates, but the journal was noticeably lacking that information.

When there was no response, Ravinia pulled the book from her back waistband and held it out flat, watching the pages riffle until they broke to a favorite page. "Want me to read it to you?" Ravinia suggested.

Still no change.

Ravinia regarded her helplessly. She wanted to shock her awake. Yes, her aunt drove her out of her mind, but she needed her to come to. *They* needed her to come to.

She glanced down at the page in front of her.

> *C., I can take D. from you. Don't think I can't. Be smart about him, or I'll prove my power to you. Give him up now, before you make me do something I don't want to. You can't keep him. I'll have him, too. J.'s husband and father.*

Ravinia glanced up from the book. A cold, eely shiver slid down her spine as she saw Catherine's blue eyes staring fixedly at her. "Aunt Catherine?" she asked, her voice wavering a bit.

Catherine's lips moved. "Mary . . . the body . . . Mary . . . the body . . . Mary . . ."

Ravinia stayed still. She kept her gaze on her aunt, wondering if there was sight behind those glassy orbs, or if she was in some other world. After a long minute, she asked, "What body?"

"From the bones . . ."

One hand reached up, clawlike, and grabbed Ravinia's arm. It was all Ravinia could do to keep from screaming. Creeped out, she gently pulled Catherine's hand from hers and asked, "Who?"

"Mary . . . the body . . . on Echo . . ."

Ravinia glanced toward the windows, which faced west, but there was only darkness beyond. "There's a body on Echo Island?" she asked carefully.

"Mary . . ."

"Who's Janet? Is she the J. Mary refers to?" Ravinia broke eye contact to look at the passage she'd read from the book, her mind racing. She thought about looking into Catherine's heart. She'd tried and failed before, but her aunt had never been in such a vulnerable position before, either. Concentrating, she tried to see what kind of person Catherine was, but even now the way was blocked.

Maybe it just meant she was neither bad nor good, Ravinia thought suddenly. That was Catherine in a nutshell.

Reading the two passages over again, Ravinia asked her, "Who's D.? Was he your lover?"

To her shock, Catherine sat straight up, and Ravinia fell back, nearly tripping over her own feet and dropping the journal. As she juggled the book and pulled it close, Catherine slowly lay back down.

Ravinia took a step forward. She half expected Catherine's head to spin around or something. Spooky.

"Miss?"

Ravinia let out a short shriek of fear and whipped around. It was a nurse, silhouetted in the doorway. "What?" Ravinia demanded, collecting herself.

"I was checking to see if she'd woken." She moved into the room, an older woman with a stern look on her face.

Ravinia glanced back at Catherine, who'd closed her eyes, as if she was faking it.

"No, she hasn't."

"Have you noticed any change?" the nurse examined the IV they'd put in Catherine's arm.

"Well, she did sit up, but she wasn't really awake."

"She sat up?"

"Uh-huh."

"Well, good. It sounds like she's coming around. I'm sure the doctor will want to keep her overnight. You're welcome to stay."

After the nurse bustled away, Ravinia looked back down at Catherine. "What are you doing?" she asked her. "Is this for real?" She watched her breathe for several moments. "Was D. your lover? Was he Janet's husband?" she asked again, pressing.

Catherine's lips moved, but no sound issued forth.

"What?" Ravinia gingerly leaned forward, trying to hear. She waited, her heart trip-hammering.

Finally, she heard Catherine say on a soft breath, "Dead gun."

"Dead gun?" Gooseflesh rose on her arms as she waited for Catherine to respond, but the only sound was her aunt's heavy breathing.

Ravinia stood in silence for long moments. She could see her aunt relax into the pillows, and she felt the release of some tension in the room she hadn't known existed. Gazing thoughtfully at the book, she riffled through the pages. Well, there were a lot more entries and a few hours left till daylight. She could get a lot of reading done.

Settling herself into a chair, she read a few more passages, and then she asked suddenly, "Or is D. Janet's father?"

Catherine just slept on.

Sunday dawned gray and cold, and Savvy turned toward the window, waking up disoriented at first, and then *bang*. She remembered everything in a rush.

She sat straight up in bed, felt muscles shriek in protest, and froze where she was in bed. A white world was unveiling itself in the patchy sunlight that filtered in after the storm. At least the snow had stopped, but the sky was still filled with scattered clouds, which looked like they might turn ominous.

There was a small overnight bag on the only chair in the room. She hazily recalled Hale coming back in and dropping it there. Gingerly, she stepped out of bed, walked to the chair, unzipped the bag, and reached inside, pulling out a neatly folded, clean dark pink sailcloth blouse. Kristina's. Savvy hesitated a moment, remembering the bag sitting in the backseat footwell in Hale's car. Well, she really couldn't put on her own soiled clothes, but the idea of putting on her injured sister's garments felt wrong somehow.

Nevertheless, she slipped her arms down the blouse's sleeves; there was no way she would even try on her bigger-chested sister's bra, although if it was ever going to fit her, she supposed it would be now. She felt a poignant rush of love for her troubled sister, and she stood there a moment before pulling on the fresh underwear and dark brown slacks. There was no way she was going to be able to get that zipper over her distended abdomen.

She made a trip to the bathroom, then carefully arranged the hem of Kristina's blouse over her gapping zipper. Catching her reflection in the mirror, she made a face at the horror show that looked back. Her hair looked like it had been through a blender, reddish-brown tufts sticking out like they were trying to escape her head, and the dark circles under her eyes were testament to the previous wild night.

Everything from the waist down was sore. No big surprise there. Though they wore the same shoe size, her sister's slip-on leather mules were a little tight. Savvy's feet had grown during pregnancy, and she wasn't sure they were going to go back to their previous size.

Anxious to find out about Declan and her sister, she headed for the door but was met by Nurse Baransky, who clucked at her and said she would get Savvy a wheelchair.

"Don't you ever go home?" Savvy asked.

"It's been one emergency after another," she said. "I'm leaving soon."

"I don't want a wheelchair," Savvy said and walked out of the room before Baransky could stop her, albeit hunched over protectively a little bit as there was definite pain involved. But she didn't care. The same kind of adrenaline rush that had overtaken her when she was ready to deliver was moving through her bloodstream again. She needed to know about the baby and her sister.

"Kristina St. Cloud is in recovery from surgery yesterday," she said to a nurse at the first station she came to. "She's my sister."

The woman looked up at Savvy, who self-consciously ran a hand over her hair. Without a word to her, she placed a call and asked for someone named Patricia, then listened for a few moments. After she hung up, she seemed to be considering her words carefully, as she directed, "Take this hall to the ICU waiting area." She pointed to the east. "Dr. Oberon will meet you there."

"Oberon's my sister's doctor?"

She gave one terse nod, said, "Her surgeon," then quickly went back to her work.

Her attitude turned Savvy's heartbeat into a hard knock, the pounding increasing with each footstep. The nurse hadn't wanted to talk to her. Hadn't wanted to answer further questions. Had wanted to be rid of her as fast as possible.

Please . . . God . . . , she thought, reaching an intersection at the end of the hall and seeing the intensive care unit sign above a closed door with a small glass window. Savvy peered through one of the windows and saw Hale in the hall beyond, his head bent, listening to a man with wavy brown hair who wore a white lab coat and a grave expression. *Oberon,* she decided, her throat dry.

She pushed through the door, and Oberon looked up. Hale turned his head at the doctor's sudden shift of attention, and in his eyes she saw the answer she was dreading.

"No . . . ," she whispered.

"You're Mrs. St. Cloud's sister?" the doctor asked.

"Yes." She could barely get it out as she read his name tag. *Yes, Oberon.* She glanced down, and the floor seemed to buckle and sway.

"She died early this morning. There was too much pressure," the doctor said, but any other words coming from his mouth were buried under a buzzing in her ears and the edges of blackness creeping into her peripheral vision.

"Savvy . . ." She saw Hale say her name more than heard it. He came to her and swept her into his arms in a crushing embrace. She leaned into him and closed her eyes. Her throat burned. She couldn't think. It was all too much.

Kristina was dead? Dead?

She'd thought she was spent of emotion. But the feel of Hale's arms around her sent up a well of tears. "My sister . . ." she said.

"I know." His voice rumbled in his chest, a comforting feeling.

And then the tears spilled over, and she clung to him, letting them silently fall onto his shirt collar.

CHAPTER 20

Catherine woke up as if she'd had an undisturbed night's sleep, blinked several times, and said, "I can't see."

Ravinia, whose chin had dipped to her chest for a moment, snapped awake, her mother's journal sliding to the floor. "Let me turn on a light." She quickly got up and walked to the light switch, pressing the toggle.

The room flooded with light, but Catherine blinked and blinked. "Ravinia?"

Ravinia walked to the edge of the bed. "I'm right here."

"I can't see you."

Ravinia stared down at her aunt, whose blue eyes were focused somewhere far away, searching. "What's wrong?"

"Where am I?" Then, "It smells like a hospital."

"I need to get the doctor."

"No, don't leave," Catherine ordered. "Please."

Ravinia regarded her with worry. "But if you can't see . . ."

"It's probably temporary," she said. "What happened?"

"I don't really know. You were out at the gate, talking to Earl, and then you never came back. Why can't you see? What do you mean, it's probably temporary?"

"It's happened before. Where's Isadora?"

"At the lodge." Ravinia quickly brought her aunt up to date on the events of the night before, finishing with, "Earl brought me here with his son, Rand. He went back to Siren Song last night to get Isadora, but he hasn't shown up again. Nobody wanted Isadora to leave. That's why I'm here instead," she added a bit uncomfortably.

"Isadora should stay with them," Catherine said.

"Yeah, well . . ." Ravinia cleared her throat. "Why did Earl come to Siren Song?"

"Why didn't he bring Ophelia?"

"Because I'm the one who went over the wall for help!" Ravinia snapped. "What the hell happened? Why can't you *see?*" She heard the hysterical note in her voice and clamped it down. She wanted to wring Catherine's neck. If they had a phone or could drive or . . .

"Sometimes stress brings it on," her aunt said, but there was something evasive in her tone.

"Did you know Ophelia has a disposable cell phone?" Ravinia asked. "She called nine-one-one while I was out looking for help. She may have saved your life."

Catherine shook her head, seeming a bit overwhelmed.

"Why did Earl come by?" Ravinia asked again. Though he was the lodge's all-around handyman, he rarely came at night. In fact, though he was the only man allowed inside the gates, she couldn't remember a time he'd ever stayed past evening.

"We had some business to take care of."

"Oh, business. That's real specific."

"What do you want, Ravinia?" she asked tiredly.

"Answers! Who's Janet?"

Catherine blinked. "What?"

"Who's Janet?" Ravinia grabbed up the journal from the floor, quickly thumbed to the first entry she'd seen, and read, "'Janet deserves what she gets. You know she took him on purpose. It's a game with her, but I'm the better player. He's mine now, and I can feel the baby already.'" She looked up at her aunt. A flush had crept up Catherine's neck. "And then it says, 'You can't keep him. I'll have him, too. J.'s husband and father.'"

"You took that journal from my room," Catherine accused angrily.

"Yes, I did. Because you won't tell us anything. And last night, when I found you in the snow, I wasn't going to wait anymore. None of us can afford to wait anymore."

"How did you get in my room?"

"What baby was Mary feeling?" Ravinia asked. "Which one of us?"

"I don't know."

"Does Isadora know?" Ravinia asked. "What else is in here?" She lifted the journal up, as if Catherine could see it. "If I spend enough time, I'll figure it out, but it would be nice to have some help."

Catherine's blank gaze flew toward her. "You're holding the journal?"

"Yes! I've been reading it all night! It's *right here.*"

Catherine's eyes flooded with water. It made Ravinia feel bad, but she held her ground. Eventually, Catherine looked away, staring straight ahead, her hands folded over one another, the fingers of one hand squeezing the other. "You had no right."

"If you would be honest, I wouldn't have to resort to stealing. Now, who the hell is Janet?"

"Janet Bancroft was Mary's nemesis. They went through school together, and Mary hated her."

"Is she the 'J.' in the journal?"

"Yes," Catherine said tautly.

"Why did Mary hate her?"

"Because Janet was beautiful and boys liked her. This is all so silly. They were high school classmates, and it was a silly jealousy."

"What happened to Janet?"

"She got married. Then I heard she was divorced. I don't know. It's ancient history, and it has nothing to do with us."

"You're lying," Ravinia asserted. She'd looked into Catherine's heart, and for just a moment she'd sensed her fear. Fear that Ravinia would learn something she shouldn't.

"I am not lying," Catherine insisted with her old spunk.

"Then you're not telling me the whole truth. What is this about J.'s husband and father? Who are they?"

"I don't owe you any more explanations."

"That's where you're wrong! Things are falling apart, Aunt Catherine. Don't you get it? This fake world you've created is over. It didn't really save us from Justice, and it's not saving us now. Be honest for once in your screwed-up life!"

"Janet is Janet Bancroft. Declan Bancroft's daughter and the ex-wife of Preston St. Cloud. Mary wanted them both, but she only got Preston," she said in rush of fury. "She took Preston away from his wife and son, and that's why Janet divorced him."

Ravinia's mind whirled. "What happened to Declan?" Ravinia said.

"What do you mean?"

"Why didn't she 'get' him, too? She acts like she could get any-body, any man. She seemed to think . . . Oh. He's the *D.!*" Ravinia thumbed through the journal again and read the second entry. "'C., I can take D. from you. Don't think I can't. Be smart about him, or I'll prove my power to you. Give him up now, before you make me do something I don't want to.'" Ravinia lifted her gaze to Catherine's ob-durate face. "She was talking about Declan. Your lover. She wanted you to give him up, or she would take him from you."

Catherine didn't respond, but she didn't deny it, either.

"What happened to Declan?" Ravinia asked.

"I gave him up," she said with forced lightness.

"Where is he now?"

"He's alive and well and running Bancroft Development with his grandson, Hale St. Cloud. He was a widower, and . . . your mother and I were both attracted to older men. I saw him on the beach and . . ." She left the thought unfinished.

"You shouldn't have given him up," Ravinia said.

Catherine turned to glare blindly at her. "Your mother was a pow-erful force. She had a sexual energy that she could lasso men with. I couldn't have her do that to Declan. Couldn't. *I wouldn't.*" She blinked several times. "Oh, there . . . there . . . I'm beginning to see again," she said in relief. "But none of this matters, don't you see? It's just a piece of Mary's past. It doesn't have any bearing on anything! Get me Isadora. Please. Ravinia. I need her. And Earl," she added as an afterthought.

"Why did Earl come to the gates?"

Her aunt eyed her carefully for several moments, but then she said, "Because he saw a fire on Echo Island, when no one should be there."

Ravinia's lips formed "Who?" but she didn't utter it.

Catherine, however, answered her as if she had. "The man from the bones."

Nurse Baransky caught up with Savvy while she was looking through the window at the babies in the neonatal center. "Ms. Dun-bar, we have further information we need to get from you. Mr. St.

Cloud gave us as much as he knew last night, but we need your insurance card, and also there are some practical considerations that need to be addressed, as well."

Savannah had zeroed in on Declan, but her mind was in a fog. *Kristina . . . God, Kristina.* "Uh-huh?"

"Are you planning on breast-feeding?"

"Uh . . . no . . ."

"Then you will want to stop your milk from coming in. You'll need to have a shot."

Savannah turned to stare at the nurse. Kristina hadn't wanted her to breast-feed; she'd been leery of Savannah bonding too much with her baby, though she hadn't said as much in words. But breast-feeding was better for the child; everyone knew that.

"Maybe you should go back to your room," the nurse said kindly as she witnessed fresh tears entering Savannah's eyes.

"No, no. I'm okay. I do want to breast-feed," she said now. "I do."

"You'll be giving the baby colostrum first, and it's very important," Nurse Baransky assured her.

Savvy nodded, unable to speak. *How would Hale feel about it?* she asked herself, then, as she followed after Nurse Baransky, decided she didn't really care. She would ask forgiveness rather than permission. Maybe Kristina hadn't wanted her to breast-feed while she was alive, but she also believed that her sister would want what was best for her child no matter what.

Hale drove carefully over the heavy snowpack on his way north from the hospital toward home. He had cleaned out his car somewhat at the hospital the night before and planned to do a better job later, but for now he just wanted to go home and sleep. He had some of Savannah's clothes still in the vehicle, too, but it was the sight of her wearing Kristina's pink blouse this morning that seemed burned on the back of his retinas.

He'd wanted to stay with her, but she'd pulled away from him upon learning about Kristina. He got it—she needed her space—but he felt like he could have held on to her forever. Now, as he drove the final miles, he was weighed down with exhaustion, his adrenaline store tapped out. The hospital was keeping both Savannah and his son till tomorrow at the very least. He needed to go home and get some energy back.

He'd expected Kristina to survive. He really had. He'd never imagined she would really die. She was resilient and tough and so alive. Once Savvy and Declan were safe, he'd been ready to fight for her and make their marriage work, no matter what it took. He'd been on such a high after seeing the birth of his son! Helping save him and Savannah . . . he was Superman! And Superman could fix the problems he and Kristina faced.

But now he was drained, untethered, completely at sea. How had this happened? How could Kristina have died?

"Crime scene," Officer Mills had said.

What the hell did that really mean? Who had killed her? Was it just random bad luck, her being inside the house at that time? Had Kristina run into a psychotic vagrant or thief at the Carmichaels'? Or stumbled into someone else's rendezvous?

But why was she there in the first place? Why crawl in through a window?

Hale sighed, squinting against the dazzling whiteness all around him as the sun slid out from behind a cloud.

No . . . she met someone there herself. A planned meeting. There was no other explanation.

And that someone had killed her.

Hale just didn't want to believe it.

By the time he was pressing the button to open his garage door, he felt as if he could sleep for a millennium, except his mind was buzzing. Buzzing and buzzing and making him feel slightly ill.

Walking into the kitchen from the garage, he threw his keys onto the island and beelined to the refrigerator, pulling out a bottle of water. He drank half of it down, then reached into the cupboard above the microwave, which held the liquor. Grabbing a bottle of scotch with one hand, he pulled out an old-fashioned glass with the other and poured himself a liberal dose. As he took a long swallow, he eyed the clock. Not quite noon on a Sunday.

Sighing, he sat down and pulled his cell phone from his jacket pocket. Text messages galore. He had no energy to answer them. Seeing his battery was almost dead, he crossed the kitchen and plugged the device into the charger on the small counter he and Kristina used as a desk.

He and Kristina.

He felt guilty every time her name crossed his mind. And sad. And boggled.

His cell phone suddenly trilled its default ring. He was still standing by it, so he picked it up and looked at the caller ID. It was Sylvie. "Hey," he said by way of answering, aware how lifeless his voice was but incapable of punching it up.

"Hey," she said back at him in a worried tone. "I saw on the morning news about Kristina. How is she?"

He had an almost uncontrollable desire to laugh at the absurdity of what he was about to say. "She's dead."

"*Dead?*" she gasped. "No!"

"I'm sorry. I just came from Ocean Park. She was in surgery, but . . ." He trailed off.

"But they said she was hurt at the Carmichael house in Seaside. That she was hit by an overhead beam. What does that mean? Where was she? God, Hale. What . . . what . . . ?" Sylvie, his right-hand woman, the clearest head in the office whenever there was a crisis, was clearly overwhelmed.

"I don't know. I don't get it. Kristina let herself in through one of the windows that doesn't stay shut."

"But why?"

"It looks like she was meeting someone. Look, Sylvie, I'm beat. I was up all night, and, oh, my son was born last night."

"He was?" She was distracted.

"He's coming home tomorrow."

"Oh . . . oh . . . good. Oh, my God. How's Savannah? Does she know about Kristina?"

"She knows."

"My God, Hale. I'm sorry. Who was Kristina meeting? Why at the Carmichaels'?"

"I wish I knew."

The front bell suddenly began its long chiming peal. Kristina had insisted on the bell, and Hale had protested that he could rotate the tires in the time it took the chimes to finish.

"Sylvie, there's someone at the door. Damn, I hope it's not a reporter," he said, realizing who might be dropping by unannounced today of all days.

"I'll let you go."

"Kristina selected a nanny," he said as he headed for the door. "I'm going to need her number, and I think it's at work. Kristina had it plugged in her phone, but—"

"Oh, yeah, yeah. Victoria Phelan. She told me all about her."

"Victoria Phelan. That's right."

"I'll go to the office and get it."

"I'm not sure where I wrote it down. . . ." If I wrote it down, he thought and then wondered briefly where Kristina's cell phone was. And her purse, for that matter.

"I'll go see what I can find," Sylvie said.

"Thanks." He hung up, walked to the front door, steeling himself to see the face of Pauline Kirby or someone of her ilk as he threw the door open.

Instead, he was greeted by two detectives from the Seaside Police Department, both of them wiping snow off their shoes as the taller one said, "Mr. St. Cloud, I'm Detective Hamett from the Seaside Police Department, and this is my partner, Detective Evinrud. May we come inside?"

Owen DeWitt woke up with a crashing headache and the dry heaves. Par for the course after a long stretch at the Rib-I. He hung his head over the bathroom sink of his dingy apartment for several minutes, debating about whether to have a cigarette. He'd given up the habit, oh, about a million times, but he'd given it up for good again six weeks ago . . . sort of. Drinking and smoking just went together, and if he ever gave up the booze, which he had no goddamn intention of doing, he might actually be able to give up smoking, too.

His jittery stomach holding firm for the moment, he searched through the kitchen drawers with no success, even the one that was off the track and got stuck halfway out. He'd tossed all the cigs out, like that was going to do the trick. All it did was piss him off now that he had to make a trip to the store.

He was going to have to get a job, he told himself morosely. He'd about run through his savings, and those investments he'd made back in the heyday of his career . . . they were all for shit already.

If it weren't for fucking Declan Bancroft and Bancroft Development, he'd still be flying high.

He found two tens in his wallet and thought he might have to make a trip to the ATM. There'd been a lot of those lately, and it scared him to think what he was going to do next. God. He'd had a career. A good one! And now he was a goddamn joke.

He needed a drink. The thought made his stomach seize and then relax. What time was it? He'd paid for a cab, rather than take a ride with the lady cop, which was just drunken stupidness, except she'd kinda worried him. He'd been a little too loose-lipped about Charlie, and that dude was fuckin' scary. Cold, dead eyes and a smile to chill the marrow of your bones whenever that mask of his slipped.

Yup. He needed a drink. Bad. It must be almost noon or so. . . . Could be in the afternoon . . . and . . .

"Holy shit." He'd opened the crappy curtains on his bedroom window, and there was goddamn snow everywhere. His car was a smooth white mound. "Damn."

Could he risk driving in this stuff? Take a chance on a fender bender with some other idiot on the road? Hell, no. He was going to have to walk to the store. *What a pisser.*

Opening the door, he gazed across the parking lot's blinding white blanket, but before he could step out, someone jumped in front of him and pushed him back inside.

"Hey!" He stumbled back in, and the door shut softly. "Charlie," he said, alarmed.

"Hey, Owen," he greeted him with a smile. He wore a black ski mask and a ski jacket.

"What the fuck are—" DeWitt inhaled sharply at the sudden pain and looked down to see the knife's hilt sticking out just below his chest. "You stabbed me! You stabbed me!"

Charlie pushed him down, and DeWitt stumbled and fell to the floor. The knife's blade was just below his breastbone. Charlie grabbed the hilt and began slicing upward with all his strength, his mean blue eyes staring at him hard. DeWitt tried to scream, but Charlie hand chopped him in the throat. Terrible pain radiated outward, and DeWitt gurgled and gazed up at Charlie in stupefied shock and fear.

"Bye, Dimwit," Charlie said with a smile, watching as the engineer's eyes bugged.

DeWitt struggled to talk, but he just moved his jaw in his last moments, and Charlie stared into his withered soul, feeling as powerful as a titan. The light slowly dimmed in DeWitt's eyes, and the man went limp, his stare fixed. Gone.

Quickly, Charlie yanked the knife back, wiped DeWitt's blood on the engineer's shirt, then stuffed the knife up the sleeve of his jacket. He pulled his ski mask down and cracked open the door. It was bright and cold outside, and no one was about.

He was so filled with good feelings that he stopped a moment, gathering his power, thinking about the voice that had challenged him. But not yet. There were still two others to take care of first. He sent his sexual power to both of them, the Bancroft man and the pregnant detective. Let them make of that what they would.

"I'm coming for you," he whispered, then slipped out the door and down to the truck.

CHAPTER 21

Savvy lay in the bed, trying to nap. She'd thought she would fall into a dead sleep after cradling and breast-feeding her little son—Hale's little son—but her dreams were dark and disturbingly sexual again, and now she was awake again and unable to stay still. She redressed in Kristina's clothes, and guilt lay on her heart like a lead weight. Survivor's guilt, for sure. But also her feelings for little Declan were crazy deep. She loved him like he was her own, and it was really, really difficult to remember that she had no claim on him whatsoever.

Her mind touched again on the swirling sexual thoughts that seemed to be invading her sleep. Was that normal? The worst of it was they seemed to be centered around Hale St. Cloud, and in a very dark, distant corner of her mind she recognized that she'd always found him attractive, in a kind of taboo, "never for you" kind of way. She'd never been worried that she would poach on her sister's husband while Kristina was alive. It never would have happened. Savvy wasn't made that way. But with her sister gone and this baby needing a mother, she was consumed with sexual thoughts about him that were downright X-rated.

"Stop it," she told herself sternly. The last thing she needed was to complicate things for herself.

With a need to keep her mind on other things, she searched through her messenger bag for her phone, relieved when her hand closed over it. In one of her few coherent moments while she'd been waiting for rescue, she'd tucked it safely inside the bag. Its battery was on its last legs, however, and the charger was in her overnight bag, which was probably still in the Escape, as she hadn't screamed for it like she had the messenger bag. Luckily, she had a spare charger at home.

Home. She would have liked to make a run there, but without a car and with the roads still covered in snow, and the hospital wanting her to stay till tomorrow, she was kind of trapped for the moment. She tried to think of a friend to call to maybe pick some things up for her, but she hadn't made any real friends in the community apart from her sister and Lang. Another pang of grief jabbed her as her thoughts touched on Kristina again. She was going to have to compartmentalize. The same way she did when investigating a case. It was the only way to manage her grief.

Exhaling, she placed a call to Lang's cell, prepared to leave a message as it was Sunday and he didn't answer calls from coworkers as a rule. If Savvy ever really needed to get hold of him on his days off, she had to call several times and/or text and/or drive over to the house that he shared with his fiancée.

"Savvy? Hello?"

She was surprised he picked up on the first ring, until she realized he must already know about last night somehow. "Hey, there," she said, suddenly damn near tears again. Hormones mixed with grief. A lethal combination.

"How's Kristina? Burghsmith said something went down at one of the Bancroft construction projects and she was injured. He met up with Bancroft at Ocean Park when your sister was in surgery."

"St. Cloud," Savvy corrected automatically, giving herself a moment to get her emotions under control.

"Right. St. Cloud. His mother was a Bancroft."

"Kristina is . . . she didn't . . ." Her inhaled breath was shaky.

When she couldn't go on, he said, "Savannah," in a strangled voice. He knew. "My, God. Are you all right? Are you still in Portland? Do you want someone to come get you?"

He didn't know about the baby. He didn't know about last night. She had tried to call him but hadn't gotten through.

"Lang, I've got a lot to tell you," she said shakily.

"I'm listening," he said.

"I'm at Ocean Park Hospital. I had the baby last night. Everything's fine. I'm just kind of overwhelmed, and I could use some things from my house, and I didn't know who to call. My extra phone charger, some clothes. I don't know."

"I'll get Claire to help me. Got a spare key?"

She told him where to find it, then said, heartfelt, "Thanks, Lang."

"The TCSD is here to serve and protect," he said gently. "I'll be there as soon as I can. . . ."

The detectives from the Seaside PD had seated themselves on two of the dining chairs on one side of the table. Hale sat across from them. He wasn't certain whether he was annoyed that they were here when he was so tired, or relieved that they were investigating Kristina's death. A little of both, probably.

The taller detective with the mustache, Hamett, was the one who did the most talking. Evinrud, his partner, was shorter but held himself straight as an arrow, with his chest forward in that way that he'd seen in serious workout aficionados.

Hamett had started out asking a number of questions about the Carmichael job, and Hale had freely told him everything he knew about the site, Ian and Astrid, the construction schedule, the workers, where they were in the permit process with the City of Seaside, and much, much more. He couldn't explain what had sent Kristina to the house or why she'd climbed inside, however, and he finished answering that question with, "She knew about the Carmichael project, but we didn't talk about my work all that much. Kristina never showed much interest."

"What did you and your wife generally talk about?" Hamett asked.

"Personal stuff. We were having a baby. . . ." He thought of his son at the hospital and Savannah and felt a growing anxiety.

"With a surrogate?" Hamett asked, prodding when he trailed off.

"Yes. Kristina's sister, Savannah. She's a detective with the TCSD."

"Uh-huh," Hamett said. He and Evinrud stared straight ahead at him, and Hale got the feeling they were trying hard not to look at each other.

"What?" Hale demanded. He was leaning toward being annoyed over relieved.

Evinrud finally spoke up. "Where were you last night, at the time of your wife's death?"

"Since I don't know the time, I can't answer exactly," Hale responded with an edge. "I was at my office till about five, and then I went to the Bridgeport Bistro for a drink before I went home."

"You were working on Saturday." This from Hamett.

"Construction isn't always Monday through Friday."

"Your wife didn't have a job?" Evinrud asked. He'd eased himself back in his chair, but he was as alert as a watchdog.

"No."

"Did you have plans together last night?" Hamett asked.

"No."

"Did you expect your wife to be home when you returned?" Hamett quizzed, pressing.

"Well, ye-es."

"You don't sound certain, Mr. St. Cloud," Evinrud noted, jumping in again. If theirs was a good cop–bad cop routine, he was definitely taking on the role of the bad one.

Hale explained, "When I got home Friday, Kristina had left me a note that said she needed some space." He hesitated, then, because it was going to come out, anyway, added, "She didn't come home that night."

Now the two detectives did share a look, and Hale could feel his pulse start to beat harder. They were acting as if he had something to do with her death. He knew that was the first assumption: the husband did it. But still, he hadn't seriously believed he would have to account for his actions.

"Was she here when you got home last night?" Hamett asked.

"No," Hale admitted.

"What time did you find the note on Friday?" Evinrud asked.

"I don't know. Around six, maybe."

"When was the last time you saw your wife?" Hamett was looking down at the notes he'd been scribbling, but when Hale didn't immediately answer, he glanced up.

"I saw her Friday afternoon, sometime after two. She came to the office." He was growing less and less interested in talking to the two detectives. He wanted to scream at them to leave him alone and go find the real killer, but that would do more harm than good.

"Was there a particular reason she came to your office?" Hamett asked.

Make love to me, and let's put some heat back in this marriage.

"She . . . thought we needed to work on our relationship," Hale said, hating the diffident tone in his voice. "The baby was due anytime. In fact, the baby came last night."

"Congratulations," Evinrud said.

Hale ground his teeth together and didn't respond.

"Do you still have that note?" Hamett regarded him seriously.

Hale nodded and went to retrieve it. He'd crumpled up the note and tossed it into the trash. Now, when he looked into the bedroom trash can, the note lay right on top.

Changed my mind. I'm not mad. I just need a little space. Kristina.

Hamett was again looking down at his notes when Hale handed him the one from Kristina. The detective studied it, then asked, "What had she changed her mind about?"

"She'd said she would be waiting for me. Like I said, she thought we needed to work on our relationship."

For the first time, Hale had time to think about that and realized that maybe something happened that caused Kristina to change her plans.

"What was the extra 'emergency' that made you leave the hospital for several hours while your wife was in surgery?" Hamett asked, bringing Hale's focus back with a bang.

He had to hang on to his escalating temper with an effort. "I went to find Savannah—Detective Dunbar—who was driving back from Portland after she heard about her sister's accident. She was stuck in the snow on the pass and couldn't get through. And she was in labor. I helped bring her to Ocean Park. A Clatsop County deputy was with me, if you need corroboration."

"I'm sure it's just as you say. We're not trying to put you on the spot, Mr. St. Cloud," Evinrud said, but there was no conviction in his tone.

"Will anyone remember you at the bistro?" Hamett asked, apparently staying away from that hot potato.

"The bartender's name is Minnie, and she called one of the customers Jimbo. They both talked to me."

"Okay." Hamett put his notebook away.

"I did not kill my wife," Hale stated flatly.

"No one said you did. We're just gathering evidence. Doing our job." Evinrud tried on a smile, but it looked false.

"You're certain it wasn't just an accident?" Hale asked. He knew better. He knew. But he couldn't help himself.

"Doesn't look like it," Hamett said. They got up from the table and Evinrud gathered up his notes. Hamett regarded Hale soberly and added, "Someone smashed your wife's head with a chunk of a four-by-four beam. Could it have just fallen from the upstairs floor? Possibly. Unlikely. There are footprints in the construction dust. Maybe from the workmen. Maybe not. When we check your wife's cell phone, we may have more answers."

"You have Kristina's cell phone?" Hale wished it were in his possession. He wanted to know whom she'd called.

"Her purse was on scene, and her cell phone was in her purse," Hamett said. "That all right with you that we have it?"

If he objected, it would only make him seem more guilty, so Hale answered, "Whatever it takes to find out what happened."

"Do you own a white truck?" Evinrud asked.

Hale frowned. "Not personally. The Bancroft Development trucks are white. Why?"

"A witness described a white truck parked down the street last night around seven p.m.," Evinrud answered.

It was all Hale could do to keep from blurting that he owned a black TrailBlazer, like they didn't know already, like that would save him from further scrutiny. Instead, he said, "Maybe she changed her mind about coming home because she was meeting someone there."

"Any particular reason you think that?" Hamett asked.

"Just the note she left."

"You don't have anyone in mind? Anyone you can think of?" Hamett asked.

Hale slowly shook his head. He had no idea what his wife did in her spare time, he realized.

Do you believe in sorcery? What had she meant by that? Did it have anything to do with this? "Most of our conversations were about the baby," was all he said.

Soon after, the detectives gathered up their things and headed toward the door. Relieved, Hale followed after them, unable to keep from asking, "You'll let me know if you find something in her phone?"

"We'll keep you informed, Mr. St. Cloud," Evinrud assured him, but something about his tone didn't inspire Hale with confidence.

As they reached the porch, Hale's cell rang. He glanced back toward the kitchen, where he'd left it, but he just wanted to get the detectives out of his house.

"You wanna get that?" Evinrud asked when it was clear Hale was ignoring the ringing. The detective's expression was bland, but he had a knack for making Hale feel like he was deliberately subverting the law. Man, he was getting tired of him!

"I can call 'em back," Hale said.

Evinrud nodded, and he and Hamett stepped off the porch and trudged back through the thick snow. They got into either side of a dark blue Ford Explorer and backed down Hale's driveway, snow crunching beneath the tires.

Hale locked the front door behind them and was heading to his phone when it rang again. Scooping it up, he saw it was his grandfather calling. Hale tried to keep the exhaustion out of his voice as he said, "I was just going to call you. I've got a lot of things to tell you."

Declan said, "I think someone's been in the house. Can you come by? I don't know what's going on."

He sounded rattled, and Hale exhaled his breath, looked at the clock and said, "It might be better if I saw you in person, anyway. I'll be there soon. . . ."

*   *   *

Savannah was standing in her hospital room, wondering if she could leave today, rather than tomorrow, but she'd tied herself to the baby with the breast-feeding. She realized belatedly that she hadn't thought that through, unusual for her, but then what was usual about the events of the past twenty-four hours?

She'd learned that Hale had left the hospital, and it had left her feeling slightly untethered. She wanted a shower—her own shower—and her own clothes, and something other than hospital food. She could go down to the cafeteria and pick something of her own choosing; she had her wallet. She knew she was running on empty sleep-wise, but she did not feel tired.

"Hey," a voice said behind her. She turned to find Lang standing in the doorway with a brown grocery bag. "Claire helped me, but we didn't see a bag, so . . ." He placed the grocery bag on her bed a bit apologetically. "Claire headed to work. They're short staffed because of the weather, but she's chained up."

Savvy smiled at him, then was horrified to feel her smile start to tremble on her lips. She was a hormonal mess! She wanted to throw herself into Lang's arms like he was the long-lost big brother she sometimes thought of him as. It was with an effort that she held her composure.

"The phone charger's there," he added, pointing to the bag.

"Thank you," Savvy said with feeling.

He eyed her pink blouse. "That doesn't look hospital issue."

"Yeah . . ." Savvy quickly brought him up to date about the harrowing events of the past hours, finishing with the fact that Hale had brought her Kristina's overnight bag, which had been in his car.

Lang just stared at her when she finished. "I don't want to be a bastard, but what the hell were you doing driving back in the worst storm we've had in years?"

"Kristina." Savvy said her sister's name and nothing else. She couldn't.

"I know, but . . ."

"You don't know, Lang. You don't."

"I know a little bit about losing a sister," he said.

Savvy drew herself up short. Lang's sister, Melody, had been killed by her psychotic boyfriend a number of years earlier. "I'm sorry," she said, heartfelt, her eyes burning.

"I shouldn't have brought it up. Never mind. You're here. Safe. The baby's safe."

She nodded, unable to find her voice immediately. Buying time, she turned to the grocery bag, pulled out her charger, and plugged her cell phone into it.

"Maybe I should leave," he said.

"No, wait. Please. I'm okay. I just want to talk about something else, think about something else."

"Okay."

Savvy inhaled and quietly exhaled, then asked, "Anything new on the Donatella homicides? I know we just met with Hillary Enders on Friday."

"This snowstorm's kinda decimated any momentum we had going, but Kyle Furstenberg did finally call me back. Apparently Hillary got through to him."

"Anything there?"

"Doesn't look like it. Furstenberg denied everything, even started waffling on whether Hillary was really involved with Marcus Donatella. Maybe that Bancroft employee who told us about Hillary Enders . . . Ella . . . something . . ."

"Blessert."

"Yeah, her. It's starting to seem like she might be one of those women who want to involve themselves in their friends' affairs. Live vicariously, or whatever. She said she thought Hillary was having an affair with Marcus Donatella, and she thought Furstenberg could be the killer, but it's starting to seem like a lot of hot air. Course, Furstenberg got on the news and made it all a big story, and he's pretty sorry about that now."

"You think this angle's a dead end."

"Kinda do," he admitted. "We all just wanted to kick-start the investigation again."

"I know." Savvy had felt that way, too. Eager for closure.

"Toonie called from the shelter. Your friend Mickey showed up once the snow started falling. He's asking for you."

"Great."

Lang smiled.

"Before the storm hit, I interviewed all the Bancroft employees again," Savvy told him. "Starting with the Seaside office, and then everyone I could reach at the Portland office, and some ex-employees, too."

"How'd that go?"

"Kind of as you'd expect." She told him briefly about meeting Sean Ingles, the architect, at the main offices; connecting with Clark Russo and Neil Vledich at the Lake Chinook home construction site; then with Henry Woodworth at the RiverEast apartment building; talking by phone to Nadine Gretz, who was apparently Henry's girl-friend; and finally meeting up with Owen DeWitt at the Rib-I steak house and bar. Her mind tripped on her conversations with Nadine Gretz and Owen DeWitt, both of whom had accused Kristina of having an affair, but she didn't say anything to Lang about their comments. Not yet. Not until she had a little more time to think about it.

But she did say, "I'd like to see the physical evidence from the Donatella crime scene again."

Lang's brows lifted. "Care to share?"

"I want to see where they found blood traces, or anything else." Like semen, maybe, on the wall. Owen DeWitt's smirking voice echoed in her ears. "He had her up against the wall. Banging her like crazy, and she was . . . man . . . in ecstasy. Head thrown back and first making these little kittenlike sounds and then screamin'! She was riding him and lovin' it."

Kristina's dead.

The thought hit her again like a bullet. Aching pain in her soul. While she was thinking and talking about the case, she could almost forget. That was what she needed to do. Keep her mind busy.

"I can get you the report," Lang said, bringing her back to the present.

"No. I'll come in tomorrow."

"Tomorrow?"

"I can't just sit around and think, Lang."

"Okay," he said slowly.

"Okay," she agreed. Then, before he could come up with some further reason for her to stay away from the station, she steered him out of the room and said, "I was just heading to the cafeteria. Do you know that you need even more calories when you're breast-feeding than when you're pregnant? It takes a lot of energy to manufacture milk."

"You're breast-feeding?"

"For the moment," she said, pushing the niggling worry about how Hale would react to the back of her mind.

"You want a wheelchair?" he asked, seeing the careful way she moved.

"Not on your life."

His grandfather wasn't in the kitchen when Hale let himself into his house, and he yelled loudly, "Hello!"

"I'm at my desk!" Declan called back, and when Hale walked down the hall and entered the office, he found him busily writing on a yellow notepad.

Declan looked up and blinked rapidly. "What happened to you?"

Hale made a strangled sound that was meant to be a laugh. "I hardly know where to start."

"Well, then, let me go first. Somebody's been around here. I keep hearing them in the house."

Hale nodded. He wasn't going to argue with Declan; he just didn't have the energy. But his grandfather wasn't as sharp as he used to be, and this wasn't the first time he'd been certain there was someone in his house. Hale had made the distinct error of suggesting that maybe Declan should move to assisted living and had been told clearly and colorfully where he could stick that idea. Declan, for being a gentleman around women, was salty enough when there were just men around.

"He says he's my son," Declan said, at which Hale, who had been feeling dozy and unfocused, snapped to attention.

"Someone actually talked to you?"

"Felt more like a dream, actually." He waved a hand, as if hearing how that sounded. "*Ach.* I'm getting the two things confused. Someone's definitely been walking around the house. Sneaking around."

"I'll take a look." Hale pushed himself to his feet with the arms of the chair.

"Be careful." Declan suddenly looked concerned.

Hale did a cursory inspection of the house, but there was no one inside. Then he walked around the home's perimeter, but there were no footsteps in the snow apart from his own. He came back inside, stamping snow from his boots.

"I don't see any signs of trespass," he said, retaking the chair across from Declan's desk, practically falling into it.

"You think I'm making it up," Declan declared.

"I don't really know."

"Someone's been here."

"I know. Your son." Hale regarded him soberly. "You keep saying things about having another child."

"I said it was a dream," he said quickly.

"Yeah, but it's not the first time you've said it, or something like it. I'm starting to think you're trying to tell me something."

"I have a daughter," Declan stated firmly. "I don't have a son. I'm not crazy, Hale. But someone's been here. He's trying to send me a message. He's the one that's out of his mind, but I swear, he's gaslightin' me."

"Dreams'll do that."

Declan stubbornly pressed his lips together and glared at him.

Hale closed his eyes. Lack of sleep was playing tricks with his mind as well. He had to cut through his grandfather's paranoia. "I've got some things I need to tell you. Then I'm going home, and I'm going to bed. I haven't slept since Friday night, and that wasn't the greatest night's sleep, either."

"Well, get on with it," Declan said irritably, glancing around again, as if he didn't quite believe someone wasn't there.

Hale took a breath, thought about how to tell Declan everything that had transpired, then launched into the tale of the past few days with, "Kristina didn't come home at all on Friday night. . . ."

As soon as Savannah and Lang entered the cafeteria, a voice called, "Detective?" and they both swung around.

It took a moment for Savvy to recognize the blond-haired young woman staring at her. Seeing her in a pair of pants, a shirt, and a jacket and so out of context had Savannah reaching through her memory to the people she'd recently seen in Portland and the hospital before the connection was made.

"I'm Ravinia," the girl said, seeing her struggle.

"Ravinia," Savannah repeated.

"What are you doing here?" Lang asked before she could say anything else. "Where's Catherine?"

"She's here. Aunt Catherine had an accident, and Earl brought us."

"Us? Who else is with you?" Lang asked.

"Earl went back for Ophelia . . . well, Isadora, but Ophelia came."

"What kind of accident?" Savvy asked.

"I guess she slipped in the snow and smacked her head on something."

"How serious is it?" Lang demanded, cutting to the chase.

"I don't really know." Ravinia's face clouded. "They don't tell me much, but they act like she'll go home soon."

"Good," Lang said.

"She should be just fine," Ravinia added, sounding strained.

Savvy couldn't tell if that was wishful thinking on her part or the truth. Lang looked past her, toward the cafeteria doors, and Ravinia, reading his mind, put in swiftly, "Oh, she wouldn't want a man coming to see her, believe me."

Lang nodded and rubbed his jaw. He had known Catherine before Savvy had, and knew the truth of that.

"I'd like to check on her," Savvy said.

Ravinia looked uncertain about that idea, but Savvy didn't much care. Catherine, and her issues, would be another distraction from her own tortured thoughts. Nailing her request home, Savvy added, "She came to the TCSD for help, and I'd like to tell her I'm following up."

Ravinia's gaze skated over Savannah from head to toe, and she said, "I saw them bring you in last night. You had your baby."

"Yes."

"But . . ." Ravinia's gaze flicked to Lang and then away. "He wasn't there."

"I'm Detective Stone," Lang said. "I'm a friend of your aunt's."

"I was with the baby's father last night, Hale St. Cloud," Savvy told her.

Ravinia reacted as if stung.

"You know Hale?" Lang asked.

"No . . . no . . ." Ravinia looked away for a moment, and Savvy could almost see the calculations going on inside her head.

Lang said to Savannah, "Fill me in later."

"Will do," she answered. To Ravinia, Savvy asked, "Can you tell me which room Catherine's in?"

"I can do better than that. I'll take you there," she answered woodenly.

CHAPTER 22

Ravinia led Detective Dunbar into her aunt's room and locked eyes with Ophelia, who was sitting in a chair, her hands folded on her lap. Ophelia had been looking out the window to the west, but as soon as she turned her head and saw them, she straightened into a stiff line. *Good.* Ravinia was pissed at her older sister. Earl had dropped her off after mumbling something about being unable to get her to come any earlier, and then he'd picked up Rand and left the hospital. Aunt Catherine had fallen into a deep sleep, and Ophelia had held her finger to her lips, so Ravinia had been unable to talk to her. Chafing at the unfairness of it all, she'd headed for the bathroom first, where she'd finger-combed her hair and gazed into her darkly clouded eyes in the mirror and wondered how, if ever, she was going to get any serious information beyond what Catherine had already told her.

It felt important that she know everything. Imperative. Who was out on Echo Island? The man from the bones?

She'd wondered if she should find a way home and question Cassandra, or Maggie or whatever the hell she wanted to be called. Maybe she had something more than her dire woo-woo predictions. Like some actual facts. Sure, Aunt Catherine clearly knew more, but the way she gave out little tidbits of information, then just clammed up, set Ravinia's teeth on edge.

Maybe it was time to leave, she'd determined as she headed down to the cafeteria. It looked like Aunt Catherine was going to be okay, and Ophelia was in charge—and Isadora, of course, was back at the house—so the urgency that had driven Ravinia since the night before had dissipated. What the hell. She didn't belong with them, all shut up in that drafty old monster of a house. It was probably time to get the hell out of Deception Bay and find out what her life was really supposed to be about.

And then she'd run into Detective Dunbar and the man, that other detective. Stone. So, here they were.

Ophelia rose and held up her hand to both Ravinia and Detective Dunbar, silently asking them to back right out the door. The detective nodded and complied, and Ravinia, feeling rebellious, opened her mouth to protest. She wanted to scream, "I was here first!" but it didn't really matter, anyway, so she followed Detective Dunbar into the hall, and Ophelia followed and closed the door to Catherine's room behind her.

"I'm Savannah Dunbar," the detective said, introducing herself. "I heard Catherine was in an accident."

"I told her," Ravinia put in.

Ophelia said, "She's sleeping. I just didn't want to disturb her. I'm Ophelia Beeman." She held out her hand, which the detective shook.

"Catherine went to the police and asked for help," Ravinia said.

"Help?" Ophelia repeated.

"Catherine asked me to come to Siren Song last week," Detective Dunbar explained.

And you weren't around, Ravinia thought smugly, meeting Ophelia's surprised eyes.

"Oh." Ophelia didn't seem to know what to say.

Ravinia took the bull by the horns. "So, maybe the detective should talk to Aunt Catherine. I mean, if something bad happened to her out there. If she didn't just slip or something . . ."

Ophelia gave Ravinia a cold look, one of those "We'll talk about this later" glares.

"Fine," said Ravinia's silent glare back. "Bring it on."

"Maybe you should talk to her," Ophelia said slowly to the detective, ignoring Ravinia's smirk of achievement.

Savannah followed the two Colony women back inside Catherine's room and gazed over at the woman who'd been so tough and in control just days before. Now, lying on her back, her eyes closed, Catherine looked older and more fragile than her actual fifty-plus years.

"Aunt Catherine?" Ophelia said quietly, placing one of her hands over one of Catherine's.

It took two more tries before Catherine's eyes fluttered open. Savvy had just opened her mouth to say that maybe it was better to wait when Catherine's gaze centered first on Ophelia, then Ravinia, then Savannah.

Ravinia said, "The detective was here at the hospital and wanted to see you."

"Savannah Dunbar," Savvy said, reintroducing herself.

"I know who you are," Catherine said in a voice that sounded dry and rusty. She cleared her throat and added, "Ophelia?"

"Earl brought me. Isadora's at the lodge with the others."

Catherine nodded her understanding. She seemed to collect herself with an effort, and when she spoke, it was to Savannah. "You . . . found out about . . . my question?"

Catherine clearly didn't want the other two to know about the knife, so Savannah answered obliquely, "I was at the hospital because I had my baby last night." And my sister died, she said to herself silently. The real reason she'd ended up at Ocean Park.

"Is he all right?" Catherine asked instantly, a look of concern on her face, and Savvy saw that she'd inadvertently telegraphed her feelings about Kristina.

"He's fine. Better than fine. Great, actually."

The older woman relaxed a bit. "What did you name him?"

"Uh . . . he's not mine to name." Another wave of sadness caught at the back of her throat. "I was a surrogate for my sister and her husband. The last I heard, she and Hale were thinking of naming him Declan, after his great-grandfather, but I don't really know if—" She cut herself off at Catherine's swift intake of breath.

"Aunt Catherine?" Ophelia asked with concern.

"Excuse me. I'm sorry." Catherine touched a hand to the side of her head, where an ugly bruise had formed near her temple. "Did you say you were a surrogate for *Hale* St. Cloud?"

"You know him?" Savannah asked.

Ravinia had been gazing at Savannah with laserlike intensity, but now she turned to her aunt. Ophelia looked a little startled, like she either wasn't following the conversation or was surprised by where it had turned.

"I know of him," Catherine said, ignoring both of her nieces. "You grow up around here, you know everybody. Girls . . . do you mind leaving me with the detective for a moment?"

Ravinia said, "Why? What can't we hear?"

"I just need a little privacy."

Ophelia hustled the resisting Ravinia toward the door. "Can I get you anything, Aunt Catherine?" she asked over her shoulder. "Something to drink?"

"A cup of tea would be wonderful," Catherine said.

As soon as Ravinia and Ophelia were out of earshot, Savvy said, "I followed up on your request. The knife's being tested now."

"Take a seat, Detective," Catherine said. "You look . . . tired."

Savvy did as suggested, sinking gratefully into one of the two straight-backed chairs in the corner. "But I put it through as a possible homicide investigation, not as a private request," she added.

"That's not what I asked for!" Catherine said sharply.

"I'm sorry, but you think someone killed your sister. That's what I'm getting from you, and it may come to an exhumation—"

"My sister's remains are not to be disturbed. I just want to know if there's any blood, other than Mary's, on that knife."

"Well, that's the problem," Savvy stated flatly. "You said she was stabbed, so it's up to the ME to determine whether it was accidental or intentional."

Catherine sank back into her pillows, an anxious expression tightening her face. "Don't name your baby Declan. It's unlucky."

Savannah almost laughed at the sudden change of subject. "Unlucky?"

"Mary used that name for one of her sons."

"Declan?" Savvy said, getting a bad feeling about that, especially considering Catherine's genetics lesson. "One of the ones she adopted out . . . ?"

"It's not what you think. Declan Bancroft wasn't his father."

"Okay . . ."

"Where's the journal?" Catherine asked suddenly. "Is it still in the room, or did Ravinia take it?"

"I don't see any journal," Savvy said, glancing around.

"It's all going to come out now that Ravinia knows. If it were just Ophelia . . ." She moved her head fretfully from side to side against the pillow.

Savannah waited a few moments while Catherine clearly wrestled with herself about something. When the older woman didn't speak for several moments, Savvy said, "I get the feeling there's something you want to tell me. More about Mary and what happened to her? But you won't allow yourself."

"Can I trust you, Detective?" She had folded her hands together and was squeezing her knuckles until they showed white.

"If you're planning on confessing to a crime, I'm bound by law to report it," Savannah said with faint humor, "but yes, you can trust me."

"Mary named her son Declan because she was playing a cruel joke on me. That's how she was, especially at the end. Cruel. And delusional. She even listed Declan Bancroft as the father on the boy's birth certificate."

"I see. . . ."

Catherine gave her a cool look. "You're wondering why it was a cruel joke. Yes, I had a . . . relationship with Declan Bancroft. It was after his wife died, and it was short-lived. My sister and I were the same in one regard. We were attracted to older men. Not that Mary couldn't go younger when it suited her." She paused a moment, then asked, "Have you ever been in love, Detective?"

Savvy slowly shook her head. "It makes you do crazy things. I didn't believe it until it happened to me. When my sister had Declan, Dr. Parnell Loman wrote out the birth certificate for her. Parnell did a lot of things for my sister that would have probably gotten his medical license revoked, but he was under her spell. He's dead now, the devil take his soul." Her voice hardened. "She named the boy Declan, then adopted him out shortly thereafter. Almost from birth, he exhibited . . . traits . . . that were worrisome."

"His gift?" Savvy suggested.

"Maybe. Something connected to it, I'm sure. Parnell helped her with the adoption, too. I don't have any records, and Mary kept that information to herself. Frankly, at the time, I was just relieved the child was gone, but now I think we need that information."

"You think this Declan was involved with your sister's death?"

"Yes." She glanced toward the window. "The boy, a man now, probably knows his birth name was Declan, and he may think Declan Bancroft is his father."

"Who is his father?"

"I don't know his name. I can see him in my mind's eye, and I know what he told us, but it was a lie. I think Mary found out, but she kept it from me. But I think Declan Jr.—Mary's son, that is—may suffer from the same mental problems as his mother, only maybe it's worse."

Savvy felt a coldness creep up her spine and actually looked behind her to see if there was something there. "When you gave me the lesson on genetics, you were thinking of him."

"I was hoping Mary's death could be explained."

"But you suspected Declan Jr. killed her."

Catherine nodded.

"And you think his blood may be on that knife," Savvy said, guessing.

"It's possible. But I don't want an exhumation unless it's absolutely necessary. I want to find him. I want you to find him and bring him in. If his blood is on the knife, then you'll be able to make a DNA match, right?"

"If he's as . . ." She almost used the word *evil,* but it sounded so melodramatic that she said instead, "As intent on causing harm as you say, he could have a criminal history already, and his DNA might be in the system."

"No. He's too careful." Catherine's blue eyes closed again, and she let out a soft shudder. "There's probably nothing on the knife other than Mary's own blood."

"How do you know he's careful?"

"By a means that would never stand up in court," she said.

"You're talking about your own gift?"

"I have a little bit of precognition. Not like Cassandra's, but a little bit."

"What else do you know about Declan Jr.?"

"He's dangerous, and I believe Mary drew him to her on the island. She set him on a path. She unleashed him, Detective. And he killed her."

Savannah gazed at the older woman and said, choosing her words carefully, "It sounds like you're asking me to start a manhunt for someone you think may have killed your sister, but you don't want an exhumation of her body. In fact, you're adamantly against that, even though you think this man could be a danger to others, as well."

"Oh, he is. To all of us."

Cassandra/Maggie's words came back to Savannah, and she shivered a little.

"What?" Catherine asked.

"Cassandra said she told you about the man and the bones. That he came for Mary, and he was coming for all of you and maybe even me, too. Is that who she meant? Declan Jr.?"

"Yes," Catherine answered after a long moment.

I see only his beauty. . . . Cassandra had said that, too.

Now, like then, Savannah felt a cold finger of premonition slide down her spine. She wasn't really buying into the whole thing; there was a lot of woo-woo and paranoia involved in the story, and she didn't see how it affected her. But it did get to her viscerally, no matter what she believed.

"When I get the report on the knife—whose blood's on it—I'll let you know."

"Detective, don't dismiss the danger. We're not the only ones in this man's sights. He believes he's Declan Bancroft's son, and he may act on that information. I don't have any idea what his timetable is, but be assured that he has one. Yes, I believe he killed my sister, and yes, I believe he's targeting us now. And his real father was a monster. . . ."

Savvy shook her head. She wasn't going to go there. "I understand, but I need something more than . . . conjecture," she said, for lack of a better word, "to launch an investigation. The knife is a good place to start."

"How would you feel, Detective, if the great-grandfather of the son you just bore was suddenly attacked, possibly killed, and you'd done nothing about it?"

"That's really a leap, Catherine."

"You'd feel terrible. Responsible. Sick at heart. You'd want to find him at all costs. Your sister's married to Declan's grandson. See, I do know a thing or two." She smiled but then saw something in Savvy's face and asked sharply, "What? What do you know?"

"My sister was also in an accident."

"Oh, no . . ."

"She died early this morning."

"How? How did she die?" Catherine sat up in bed, her eyes filled with horror.

"A beam fell on her at a construction site."

"*Fell* on her?"

"There's speculation that it was something more. The Seaside police are investigating, but it could just be an accident."

"You're trying to tell yourself that because you don't want it to be murder. Because you, an officer of the law, couldn't save your sister."

"That's not how it is," Savannah said sharply.

"Don't you see? It's him! It's *him.* Was your sister sexually involved with him? That was Mary's downfall, and in her son it could be worse. It *would* be worse. I've had feelings about it. He casts a spell, just like Mary did, only it's a thousand times worse!"

I asked Hale earlier if he believed in sorcery. . . .

Savannah felt a pounding in her head. Like hoofbeats clattering across her brain. "I've got to go, Catherine. I've got a baby to take care of," she murmured. She suddenly wanted to scoop up that little boy and hold him close.

"Running away won't stop him," Catherine said, the words singeing Savvy's ears as she stumbled blindly out of the room. "When you want to do something, come to Siren Song. I'll be there. I'll help you. . . ."

He was escalating. He got that. The thrills weren't as high, and he didn't want to wait as long between kills. In the back of his head he knew he was really in trouble, because his kills had been working out to more than one a day, what with Garth and Tammie, and then

Kristina, and now DeWitt, and hopefully, tonight that bastard at Bancroft Bluff who'd talked to him about the detective with such interest, kept bringing her up almost like he'd been digging at Charlie. Almost like he *knew*.

He was going to have to take care of that fucker tonight, kill ratio or no.

He drew down his ski mask until his eyes were all that was visible. The weather was complying. Goddamn terrible storm made it okay to bundle up like a robber. Ha.

He looked around the tiny studio apartment that he'd called home since he left the coast. Squalor. Damn near a cell. But he never cared. Sleep, rest, a warm and *happy* home . . . no, that wasn't Charlie's fate or future. He was destined to roam the world, to keep moving or die, like a shark.

He knew where the asshole was. Like Dimwit, he habituated the same kind of tired dives, rarely moving outside a range of three or four. There was no work on Sundays, as a rule, but that wouldn't keep his prey from hitting his favorite happy hours.

Charlie spotted him at the second place he stopped in: Bernadette's. Just Bernie's if you were one of the regulars. Big fuckin' deal. Sometimes it almost hurt that there were such losers in this world.

He pulled up his ski mask when he walked in. Otherwise he'd be too memorable later, after the fucker was a corpse and the stupid police started sniffing at his trail. Still, his hair was covered and ski masks were the attire du jour in this dead-end place. Yep, it was all good, so he sidled right up to his prey and sat down on a nearby bar stool.

"Hey," the man said, looking up from a game of pool. Charlie took note of the cue still in the asshole's hand and threw on a full-wattage smile.

"Man, this weather, huh? I wasn't gonna stay inside like those pussies who won't drive in this shit," Charlie said.

"You got that right." The man sounded kinda relieved as he leaned over the cue ball and took aim.

Did he scare people that much? Charlie wondered. Was he changing somehow? In some indefinable way? He'd always been able to pull off the Good Time Charlie persona, but something was different here somehow. . . .

"So, what are you doing here?" the man asked casually, sighting down the cue.

Was that a flutter of fear Charlie was sensing? His grin widened as he answered, "Oh, just thought you might be here on a Sunday night. Maybe there'll be another storm and there won't be work to-morrow."

"Supposed to be clear." He pushed the cue hard and smacked the cue ball into the fifteen, which careened off the eight, sending the solid black ball into the pocket.

"Too bad," Charlie observed.

"Yeah." He dropped the cue stick on the table with more force than necessary, disgusted.

"Let me buy ya a beer."

He glared at Charlie belligerently. "Yeah? What the fuck are you doing? Huh? This ain't no casual drop-in, buddy. I'm not buying it for a minute. I got a woman waiting for me. I don't need this shit. I don't know what your deal is, but I'm out."

"Whoa." Charlie lifted his hands in surrender. Inside he was grin-ning and grinning. Couldn't stop himself.

With that, his target grabbed up his ski jacket, shrugged into it, and stomped toward the door.

The man he'd been playing against observed, "Poor loser."

Charlie didn't engage with him. Didn't want to be remembered that well. He followed his prey leisurely toward the door and watched him get into his truck, spin out in the slushy snow of the parking lot, then *chink, chink, chink* away, his chains biting down to the pavement.

Pulling down his ski mask, Charlie got in his own vehicle and fol-lowed. He knew where the guy was going. He would just have to lie in wait . . . and maybe he'd get a twofer. The asshole and his woman.

His cock stirred, and he thought of the detective. She was climb-ing up Charlie's top ten hit list. Actually, she'd just leapt over Pops.

He was going to get them both soon. *Top ten? Top one hundred,* he thought with a laugh. He had a long way to go. Yessirree. No one was going to stop him.

"You feel me, bitch," he whispered, sending the detective his sexual desire in a hot, snaking wave.

Then he sent another message to his father, too, reaching in his pocket to slide his thumb along the edge of the knife tucked inside. *It's long past time for a family reunion, Pops. I'm coming for you. Soon.*

CHAPTER 23

Late Monday morning Savannah stood with Hale outside the Hertz rental agency in Seaside in a blowing wind mixed with a slap of rain, the keys to a blue Ford Escape in her gloved hands. The temperature was above freezing and rising, and the snow was off the main roads, but it felt cold as the Arctic.

Hale had come to her room this morning, early, and had caught her breast-feeding his son. She'd looked up at him, worried about his reaction, but he'd swallowed once, hard, and said, "I'm so glad he has you," and that had sent Savannah's hormones into overdrive and she'd felt the sting of tears once again.

He'd offered to take her home, but she'd asked for a ride to Hertz. Her own Escape was in the process of being picked up by Isaac's Towing and taken to a repair shop in Seaside. Baby Declan was still at the hospital; Hale was planning to pick up the car seat he and Kristina had purchased and fit it into his car this afternoon. The new nanny was meeting him at the hospital, as well.

Now, as they stood together under the meager protection of the front awning, Hale asked, "You sure you're up for this?"

Savvy was standing a little hunched over, the way she had ever since she'd gotten on her feet. The tender areas were becoming less tender, but she was still definitely sore. "I can't wait to get home and take a shower in my own shower."

He half laughed in agreement. "Yeah."

"Thanks for bringing me here."

He nodded, then asked cautiously, "Do you know what your long-term plan for Declan is?"

"You mean the breast-feeding?" Savvy asked.

"That . . . and you are his aunt, among other things. . . ." He flicked her a look, his gray eyes sober. "I always figured you'd be a big part of his life, but now . . . maybe even bigger."

"I want to be," Savvy responded. "Absolutely."

"But your job . . . it has a lot of hours, and you're with the Tillamook County Sheriff's Department. . . . It's not right around the corner."

She wanted to argue with him about everything, when in fact he was right on all counts. "I'll figure out how to pump," she said. "But I guess you'll have to use formula, too."

"I think Kristina bought some. I'd better head home and do some inventory before I meet Victoria at the hospital."

"Okay."

He bent his head to the rain and walked quickly to his TrailBlazer. She did the same, sliding into the Escape and familiarizing herself with everything inside as the vehicle was a few years newer than hers.

She didn't need chains on the main road, so she made good time down Highway 101 to Deception Bay. She'd been on the road forty minutes when she drove past the turnoff to Siren Song, and she looked up as she passed. The top floors of the lodge were visible from the road above the Douglas firs, and the place looked forbidding and cold. Or maybe that was just her imagination.

How would you feel, Detective, if the great-grandfather of the son you just bore was suddenly attacked, possibly killed, and you'd done nothing about it?

She couldn't get caught up in Catherine's craziness. And yet . . .

It's him! It's him. Was your sister sexually involved with him?

"Stop it," Savvy snapped at herself. Maybe there was someone out there named Declan who thought Declan Sr. was his father. Maybe he *was* his father. Catherine liked to spin tales, but maybe Hale's grandfather had been involved with Mary, too. Why not? If she was as sexually luring as Catherine made out, anything could have happened.

Or maybe it was true that Declan Sr. had had a love affair with Catherine Rutledge.

"Or maybe it's all fantasy," Savvy said aloud.

And yet . . . and yet . . .

When Savvy drove up the small hill to her house, the snow was still deep and undisturbed, but the Escape's four-wheel drive made it easy. She pulled into the garage, and before she hit the button to send the garage door back down, she looked at her tire tracks. The snow was already melting around them. *Good.*

Gathering up Kristina's clothes, her messenger bag, and other personal items she'd taken from the hospital, she headed up the back steps. She was sick of this weather. Sick of herself. Sick of everything. Except little Declan . . . and maybe Hale . . .

Hale.

She grimaced, remembering the sexual thrill that had shot through her last night, just after she'd finished breast-feeding the baby. Shaking her head, she aimed straight for the shower. Embarrassing, that was what it was. And weird. This wasn't normal. It wasn't . . . *her.*

An hour and a half later she was through with the shower and was blow-drying her hair. Combing it into a ponytail, she gave her body a hard look in the mirror, turning sideways. Yes, there was some pooching out. No denying that. But with exercise and a decent diet, she believed she would be back to her old self soon enough.

Feeling better, she opened her closet doors, pulling out black slacks, a dark gray shirt, and a long overcoat. She gathered up the clothes she'd brought in from her car and took them to the alcove off the kitchen, which served as her laundry room. She threw her ski jacket in the washer along with some detergent, then piled Kristina's clothes into the laundry bin that sat on top of the dryer.

So, now what? she thought. Baby Declan was being taken care of by his father and the nanny, who evoked feelings of jealousy in Savvy, which made her groan aloud at herself. "Get a grip," she told herself in disgust.

A little over a half hour later she put the wet laundry in the dryer, threw a look at the clock. Two p.m. She needed to buy a breast pump tout de suite, so she drove into Tillamook and purchased one, trying it out in the front seat of her rental, beneath the overcoat, which she'd taken off and laid over her body. Twenty minutes later she thought, *What a pain in the ass,* when it was a total trial and nothing much came out.

After that, she sat staring through the windshield for another ten minutes. Then she drove to the station.

O'Halloran had told her they would talk about whether she would be chained to desk duty on Monday. Might as well find out if that decree still stood.

Catherine refused to head upstairs to her room, partly because she wanted to put off going up those steep steps when she still felt somewhat shaky, partly because she was waiting for Earl, who was on a second trip to the hospital to pick up Ravinia and Ophelia.

Isadora said to her, "Let me get you something to eat."

"No, I'm not hungry. I just need a little time."

"I'll just get some tea and crackers." Isadora hurried off, clearly needing to do something. Catherine inwardly sighed. Everyone's solicitousness was about to kill her.

Lillibeth had parked her wheelchair directly in front of Catherine. "What happened? You don't have to go back, do you?"

"I'm fine," Catherine assured her.

"You're sure?" Cassandra asked. "It was just an accident? Just a fall?"

"Yes," Catherine said firmly. "I have a concussion. I slipped, and my head hit one of the flagstones."

"Don't do that again," Lillibeth begged.

"I don't intend to," Catherine answered with asperity.

As much as she loved her nieces, she really needed them to give her some space. There were things that needed to be done, problems that needed to be addressed, and she needed Earl's help to accomplish them.

Like exchanging the bones in the grave marked as Mary's with those in the unmarked grave, where Mary's bones actually lay.

But how to accomplish that, with all the girls—women—so attentive and aware of Catherine's every movement now?

She was pretty sure she was going to have to confide in one of them, and with God as her witness, she thought it might have to be Ravinia.

Cassandra was sitting in one of the chairs across from the couch, the side of her face fanned with jeweled light from the Tiffany lamp, which was cutting into the afternoon's gloom. The prism of colors against her cheek gave her an otherworldly look. Like Lillibeth, she questioned, "It was just an accident?"

"I'm sorry I had to leave," Catherine said, trying to assure them. "Sometimes things just happen."

"There's always a reason," Cassandra argued.

"No, there isn't." Catherine would've gotten to her feet and stalked away from them, but she was blocked by Lillibeth, and honestly, she wasn't 100 percent yet.

Isadora returned with a tray of tea and crackers and several tiny ceramic pots of strawberry and apricot jams. Nobody touched it, however, and Catherine swallowed her frustration, picked up a wafer-like cracker, and spread it with apricot jam. Isadora poured her a cup of tea, and once she was eating, everyone else finally stopped staring at her and joined in.

Ravinia had the journal, and with her nosiness, it would only be a matter of time before she started asking about the man in the grave. Maybe Catherine could head her off at the pass, but there were other issues pressing upon her.

She needed Earl to go to Echo Island and find out who was there. As far as she could tell when Isadora and Cassandra helped her into the lodge, there was no fire visible any longer; hopefully it had burned out. If at all possible, she would like to meet Earl outside the gate, where they could both see across to Echo and mark out a plan.

An hour later Earl's truck could be heard approaching, and Catherine got to her feet with relief. Lillibeth reluctantly moved her chair away, and Catherine went to the door.

"You sure you feel steady enough?" Isadora asked. Normally, she was the rock-solid lieutenant Catherine could rely on, but even she'd been rattled by Catherine's injury and trip to the hospital.

"Why did Ravinia get to go?" Lillibeth asked, a question she'd asked before.

"She came on her own," Catherine answered her, again.

Cassandra said, "I don't want you to go outside."

"Cassandra!" Catherine was at her wit's end.

"Maggie. And there's something out there. You know it, too, but you're ignoring it."

"I'm not ignoring it." Catherine was brusque. "I have things I need to do, and I appreciate your concern, all of you, but I need some space. Some time to make plans for us."

"He's coming," Cassandra said, and Lillibeth squeaked with fear and stared at her sister.

"Right now Earl's here," Catherine said. "I'm going to meet with him outside. Just . . . let me," she said in a rush of frustration.

Isadora opened the door to Ravinia and Ophelia, who entered in a blast of cold air. Immediately, Ophelia said, "Where are you going?"

"Just to talk to Earl. I'll be right back," Catherine told her.

She brushed past them, choosing her steps carefully, still faintly dizzy. She felt someone take her arm and guide her and realized Ravinia was beside her, leading her up the flagstone path to the gate.

"I'm not going to have you fall again," Ravinia said.

"You just want to know what I'm going to talk to Earl about," Catherine accused.

"That too. But you're not steady enough to walk by yourself."

Catherine pressed her lips together, conceding the point. Time was racing by, and she didn't have the luxury of arguing with her, a losing game with Ravinia in the best of circumstances.

Earl was waiting patiently outside the gates, though they were un-locked and Catherine passed through to meet him. He had a key of his own, which he used only when he came to do yard work or re-pairs. With Ravinia beside her, Catherine felt oddly unsure of what to say. Earl frowned upon seeing the girl, but there was nothing to do.

"I need someone to go to Echo and find out who's there," Cather-ine said. She glanced toward the island, which was a dark mound.

Earl's frown deepened, but he nodded slowly. "I will see if I can."

"But then there's that other matter," Catherine said. The one she'd told him about when he drove her from the hospital: switching the bodies in the graves.

"When can that be done?" Earl asked her. Like Lillibeth, he'd asked that question before, several times, and Catherine had never had an answer.

"What other matter?" Ravinia asked.

Catherine felt a faint stirring inside herself, the harbinger of pre-cognition. She waited, and thought, *He's coming. . . .*

It might be dangerous to go to Echo Island, and not just because of the weather and the approach, she thought with an inward shudder.

"What other matter?" Ravinia repeated.

"The graves," Catherine said suddenly. "If you can't get to Echo, let's take care of the graves first."

"All right," Earl said.

"Tonight," Catherine replied, pressing.

"Tomorrow," Earl said after a moment of thought, and then he locked the gate and headed out.

Catherine turned back toward the lodge with Ravinia at her side. "What's with the graves?" Ravinia asked.

"Detective Dunbar says there will be an exhumation, so I need to make sure your mother's bones are in the ground beside her headstone."

Ravinia looked at her carefully. "They're not now?"

"No. They're in a separate place in the graveyard."

"So, whose bones are in there?"

Catherine felt her stomach tighten. She hadn't talked about it. Ever. Not even with Mary, who'd been there, who'd saved her . . . "The bastard who tried to rape me. The one your mother killed in order to stop him."

"My mother killed someone?" Ravinia asked in surprise.

"And he deserved to die," Catherine responded tautly.

"My God, Aunt Catherine . . . who? One of our . . . fathers?"

Catherine thought back to the evil monster who'd pushed her into the closet, his hot breath stinking of bourbon, his eyes a malevolent blue flame that burned into her as his hands crawled all over her and he bit at her neck and breasts. "Yes," she stated flatly. "But he sired a son, not a daughter. And I think he's out there on Echo, biding his time. Waiting to come for us." She looked to the west, but there was no fire tonight. Then she turned to Ravinia, who was standing immobile, waiting for more. "I may need your help in this endeavor."

"Just tell me what I have to do," Ravinia said, on the same wavelength as Catherine for possibly the first time in her life.

* * *

Conversation stopped as soon as Savvy eased into the chair behind her desk. Lang wasn't immediately visible, but she'd seen his car in the back lot. Burghsmith looked to Deputy Delaney, who'd been off for a week on a pre-Thanksgiving vacation, and Delaney looked to Clausen, who finally said, "Lang filled us in. Real sorry about Kristina."

"Yeah." If Savannah said anything more, she risked those tears that were hovering behind her eyelids, ready to jump out at a moment's notice.

"Congrats on the baby," he added. "O'Halloran really put the fear of God into you about desk duty, huh?"

He was trying to keep things light, but his eyes were serious and she could feel the empathy, even if he wasn't showing it. This was not good. If they were going to be *nice* to her, damn it, she was not going to make it through the day.

Lang appeared from the break room with a cup of coffee and an individual-size bag of barbecue potato chips from the vending machine. Seeing Savvy, he put the cup and chips on his desk and sat down across from her. "You really did come to work."

"I said I was going to."

"Think you and I could talk alone for a moment?"

"Sure," she said slowly, wondering what was coming. She looked around, but before she could get up from her seat, the other officers left in a herd, as if they knew what was coming and didn't want to be anywhere around. "Uh-oh," she said.

"You didn't mention yesterday that Kristina's death was a homicide."

"That hasn't been fully determined yet," she said.

"Yeah, it has." Lang looked at her with sympathy. "O'Halloran took a call from Detective Hamett out of Seaside. They interviewed Hale Bancroft yesterday."

"St. Cloud, Lang. St. Cloud," she said, her face flushing from growing fury. "I just saw Hale, and he didn't say anything about it."

Lang lifted his palms. "Maybe there's a reason for that."

"Don't play word games. What are you suggesting?"

"That maybe he didn't want you to know that they were looking at him."

"Looking at him," she repeated. "You're kidding. You have to be kidding. Hale? It's not him."

"He is her husband," Lang pointed out, "and by his own admission, they were working on their marriage, so something wasn't right between them."

"Hale said that? To Hamett?"

"And his partner, Evinrud. They went to Hale's house yesterday afternoon and asked him where he was Saturday night, and he said his wife never came home Friday night at all, and that he hadn't seen her since Friday afternoon."

"Hale did not kill my sister."

"A neighbor saw a white truck outside the crime scene that night. Your sister's car was parked there, and the truck was just down the street."

"Hale drives a black TrailBlazer. I just saw him getting into it."

"Bancroft Development trucks are all white. That was confirmed by St. Cloud as well."

"Jesus, Lang."

"I'm just telling you what I know."

"Then it's someone else. Someone . . . maybe . . . Kristina was involved with."

Lang gave her a long look. "Are you saying she was involved with someone?"

"I'm saying that I have some other ideas. Not Hale St. Cloud. Where's the evidence report on the Donatellas?"

"You still want that?"

"Yes, I want it." Savvy was sick of being treated like she was somehow deficient in her skills as a detective.

"Okay, but I want to know what you're thinking about your sister. Hamett and Evinrud already want to talk to you."

"I need to talk to Hale first."

"Savvy. What the hell? I'm telling you he's a suspect. You can't talk to—"

"Not about the case," she snapped in frustration. "About his wife. My sister. And whether he thought she might be having an affair. That's what I want to talk to him about. If he doesn't know, I want to be the one to tell him."

"Let Hamett and—"

"No! That's just what I'm saying! You're not listening. Owen DeWitt suggested that Kristina might have met someone . . . at the Donatellas. Someone she was meeting there."

"Holy shit . . ."

"That's why I want to talk to Hale first. I don't think he killed my sister, but believe me, if he did, I'll be first in line to string him up."

"You're too close to this."

"God damn it, Lang." Savvy jumped to her feet just as O'Halloran looked into the squad room.

"When you have a minute, want to come to my office?" he said.

"We're not done," Lang said as Savannah headed after O'Halloran. When Savvy ignored him, he added, "You said you got some files from Bancroft Development?"

She stopped at the door to the sheriff's office and called back, "They're in my Escape, which is at Isaac's Towing by now, most likely."

"Ah. Okay. I'll get somebody to retrieve them."

"I looked them over. I don't think there was anything there."

He nodded as if he heard her, but she realized, with another spurt of renewed anger, that he thought she was just covering up for Hale some more. Her heart was pumping wildly, she realized as she entered O'Halloran's sanctum. Hale wasn't involved. He wasn't. But he was being targeted like a main suspect, and what did that mean for little Declan? And how come he hadn't told her about the interview with the cops?

And who could have wanted to kill her sister? Kristina had had her issues, yes, but she wasn't a bad person. Was it Declan Jr.? Whose sexual lure might be as powerful as his mother's. Who maybe had drawn Savvy's sister under his spell so powerfully that she thought it was *sorcery*. Whose sickness and lust for revenge or payback or blood-lust, or whatever, had put them all in his sights, the women of Siren Song and Declan Bancroft, and herself as well.

Did that even sound like a sane argument?

She needed to talk to Hale. And she needed to talk to Declan Sr.

"Take a seat, Savannah," the sheriff said, gesturing to the chairs on the opposite side of the desk as he settled his bulk into his desk chair, which creaked and groaned under his weight. When she did as instructed, he said, "Last week we were going to put you on desk duty today, as I recall."

"We were going to meet today and discuss it."

"And how are you feeling?"

"A lot of things have happened. I'm . . . still processing," Savvy admitted.

"But you're here at work."

"This is the one area that I feel certain about right now. My job." She gave him a weak smile. Lang's words still rang in her ears, and her head was full of thoughts of Hale . . . and little Declan . . . and Catherine's warnings. . . .

"You still want to be out in the field."

"Yes." She was adamant.

"If you feel ready, I don't see any reason to hold you back," he said.

"Thank you," she said with feeling.

"I'm sorry about your sister. We all are."

Savvy nodded as she got to her feet. Feeling like she'd gotten past a huge obstacle, she walked back toward the squad room and then felt something wet on her chest. Looking down at her gray shirt, she saw two wet spots spreading across her breasts.

May Johnson was just coming out of the break room. "What?" she asked, seeing Savvy had stopped short.

"My milk just came in," Savannah said.

"What did you say?" Hale asked, the receiver of his landline pressed to his ear, as he watched the nanny, Victoria, carry the baby toward his nursery, cooing to him.

"Your mother's on her way," Declan repeated, sounding pleased.

Hale let that information process slowly. He'd figured out how to put in the new car seat, and he'd driven Declan home, with Victoria following behind in her car. His head was full of thoughts of bringing the baby home and settling him in. Thinking of his mother, who, in her way, was as bullheaded as her father—probably why they didn't get along—made him feel like the precarious merry-go-round he'd been riding was about to spin out of control. "My mother is flying in from Philadelphia?"

"I told her about little Declan. She should be here in Portland tonight."

"How's she getting to the coast? The roads are still a mess."

"Oh, they're fine. I saw it on the news. She's a grandmother, Hale," he said, as if that explained away irrational behavior. "She's going to want to see the boy. I do too. I'm getting out of my driveway this afternoon and coming up there to see him. Maybe I'll stay overnight."

"I'll have someone come get you," Hale said quickly. His grandfather's driving ability was suspect as best and didn't allow for any unexpected changes, like hazardous weather conditions.

"The roads are clearing. It's fine."

"They're not that fine." Hale thought his grandfather's anxiousness could also be attributed to his belief that someone had been at his house.

"All right. Have someone come get me," Declan grumbled. "But I want to be there when Janet shows up."

"Mom shouldn't drive over the mountains yet. It's not safe."

"Well, you tell her that when she lands. See how that goes over."

Though Hale rarely saw his mother these days, he knew of her formidable will. What the hell? He'd inherited some of that, too. He could handle her. But he sure wished Declan would have let him tell his mother about the baby first. The surprising part was Janet and Declan rarely talked to each other. They'd been damn near estranged for all of Hale's adult life.

"What time is she getting in?" Hale asked.

"Seven or so."

"I'll leave a message on her cell. What made you decide to tell her about the baby?"

"Well, you didn't seem to be picking up the phone."

"I've been a little busy," Hale said dryly.

"*Ack.* For your own son?"

Hale held on to his temper with an effort. While visiting his grandfather the day before he'd laid out all the events that had surrounded baby Declan's birth, the terrible weather and Kristina's death, expecting a different reaction from Declan's rather befuddled "Well, why couldn't you just wait for the ambulance, son?"

With his grandfather, sometimes explanations were a waste of breath. Hale had left him then, heading home to take a shower, drink a glass of red wine, and fall into bed. Sylvie had left him a message with Victoria Phelan's number, and he'd made plans to meet with the nanny at the hospital this afternoon. As soon as he got up, he'd gone to see Savannah and the baby. Savvy had been on one foot and the other to get home, so he'd taken her into Seaside so she could rent a car. Then he'd headed to Ocean Park to meet Victoria and pick up baby Declan.

"I'll come get you," he said to his grandfather as Victoria cruised into the kitchen.

"I'll get my overnight bag ready," Declan said.

"You have formula?" Victoria mouthed, holding up a baby bottle, and he pointed to the cabinet that Kristina had chosen for baby supplies.

Victoria was slim and attractive, and he hoped she was going to be good for the baby. She'd signed a contract with Kristina, so now he and she were forging ahead, seeing how things worked out. There was nothing wrong with her. She just seemed kind of . . . young . . . and, well, he wished that Savannah were here. He wanted her to be with Declan, to be at the house. He wanted her to be Declan's mother in Kristina's place. But that was never the way it was supposed to be. He was just . . . wishful.

"What?" Hale asked, realizing his grandfather had said something that he'd missed.

"I said, your father was a good man. I'm just sorry Janet never saw that."

"Yeah."

Hale's mind moved to the call he'd received from the medical examiner's office. They'd done an autopsy on Kristina's body earlier today. As far as he knew, there had been no surprises. Death was caused by blunt force trauma to the head. Kristina's body had been sent for cremation, and Hale needed to think about a memorial service. But he wanted to talk to Savannah about that.

"I never wanted her to marry Preston, but he was the right man for her," Declan was going on.

"We can talk about this later."

"Sure, sure."

"I'll be there in about an hour," Hale said, hanging up.

Declan was thinking about Preston because of the baby's birth. Hale's father had been in the back of Hale's mind, too: how he wouldn't be able to meet his grandson, how his slow death from liver cancer had robbed him of that chance, how the cancer had come on almost immediately after Janet divorced him. Though separate, those two issues always collided in Hale's mind: his parents' divorce and his father's declining health. Janet had split from Preston St. Cloud when Hale was about eighteen, and she'd met her current husband, Lee Spurrier, whose family was in the banking business in Philadelphia, almost immediately afterward. While Hale was in his first year of college, Janet Bancroft St. Cloud became Janet Bancroft St. Cloud Spurrier and moved to the East Coast. Preston's health started declining at the same time, and as soon as Hale graduated, though he started working for Declan, he was half taking care of his father at the same time.

Kristina crossed his path at the Bridgeport Bistro one night, at his lowest point. She knew of his grandfather, having grown up around Tillamook, which was just south of his grandfather's Deception Bay home, and she'd heard about Hale's father's illness. She'd been a willing ear and a godsend while Hale juggled all the pieces of his life. He'd been damn near overwhelmed, and Kristina had come into his life at the right time. He'd married her shortly after Preston passed away, only later realizing that he barely knew her.

He watched Victoria heat up a bottle of formula in the microwave. Her hair was long and dark brown, and she wore a skintight T-shirt and skinny jeans.

She sensed him looking at her and turned to give him a bright smile. "He's a beautiful little boy."

"Thank you." Hale hesitated, then asked, "Have you had much experience as a nanny?"

"Oh, it's all in my profile. The one I gave to your wife. Oh. Sorry. It's just so weird that she's gone."

Hale nodded. "How long can you be here today?"

She blinked at him. "Ummm . . . I thought I was living with you." A red flush crept up her skin. "I mean, I'm moving here, right?"

"I'm just catching up slowly. Do you have a copy of your profile? And the contract?"

"Sure. It's in my room."

She walked down the hall to the spare bedroom across the hall from the nursery. Magda, their cleaning woman, had come in today and had changed all the sheets, crying and crossing her heart as she did her work, saying, "Mrs. St. Cloud said she wanted the beds changed for the baby and maybe some guests. I was going to do it last week . . . but, oh, now . . ." When she trailed off into more tears, Hale had assured her that she was doing what Kristina had wanted and that was a good thing.

It had reminded him again, like almost everything did, that the world had changed in the last two days.

Hale started thinking about his four-bedroom house and did a mental head count: one for the baby, one for Victoria, one for his grandfather, one for his mother, maybe, and one for himself. Not enough. When Janet showed, somebody was going to be sleeping on the couch. Of course, maybe it was a moot point, if Detectives Hamett and Evinrud decided he'd killed his wife, and hauled him off to jail.

Grabbing up his cell phone from where he'd left it on the counter, he went to his favorites list and touched the number for Savannah's cell. Maybe she could give him an idea what the hell was going on.

CHAPTER 24

Savvy heard Hale's ring tone and dragged her attention from the physical evidence report on the Donatella homicides. She scrabbled around in her messenger bag until she found the phone. "Hello?" she said a little cautiously. She was in the squad room, and she really wanted to talk to him without anyone overhearing.

"Hey," he said, sounding relieved. "How's it going?"

"Not bad, I guess."

"Are you at home?"

"No, I'm at the department."

"You went back to work already?" He didn't try to hide his surprise.

"Yeah. How's the baby?" she asked.

"Good." He gave her a quick rundown of picking Declan up from the hospital and how the nanny was settling in, and the fact that his grandfather and his mother were heading his way.

"You're going to have a houseful," she said, her mind already moving ahead. "I hear you were visited by two Seaside detectives."

"Yeah."

There was a moment when neither of them said anything. Then Savvy said, "I'm working on some other angles."

"To Kristina's murder? Is that allowed?"

"Not really. No. But there are some questions that cropped up when I was in Portland that I wanted to go over with you."

There was a weighty pause. Then he said in a cooler voice, "Are you buying this? That I had something to do with Kristina's *death?*"

"I talked to a couple of people who believe Kristina was having an affair. That's more where I'm going."

"Who said that?"

She ignored the question and asked, "You never thought that? Never had a suspicion?"

"Kristina having an affair? No . . ." She could practically hear the wheels turning in his mind. "No," he said again, then added, "One of the reasons I called was to talk about a memorial service for her."

Savvy felt like a heel. "Absolutely. I'm happy to help any way I can. I'm sorry, Hale."

"I know."

"Look, I don't mean to be a dog with a bone, but you never even got the inkling that she might be seeing someone?"

"What I thought was, she's acting crazy. That's about as far as it went. *She* thought she was going crazy."

"It doesn't seem right to me, either, but then I don't know," Savvy admitted. "I've got this strange theory, and it's . . . I don't want to talk about it now. I'll come to your house."

"Okay."

"I'm going to wrap things up here," she said, thinking about the breast pump and a trip to the ladies' room. "I've got a few things to do. Then I'll come your way."

"Bring an overnight bag, just in case. It's terrible weather, and you might want to stay," he said before he hung up.

Savvy replaced her phone in her messenger bag. No, she wasn't going to stay over at Hale and Kristina's house. There was a nanny in place for the baby, and she couldn't suffer any more of the dangerous thoughts that seemed to infect her reason whenever she was too close to Hale.

Dragging her attention back to the case, she glanced back down at the report again. There was nothing in it she hadn't seen before. In her mind's eye she thought about Owen DeWitt's comment about Charlie with Kristina at the Donatella house. "He had her up against the wall. Banging her like crazy . . ." She checked again to see if the techs had found anything—blood, tissue, semen—other than that of the victims themselves, but there was no mention of it. The techs had taken fingerprints and had used luminol over most of the house, looking for blood traces from tissue or semen or actual blood from the perpetrator, but there wasn't anything definitive.

Catherine had said Declan Jr. was too careful to leave any evidence.

Was he the man Kristina had been with, if she'd been with anyone at all . . . ?

Savvy thought about that hard for a few moments, testing her own gut feeling on the subject. She did believe Kristina was having an affair, whether Hale knew it or not. She also believed that affair had gone sour; Kristina had wanted out. She'd said as much to Savannah, and all her talk of sorcery, of feeling weird, and not being herself, seemed to add credence to that theory.

Lang had been gone for a while, and now he returned, running his hands through his damp hair as he retook his seat at his desk. "Cold rain," he said. Savvy was considering how to tell him she'd talked to Hale, when he added, "Finally reached Curtis about those deaths outside the Rib-I last Thursday."

"Yeah?"

"Nothing. The guy who killed those two is a ghost. Meets 'em outside, then pops 'em. End of story."

"Hmmm."

"There was a gal inside the bar who saw Garth, the male victim, get in some guy's grill about hitting on his date, Tammie, the female victim. Curtis asked for a description, but all she said was that she thought he was good-looking. Had a big smile. Tammie and Garth must've made up, because they were having sex in the parking lot when the killer attacked them."

Savvy thought about her meeting with DeWitt. "A lot of restaurants and bars in Portland, and I was at the Rib-I two nights later, meeting with Owen DeWitt."

"I know."

They looked at each other. "DeWitt said some things about my sister," Savvy admitted.

"Uh-oh."

She smiled faintly. "Yeah. Like she was having sex with somebody up against the wall in the Donatella house on which the killer spray painted *blood money*. Said he saw her there with the same guy a couple of times when he was at the site, looking for some proof that it wasn't his fault the dune failed. DeWitt's like that. A blame shifter."

"That's why you wanted to recheck the physical evidence?"

She nodded. "I didn't find anything. I don't even really know if I believe DeWitt's account."

"Have you told St. Cloud this?"

"Not all of it. I asked him if he thought Kristina had a lover, and he acted like it was news."

"You talked to him today?"

"Yep." She related her conversation with Hale, and his expression darkened until she finished with, "We have a memorial service to plan together. I'm going to talk to him today, tomorrow, every day."

"Don't get in Hamett and Evinrud's way. I'm just sayin'."

"I'm just sayin' that someone other than Hale killed my sister. I want to talk to DeWitt again."

"Hell, no. Savannah," he said, spreading his hands in a "What gives?" gesture.

"If Kristina's death has anything to do with the Donatella homicides, that's our case."

"*I'll* talk to DeWitt."

"Okay, fine."

She'd already moved on to another thought: Paulie Williamson, the ex-Portland Bancroft Development manager who'd moved to Tucson. Clark Russo had given her his number.

For a brief moment, she thought about telling Lang what Catherine had said about Mary's son Declan. How he was coming after them, and Declan Sr., too. How he might have been "gifted" with Mary's strange sexual lure. How the boys were so much more affected than the girls. Lang knew Catherine well. Knew about the woo-woo. He might give the whole thing some credence, even.

"Have Hamett and Evinrud reached you yet?" Lang asked.

"No."

"They will. Be careful what you say to their prime suspect," he said before heading toward the break room with an empty coffee cup.

Savvy gritted her teeth, and then the phone on her desk rang, and she answered, "Detective Dunbar," checking the clock on the wall. Four p.m.

"Hey, Savvy," a female voice said. It was Geena Cho, who worked dispatch for the TCSD. "You gotta call from Toonie at the shelter. She said someone there named Mickey really needs to talk to you."

"Yeah, I know."

"You gonna call her?" Cho asked, hearing Savannah's lack of enthusiasm. "'Cause if you don't, she'll keep calling and calling and calling."

"I'll stop by there tonight," Savannah promised, adding it to her list of errands to run before she could make her way to Hale's house.

"You sure?" she asked.

"Yes! I'll go. If Toonie calls again before I get there, let her know I'll be there within the hour."

Ravinia watched as Catherine began the trek upstairs to her bedroom, looking exhausted. With much solicitation, Isadora and Cassandra helped her to the second floor, while in the great room below, Ophelia, Lillibeth, and Ravinia watched their progress.

"Aunt Catherine wanted to see Earl again," Lillibeth said, sounding worried.

"She always wants to see Earl," Ravinia answered with a shrug. She didn't want anyone questioning what had transpired between her aunt and Earl. Not with some grave digging in her near future. She suppressed a shiver at the thought.

"Did they say anything while you were with them?" Ophelia asked casually.

Ravinia slid a look at her sister, but Ophelia's bland expression gave nothing away. *Careful,* she warned herself.

"Not particularly. Let's turn the TV on," Ravinia said and walked over to the old set, switching it on. Lillibeth's attention span was such that she would tune in to just about anything.

She half expected Ophelia to keep badgering her, but she just stood by while Ravinia channel surfed until she found something their antenna would pick up other than news: an ancient episode of *Gilligan's Island.*

"We are going to get cable TV," Ravinia stated, a challenging tone in her voice, as she left the room, heading toward the kitchen. Ophelia followed after her immediately, but Lillibeth stayed with the television program.

"I thought you were leaving," Ophelia said.

"You sound kind of anxious to get rid of me."

"That's not it."

"What's your deal?" Ravinia demanded, taking in Ophelia's long dress and the loose bun in her hair. "You've been drinking Aunt Catherine's Kool-Aid a long time, but you've got a cell phone, and you've been sewing me pants and shirts like it's your job. Yet you look like that." She swept her hand up and down, pointing out her sister's dress.

"Well, you've certainly picked up some idioms and colloquial terms from outside the gates. Part of your new friendships?"

"You'd better believe it," Ravinia said with a snort. "Last summer I thought this imprisonment was over, but then you and Aunt Catherine and Isadora decided it wasn't. I'm not going to live like this."

"You know it was Aunt Catherine's idea to shut the gates again."

"Well, it hasn't worked. Whoever she's trying to keep out is coming. Just ask Cassandra. 'He's coming.' She damn near can't say anything else."

"That's not true."

"Yes, it is, Ophelia," Ravinia said, exasperated. "This whole thing is screwed up!"

"You want cable TV?" Ophelia shot back. "Fine. You're talking to the right person. I run the books for Catherine, for all of us, and yes, I think we need a new television, and yes, maybe the gates should be opened again."

Not yet, though, Ravinia thought with a stab of fear. She'd gone into her rant because it was what she always did, but she needed to help Catherine move the bones before anything changed. Still, she had to play a part. "Hallelujah. She sees the light!"

"Do you know how we survive here? How we get the money to pay for the electricity and the food we don't grow and store on our own?" Ophelia demanded.

Ravinia's fear turned to irritation. "We have lots of property. We get rent. I don't need an economics lesson."

"Somebody has to run things around here. Catherine can't do it all."

"She pretty much has so far. And she has Isadora, too."

"Isadora helps with housework and meals. She doesn't work with the finances at all. You want better television? How about electricity on every floor? How about you learn how to drive a car, like I did." Ophelia's blue eyes glimmered.

"What? You don't know how to drive."

"Last summer I studied and practiced, and then I took the test with the Buick and passed."

"Bull. Shit."

"You were just too busy running away to notice."

"Somebody here would have known," Ravinia retorted in disbelief.

"Aunt Catherine knew. She took me out for driving lessons. You were gone all the time. Locked in your room, or out running around at night with all your new friends."

"You made me these clothes so I could!" Ravinia glanced down at the pants and shirt that covered her slim body.

"I know what you want. I know you think you need to be free of these walls. So I helped you. When Catherine asked me about it, I told her what I'm telling you now. That you need to be free of these walls."

"She told me if I left, I could never come back."

"She's afraid, Ravinia. For all of us, and there are people out there that want to really harm us."

It felt like Ophelia was trying to tell her something. Something she didn't want to state aloud. "How do you know that?" Ravinia asked.

"History. Justice was bent on killing us, and we're lucky he was killed, because he would have never given up."

"That's not all it is. You know something."

Ophelia pressed her lips together, her blue eyes holding Ravinia's. She had opened her mouth to say something when they heard Isadora and Cassandra coming back down the stairs.

"Ophelia, what do you know?" Ravinia hissed.

She shook her head and threw back, "What did you and Catherine and Earl talk about?"

Stalemate. She wasn't going to even hint at the future body switching. She didn't know when and how that was going to happen, but she wasn't going to trust Ophelia with the information just yet.

Something crossed her older sister's face—a flicker of surprise and alarm—just as Cassandra and Isadora entered the kitchen and Cassandra asked, "What are you two whispering about?"

Ravinia waited for Ophelia to say something, but she seemed too distracted to answer. "Ophelia has her driver's license," Ravinia said into the gap.

Cassandra's large-pupiled eyes moved from Ravinia to Ophelia. "You're leaving?" she asked tremulously.

"No. We were talking about . . . destiny," Ophelia said, still locked in her own thoughts.

"Whose destiny?" Cassandra asked.

"Yours, Cassandra," Ravinia snapped, sick of this conversation. She needed to get away from all of them.

"My name's Maggie now," she cried. "Why can't you call me that?"

"Because I just can't, okay?" Ravinia strode out of the room and ran upstairs, grabbing her bag from her bedroom closet that held the items she needed to leave: a change of clothes, a flashlight, the few dollars that she'd taken from Catherine's purse. Yes, she was a thief, but she'd pay them back someday, when she was able to. And as soon as she got some real money, she was going to buy some real clothes from real stores.

This graveyard rendezvous couldn't come soon enough. Earl had said tomorrow night, but Ravinia wanted to leave *now*. Every nerve in her body felt like it was jumping around. She just had to go. But she couldn't. Not yet. Not till after tomorrow night.

Exhaling heavily, she touched a match to her oil lamp, as the evening light was all but gone. Then she sank onto her bed and felt the journal tucked beneath her shirt at the back of her waistband.

She would keep reading her mother's diary, even though apart from a few strange passages whose meaning she hadn't yet figured out, it was kind of a snooze.

But then . . . after tomorrow . . . she was outta here for good.

Savvy made two stops before heading to the shelter: the pharmacy where she'd gotten the breast pump, this time for some nursing pads; and then back to her house for a quick freshening up and a peanut butter and jelly sandwich. Then she was on her way north again, and she would have skipped Mickey and the shelter entirely except for the niggling sense of duty that she couldn't ignore. She'd said she would go, so she might as well follow through. She had a feeling Mickey was the type to keep calling until she did.

The Savior's Lighthouse was a long, low building that had once been a mom-and-pop grocery store on the north end of Tillamook. Althea Tunewell was the force behind the shelter's existence, and she was fiercely devoted to taking care of the homeless men, women, and children who passed through her door. Toonie had been homeless herself for a short time in her youth, and she'd made social work and teaching others about the goodness of God and his son, Jesus, her mission in life.

Savannah ducked her head against a very cold and insistent rain as she headed inside. She wasn't really sure why she was even here, but Toonie generally didn't call the TCSD without a good reason.

Inside the place smelled like canned corn and cigarettes, the cigarette odor seemingly embedded in the walls, as no one was allowed to smoke indoors. Savvy's stomach reacted with an uncomfortable lurch, and she determined to make this visit short and sweet.

Toonie was talking to a woman whose hair looked in need of a serious washing and who also had her own aroma, nothing good. The woman smiled when Savvy approached, and asked, "You here for the meetin', sister?"

"No, she's here to see me. Go on now, Jolene. Join the others," Toonie said before Savannah could answer.

"Jesus loves you," Jolene said as she turned away, touching at her hair after seeing Savannah.

"I'm so sorry about your sister," Toonie said. "How are you doing?"

"I'm okay."

"You're not okay by a long shot, honey. We both know that. I don't mean to add to your troubles, especially since you just had your baby, but I felt that you needed to talk to Mickey."

"I'm not sure I can help him—" Savvy said, starting to demur, but Toonie interrupted quickly.

"Oh, I thought you understood. I think Mickey may be able to help you with that investigation of yours."

"I didn't get that message," she said.

"He's been talking about you and your baby. Talking about Bancroft Bluff and that house he was found in."

The Pembertons' house, before it was purchased back by Bancroft Development. "He was trying to start a fire inside it," Savvy said.

"Yes. I know." She thought about something for a moment, then nodded, as if she'd come to a conclusion. "Could you come into my office for a moment? This won't take long."

Savvy just managed to keep herself from checking her watch as she followed Toonie through the kitchen to a small room beyond, which might have once been a large supply closet but was now crowded with a desk, a chair, and a fairly new laptop computer. Bookshelves held several copies of the Bible, books on theology, and a few on institution management.

Toonie gestured to a seat, and Savannah sat down on the edge. She wanted to get going soon and didn't want to give the wrong impression.

"I'll make this quick," Toonie said in response. "Mickey has issues with reality, as I'm sure you noticed, but I believe it's only recently that he couldn't handle the pressures of his life. His family's been in touch with him, but he's unable to accept them yet. He needs medication, and he won't take it. Says it's too expensive, and he's right, but he could get dispensation if he filled out the right forms."

"I hate to be pushy, but you said he could help me."

"Just bear with me a small moment or two more." She pressed her forefinger and thumb together to show Savvy just how small it would be. "Mickey's a Foothiller. Not a term I would call the mix of Native Americans and whites who live in that area around Deception Bay, but it's what they call themselves."

"I know about the Foothillers," Savvy said.

"Do you know that they possess some . . . oh, ESP, I guess you'd call it?"

Savvy held her gaze. "Like psychic gifts?"

She lifted her hands as if to negate the words that she was forcing herself to say. "I only believe in God's gifts to us. Our souls. Our integrity. Our concern for our fellow man, but . . ."

"But?"

"Mickey believes in God and Jesus and a whole host of other religious figures associated with the Native American culture and, well, you name it. I'm sure Buddha's in there somewhere, if you asked him. I don't pretend to understand it all, but he is surprisingly accurate in predicting . . . coming misfortune."

"Okay." Over the past week Savannah had been so inundated with talk of psychic gifts and paranormal woo-woo that she was beginning to become inured to it.

"He says, and I'm paraphrasing here, that the devil is coming and you need to burn him to send him back to hell. He says that he saw him at Bancroft Bluff."

"Mickey saw the devil at Bancroft Bluff?" Savvy asked. She wanted to say, "The devil was already there and killed the Donatellas," but she waited for Toonie to finish, as she was obviously coming to a point. *Small moment, my ass,* she thought.

"He sings 'Jesus Loves Me' to ward away the devil. He thinks it keeps him and people around him safe."

"He was singing it when we took him into custody."

"Trying to save you and your baby, too, I'll wager." She cleared her throat. "Several nights ago he caught the news, and he saw a picture of your sister. He said, 'That's her. That's the one Satan's taking to the bluff,' or something like that. I asked, 'Who?' and he pointed to your sister and said, 'We need to tell that nice police lady who's having the baby Jesus. She'll send him back to hell. Tell her to burn him.'"

Savvy's throat tightened. "He saw my sister inside one of the houses at Bancroft Bluff?"

"That's what he says."

"Do you believe him?"

Toonie struggled to come up with an answer. "I don't believe he saw the devil in corporeal form, no. But I think he saw something that frightened him."

"How long has he been going to the Pemberton house? I didn't think it was the first time when we picked him up."

"Would you like to speak to him? I know he'd like to talk to you."

No, she didn't want to talk to him. But if he'd seen Kristina somewhere at Bancroft Bluff . . . "Sure," she agreed.

"We're just getting ready for dinner, so I'll take you to the dining room."

Savvy followed Toonie down a short hallway that connected the main room to the kitchen and Toonie's office and ended at another large room, full of folding tables with white plastic covers. A line of men and women was forming, and about three people from the end stood Mickey. His hair had been combed, but his beard was still straggly, and his clothes didn't look much cleaner. Toonie instructed Savvy to take a seat on one of the benches that lined the perimeter wall, and she went over to Mickey and said something to him. Immediately, his attention jumped to Savannah, and he left the line and racewalked across the room so fast that Savvy tightened her grip on the messenger bag, which lay over her shoulder and currently held her gun.

He leaned in close, and she couldn't help but pull back slightly. "I saw her with the devil," he whispered intensely.

"You mean my sister, somewhere at Bancroft Bluff?"

He blinked rapidly. "Your sister?"

"The woman you saw on the news," Savvy explained.

"Oh, yes! Yes. The pretty lady. She was with *him*."

"Where did you see them?"

"They went inside the house." He looked around nervously.

"The house you were in when I saw you last week?"

"That's my house," he declared strongly. "They were in the other one, with the red tile roof."

"The Donatella house is a Spanish Colonial, and it has a red tile roof," Savvy said.

He nodded gravely. "The house where the people died. Marcus and Chandra Donatella."

"Yes," Savvy said, surprised that he knew their names.

"Yes," he repeated, then said, "They went inside, but Marcus and Chandra weren't there yet."

Savvy blinked at him. "What?"

"They got there first. The pretty lady and the devil." He leaned even closer. "I had to hide. Couldn't make my fire while they were there, because they would know I was there, you know?"

"You saw Marcus and Chandra Donatella come later, to join them?"

"The devil killed them. Bang, bang!" His sudden yell made Savvy jump.

After a moment, while she waited for her heart rate to stop thundering, she asked carefully, "You heard the shots when the Donatellas were executed?"

"Bang, bang," he said again, much softer. "And then the pretty lady came out again, but you can't run from the devil." He turned away, his lips quivering. "'Jesus loves me! This I know, cuz the Bible tells me so. Little ones to Him belong. They are weak, but He is strong. . . .'"

Savannah couldn't take it in. Kristina was on-site when the Donatellas were murdered? She hadn't fully believed Owen DeWitt. She'd ignored Nadine Gretz's comments about Kristina, as well. But something had gone on between Kristina and another man. Something that maybe was connected to the Donatella murders? Who was this mysterious other man?

Declan Jr.

"I'm sorry about your sister. She was very pretty. I saw her on the television."

"Thank you," Savvy said distractedly.

"Where's your baby? What happened to your baby!"

"I had the baby. The baby's fine. He's at his father's house, doing just fine."

"Keep baby Jesus safe," he advised.

Steeling herself, Savvy asked, "What were they doing, my sister and the devil?"

"Fucking."

Mickey's matter-of-fact tone felt like a hard slap. "Does the devil look like a man? Someone you might recognize?"

"It's a disguise."

"But if you could describe him, what would you say? Look behind the disguise."

"Oh, the devil is her husband. That's who he is. He took her to his mansion and made her his. . . ."

CHAPTER 25

Savvy ran through the rain to her rented SUV and scrolled through the list of numbers on her cell phone, looking for Owen DeWitt's. She didn't have it, she realized. *Damn.* She had the list she'd been given of all the Bancroft employees and former employees, and she had almost all their contact numbers, but she hadn't gotten DeWitt's when she met him Saturday at the Rib-I. She'd only given him hers.

But she had Clark Russo's, so she quickly phoned him. He answered just before the call went to voicemail, and she quickly told him what she needed.

"Let's see," he said, taking a moment to look up the number on his own phone. "I'm really sorry about your sister, Detective Dunbar. I always liked her."

"Thank you."

Savvy visualized the handsome project manager, remembering that Sylvie Strahan from Hale's office had recommended him for the job when Paulie Williamson, whom both Russo and Vledich had jumped in and denigrated, quit and moved to Tucson. She'd been interrupted before calling Williamson by Geena Cho, and then everything had gotten crazy. She sure as hell wasn't going to wait for Lang to call DeWitt, not after what Mickey had said.

"I talked to Hale," he added. "He sounds pretty broken up."

She sensed he was fishing for information, but she wasn't going to go there. Mickey's screwed-up but scary report on Kristina and her trysts—plural, apparently—filled her head. She absolutely didn't believe he was right about Hale. But she needed to nail down who

Charlie was. "Beelzebub," DeWitt had said. On that he and Mickey agreed. Both of them thought Kristina's lover was the devil.

Russo gave her DeWitt's cell number and said casually, "Thought Woodworth steered you toward the Rib-I to find DeWitt. He wasn't there?"

"I just need to talk to him again."

"So you did see him."

"I've really got to get going, Mr. Russo. Thank you."

"Okay. Good luck with that new baby," he said as he rang off.

Savvy quickly placed a call to DeWitt, but his phone went straight to voicemail. She hung up and called right back, in case he'd just missed the call, but again she heard his voice telling the caller to leave a message, and she did, identifying herself and leaving him her number. She suspected Lang had left his callback number, too. When DeWitt heard the messages, he'd wonder what had put a fire under the TCSD.

She drove north with controlled concentration, feeling time ticking by, as if she had a clock inside her head. She was tired, too, and her breasts felt like heavy bricks. She would have called Hale, too, but she was driving without Bluetooth, and frankly, she just wanted to get there.

Hale waited for his grandfather as Declan worked his way out of Hale's SUV and through Hale's garage, leaning heavily on his cane. Hale hit the button to lower the garage door as a whipping wind sent a rush of rain their way. Already the driving rain had melted half the snow. A few more hours, and the snow would be a memory on the coast, though what that meant for the mountains was another story.

"I got it. I got it." Declan waved him inside as Hale held the door for him. Ignoring him, Hale stayed where he was as Declan navigated the few steps to the kitchen.

Victoria Phelan was standing just inside, and baby Declan was in full squall behind her in his car seat, which was sitting on the counter. "I tried giving him a bottle, but he's not taking it. I don't know what to do."

Declan gave her the once-over as he found one of the kitchen table chairs, his eyes taking in her thin T-shirt, which hugged her breasts, and her skinny jeans. She'd taken off her shoes and socks, and her bare toenails were painted black, the black on both big toes painted with a gold peace sign.

The look on his grandfather's face as his gaze took in the design made Hale want to laugh out loud. But baby Declan's wailing cries took his attention, and he went to the baby and gathered him up. He kept crying, but it wasn't quite as loud as before as Hale, rocking him gently, walked him into the living room. "Do you have a bottle ready?" he called to the nanny as he kept moving.

"Umm . . . yeah," she called back. "He did take some formula earlier," she yelled a bit defensively.

At that moment a wash of headlights lit the room, and Hale looked up to see Savvy's rental SUV pull into the driveway. His relief was mixed with pleasure, and when Victoria came with the bottle, he handed over the baby and headed for the door. He walked outside into the pouring rain as Savannah stepped from her car, her face half covered by the large hood of her raincoat.

Hurrying to meet her, he simply wrapped his arms around her in a bear hug. "Thank God," he said. "The baby needs you. Or maybe I need you. . . . I'm just so glad you're here."

Savannah looked up, the golden living room light shining on her blue eyes, making them glow. It struck him how beautiful she was, and for a moment they just stared at each other. Everything slowed down for Hale, and he felt his blood moving heavy in his veins. Heightened emotions over these past days. Strange events. Incredible highs. Devastating lows. For one crazy second he stepped forward and put his hands on her shoulders, gazing down at her with a kind of wild desire that was reflected in her expressive eyes. Dangerous . . .

And then the wind blew her hood back, and her dark auburn hair flew in front of her face, and Hale dropped his hold on her and grabbed her hand instead, tugging her toward the front door. Once inside, he slammed it shut behind them, but not before another heavy slap of rain followed them in.

"Wow," he said, running his hands through his own wet hair. Declan's cries greeted them both.

Savvy asked, "What's going on?"

"He's hungry. Doesn't seem to be taking to the formula that well."

She moved past him into the other room, shedding her coat as she went, folding it over her arm. Hale took the coat from her and felt moved by the way she beelined for Victoria, reaching for the baby. For a moment Victoria looked like she might resist, and Hale told her, "Savannah gave birth to Declan," so Victoria turned the baby over, albeit reluctantly. *Hopeless,* Hale thought. He was going to have to do something about replacing her, despite her one-year contract.

"Is there somewhere I can feed him?" Savannah looked to Hale, who led the way into the master bedroom. The lamps were on, and the room was bathed in soft light. Hale could see the vacuum cleaner tracks in the carpet and could smell the faintly citrus scent from the cluster of candles sitting on a silver tray on the dresser.

"Magda cleaned today," Hale said as Savvy sat down on the cream-colored occasional chair in the corner. "There's a rocker in the nursery," he added, remembering it.

"This is fine."

She sounded weary, and he nodded and left her in the room, closing the door softly behind them. He thought about his earlier reaction to her and decided he might need a drink.

His wipers rhythmically slapped at the driving rain as he drove south from the St. Cloud house. He'd seen them. He'd seen *her.* He'd been waiting for her up around a bend, with binoculars on the drive that led to the house. He'd been lying in wait for the old man, aware that his grandson had brought him to the house, and then because he was lucky, she'd shown up, the lovely, ripe detective with her swollen breasts and earthiness that dug right into his loins.

Seeing her, his dick had jumped right up, so while he'd stroked himself, he'd sent her another message, sweet and irresistible. *Lover. Soon. We'll be together soon.* He'd waited for her to respond, but something had gone wrong. He'd opened his eyes to see what it was, and she'd been looking up at goddamn Hale St. Cloud like *he* was some kind of fucking god! That wasn't the way it worked. That wasn't right. Had she been feeling this all along, this transference to the wrong man?

Charlie's blood boiled with frustration and rage. He watched them enter the house together, and he knew they were all over each other. He could *feel* it.

He'd netted her, and somehow she'd slipped away!

No!

A car drove by him, and he had to put his truck in gear and ease back onto the road and drive past the house. He couldn't be remembered. Had to stay under the radar.

In his dark mood, he was surprised when a message suddenly blasted across his mind, the first time his secret lover had contacted him first. *I have something for you.*

Charlie's attention snapped back. *What? Where are you?* he asked her.

Close. I'll see you soon. Wait for my call.

Fuck that, Charlie thought. He was going to find her. And then he was going to kill them all: her, the luscious detective, all the sisters at Siren Song, and, of course, Pops, the creaky old bastard who'd climbed atop that bitch Mary Beeman and sired him.

She was asleep in the chair when Hale returned to his bedroom. Baby Declan was lying in the center of the king bed, wrapped up in a blanket, sound asleep, but Savannah had curled into the chair, her head lying against the back of it. Hale gazed down at her, noticing the sweep of her lashes against her cheek. He debated about finding her a blanket, but instead he half woke her and guided her to the bed while she protested that she wasn't going to sleep in his bed. Ignoring her, he pulled back the covers and tucked her in. For a moment, he thought she was going to wake completely; she looked tense and ready. But then she gave up with a deep sigh, and when she was lying quietly, he scooped up baby Declan and took him to his bassinet in the nursery. Victoria was in her room, but she heard him and came into the hall, standing in the doorway and watching him settle the baby. He cracked the door open and joined her in the hall.

"I'll keep an ear open for him all night," she promised, heading back to her room.

Hale just nodded and then rejoined his grandfather in the kitchen. Before he could say a word, his cell phone buzzed. Glancing at the screen, he saw it was his mother. He almost didn't answer it.

* * *

Savvy woke up with a start, confused for a moment. *Where am I?* And then her memory came back in snapshots, the most memorable being standing outside Hale's house and staring up at him, sensing that he was feeling something of what she was.

And then baby Declan's cries. It was as if she'd been scripted to take him from the young woman's arms and into the safe haven of Hale's bedroom.

Hale's bedroom. Kristina's bedroom . . .

Savvy tossed back the covers and got to her feet. She was fully clothed except for her shoes and socks. Vaguely she remembered being helped to the bed from the chair, and she realized, a dark pink flush climbing up her neck, that it had been Hale, his strong arms around her, who'd pulled back the covers and tucked her in.

Guilt flared inside her. He was still Kristina's husband, and it didn't matter that she was gone. It didn't matter what she did, or didn't, do with Beelzebub before her death. It didn't matter that she might, or might not, have been on-site when the Donatellas were killed . . . not when it came to Hale. Savannah had always prided herself on being the sane sister, the discriminating one, while Kristina had been flighty and impressionable.

So what the hell was this all about?

Hating herself a little, she stumbled into the master bath and took a look at herself in the mirror. She groaned upon seeing her tangled hair and dark-circled eyes.

And then she heard the baby crying again and wondered if that had woken her up. What time was it? She glanced back into the bedroom and realized it was 9:00 p.m. Quickly, she finger-combed her hair, found some toothpaste and rubbed it on her teeth with her index finger—wasn't going to poach either her sister's or Hale's toothbrush—and then hurried out to see where Hale was and to find the baby.

Hale had heard baby Declan's cries and was just coming down the hall when Savannah appeared from the master bedroom. Victoria's door was shut, and she was nowhere to be seen.

"I think he's hungry again," Savannah said.

"Looks that way," Hale said.

"I'll get him and take him back to your room . . . if that's okay."

"Absolutely. Thank you."

He stood outside the nursery door and watched her pick up the baby and carry him back to the bedroom, giving him a quick smile as she closed the door. Hale stayed where he was for a moment, then headed back to the den off the kitchen, where his grandfather was ensconced in a chair and the television was turned on to a sports channel, the volume on low.

"When did Janet last call?" Declan asked him.

"An hour ago."

"Maybe she shouldn't be crossing the mountains," Declan said fretfully. "Could be a lot of snow."

Hale didn't remind him that he'd had exactly the opposite opinion just hours earlier. Both of them were worried, though Hale had channel surfed around for an updated local weather report an hour before and had learned it was mostly raining in the Coast Range. He just hoped it stayed that way.

In truth, his attention was fractured; his mind's eye pictured Savannah in the chair in his bedroom, breast-feeding his son. He yearned to be in the room with her, yet that wasn't the way it was supposed to be.

"What're you gonna do with that bimbo who calls herself a nanny?" Declan asked in a whisper.

"Shhh."

"She doesn't know a damn thing about being a mother."

"She's the nanny Kristina hired."

"*Ack.* Kristina wasn't a good decision maker. Don't want to speak ill of the dead," he added quickly, when he could see Hale was about to object. "But I'm not telling you anything you don't know. She wasn't for you, son."

Hale stared at his empty wineglass. He'd moved from bourbon, which he'd been drinking much too quickly, to cabernet. He and Declan had eaten some of the casserole that Magda had brought from the office, one of many, apparently, that were showing up from business associates, Hale and Kristina's only real friends. Neither he nor his grandfather had much of an appetite.

Half an hour later Savannah joined them. "I put him back down. He's asleep."

"How're you going to do this, girl?" Declan asked. "With your job."

"Declan . . . ," Hale warned.

"I don't know," Savvy answered. "Things are . . . confusing at the moment."

"Clear as glass to me," Declan said, ignoring Hale's glare. "Quit that job. Become a full-time mother. Most important job in the universe."

Savannah broke into a wide smile, unnerving Declan a bit, apparently, as he demanded, "What are you grinning at?"

"I'm not going to argue with you. You're . . ." She seemed to bite off what she was going to say. "I like my job, and I need to support myself, and no, I'm not going to live off Bancroft/St. Cloud money, so you can just forget that before you even get started."

Declan had opened his mouth, and now he snapped it shut into a thin line of disapproval.

"I'll feed Declan as much as I can. I want to. But I can't be with him all the time."

"Maternity leave," Declan said flatly.

"We're all figuring this out," Hale said. "We'll take it an hour at a time."

Savannah shot him a grateful look, then asked, "Could I talk to you alone for a minute?"

They returned to the master bedroom, and Hale closed the door behind him while Savvy walked back toward her chair but didn't sit down. "You know I've been following up on some leads at work, on the Donatella case."

"I thought you were going to tell me something about Kristina," he said.

"That too. This is going to sound strange, but the two cases may be dovetailing. Several sources told me that Kristina was having an affair, and that she was . . . She'd been seen with a man at the Donatella house, apparently after Marcus and Chandra moved out or weren't there."

Hale thought about his wife, her strange behavior the last weeks and months of her life. "She and I were friends with the Donatellas. . . ."

"I know it doesn't sound like her," Savvy said, picking up his train of thought. "I'm having trouble believing it myself. But it gets stranger, and more . . . and more . . . terrible."

Hale felt himself go still. "What is it?"

Savannah took a breath and launched in. "Last Thursday, before I came here to see Kristina, I stopped by Siren Song and met with Catherine Rutledge. . . ."

Savannah didn't know how much to tell Hale, whether she should go through every detail or hit the highlights. In the end, she settled for somewhere in between, telling him about Catherine's worry that Mary's son, who'd been adopted out when he was still a baby, apparently, had been lured to Echo Island, where Mary was exiled, and had ultimately killed her there, stabbing her to death with a knife, which was currently being tested for DNA evidence from the blood residue on its blade. She then added that Mary had named the boy Declan as a means to get back at Catherine, who'd apparently had a relationship with Hale's own grandfather at one time. Catherine believed that Declan Jr., as they were calling him, was as mentally unstable as his mother had been, or worse; that he was the one who had had an affair with Kristina and had killed her; and that he was now setting his sights on his half sisters, the women of Siren Song, on his father—or the man he assumed was his father, Declan Bancroft—and maybe even on those who were delving into his life in some way or investigating the Donatella homicides, a crime that might ultimately end up being laid at his feet, as well.

Hale absorbed all the information, a look of incredulity on his face when Savvy finished. He started to ask a question several times, stopping himself, then approaching it from another direction, only to stop himself again. In the end, he asked, "How did this Declan Jr. meet Kristina?"

Savvy said, "I talked to Owen DeWitt, and he implied that he knew someone who calls himself Charlie, not his real name, and who, DeWitt thought, is the devil incarnate." Hale made a disparaging sound, and Savvy couldn't blame him. "If he's the same person Catherine calls Declan Jr., and I kind of think he is, then I'd say he met Kristina here on the coast. I've put in a call to DeWitt. I didn't know on Saturday, when I talked to him, that my sister had been killed. I didn't press him on Charlie. It seemed . . . I don't know . . . untrue that Kristina was having an affair."

"But now you think it's fact."

"Several people saw her with someone at the Donatellas. I'm not sure exactly what nights, but sometime close to their deaths." Savvy couldn't hold his gaze and looked away. "I just want to talk to this Charlie—DeWitt called him Good Time Charlie—and see who he is and how he's connected to this all."

"What aren't you telling me?"

Savannah recalled Mickey's comment about Kristina being with her husband. "I need to talk to DeWitt before I say anything else. I was hoping he'd get back to me by now. Lang is trying to reach him, too. Maybe already has. I just want to know more about Charlie."

Catherine lay awake in the dark, staring toward the beamed wood ceiling. She was torn over whether to trust Ravinia, but what choice did she have? She'd set the investigation in motion by giving Detective Dunbar the knife because she wanted to know who'd killed her sister. But that was last week, and what had been a question mark last week was almost a certainty now. It was Declan . . . Declan Jr.

She wished she could get to the island. She would kill him, she thought. She would. He'd taken her sister from her, damaged though she was, and Catherine was all about payback. She knew she should turn the other cheek, but it wasn't in her.

She wasn't sorry that Mary had killed Declan Jr.'s real father . . . *the devil who gave me D. . . .* She'd hated him on sight.

He'd come to Siren Song with a swagger, even though he was old, way past the prime of his life, but then, as she'd told the detective, she and Mary gravitated toward older, more experienced males.

But not the man Mary called Richard Beeman. At least not for Catherine.

Mary, however, had regarded him with sloe eyes, wary and sexy at the same time. She threw over her previous lover, Dr. Dolph Loman, Ophelia's father, the only one of Mary's lovers who Catherine knew was one of the girls' fathers. Mary had stuck with Loman for several years, an eternity for one of her sister's relationships, much longer, in fact, than she'd entertained his brother, Parnell, but in the end the rigid, stone-faced doctor was tossed aside, as well. However, she'd given the new man a run for his money, too. She liked the chase.

They'd never gotten around to asking Earl for a coffin, so Beeman's bones lay moldering in the ground. It was these bones that Cassandra had seen in her vision, the bones of the man who'd sired Declan Jr. "He's coming," Cassandra had said, and Catherine had sensed the same thing.

Well, she wasn't about to sit by and cower any longer, like she had when Justice was terrorizing them. And she could admit that her methodology to keep them all safe—living in this isolated state, a *cult,* if you listened to the ignorant locals—hadn't really worked. The damage had been done long before her decision to lock the gates, even long before her promiscuous sister had dropped a dozen children. Her ancestors had sowed dangerous oats for centuries, the seeds of which had sprouted not only in the circle of land around Siren Song, but also beyond, in the Foothillers' territory, in the state of Oregon, and God knew where else.

And who was to say that Mary hadn't borne even more children . . . out on her island, luring the brave and incautious and horny males to her with her siren's song. Catherine had suspected and worried and fretted about Mary's ability to draw in the opposite sex, even out on Echo, and it was one of the reasons she'd seen her sister so rarely, even when the weather was fine.

Now she rose from her bed and walked to the window, staring out across the Pacific to where she knew Echo Island was, though with the wind and rain and darkness, it was indistinguishable tonight from the extended blackness of the ocean. What did the fire mean? What was Declan Jr. up to? He'd clearly found a way over to Echo. She hoped with all her heart that Earl would, too.

What if it's not Declan . . . ?

This was the thought that had been hiding in her brain, afraid to appear. As much as she feared Richard Beeman's offspring, there was a chance that whoever was on Echo was someone else. Maybe someone with ill intent. Maybe even another of Mary's children. Declan Jr. wasn't Mary's last child, nor was he Mary's last son.

Catherine turned away from the window and went to the locked drawer in her closet that held her own leather box. The key was inside the heel of one of her boots, and she reached down and grabbed up the shoe, twisting the heel sideways. The tiny key dropped to the floor with a soft *ping*. Bending over, she was slightly panicked when she couldn't find it, but then her groping fingers touched it, and she picked it up and fitted it into the lock.

Inside the drawer was the leather box, and inside the box was her own journal. It did not contain the dark mysteries that were within the pages of her sister's diary, but it did hold her younger dreams and the one secret she didn't want to share. Mary had known, but Mary had been oddly careful not to hurt Catherine with it. They were sisters, after all.

Catherine opened to a well-worn spot toward the end of the missive.

> *I gave birth to her today with Mary's help. She's the most beautiful child ever born. I want to keep her so much, I would kill to do it, but Mary's good days are fewer and fewer, and her bad days are unspeakably dangerous.*
>
> *I have to give her up. I have to.*
>
> *Elizabeth, my one true love. I promise I'll see you again.*
>
> *Your loving mother, forever and always,*
> *Catherine*

She read the message to her daughter over ten times, a ritual she went through whenever she needed strength. Feeling better, she put the journal into the box and relocked the drawer, replacing the key in the heel of her boot. Ravinia might have found Mary's journal, which was unfortunate, to say the least, but she hadn't known to look for Catherine's own.

Catherine moved back to the nightstand and extinguished the flame in the lamp. Then she climbed back into bed and thought about what was ahead with less trepidation. Tomorrow night she and Earl, with Ravinia's help, would move Richard Beeman's bones to the back of the graveyard, behind the rhododendrons, and would set

Mary in the grave already marked with her name, where she should lie in eternal rest.

Once that was done, she would think about what to do about Declan Jr. One way or another, she was going to deal with him, whatever it took.

And if it turned out he wasn't the menace she sensed on the island, she would figure out who was, what they intended, and if and why they had started the fire.

CHAPTER 26

It was almost eleven when the sound of a car pulling into the drive awoke Declan out of his sleep with a snort in the den chair. Savvy was seated across from both Hale and Declan, half watching the news, half worrying about what Hale was thinking about what she'd told him. He'd basically shut down after she told him about Declan Jr. and DeWitt's comments about Charlie and Kristina; he was still clearly processing everything. When she'd tried to go to her car to bring in her bag with the breast pump, he'd stopped her and gone to get it himself. She had the feeling he didn't want her to leave, and she didn't want to leave at all, but as the hours stretched by, she wondered what the hell she was doing. Marking time. Locked in this cocoon of safety.

But there was a killer out there. Her sister's killer. And she could pretend only so long that she was Hale's "wife" before reality jabbed at her conscience. She was a cop. She wasn't really little Declan's mom. She was living in a fake world, and though she longed for it in a way that surprised her, it wasn't her reality.

Owen DeWitt hadn't phoned her back. Maybe he was purposely ignoring her voicemail. Maybe he'd already talked to Lang. Whatever the case, he was her main priority, and tomorrow morning she was going to do something about it.

She'd told Hale almost everything she knew about the investigation into Kristina's death. She'd held back only Mickey's accusation that Kristina had been with Hale at the Donatellas' house. She hadn't told Hale she'd talked to Mickey at all. She didn't believe the homeless man's story, anyway; Mickey was hardly what you'd call a credible witness. Whatever he had seen or hadn't seen, or thought he saw or possibly dreamed . . . none of it mattered. The only thing that did was that he'd echoed Owen DeWitt's claim about seeing Kristina with someone in the same place DeWitt had.

"Who's that?" Declan asked, clearing his throat and straightening in his chair. "Someone here?"

"Looks like she made it tonight, after all," Hale said. He'd been quiet since their conversation, not saying much of anything while he offered Savvy some dinner from the well-stocked refrigerator. She had chosen a chicken pasta salad and had made small talk with Declan while she ate it.

Savvy realized Hale's mother had arrived.

Hale walked out to meet Janet, and Savvy heard him exchange hellos with her, sounding a bit stiff. Declan was finally on his feet and would have tottered out to see them, but they appeared in the doorway, driven by a blast of frigid air, which followed them into the house and swirled tendrils of cold into the den.

"What horrible weather," Janet declared, shrugging out of a long black coat. Underneath she wore black slacks and a gold cowl-necked sweater. She was middle-aged, tall and sturdy. Her hair was short and dark, heavily threaded with gray, attractively layered.

"Janet!" Declan greeted his daughter with delight.

"Hello, Dad," she responded, not so enthusiastically. She did not move forward to embrace him, but that didn't stop him from hugging her.

"How's Peter?" Declan asked.

"Fine. Working." She dismissed her husband with a small shrug, then, catching Savvy's glance, said, "Hello there. You look a lot like your sister. I'm so sorry about her accident. I didn't know anything about it until Dad called. And the baby . . ." She glanced at Hale and added, "You can't pick up a phone?"

"I was going to call you when I had more information. Kristina's accident appears to be something more," Hale responded coolly. Unlike Declan, he didn't seem thrilled to see his mother.

"What do you mean?" Janet asked with a frown.

"Someone may have killed her."

That stopped her cold, and she simply stared at Hale as if he'd said something so completely outrageous that she couldn't process it. Instead of addressing it, she turned away, glancing down the hall-way. "I've been traveling all day and I'm tired and hungry and I want to see that baby. Let me have a peek at him."

Hale shot Savannah a glance and said, "Don't leave," and then he took his mother down the hall, with Declan following at a slower pace, leaning heavily on his cane.

Savvy did want to leave. Now that Janet was here, she definitely felt like a guest who'd overstayed her welcome. Maybe she could pump some milk and then head home.

Twenty minutes later Hale and Janet returned to the den, Hale gazing hard at Savvy as if he'd expected her to bolt at the first oppor-tunity. "Declan's down for the night in the other guest room," Hale said.

"Which means I have the couch?" Janet asked. "Since you have the nanny tucked into one of the spare rooms and your grandfather in the other. I don't really care, you know, but I'm sure your grand-father needs a real bed."

Her tone was somewhat disparaging, as if Declan didn't deserve it, and Savannah wondered what that was about. But she saw now that if she'd even entertained the idea for a moment that she might spend the night, there was no chance of that. Which was just as well, as sleeping in Hale's bed had been too seductive, had felt too safe, and she knew she couldn't let her guard down.

"Tell me what happened to Kristina," Janet said to Hale. "My God. Killed? Who would kill her? Why?"

"That's what the police are trying to figure out," Hale said.

Janet's attention turned to Savvy. "You're a cop. What's the think-ing here?"

"I'm not investigating my sister's death," Savvy pointed out neu-trally.

"It looks like Kristina was having an affair," Hale said when Janet's gimlet-eyed appraisal of Savannah went on too long.

"An affair? With who?" She looked aghast. "I don't believe it." Then, "This lover killed her?"

"I'm on the suspect list," Hale said, which caused Janet to turn red with disbelief.

Savannah felt her pulse speed up a little at Hale's casual com-ment. She looked down at her overnight bag, which held the breast pump. She should have told him what Mickey said, she realized. She should have laid everything out there—the good, the bad, and the ugly—and let him mentally pick through it. But then she'd given him a lot to think about already, half of which she didn't believe herself.

"Oh, for God's sake!" Janet turned to Savvy and asked fiercely, "Is that right, Detective? Hale's a suspect?"

"We always try to rule out the family members first."

"Well, Hale obviously didn't kill your sister. He wouldn't hurt anyone, for any reason. He's good that way, not like his father or mine." She seemed to be waiting for some kind of reaction out of her son, as if they'd gone over this particular territory many times already, which Savvy guessed they probably had by the annoyance that flickered across Hale's face.

When he didn't respond, Janet got tired of waiting. "You got anything to drink around here?"

"Whatever you want." Hale was stiff.

"Wine?"

Hale flicked a look Savvy's way before going to fill his mother's request. As soon as he was out of earshot, Janet's gaze narrowed on Savannah, and she sensed an inquisition coming.

"Hale doesn't like me denigrating Preston or Declan, but as far as I'm concerned, they can both rot in hell. I'm sure Preston's already there, and Dad's not far behind." When Savannah remained silent, Janet said, "I've shocked you. You're just too well trained to show it."

Savvy could faintly hear the sounds of Hale getting another bottle of wine open for his mother. "I already told you I can't talk about the investigation, if that's what you want."

"Do you know who your sister was having an affair with?"

"No."

"My husband had an affair when we were married. Did you know that? That's why I divorced him. He knew how I felt about her, but he just couldn't resist the conniving bitch. He said he tried, but come on . . . He wasn't that powerless. He could have let it go, but he wanted her."

Hale returned with a glass of wine in a large goblet for his mother, the dark red fluid catching the light in a ruby glow. "Leave Dad alone," he said shortly.

"I know. You think I should have stayed with him, even after he screwed that crazy witch." She settled her bitter gaze on Savvy. "You grew up around here, right?"

"The Tillamook area," Savvy admitted. She eased a hand toward her bag. She could probably steal into the bedroom for some privacy for a few minutes before she hit the road and headed home.

Janet was on her own track, however, about to launch into a tale she'd clearly told often, the needle groove deepening in the record with each telling.

"So you know that freak show they call Siren Song?"

"Savannah and I were just talking about Catherine Rutledge," Hale said.

"Oh, yeah? Why? What's she done now?"

Savannah looked at Hale warily, wondering what he was going to say. He hadn't said how he felt about what she'd told him of his grandfather and Catherine's relationship. Nor had he mentioned what he thought of Mary's son, Declan Jr., who, according to Catherine, believed Hale's grandfather was his real father. Nor had he responded to Catherine's fear that he was targeting her nieces, Declan Sr., maybe Savvy, and God knew how many others.

He hadn't said anything at all.

But now Janet had brought up Siren Song, and the topic was on the table. Hale didn't react for several long moments, and instead of responding to Janet's question about Catherine, he said, "I put your suitcase in my bedroom."

"Oh, for God's sake. I told you I'd sleep here."

"I'll take the den," he stated firmly.

"We'll see." But if Hale thought he'd effectively turned the conversation away from Siren Song, he found out that was wishful thinking, as Janet said, "Catherine's not near as saintly as she would have everyone believe. What a goddamned hypocrite. Those *dresses!* That hair. That holier-than-thou attitude. She had a *thing* for Declan, only that bitch Mary took him away from her, too. First my husband, then Declan. Mary had to have them both. I don't care that Mary's been dead for years. Whenever I think of her, it's like I want to rip her eyes out."

Hale made a sound of disgust, but Savvy found herself riveted. On the heels of Catherine's revelations about her relationship with Declan, and the son of Mary's who she believed was responsible for Kristina's death, now Janet was saying Hale's father, Preston St.

Cloud, had had an affair with Mary Beeman? She was afraid to meet Hale's eyes, so she just kept her gaze pinned on Janet.

"I know, I know," Janet said. "You think I'm making it all up. But Mary had sex with both of them. I already knew about Declan, but then I caught Preston with her, and the look on his face . . . And this was years after they'd had the affair. We were in a coffee shop, and she walked in, and he . . . he was still dying for her. And she was so fucking smug." Janet bared her teeth at the memory. "I went through school with that sick bitch, and she stole every boy I ever had a crush on. Preston wasn't from here, but we stupidly stayed around Deception Bay, even though I *begged* Preston to leave, but no . . . Declan talked him into working for him at Bancroft Development. Just like he did Hale. And when Mary found out I loved Preston, she took him, too. Just because she could."

Janet almost echoed Catherine's words to Savvy about Mary, how Mary had warned Catherine to let Declan go, or she would take him from her. How Mary had gathered men like trophies all her life. Just because she could.

"It's lucky she's dead, or I don't doubt she would have come for you, too," Janet said to Hale.

"You're obsessed with this. Let it go," Hale told her flatly.

Savvy saw that he'd never credited anything his mother had said before; maybe he'd even felt she divorced his father for crimes he'd never committed. She wondered what he was thinking now, after the things she'd told him about Declan and Catherine and Mary.

"Your saintly father screwed Mary Rutledge," Janet declared coolly. "I know you never wanted to believe it, but I'm not making it up. I didn't find out myself about Preston until years later, but when I did, I left him and your grandfather and Deception Bay. Thank God for Peter. He took me away from this hellhole before Mary could find out about him, and I still won't bring him anywhere near that lodge and her demon-seed daughters." She drank half the glass of wine as if it were water, looked down into the wine that was left, then knocked the rest back. "God, I forgot what it feels like being so close to them. You've got to move, Hale, before one of them turns into their mother and comes for you."

"You're really over the top," Hale told her.

"I wish that were true," she answered, then held out her wineglass for a refill.

*   *   *

Ravinia riffled through the pages of her mother's journal. She'd skipped around, letting the book open to its most used places, but now she ran back to the beginning, examining her mother's younger entries. The "J." she'd written about, Janet Bancroft, was featured prominently when they were in grade school and high school. "J." could easily stand for *jealousy,* too, Ravinia realized, because her mother was consumed with it whenever Janet was mentioned, which was on a regular basis for a number of years.

From Mary's point of view, Janet Bancroft had everything. She was beautiful and rich and looked down on Mary and Catherine, who were considered outcasts by virtue of their odd family history. It must have shown in their dress, because Mary accused Janet of calling her "tawdry and embarrassing" and, later, "a psycho whore" and "sick in the head." Ravinia found herself stirred to anger at Janet, but then her mother certainly had had her issues. Mary had then zeroed in on Janet as her enemy. She cast her web on every boy who showed an interest in Janet, though she clearly wasn't interested in them herself. She called them "stupid larvae" and "immature sperm," which Ravinia found kind of creepy when she considered this was her own mother's writings.

The journal entries about "J." slowly trailed off as Mary grew older. But then she found one passage that was full of her mother's excitement.

> *J. got someone to marry her, and he's here! Preston St. Cloud. He's working for Declan. Cathy, are you reading this? I'm going to take them both. . . . I swear I will, if you don't give him up. You'll be sorry.*

Ravinia shut the journal and set it aside. She hated to admit it, but she was kind of seeing Aunt Catherine's side a little bit. No wonder her aunt had tried to shelter them so much. Screwed up as Aunt Catherine's plan had been, maybe it was all she could come up with, and given what a complete nut job Mary was, it wasn't half bad.

Savvy finished pumping both breasts, set the bottles aside, then rinsed out the equipment in Hale's master bath before putting it all away. Grabbing up her bag, she headed down the hall and toward the front door. Janet had ranted on a while more, but the wine and the long day had finally done their job, and she was now either asleep or watching television in the den.

She moved quietly to the front door, but Hale suddenly materialized before she could twist the knob.

"You sure you don't want to stay?" he asked with concern.

And stay where? she thought. *In bed with you?*

"I'd better get home. It's after midnight, and there are things I need to do tomorrow. Oh, I left the breast milk in your bathroom."

"I'll get it." Then, "It's dark and wet and cold outside."

"And I'm perfectly capable of taking care of myself. Thanks, Hale. Good night."

"Nothing I can do to get you to stay . . . ?"

He had no idea how tempting the thought was. Or maybe he did.

Her cell phone rang at that moment, muffled inside her messenger bag. It brought her back to her senses, as she'd been teetering. Recognizing Lang's ring tone, she reached inside her bag. Given the time of night, that didn't bode well.

"Hey, Lang," she answered.

"Savvy, I just got a call from Trey Curtis. I asked him to go to DeWitt's apartment and see why he hadn't answered any of my calls."

His unemotional tone told her more than she wanted to hear. "Uh-oh . . ."

"DeWitt's dead. Stabbed in the chest. The doer put the knife in and sliced upward in a way that . . . Well, Curtis thinks he liked what he was doing. I'm going to Portland in the morning."

"When . . . did this happen?"

"Not sure yet, but the body's passed through full rigor. Yesterday sometime, probably." A pause. "You sound wide awake. You're not in bed?"

"Not yet. I want to meet you. I can come to Portland tomorrow."

"Nah, stay put. But it looks like you may have stirred up a hornet's nest. I know, with everything, you probably haven't had time to write up a report on the interview with DeWitt, but do it now. And all the other interviews, too. Something happened when you were in Portland. Something that got somebody worried. Let's figure out what it is."

CHAPTER 27

Savannah was at her desk by eight thirty, too tired to think straight, too tense to sleep. She knew Charlie had killed Owen DeWitt. Knew it like she'd never known anything else. But Good Time Charlie was practically a figment of the imagination, a faceless demon with a Cheshire cat grin, a wizard who had cast a spell on Savvy's own sister and then had murdered the only man who could finger him and therefore possibly bring him to justice.

Was Charlie Mary's son, Declan Jr.? The more time that passed since Savvy's improbable talk with Catherine, the more she wondered if she hadn't checked her sane cop brain at the door when she entered Catherine's hospital room and listened to more of her tales of strange and awe-inspiring psychic gifts, some with their own terrible backlash. Dark magic. That was what it all felt like now.

To hell with it all. She'd skipped breakfast this morning, a first since the onset of her pregnancy, and now, as she typed in her report on the interviews with the Bancroft Portland employees, she was feeling low on energy. She'd been staring at the computer screen for a solid fifteen seconds without moving, and now she saved the file and swung away from her desk. She'd laid her cell beside her desk phone, and now she looked at both phones, willing Lang to call her with more details, even though he probably hadn't even made it to Portland yet this morning.

Stretching, she walked into the break room and raided the vending machine for a bag of potato chips. She grimaced, realizing she was going back to some of the bad habits she'd had before her pregnancy. Not good, but chips were what she felt like. Breaking the bag open, she headed for the coffee machine and poured herself a large cup of decaf. She dug into the bag of chips, munching slowly, contemplating the steaming cup of coffee she'd just poured. A few minutes later she crumpled the bag and tossed out the rest of the chips, then picked up the decaf and threw it down the drain. She then got herself a cup of regular coffee. She needed *something.* Good news would be the best antidote, but she couldn't even think what that might constitute beyond the capture and conviction of Kristina's killer.

She wanted her sister back.

An hour went by, and Savvy finished up her report. She stared into space for a moment, reviewing what she'd written, trying to put things together in her head. Outside the windows wind and rain were still lashing violently, but she'd caught an early morning weather report, which said that things were supposed to dry out by sometime tomorrow.

She slowly remembered that she hadn't called Paulie Williamson. Like everything else the past few days, it had fallen through the cracks when she'd been distracted, and she'd been constantly distracted. Maybe it was finally time to follow up.

Plucking her notebook from her messenger bag, she flipped to the list of names and numbers she'd written in for Bancroft Development. Picking up the desk phone, she placed a call to the number Clark Russo had given her for Williamson. The phone rang on and on, and she prepared herself to leave a voicemail. Instead, after a long, long time, a man picked up and said, "Hello?" in a cautious voice.

"Mr. Williamson?"

"Yes." More cautious.

"I'm Detective Savannah Dunbar with the Tillamook County Sheriff's Department. I'm doing follow-up interviews on the Marcus and Chandra Donatella homicides, which took place at Bancroft Bluff in Deception Bay." She paused, but when all she could hear was his breathing, she went on. "I understand you were the manager of the Bancroft Development Portland office at the time."

"That's right." Again, very cautiously.

"Clark Russo, the current Portland manager, gave me your name and cell number. Do you have a minute?"

"Look, whatever it is, I can't help you with it. I'm at a job site now, and I'm busy."

And he hung up.

Huh.

Burghsmith and Clausen entered the squad room in the midst of a loud discussion in which Burghsmith, deep into a new diet regime, was extolling the virtues of gluten-free doughnuts and Clausen was talking over him with a series of rude noises and comments.

She almost missed Hale's ring tone in the midst of Clausen's contention that Burghsmith had "been taken over by faddist aliens and had moved to the dark side." Sweeping the cell from her desk, she turned her back to the argument and answered, "Good morning. Everything okay?"

"I was just going to ask you the same thing. . . ." He trailed off, then asked, "You're at work?"

"Had to write up a report, and I couldn't sleep much, anyway. How'd it go with little Declan last night?"

"Victoria actually got up and fed him, but my mother took over this morning. Declan seems to be taking some formula."

"Good," Savvy said, though she felt a twinge of what? Jealousy? *Down, girl,* she told herself.

Hale was going on, "She was holding him and actually crooning to him when I left. Can't tell if she's really into the baby, or she just wants me to get rid of the nanny."

"Maybe a little of both," she said. "So, you're at work, too."

"I feel like I've been on a sabbatical. I needed to refocus."

"Yeah."

Savannah's desk phone suddenly rang. Clausen and Burghsmith had moved down the hall to the break room, but the doughnut discussion had yet to abate. Burghsmith had made some insulting comment about Clausen's waistline, apparently, because the discussion was quickly turning into a heated argument.

"I've got to go," Savvy said.

"Do you have a plan for today? About the baby?" he asked.

"I want to stop by this evening with more breast milk, but if he's taking formula better, then I don't know. . . ."

"Come for dinner," he said. "I'll pick up from Gino's. Chicken and artichoke linguine . . . ?"

She almost asked if his grandfather and his mother would still be there, but they probably would, and, anyway, what did it matter? She wanted to go. "I can't say no to that. Thanks. I'll see you later." She clicked off and grabbed her desk phone receiver. "Detective Dunbar."

"There's a Nadine Gretz calling for you," Cho's voice said. "She wanted to know if this is where you worked."

"Put her through," Savvy said. Nadine Gretz. Bancroft Development's ex-employee to whom Savannah had spoken through Henry Woodworth's cell phone.

"Hello?" Nadine's voice asked uncertainly.

"Hi, Nadine. This is Detective Dunbar."

"Look, this is going to sound weird, and I probably called too early, but something's happened to Henry."

"What do you mean?"

"We were supposed to meet Sunday. He said he was on his way, and he never showed. He didn't go to work yesterday. I've called and called, and he hasn't picked up. I actually went over to the work site. RiverEast? They start at seven or seven-thirty, but he's not there today, either."

"Have you talked to Mr. Russo?"

"I tried to reach Clark yesterday, and I tried again just now. I just know something's happened. And it was after you were here," she said with an accusing tone. "He said . . . he said, I should've been nicer to you. That you were just doing your job. Well, I don't know, but maybe you doing your job is why he's missing!"

"Have you been to his home?"

"Of course I have! He doesn't answer my knock! He's *not there!*"

"And you reported him missing?"

"God! That's what I'm doing *now!*"

Savvy said, "I'll talk to the Portland police and let them know. Can you give me Henry's address?"

"Yes . . ."

When the call ended, Savvy started to call Portland, then stopped, thinking back to her conversation on Saturday with Henry, and then Nadine, through Henry's phone. She'd just written up a report on that interview and call, so they were fresh in her mind, and the gist of it was Henry had been friendly and not too informative, and Nadine had gotten on the phone and accused Kristina of slavering all over Marcus Donatella and coming on to other Bancroft employees, including Henry. She'd also blamed Hale and "that old lech" Declan of knowing about the dune's instability and building Bancroft Bluff, anyway.

Now Savannah pulled up the file on her computer again and looked at what she'd written. Grimacing, she changed a few words, putting in Nadine's "slavering over Marcus" comment, knowing that trying to protect her sister's memory and Hale's reputation wasn't going to help find Kristina's killer.

As soon as she finished, she put in a call to Lang and left a message on his voicemail that included Henry's address and Nadine's fears about him being missing. Lang was headed straight for the Portland PD and could deliver the message in person.

For a moment, she recalled the Bancroft worker who'd stared at her at the job site. It had seemed so pointed at the time, so intent. Who was he? And was that simple curiosity she'd felt, or was it something else?

Going back to her notebook, she looked down the list of temporary employees. Henry Woodworth's name was at the top of the list; she recalled that he'd been angling for Neil Vledich's job, according to both Vledich and Russo. They'd both made disparaging remarks about Henry. The other employees' names were listed with their phone numbers. Maybe she should start with the name under Henry's, Jacob Balboa, and go down from there.

She picked up the receiver, then glanced back to her notes on Russo and Vledich, wanting to see if what they'd said about Henry Woodworth was how she remembered it. Yep. They weren't fond of him, and he hadn't been of them, either.

A notation in her own handwriting suddenly caught her eye. It was small enough that she had to take a moment to decipher it. She saw the notation *Williamson a friend of DeWitt's.*

Savvy's brows rose. She glanced rapidly over her notebook again. Clark Russo had given her the previous manager, Paulie Williamson's, phone number. Williamson had quit and moved to Tucson soon after the dune debacle. Russo had then taken over Williamson's vacated job in Portland at Sylvie Strahan's recommendation.

Savannah's pulse sped up as she concentrated hard on exactly what Russo had said in that conversation with her about Williamson. What was it?

Working on his tan and drinking mojitos . . . ran like a rabbit after the Donatellas were killed . . . He's the one who awarded the engineering job to DeWitt. . . .

Was that why he'd hung up on her? Because he knew something?

Quickly, she phoned Williamson again. Once more she was made to wait long, anxious minutes for either Williamson or his voicemail or an answering machine to pick up. To her surprise, it was Williamson himself who answered, and she realized this time she'd called him on her cell. His caller ID hadn't given him any information other than her phone number, and he hadn't realized who was calling.

"Mr. Williamson, this is Detective Dunbar again. I need to talk to you, and if you can't find the time, I'll have someone from your local precinct get in touch with you in person."

"What do you people want?" he declared in exasperation. "I talked to you before! Did I know the dune was unsafe? No! Did the Bancrofts? Yeah, I think so. And they went ahead, anyway! But it's not my fault."

"I understand you awarded the engineering contract to Owen DeWitt."

A pause. "We used him all the time."

"'We' meaning Bancroft Development?"

"What are you getting at? What is this?" he demanded.

Savvy hesitated a moment, knowing she hadn't been cleared to release information on DeWitt, also knowing that the word would be out within a few hours. "Mr. Williamson, we're investigating the homicide of Owen DeWitt, who was killed sometime between Saturday night and today."

His sharp intake of breath was a sound of pure fear. "*What?* How? Who did it? Do you know?"

"We're hoping you can help."

"Oh, my God." He was rattled, but he was still on the phone.

"Do you know anything about a man who goes by Charlie? Even sometimes Good Time Charlie?"

"Charlie . . . no . . . I never heard that. . . ."

"It sounds like there might be something else." Savannah gripped the receiver tighter.

"There was a guy from work that Owen saw sometimes . . . a real scary dude, but in a way Owen kinda liked, y'know? This guy bragged all the time about stuff he'd done, and lots of times it was kinda . . . raunchy."

"Sexual?"

"Like *real* sexual," Williamson agreed. "Owen was messed up after what happened with Bancroft Development. Kept trying to prove he was right and the dune was safe, but that was a lost cause. Jesus . . . I can't believe he's dead," he whispered in disbelief.

"I spoke to Owen last weekend. He said he went back to Bancroft Bluff several times."

"Oh, shit . . . oh, shit . . ."

"What?"

"He said the dude was there with some chick, at the Donatella house! Bangin' her brains loose against a wall."

Savvy's throat felt hot. "Did he say that the woman was Kristina St. Cloud? Hale St. Cloud's wife?"

"Holy . . . God . . . no, he didn't say that. . . ." Williamson sounded horrified. "But . . ."

"But?" Savvy pressed when he trailed off.

"But there was something funny going on. Owen was kinda tick-led about catching them. Like it was a big joke on the Bancroft clan. He didn't like them much. Coulda been the wife, I suppose," he said, rolling that over. "Makes sense, now that I think about it."

"He intimated that he saw them more than once," Savvy said, struggling to keep emotions under tight lock and key.

"Yeah, I think that's right."

"Did he ever act like . . . maybe there were more people there with them at any time?"

"Like, what do you mean? An orgy?"

Savvy hung on to her patience with an effort. "More like this friend of Owen's was meeting other people there, besides his . . . date."

"He was no friend of Owen's. Believe me. The dude was just in-teresting, but in a way that, like, you wanted to stay ten feet back from him, wherever he was. Just enjoy the show, but keep out of range. That's the impression I got. Man. You say his name is Charlie?"

"We don't know his real name," Savannah said.

"But you think this dude is the one who killed him."

"It's a possibility."

"Shit, I'm glad I got outta there. Those Bancrofts . . . that fuckin' scary town with the cult and all. I was glad to be on the other side of the mountains from them, but even Portland was too close. Tucson is just fine."

"Thank you, Mr. Williamson."

"You get the bastard that killed Owen, Detective. String him up by the balls."

And maybe the bastard who killed my sister, Savannah thought as she hung up. If she found him, she'd be happy to string him up by the balls herself.

Hale fielded calls from all the projects he had going, and it took most of the morning and all of lunch. The rain lashed at the window-panes, driven by a raging wind. He ignored the weather as he systematically returned calls and took some more, mainly from business friends who hadn't been able to reach him the past few days and who offered condolences. Most knew about Kristina, but fewer knew he'd become a new father. He kept the calls as short as possible, mainly because he just needed to keep moving forward.

Ella knocked on the jamb of Hale's open door. He looked up, and she said, "You missed lunch. Can I get you a sandwich?"

"No, thanks, Ella." In truth, he wasn't that hungry.

"It's no trouble. You need to take care of yourself. You're a father now." She hesitated, her face crumpling. "A single father."

"Ella . . ."

Tears welled in her eyes. "I'll just go to the Bridgeport Bistro. You like that crab and Havarti one, don't you?"

"Yes, I do." It was easier to just say yes than get in the way of Ella's mothering.

"I'll take money out of petty cash," she said on a sob, and then she was gone.

Hale pushed back from his desk and walked to the windows. A

few minutes later he saw Ella beneath her lavender umbrella, making her way to her car through the driving rain. Maybe the showers would stop, as the weatherman had predicted, but it wasn't going to be today.

He thought about what Savvy had told him about Catherine Rutledge and her hunch about Kristina and Mary Beeman's son, Declan Jr. Catherine was adamant that Declan Jr. was not truly Hale's grandfather's son, but Declan Jr. believed he was because that was what his mother, Mary, had told him. What a screwed-up family that was, he thought. And homicidal, too, if Catherine was to be believed. And maybe flat-out crazy. His mother certainly had nothing good to say about the Rutledge sisters, but then she had a tendency toward hyperbole. Hale did not believe his father had cheated on his mother with anyone, least of all Mary Beeman, but then he wouldn't have believed it of Kristina, either. His wife had been fastidious and choosy, and, okay, maybe she did make some bad choices, but even so, she was about the least likely person to get involved with someone as dangerous and unhinged as this Declan Jr., as Catherine called him, seemed to be.

But someone had killed Kristina. And someone had now killed Owen DeWitt, the man who'd told Savannah he'd seen Kristina with a man he called Charlie, pounding it out together at the Donatellas' house. Were the two murders related? It made more sense that they were than that they weren't.

But Kristina with this Charlie, or Declan Jr. or whoever, having sex at the Donatellas'? That didn't sound like her at all.

Do you believe in sorcery?

"No," he said aloud. But he believed there was some nebulous danger out there, and if Catherine was correct, and it was headed for his grandfather and Savannah, among others, he was going to be on heightened alert. He didn't know what had brought the danger to his doorstep, but he sensed it was real.

And nobody else was going to be harmed. He was going to see to that.

It was after four before Lang called Savvy, and she damn near screamed at him, wanting to know what took him so long. Instead she swallowed back her frustration and answered, "Okay, finally. What's going on?"

There was noise in the background, and Savvy was immediately suspicious that Lang was at a bar with his good buddy Curtis. But he was sober and terse when he said, "Looks like DeWitt was killed sometime Sunday, like we thought. ME's still nailing it down. Probably less than a day after you met with him."

"The two things are connected," Savannah said. "Charlie did this."

"You certainly got someone's attention. Did you write up that report?"

"I did. I can e-mail it to you."

"Do that."

"Did you get my message about Henry Woodworth?"

"Yeah, and Curtis and I went over and checked out his place. Nobody there. Pretty spotless, but there was a broken cup on the kitchen floor."

"Like . . . a struggle?"

"Maybe. There was nothing else, though. No other signs. Coulda just fallen off the counter. I talked to Gretz and told her to file a report with Missing Persons."

"You think she's jumping the gun?" Savvy asked. Her mind traveled back to the list of the other temporary employees. Was she making connections when none were there?

"Maybe Woodworth just decided to take a few days off."

"I'll check with Russo about his employment record," Savvy said, adding it to her mental to-do list. She would check on the rest of the temporary employees, as well, see if she could figure out which one was the guy who'd stared so long at her.

"We up to date now?" Lang asked.

"Almost. I talked to Paulie Williamson today, the ex–Portland manager for Bancroft Development. He was a friend of DeWitt's, and he confirmed that DeWitt had a friend, more like a frenemy, whose sexual exploits apparently gave DeWitt vicarious thrills. Williamson said the guy—he doesn't know his name—was one of those people you want to stand back from."

"Like he's a walking disaster?"

"Like he's unpredictable and dangerous."

"You think this is the guy DeWitt said was with Kristina?"

"Yeah. Charlie."

"Charlie?"

"Good Time Charlie. Not his real name. I've got him at the top of my list as the doer for DeWitt."

Lang mulled that over. "All right, I'm coming back tonight."

"Where are you now?" Savvy asked.

"A place near the station. Dooley's. Don't worry, Mom. I just had one beer. I already told Claire the same thing."

"I was thinking maybe you can stick around and do a little checking for me. I kinda think Charlie's associated with Bancroft Development somehow. I've got this list of temporary employees. Mostly construction workers. Henry Woodworth's name is at the top of the list. I didn't meet any of the other ones, but one of them was looking at me pretty intently when I was interviewing Henry at the RiverEast Apartments building site."

"E-mail me the list when you send the report. I'll pick it up on my phone."

"Does that mean you're staying over?" She would have to scan the list into the computer from her notebook, but that was easy enough.

"Get me another beer," Lang yelled to someone across the hubbub of the bar. Then to Savvy, "Yep. Anything else?"

"When you get back tomorrow, let's have a sit-down. I had a talk with Catherine Rutledge about some stuff, and I want to go over it with you."

"Oh, God," Lang groaned. "You know, you're Clausen's partner."

"I think he dropped me when I was pregnant, so now I'm yours." Savannah smiled, knowing that wasn't the way it worked and not caring. It was the first time she'd really felt like smiling since Kristina's death.

"Talk to you tomorrow," Lang said, and Savannah settled back into work, putting the finishing touches on the interview report, scanning the list of temporary employees, and sending the whole thing to Lang's e-mail address.

Her rumbling stomach was the first indication that time had

passed, and when she looked up again, she realized it was after lunch and she really needed to get something to eat.

And then tonight . . . chicken and artichoke linguine with Hale . . .

Charlie shook rain off his black jacket and ran his hands through his hair as he stepped inside the door to the Crab Shack, a dilapidated board-and-bat hovel crouched on the edge of Nehalem Bay, a place so weathered and decrepit that it made Davy Jones's Locker, his favorite dive bar along the coast, look like a four-star restaurant. But no one knew him at the Crab Shack—at least that was what he was banking on—whereas he would be recognizable at Davy's.

And he needed somewhere to hunker down for a few hours. He'd given up his apartment in Seaside when he'd taken the job in Portland. Couldn't afford to maintain two places, even with the money from Bancroft Development.

Bancroft Development. The company that was rightfully his. Only Pops refused to recognize him. *Ha.* The old man would learn what dismissing his son would get him soon enough.

But first . . . some fun.

Charlie moved up to the bar and ordered a Bud. He didn't drink as a rule, but if he strode in and ordered up a soda or water, the bartender might take note of him, and then if the cops came around, a blurry memory might suddenly turn into a sharp recollection. Couldn't have that.

And let's face it, he'd been making a few decisions lately that hadn't been all that well thought out. *Damn.* He'd been so careful for so long. But something had been triggered, and it wasn't going away. Hell, he didn't even want it to! A slinky, hot thread of desire was winding inside his blood, moving through his system, and it felt *good.* Ever since sliding that knife into his mother, he'd been infected, and well, he could admit, he'd gotten a little careless. Looking for that next thrill ride all the time, instead of lying back and waiting.

Escalating. Yep. That was what he was doing. But there was no going back.

And why should he? He'd told Mary he'd take out those juicy women at the lodge, and he would. He just needed a plan, and right now he didn't want to take the time. He wanted something fast. Fast and hot.

The luscious detective flashed across his mind, and he felt a blinding rage. Transferring her desire for him—the attraction he'd sent her!—to Hale St. Cloud? The bastard who'd taken Charlie's place in Pops's affection? Charlie's fucking boss, for fuck's sake? She deserved to die. A slow, sensual, spiraling death while he made love to her with all the power of his sexual gift.

His hard-on was immediate, and he crouched over the bar, drinking at the beer, making it look like he was gulping it down, but not making much of a dent. Couldn't do that too long without someone getting wise, but no one was looking, anyway. There was one skanky-looking woman with long, dark, stringy hair swaying to a country-western song he thought he should know but couldn't place, and there were a couple of guys in cowboy boots and plaid shirts watching her, but otherwise the place was empty.

Charlie's mind slithered back to the detective. Not pregnant anymore. Focused on another man. Thinking about being a mother and stepping into Kristina's shoes and becoming a wife, too.

Not gonna happen.

He went into the bathroom with vague thoughts of masturbating and taking care of this woody. *Jesus.* But he didn't have a plastic bag with him. That was out in his white truck, the Bancroft Development truck, so he was stuck trying to mentally get himself under control, a real bitch.

A few minutes later he hurried out to the truck, grabbed a bag, and stroked himself in the gloom of late afternoon, the dark red-haired detective in mind. It took seconds, and when he was finished, instead of release, he felt building fury. She was *his.*

The skank swayed out of the bar with one of the cowboys, and they moved to his truck, a black Dodge Ram. Watching them, Charlie popped open the glove box and slid out his knife. He was hard again already.

But just as he was opening his door, another truck came splashing through the mud puddles and the rain and came to a stop between Charlie and the couple in the Dodge truck. Charlie hesitated, and two women jumped out of the truck, whooping and hollering as they ran inside the Crab Shack. Right behind them came a couple of cars and more women. Goddamned happy hour.

By the time they'd all gotten out of the rain, the Dodge Ram was rumbling out of the parking lot and back up to 101.

Briefly, he thought about going back inside and juicing them with some Good Time Charlie pheromones. He could probably pick up two or three easily.

But there was danger in crowds . . . and besides, he was getting a real cranking hard-on for the detective. With a vision of her swaying in front of his eyes, he followed the Ram onto the highway and headed north, because she would be panting her way to Hale St. Cloud's house soon enough.

He was going to have to ditch this truck soon. It didn't have the Bancroft logo on it, but he wasn't really supposed to even have it. He had appropriated it for the RiverEast project and had just kind of kept it. That project was being overseen by a larger construction company that dealt with high-rises; they had been hired because Bancroft Development wasn't in that kind of commercial construction. They were strictly penny-ante, in Charlie's opinion, and had to rely on experts to actually build the structure. But Bancroft Development owned the land, so Charlie and some other guys were on-site to monitor the construction.

But, well, now things had changed. Charlie was through working for the company that, by all rights, should be his. He was going to have to ditch the Bancroft truck sometime soon, but that meant stealing a car or renting one, and he just didn't have time.

He needed to lure that detective to him.

Pulling out his cell phone, he saw that his hands were shaking, and he gazed at them in wonder. What the hell? He was morphing into something else. Something more powerful.

It was . . . *awesome.*

CHAPTER 28

Ravinia knocked on Catherine's bedroom door, tried the knob, and when it turned in her hand, she stepped inside the gloomy space. She heard Catherine rustle in the bed and reach for the lighter to light the lamp.

"Ravinia," Catherine said when the wick was lit and the soft glow pushed the evening shadows back to the corners of the room.

"When is Earl coming?" Ravinia asked.

"Tonight, late." She threw a look toward the windows that faced west. "I don't think he made it to Echo in this weather."

"But he is coming tonight, here, to . . . switch things around?" Ravinia asked.

"Yes. And I'm afraid you'll have to help him. I don't have the strength, and someone needs to stay inside the house. They won't expect you to stay around. You never do."

Ravinia had no problem with the task. Her only complaint was the blasted weather.

"Be patient," Catherine warned. "Unless something unforeseeable happens, Earl will be here." She exhaled heavily. "I may need you to do something else for me, too."

"What?"

"Let's wait until after . . . everything gets taken care of. I'll be coming downstairs in a few minutes. I can smell that Isadora's making dinner. Chicken? We'll eat and then move to the great hall, and I'll let everyone fuss over me. You'll leave early, as you always do. Go to your room and wait. When everything quiets down and everyone's in bed, watch out your east window, toward the graveyard. Earl will give you a signal. A quick flash of light."

"What if someone else wakes up and sees it?"

"I'll leave my door open a crack, so they'll come to me first."

"But what will you say?" Ravinia asked.

"I'll tell them it's you, going over the wall again."

Savannah drove north through the rain, which seemed to be lessening a little. At least she hoped it was. There was water rushing in a thin film across the road. The snow was completely gone, washed away.

She couldn't wait to get to Hale's house. Hale and Kristina's house. It wasn't right, but it was all she could do. She drove through Deception Bay, past the turnoff to Bancroft Bluff, and then a few miles farther, she saw the entrance to Declan Bancroft's house. Had Declan had an affair with Catherine or, despite all Catherine's claims to the contrary, with her sister, Mary? Could the boy whom Catherine called Declan Jr. really be Declan Sr.'s son? How would you know? There was no listing of the fathers of the Siren Song girls, again, according to Catherine. There was only *A Short History of the Colony*, and that had been written by a man who, even within the text of the book, freely admitted that some of it was conjecture. Herman Smythe was no historian. He was just an older man who was living out his days at . . .

"Seagull Pointe," she said aloud. The assisted living facility/nursing home would be coming up on her right very soon. She hadn't been there since Madeline "Mad Maddie" Turnbull's death, but Smythe was a resident, too. She'd planned on stopping in and talking to him, but, well, she'd been kind of overwhelmed with the changes in her life.

But now here she was.

Might as well try to see him.

Hale looked down the length of the dining table at the cartons of food he'd brought from Gino's. His grandfather sat at one end; his mother at the other. Janet couldn't forgive Declan for, at least in her mind, contributing to the failure of her marriage by having any kind of relations with the Rutledge sisters. Declan seemed perplexed by her cold distance, but it had been the same between them for years, so Hale suspected he had to have some clue.

Victoria was feeding the baby a bottle, but little Declan was starting to fuss, and the nanny heaved a huge sigh. "I don't know what's wrong with him."

Janet rolled her eyes at Hale, silently saying, "How long are you going to let this go on?"

"I'll take him," Hale said, and he carried the baby back to his bedroom and walked him around until he fell asleep.

He wondered what was keeping Savvy. Work, maybe. He wondered if she'd talked to Hamett and Evinrud. Probably. It gave him a slightly sick feeling to think what they might be saying about him, but Savannah was a cop and knew better than he did what to expect in a murder investigation. She could separate fact from fiction, good cop from bad, truth from lies.

He snuggled baby Declan back into his bassinet and then returned to the dining room to find Janet standing on her feet, back rigid, glaring at her father, who was still sitting. "Do you know what he said?" she asked, swinging around to Hale, her eyes bright with fury. "He said he has a son!"

"I said I have a grandson," Declan said, sweeping a hand toward Hale, then bringing it back to rest on the tabletop, but not before waving it at Janet, as if she were a noxious fume.

"You said *son*. Who with? That whore, Mary Rutledge . . . Beeman . . . or whatever the hell?"

"I do not have a son." Declan's face was turning red with anger.

"I'm leaving," Janet said. "I love the baby, Hale. He's so precious, but I can't stand this." She swept toward the den.

"I don't have a son!"

Hale followed after her, recalling how just the other day his grandfather had mistakenly said he had a son. Was he just losing it a little, like Hale had thought at the time? Or was Janet right and there was something more . . . like Declan Jr. . . . ?

"You're leaving tonight?" he said to her.

"I sure as hell am. And you need to do something about that girl. She's hopeless. If she's the best they're offering at that nanny school where Kristina picked her out, that place should be written up!"

"She was pretty," Hale said.

"What?"

"I told Kristina she could pick whomever she wanted, and she picked Victoria from some résumés the school sent. Victoria was the prettiest."

"That's sick, Hale. Really."

"I'll figure it out."

Janet zipped up her bag and straightened. "I notice you're not dying to get me to stay and help you. Is it because I can't get along with my father, or do you have someone else in mind, hmmm?"

"If you're talking about Savannah, don't let your imagination run wild."

"It's not running wild, dear." She leaned forward and gave him a quick kiss on the cheek. "I've got a pretty clear idea of what's going on, and for the record, I don't approve."

Hale felt anger rush through him. "What the hell?"

"It's too soon. And this incestuous relationship you have going reminds me too much of your father and grandfather, hanging around Siren Song with their tongues out. It's sick."

"That's not my relationship with Savvy."

"Yet." She picked up her bag, but Hale took it from her. Then he followed her back toward the dining room, where she threw a baleful look at Declan, who declared, "I don't have a son, Janet!"

"Well, Mary had one about nine months after her affair with you. When I learned about her and Preston, I checked. If he wasn't your son, are you saying he was Preston's?"

"I'm not saying anything. *Ack!*"

"Maybe you don't know," she said tautly, heading for the front door. Before she twisted the knob, she said, "But I think you do."

Herman Smythe was tickled pink that a young lady cop had come to see him, and he waved his guest to a chair in his meager room while he sat in a wheelchair. Savvy did as he bade her, though somewhat reluctantly. Her steps had slowed as soon as she was about to enter the building, because she'd wanted to turn around and jump in the car and race to see Hale and the baby. It was precisely her own eagerness to hurry to them, the two men in her life, that got her feet moving again. She was worried about how much it mattered. She needed to get a grip on her own emotions and fast.

And then she'd gotten the call from Detective Hamett, asking her to come in the next day and talk to them about Kristina and Hale St. Cloud.

That was what was preying on her mind now, while Herman was going on about his daughter, Dinah, who came to see him regularly.

"I'm dying, you know," he said, snapping Savvy's attention back to him. "One of those cancer things." He shrugged his thin shoulders. "First, it was this kind, and then it was that kind. Dinah has some herbal remedies, but when your number's up, your number's up. So, what did you come to see an old man about?"

"I recently read *A Short History of the Colony,* and I thought I'd like to meet the man who wrote it."

"You investigating something that involves Siren Song?" he asked keenly, his bushy eyebrows lifting.

"Well, not really . . . I met with Catherine Rutledge, and it reminded me that I'd been meaning to read your book," Savvy said, stumbling around.

"Ah, Catherine. You know about her sister, Mary, don't you?" He smiled in remembrance. "I should probably be ashamed of it. My exwife certainly thought I should, but I was one of Mary's lovers. I think I shared that in the book."

"You mentioned her sexuality," Savannah said.

"Mary was something, all right." He winked at her. "Dinah gets tired of me saying it, but I was quite a swordsman in my day." While Savvy was wondering how to respond to that, he went on. "Mary got crazy, though. No doubt about it. It just got worse and worse."

"You say in the book that many of Mary's children never knew who their fathers were."

"That's right. I think maybe one or two of them's mine, but Mary would never let anyone know. I could get a test now, I suppose, but Catherine keeps those girls locked up pretty tight, and, well, it's just never happened."

"Catherine told me that Mary put down Declan Bancroft as one of the possible fathers of a son that she named Declan."

He frowned. "She adopted her sons out."

"Yes. And one she named Declan."

"No, I don't remember that. . . . She did name one Silas, I thought."

"Silas?"

"I don't remember Declan," he said, mulling that over. "Someone said that Declan Bancroft was spending a lot of time there for a while. That was after my time. Mary would suddenly be tired of whomever she was with and would just give one of us the boot." He chuckled. "You always hoped it was some other guy getting kicked out, but it happened to us all eventually."

"Did you ever interact with the children?"

"Nooo . . . Catherine would never have allowed that, and we didn't want it, either. She finally burned that bunkhouse down, just to get rid of some of those guys who wouldn't leave. Then she locked the gates."

Savannah remembered the passage about the bunkhouse. "You're sure that was Catherine? You didn't say that in the book."

"Catherine said, 'You have to burn them out.' If she didn't do it, she had somebody who did. Not that it was a bad thing, I suppose. Mary was getting crazier, and Catherine wanted a better life for the girls."

They talked for a few more moments, with Herman reminiscing some more, and then Savvy stood up and said she had to leave.

"You made an old man happy, Detective," he said, clasping her hand. When she was almost out the door, he said, "Oh! Did I tell you she had a son named Silas?"

"Well, you said you thought so."

"He wasn't Declan's boy. He was Preston's. Mary always hated Janet Bancroft, and she got her hooks into Janet's husband and woo-wee. . . ." He mock shuddered. "Lucky one of 'em didn't kill the other."

Well, someone killed Mary, Savvy thought while driving the rest of the way to Hale's. She wasn't sure whether she believed Herman's account that Preston St. Cloud had fathered another son besides Hale. He'd said himself there was no proof about the paternity of most of Mary's children. And she sure as hell wasn't going to lay that one on Hale without proof.

When she got to the St. Cloud house, she saw the outdoor lights had been left on for her. She glanced down at her watch and groaned. She'd told Hale she would come for dinner, and though they hadn't set a time, it was pretty late.

As she pulled into the drive, she noticed Janet's rental was gone, and then she looked over to see Hale coming through the front door. It gave her a warm feeling to think he'd been waiting for her, but then again, maybe he'd been worried.

Savvy stepped out of the car into the faintest of drizzles, the outdoor lights shining in her face. Hale came toward her, a smile of greeting on his face.

"I'm sorry I'm late," she apologized.

"No set time," he assured her easily. "Just glad you're here. You need me to bring anything from your car?"

She patted her messenger bag, which was slung over her shoulder. "My pump's in my messenger bag. I'm good."

"If you want to spend the night, we have more room. Mom left about twenty minutes ago."

Savvy was surprised. "She just got here."

"I know. The problem is, she and Declan have a lot of issues that neither of them will let go of."

They walked along the sidewalk to the front porch together. Being this close to Hale, with the misting rain surrounding them, feeling now more like a soft caress, Savvy tried to hold down her racing heart. She seemed to be infected with a kind of sexual madness herself.

He gazed down at her, and his lips parted, as if he were about to say something.

Savannah focused on his lips. A thrill shot through her at the thought of them crushing down on hers. Good God, but she needed to get a grip.

Victoria came out to the porch, wearing a jacket, her purse over her shoulder, heading for her blue Toyota, taking a break from nanny duty. "Your mom left? It wasn't because of me, was it?" she asked anxiously.

"No," Hale told her and then indicated that Savvy should enter the house ahead of him. She stepped inside, both gladdened and a little disappointed by the nanny's appearance. She'd thought for just a moment that he was going to kiss her.

* * *

The light flashed quickly. A small jet of illumination into the black night and rain. Ravinia almost missed it, it was so brief, but she was already dressed in her darkest pair of pants and a blue shirt. Her boots and cloak were hanging in the storeroom, and she crept down the stairs and through the kitchen, banging her shin in her haste, enough that she had to bite back a cry of pain. *Damn.* How many times had she sneaked away with no problem at all? She had to relax. Stop hurrying.

The wind had turned into a rustle when Ravinia stepped outside, sliding a little in slippery mud that had mired onto the flagstone path that ran around the east side of the lodge. She hurried as fast as she dared toward the graveyard, then picked her way carefully through the headstones to where she could see a faint glow. Earl had turned the flashlight beam toward the ground and behind a boulder and a rhododendron toward the back of the plot where he had already been digging.

"What's this?" she whispered when she reached him.

He pointed downward, his finger barely visible. "Mary."

"Oh."

When she saw the pine box that held her mother, she felt a strange guilt. Like she was betraying this woman that she didn't even know. But then Earl needed her help to carry the box toward the lodge. Ravinia strained with all her might. She was barely up to the task and just managed to hang on to the slippery wood, her arms aching from the effort. They worked their way slowly to where her mother's real grave lay and set the box down.

The rain had finally abated to a soft drizzle. Earl looked at the ground in front of Mary's headstone and laid a hand on the wet earth.

"What?" Ravinia whispered.

"It was dug up recently."

"No. It's just messed up because of this damn rain."

"We needed the rain to explain why the earth will be disturbed," he muttered.

She gazed down at his damp blue baseball cap and the slick black jacket he wore. She needed better clothes for the weather. Something more weatherproof than this wool.

"Someone's been here," he said, his words so quiet, she had to strain to hear. Then he went back to the first grave, smoothed it over, then returned with his shovel.

"No one's been here," she told him, certain he was imagining it.

Earl bent down and began shoveling the dirt. He placed careful shovelfuls on the ground beside the grave while Ravinia watched and shivered. It felt like forever before Earl slowed down and finally stopped. Ravinia looked into a deep hole.

"Shouldn't there be a casket by now?" she asked.

"There never was a casket."

"So . . . where are the bones?"

Earl looked toward the west, and Ravinia followed his gaze, getting a bad feeling.

"Earl?" she asked, her shiver turning into a deep body shudder.

"He's gone," was all he said.

Ravinia was still shaking by the time she entered Catherine's room. Though she had shed her cloak and boots, the hems of her pant legs were soaking wet and left a damp trail up the stairs and into her aunt's bedroom.

"Well?" Catherine asked tautly.

"We moved Mary's casket into the grave with the headstone. Earl says, with all this rain, the police won't notice that it's been recently dug. Although, he sure seems to be able to tell those kinds of things. He says they won't be looking, though."

"What are you talking about?" Catherine struggled out of bed and lit the lamp again. "Close the door," she ordered in a harsh whisper.

Ravinia did as she asked, then turned back to her, her whole body feeling like it was clenched. "The bones were gone."

"What?"

"They weren't in the grave." Catherine stared at her hard, and Ravinia added, "Even before we started digging, Earl noticed something. He said someone had been there."

Catherine got to her feet, steadying herself for a moment. When Ravinia stepped forward, she snapped, "No, no. I'm fine. Just got up too fast. I hate being so feeble."

"But you're getting better."

"Yes, yes, of course. Don't worry. What else did Earl say?"

"Nothing. He just said, 'He's gone,' and then we put Mary's casket in the grave and covered it up."

"This wasn't Declan Jr.," Catherine said, her expression hard to read. "This isn't right."

"Who's Declan Jr.?"

"The son of the man who tried to rape me."

"The one whose bones should have been in the grave? If it's his father, maybe he did take them. I mean, who else would want them?" Ravinia demanded.

"He doesn't know. He thinks someone else is his father." Catherine waved her to silence, her face a study in concentration.

After a few minutes of complying, Ravinia had had enough. "What do you want me to do?"

"I'm still thinking."

"Stop keeping me in the dark. Give me a clue. Something."

"I've been wrong about the fire on Echo. I thought it was Declan Jr.'s doing. It's got to be . . . someone else."

"Why?" When she didn't answer, Ravinia asked, "Okay, then, who?" When Catherine still failed to engage with her, Ravinia said, "You said you needed me to do something for you. What?"

"When are you leaving?" Catherine asked her.

"Leaving . . . what? For good? I'm not sure I am. What are you saying?"

"Cassandra's seen you on the road with a friend. I'm asking you, when are you planning to go?"

Ravinia stared at her aunt. She realized she'd been entertaining ideas of staying ever since Catherine's accident, like she could change things for the better at the lodge. But Ophelia was already making plans to do just that, and Ravinia's reason to stick around had become no reason at all. It would take a long time to really change the atmosphere around Siren Song, to really instigate changes. And Ravinia couldn't wait that long.

"Tomorrow," she heard herself say, and Catherine nodded once and said, "Then you'll need some money."

CHAPTER 29

Savvy awoke to unfamiliar surroundings and the distinct smell of leather. She sat bolt upright, and her memory flooded back. She'd taken Hale up on his invitation to spend the night, but she'd refused his bedroom. That was just . . . not a good idea, and instead she'd insisted on the couch.

And her sleep had been interrupted by the baby enough times to make Savvy feel tired, yet happy. Victoria had managed to stumble awake once, but seeing Savvy, she'd turned back to her bed with a desultory wave.

Now she heard someone in the kitchen. She'd slept in her shirt and pants, which was all she had, and she ran a hand through her tousled hair as she walked out barefoot to meet them. But it wasn't Hale; it was Declan. He was in a robe over pajamas, and he, too, ran a hand through his white hair upon seeing her.

"Going to the office today," he announced. "Time to get back to work." He eyed her keenly. "But you, now. You're not going to want"—he turned around and motioned down the hallway—"that girl taking care of the boy." He harrumphed. "She doesn't have the good sense that God gave her."

"Hale's working on it and the memorial service," Savvy said diffidently. If Hale hadn't told Declan what his plans were, there was probably a good reason. And she was telling the truth. Hale had told Savvy that he had a call into the nanny service that had supplied them with Victoria and arrangements were being made. They'd also talked over the memorial service. He was thinking of having something at the house, although it would be tight if they got a crowd. Ian and Astrid Carmichael, who had found Kristina unconscious in the living room of their home, had suggested a hotel in Seaside that had meeting rooms. Astrid, though pregnant, seemed to want to take over all the planning for the service. She was, in fact, a little manic about it. Survivor's guilt again, Savvy felt. They were all suffering from it.

But she said none of that to Declan, whose voice was rising as he warmed to his theme of Victoria's shortcomings. "Witless, that girl is. Nice enough, sure, but you could fill a continent with nice people, and if they don't have it up here . . ." He tapped his skull with his finger. "It doesn't count."

"I'd better get home and take a shower," Savvy said before he could go on.

"You can use mine," Hale's voice said casually. She looked over as he appeared from the hallway. His hair was still damp from the shower and curled dark and wet at his neck.

"Thanks, but I don't have any fresh clothes." She slipped away from him and into the den and gathered up her things. It was downright annoying, the way she noticed everything about him.

Had it really been less than a week since she'd thought him cold and uncommunicative?

"What are you going to do about that girl?" Declan was complaining when Savvy returned a few minutes later, back in her shoes and socks and with her coat slung over her arm.

"Leave it alone," Hale told him. "Declan's safe with her for now."

"You sure?" He squinted up at Hale as he leaned on his cane.

"I heard you say you're going to the office," Hale said, changing the subject.

"Well, I can't sit around here all day, now, can I?" he demanded querulously.

There was just no way to win with Declan, so Hale gave up and turned to Savvy. "Call me later, and let's get this memorial service nailed down."

"You got it," Savvy said and let herself out into a crisp, cool morning, for once without a hint of rain.

Ravinia crawled over the wall, her hand slipping a little on the railing. But it was dew, not rain, and she caught herself and dropped lightly to her feet. She probably could have asked someone to open the gate, but she couldn't bring herself to do it, for some reason. It felt too much like begging, and, anyway, this was nearly the last, if not the last, time she would sneak away.

Money. Catherine had given her a stash that had made her eyes widen. The speed at which things were going, now that Catherine had accepted she was leaving and was okay with it, boggled Ravinia's mind. Her aunt hadn't once decreed that Ravinia could never come back since they'd made a tacit pact to work together. It was just a fact that Ravinia would go and Catherine would remain with the others, and they would work together to keep Siren Song's secrets safe.

She'd told Aunt Catherine she was leaving today, and she found the idea kind of scary. Where would she go? What would she do? She was taking a trek out this morning to Deception Bay, and with the money she now had, she was going to buy herself a few things. Some new clothes. Some of those energy bars. A knife—you never knew when a weapon might come in handy. A new pair of hiking boots. A disposable cell phone.

She'd left early, because it would take some time to get to town on foot and she really wanted to be alone with her thoughts. Inside, she was brimming with a kind of repressed excitement she was afraid to let out. She was free! It was what she'd wanted for too long to remember. It was . . .

She walked around a corner and saw the figure of a man at the next rise, right in the middle of the road. There was something familiar about him, and she realized it was her friend, the man she'd dreamed of running away with. Briefly, she thought of Rand and wondered if she should make a point of saying good-bye. Why, she wasn't sure. She barely knew him. But seeing her friend again made it just all the more clear that she was going to go away, and if she ever did come back, it wasn't going to be for a long time.

She hurried toward him, vaguely aware that something about him seemed different.

She was puffing by the time she reached him, little poofs of her breath visible in the cold air. "What are you doing?" she asked him.

"Waiting for you."

"Like you knew I'd be here," she said dryly.

He smiled as they walked to the side of the road together. He wore a dark blue Gore-Tex jacket, and his hair was covered by a hood. But she could see his blue eyes. Crystalline. Almost silvery. She realized that it was a week's growth of beard that darkened his jaw that made him seem different. Older. More sexy in some way that reached right down to Ravinia's toes.

"I have something for you," he said.

"Yeah? What?"

He slid the pack from his back. She had a sense it was all he owned, that he was a vagabond of sorts. Well, so would she be by the end of the day.

To her confusion and disappointment, it was a sheaf of papers, rolled up and rubber banded together. "Take these to your aunt."

Ravinia shot him a startled glance. She'd never told him her name, and he'd never told her his. They'd just run into each other a few times, and though she thought she could follow him anywhere, she knew next to nothing about him. "How do you know who my aunt is?"

"The middle-aged woman who wears long dresses and puts her hair in a bun and runs the cult in that lodge where you live? Catherine Rutledge. She's more well known than the mayor in Deception Bay."

"What is this?" Ravinia asked, looking down at the papers.

"Something she's been looking for."

"It's you," she said, realization dawning. She looked toward the outlines of the island far out in the water. "You were on Echo. You set the fire. Why?"

"Sometimes you have to burn things," was his unsatisfying answer.

"Who are you? What do you want?"

"I'm a friend, Ravinia. Take Catherine the papers. She'll know."

"Can I read them?"

"If I said no, would it do any good?"

"Probably not," she admitted.

He smiled again, his teeth very white. "Just make sure Catherine gets them."

"Where are you going?" she asked when he turned away as if their meeting was over.

"I've got some things to do, but I'll be around."

"Will I see you again?" she blurted out as he headed in the opposite direction from Deception Bay.

"You never know," he called over his shoulder. "Maybe it's our destiny."

She watched him for a long time, torn between wanting to chase after him and the equally strong desire to go into town and prepare for her own adventure. She looked down at the sheaf of papers, then shoved them inside her coat. Maybe she would wait and read them after she'd shown them to Aunt Catherine.

It had taken Charlie all night to come up with a foolproof plan, but by the time he did, he was grinning to himself. He knew how to get to the luscious detective, Savannah Dunbar. He knew what to do. And now the plan was in place, and he just had to wait.

Thinking of her made him horny. Her lovely milk-engorged breasts. Her cool, efficient demeanor. Her belief that he was the hunted and she was the hunter. *Ha!*

He closed his eyes, dreamed of sliding himself all over her. There were others to take care of, too, but he wanted her first. Now. Today. In his mind's eye he saw himself riding her hard, and his cock jumped to life so fast, he could almost hear the cartoon *boing* sound.

But it was the thought of the killing afterward that really got him cranked up.

And now everything was in place. He literally rubbed his hands together and laughed aloud when he realized it. He couldn't wait for the lovely Detective Dunbar. He envisioned her lying on her back, tied down, writhing for him, while he stood by and watched her.

An unwanted thought sizzled across his brain, shattering his delicious fantasy, infuriating him. It was his secret lover calling. *I know what you're thinking.*

Charlie's teeth ground together. Bullshit. No one knew what he was thinking. His thoughts were his own. He was getting tired of her and her game playing. She was just toying with him, not letting him see her. To hell with her. He was going to play the game on his terms, not hers.

He could feel his carefully constructed Charlie mask start to crack and split on his face.

You getting wet, bitch? he asked her. *Getting ready for me?*

Name the place, was the answer that came back to him, faintly haunting, carried on the wind.

He clamped his mind shut. No! Not yet. He wasn't going to let her see his perfect plan. First, he was going to have his time with the hot detective; she could just goddamn wait.

He hated her, this sneaky secret lover. He didn't like being watched from the shadows.

After the detective, she was next. He would lure her out, and then they would see who the master game player was.

Savannah phoned Lang as soon as she got to work. When he didn't answer, she called him every hour on the hour, knowing she was being flat-out annoying, uncaring that she was. She wanted answers from him. She'd sent him the report; the least he could do was get back to her about *something*.

Detective Hamett had phoned again, and this time she'd taken the call. He'd asked her a number of roundabout questions that all had to do with Hale, which ratcheted up her anxiety, even though she knew the routine. She told him that she felt Kristina's killer could be the mysterious lover her sister had met at the Carmichael house. She was debating about telling him about Kristina's liaisons at the Donatella house, but he was called away before she could go into the story, so she settled on writing down the information instead.

Finally, Lang called back in the late afternoon. "Looks like Woodworth isn't the only missing employee. Jacob Balboa's been gone since Saturday."

"Balboa," she repeated. The next name on the list. "But he did work Saturday?" Savvy asked, thinking of the cold eyes that she'd felt staring at her from afar at the RiverEast Apartments construction zone.

"Yeah, he was there. Apparently, he even talked to Woodworth about you. One of the other guys thought he overheard them mention a female detective."

"I noticed one of the workers staring at me from a distance."

"Bet it's the same guy."

"Where does he live?" Savvy asked.

"Some place south of Oregon City, more rural country. I'm heading there with Curtis now, and we've contacted the sheriff. I don't know. . . ." He sounded uncertain.

"What?"

"I don't like thinking they had a conversation about you and now they're both missing."

Savvy felt a flutter of fear travel up her spine but said, "I'm fine. Maybe Balboa's worried that I'm on his trail."

"Stay close to the phone," he said.

"Hey, I'm like a teenager in love, waiting all day for you to call."

She scared a chuckle out of him, which had been her intention. "Okay. I'll let you know what we find at Balboa's."

She hung up slowly, feeling like they were getting close. Was Balboa Charlie? Had he killed DeWitt and possibly Henry . . . ? She thought of Nadine, how she'd sounded on the edge of panic that Henry was missing. Did she maybe suspect something? She'd still been filling in at Bancroft Development. Maybe she knew Jacob Balboa and sensed he was dangerous.

Maybe he was Kristina's lover . . . Mary's son, Declan Jr.?

She jumped when her desk phone suddenly rang, another call through the switchboard. She picked up the receiver. "A Victoria Phelan wants to speak to Detective Savvy somebody or other," Cho told her.

Victoria? "Put her through," she said, immediately worried about the baby. As soon as she heard the click that confirmed they were connected, she said, "Victoria? This is Savannah Dunbar. Is there something wrong?"

"Yes . . . ," the girl said on a gulp.

Her heart squeezed hard; her pulse pounded in her ears. "What?"

"I found . . . a gun."

Savannah blinked hard, pulling herself back from a full-on Mommy panic attack. "What kind of gun?"

"I don't know. A little one? A . . . handgun, I guess."

"Oh. Well, it must be Hale's," she said.

"Uh-uh. I think it's his wife's. . . . It was in her things, but kinda . . . hidden a little," she said slowly.

"Where did you find it?" Savvy asked, realizing that Victoria had most likely been snooping in Kristina's belongings. A slow burn started inside her at a deep level.

"There was this bag of clothes in the closet? For long dresses and stuff, to protect them? I just wanted to see and I unzipped it and the gun was lying on the bottom, sort of. Kinda tucked back."

Savvy pushed her anger at Victoria to the back of her mind. Kristina had had a gun? That was news to her, but then her sister had become so cagey and secretive, it was possible she hadn't known. "You should let Hale know," Savvy said, but a dark fear swirled into her thoughts. *Kristina with a gun . . .*

She thought of the evidence file on the Donatellas. The murder weapon was never discovered.

"Have you touched it?" Savannah asked swiftly.

"Well, uh . . . I picked it up, but I put it back."

Her Mommy panic was back, only in a different form.

"Should I bring it to you?" Victoria asked.

"No! Don't touch it again."

"You're scaring me," she said, her voice starting to quaver.

"Just . . . stay with Declan, and don't do anything. I'll be right there."

Savvy grabbed her messenger bag, checked her own gun at her hip, then headed toward the back door of the station.

Ravinia pulled the sheaf of papers from her pack, where she'd had them stowed ever since her friend had handed them to her. She'd intended to turn them right over to Catherine, but then she'd been reluctant to. No, she hadn't read them, and she couldn't rightly say why.

She'd purchased several pairs of jeans and some dark green dungarees, three shirts, a sweatshirt, and yes, a black Gore-Tex jacket. She had new underwear; several new bras, the store-bought kind, which actually cinched you in; a new pair of sneakers; and the boots on her feet, with some heavy socks. She had bought some snacks, too, and thought Hot Tamales could almost be the perfect food.

Lastly, she'd purchased a disposable cell phone.

But after she'd returned, she'd spent the day in her room, reluctant to leave it until she was actually on the road. She was delaying for reasons she couldn't quite fathom, but she knew it was because she was going to miss her sisters. Not that she was spending these last hours with them. That was what she should be doing, but it seemed too hard, somehow.

She'd decided that when she did leave, she was going to tramp up the road that ran in front of the Siren Song drive and led to the Foothillers' village. She wanted to see Rand one last time, see if he could tell her anything more about her family's connection to his.

Of course . . . her eyes strayed to the pages. Her friend had told her Catherine had been looking for them, so maybe some of the answers were right here.

Getting to her feet, she looked into the small mirror above her ancient vanity and made a face. She'd always been rather proud of her hair. Had combed the dark blond tresses and tossed them about her head, lost in self-admiration. Now that just felt . . . stupid . . . and so she'd plaited her hair into one long braid down her back.

Grabbing up her pack, which was a little heavier than she would have liked, but no pain, no gain, Ravinia slung it over one shoulder, picked up the papers, then headed down the hall to Catherine's room. She raised her hand to knock but heard voices inside. For a moment she was undecided. She wanted Aunt Catherine to be alone when she turned over the pages. She was just turning back toward her room when Ophelia burst through the door, nearly running into her.

"I was just coming for you," Ophelia said, taking in Ravinia's attire and backpack with raised brows.

"I'm just saying good-bye," Ravinia said, lifting her chin in challenge.

"What's that?" Ophelia asked, zeroing in on the pages clutched in her left hand.

"Something for Aunt Catherine."

She was annoyed when Ophelia walked right back into Catherine's room ahead of her instead of leaving. And then she was further annoyed when Ophelia said, "Ravinia has something you've been looking for."

"How did you know?" Ravinia wanted to scream, but she swallowed the words, knowing full well there were other forces at play in her family.

"What is it?" Catherine asked. She was seated at her desk, not lying in bed, which was a good sign.

For an answer, Ravinia handed over the papers, giving Ophelia a hard look when it appeared she might try to grab some for herself. Ravinia had waited all day to share this moment with her aunt, and now she had to deal with Ophelia.

But then Catherine suddenly handed the top page to Ophelia, anyway, saying, "The adoptive families! Mary had these on Echo." Then, to Ravinia, "How did you get these?"

"Maybe this'll lead us to Declan Jr.," Ophelia said.

Ophelia swept out of the room, but Ravinia felt her comment like a blow. She shouldn't be surprised that she wasn't the only one Aunt Catherine had confided in, but it bothered her deeply. One more reason to go.

"Good," Aunt Catherine said, glancing down at the other pages, which looked as if they were lined notebook paper, their holes tied together with orange thread. "She didn't have a journal on the island," Catherine mused. "She put it down on paper. How did you get this, Ravinia?" She looked up at her, demanding an answer.

"He gave it to me."

"Who?"

"I don't know his name."

"How . . ." Catherine swallowed, then asked sharply, "What did he look like?"

"I don't know. Dark hair. Blue eyes . . . I guess. Handsome," she said reluctantly.

"His hair was dark? Not any shade of blond?"

"He's not one of us, is he?" Ravinia asked on a gasp.

"Was he on the island? Was he the one who found these pages on the island?" Catherine demanded.

"I guess so. He's the one that built the fire."

"He said that? He admitted it?"

"Pretty much."

"Ravinia, what exactly did he say?"

"He said he was a friend, and that sometimes you just had to burn things."

Catherine seemed to melt into the chair, as if all her energy had been expended. "He burned them," she said in wonder. "He took the bones, and he burned them."

"Are you sure? Why would he do that? Why would anyone do that?"

To her surprise, her aunt actually smiled. "It's how you kill the Hydra. Burn it, so it doesn't grow another head."

"Who is he?" Ravinia said. "Is he some relative?"

"I think he's your brother Silas. Mary's last son, like you're her last daughter . . ." A cloud marred her expression. "Unless she had more children I'm unaware of."

"On the island? How?"

Her gaze had dropped to the tied pages. "Never mind. I'm just borrowing trouble."

"So, he's my brother Silas?" Ravinia repeated. "And he's not like Declan . . . ?"

"The remains that Silas burned were once Declan's father, not Silas's. I don't think Silas means us harm."

"He doesn't," Ravinia assured her.

Catherine nodded, accepting her answer as the truth, which was surprising in itself. "Silas wouldn't have given you the pages if he wanted to keep his past secret. Ophelia will check with their adoptive families."

They stared at each other a moment, and then Catherine got to her feet. She looked down at the desk and picked up a piece of paper, staring at it a moment before turning to Ravinia and holding it out to her.

"What's this?"

"It's what I'd like you to do for me. It's comforting to know that Silas appears to be helping us, but I can't take the chance. Declan Jr.'s too strong, and if he senses that there's someone vulnerable out there . . ." She pressed her hand to her mouth and shook her head. "I couldn't keep her. Not with Mary so dead set on me giving up Declan. I did as she asked, but fertility is one of our assets."

"You had a baby," Ravinia realized.

"Elizabeth. I gave her away at birth, but now I want you to find her." Ravinia took the piece of paper and read the name: Elizabeth Gaines. "She could be married now," Catherine went on. "The Gaineses lived in Northern California. I don't know if they still do. Robert Gaines was in real estate, and Joy was a stay-at-home mom."

"How old is Elizabeth now?"

"Twenty-six."

"I'm not sure how I'll find her, but if I do . . . ?"

"Let me know she's all right. And keep her safe."

Ravinia saw the glimmer of moisture in her aunt's eyes, but Catherine turned away, back to the papers. As she left the room, she thought she heard her aunt say, "I'm going to miss you," but she wasn't really sure.

Savvy drove fast and hard. The roads were dry, and though water stood in puddles all around, her tires gripped the road.

She'd tried to call Hale several times, but he had been at a job site and then had gotten on the phone hurriedly once, saying Astrid Carmichael was in his office, working on the memorial service, and asking if he could call her back.

She should have just told him about the gun, but she'd let the thought slip away. She wanted to see it for herself, anyway. She would call him from the house.

She turned into the driveway, her tires giving a squeal of protest. Victoria's small compact was parked in the turnaround, as it had been each time she'd arrived. Savvy jumped out of the car.

And immediately sensed a presence behind her. She turned, one hand reaching automatically for her gun, and then stopped cold, seeing the familiar man with the wide smile.

"Mr. Woodworth," she said, surprised. "Nadine Gretz put out a missing person's report on you."

He took a step closer. "Call me Henry. Or, better yet, Declan. How's that? Or how about Charlie . . . ?"

She was already reaching for her gun, adrenaline sizzling through her like a jolt of electricity. Not Jacob Balboa. Henry Woodworth.

He jumped forward and grabbed her arms. Her fingers slipped on the butt of her gun. His hands were steel, squeezing so hard, she couldn't move. Then he let go of one hand to yank her hair, snapping her head back. He slammed his fist into her jaw with the other, and she stumbled backward. Pinpoints of light flickered behind her eyes.

Go for the nose and eyes, she thought. *Elbows are weapons.*

She twisted, hard. Tried for the gun again. Failed. Jabbed her right elbow into his nose. A gush of blood sprayed her as he howled in surprise and pain, but then his hands were around her throat, choking her. They fell to the ground together. Savannah pried at his strangling fingers, flailing, struggling to breathe. He was holding her down, pressing his weight on her. Kissing her. Biting her. Making her stomach revolt and her throat gag.

"I knew you'd be a hellcat. Give all you've got. I'm going to have you. Forever," he cooed. He released her long enough to rip at her shirt. She gasped for air as one of his hands caressed her breast, squeezing hard.

"C'mon, Mama," he whispered, and she tensed. She wasn't going to let him rape her. She would kill him. Smash his head. Find a way to get her gun. Shoot the son of a bitch in the heart.

And then she felt something cold and insistent slide through her skin, into her bloodstream, along her nerves, firing up all the sensors in her brain with a wild, rampant sexual desire that froze her where she lay.

No . . . oh, God . . . , she thought, inwardly panicked, unable to move. *Kristina . . . this is what you felt . . . !*

His hands were around her throat again, squeezing. She sensed his blue eyes boring into hers. Then her consciousness spiraled downward, funneling smaller and smaller, compressing down until blackness surrounded her and she was gone.

CHAPTER 30

Savannah's first conscious thought was that she was lying on a cold slab. Every muscle ached, and she was freezing. She slowly came awake to realize she was lying naked atop a granite kitchen island. Bluish moonlight left a hard rectangle across her feet, the only illumination in an otherwise dark room.

She tried to lift her hand, but it was tied down. Both hands were. And her legs.

"Been waiting for you . . . ," a voice said silkily from across the room.

Savvy turned her head sharply and saw he was standing by the fireplace. She could just make out a jumble of wood inside the hearth, but Charlie didn't seem to be in any hurry to light it. He probably hadn't put it there, she realized. The house had a cold, empty feel and a faintly musty smell.

The Donatella home. Left to rot and fall into the ocean.

He'd brought Kristina here.

"I know what you're thinking," he said, coming closer. He was still wearing his dark jacket and jeans, while she was completely nude, and his nose, though swollen, had stopped bleeding. Just looking at him, her teeth started chattering. "Don't worry. I'm gonna get you real warm," he said, running a finger along her jawline and down her neck, along the curve of her breast and down her hipline. She was afraid she would feel that noxious sexual thrill again. No wonder Kristina had been so desperate and crazy! He'd put her under his spell, somehow, just like Catherine had predicted.

He was Declan Jr. He'd said so. He'd killed Kristina and he'd killed Owen DeWitt and he'd probably killed his mother, too.

His grin was so malevolent, she had to remind herself that he was just a man. Not a demon. Gift or no gift, he was still just a man.

Savvy had to keep him talking. She had to buy time until what? Victoria saw her car in the driveway? Hale came home and wondered what had happened to her?

"What name do you go by?" she asked him, trying to stop her shivering.

"Henry Charles Woodworth. That's what my adoptive parents called me, before my 'mother' committed suicide, that is. Think I should change it to Declan, like my birth certificate?"

"You're not Declan Bancroft's son," Savvy said. "That was just something Mary told Catherine as a means to hurt her. Your real father is someone else."

"You're wrong."

"I don't think so."

"He's my father. Why do you think I'm working for him? Because I love the job? Bancroft Development is rightfully mine." He made a disparaging sound. "I've been letting the old man know he shouldn't have ignored me."

"What do you mean?" She'd turned her head toward the window at the front of the house, and though he'd pulled the drapes closed, there was a sliver of moonlit porch and driveway visible beyond. And her car sat in front of the house.

Her car.

She felt despair. Maybe Victoria didn't even know she'd come by.

"I mean, I'm a Bancroft and I deserve what's mine. Oh, don't shiver. I've got what you need right here." He grabbed his crotch and grinned some more. "But you gotta be patient, like me. I've been thinking about you ever since you came to the job site. Couldn't get you outta my head. It's too bad, because I treated Nadine pretty badly afterward, but she always comes around."

"What about Jacob Balboa?" Savvy asked. Her thoughts were on Kristina, but she couldn't go there. She didn't think she could stand hearing what he said about her.

She'd surprised him with the name. He blinked several times and asked sharply, "What about him?"

"My partner's at his house. Did you kill him? Why?"

"Now, hold on. I didn't say I killed him."

"You did, though," Savvy realized, reading between the lines. Would anyone be looking for her? The only one who was expecting her was the nanny, and she had no faith in Victoria.

"Balboa was asking all about you. And he knew a little too much about Good Time Charlie. I had to . . . take care of things."

"And then you came to the coast, after you killed both him and DeWitt," Savvy said.

"Dimwit! If anyone deserved to die, it was that piece of human garbage." He leaned closer. Savvy would have shrunk away if she could have. "But it's their black souls that hold the mysteries. I look into their eyes and . . ." He closed his own eyes and sucked in air with a sigh of pleasure. "I can see every part of them. Your sister was so easy, but she knew too much, too."

"That's why you killed her."

"She was a part of it. She was right here." He looked around himself.

"She was here the night you executed the Donatellas?" She wanted her voice to be steel, but there was a quiver beneath it she couldn't contain.

"Oh, sure. She liked coming to Bancroft properties and fucking me," he said, and Savvy knew it was a lie. "She liked the danger. Marcus wasn't invited, but he showed up with Chandra. They caught us, and they would have told the old man, which wasn't part of the plan."

"Their deaths never had anything to do with the dune failure," Savvy said.

"That was what everyone wanted to believe, so I pushed 'em there. 'Blood money' was a nice touch."

She felt soul sick for her sister, seeing how terribly she'd been used and abused by this human aberration.

"I like you, Detective. I really do. It's too bad you couldn't be like Nadine or Kristina and hang around awhile, but you're not the type to play along, are you?"

"Kristina never played along."

"Oh, she did. She did. She helped me haunt the old man. She despised him."

Fury licked through Savannah. "That's a lie. She liked Declan."

"That's why I picked her, y'know. 'Cause she married St. Cloud. His grandson. My nephew," he said, chortling.

"You're not a Bancroft," Savvy said again. "Catherine said your father was a monster."

He flew forward and slapped her hard. Her senses spun. How long had it been since he'd abducted her? It had been afternoon, and now it was night. She'd called Hale, and he said he would call her back. How many times had he tried?

"My father is Declan Bancroft!"

"No."

This time his answer was to pinch one of her nipples, hard. Savvy shuddered but was too cold to react much, and, anyway, it was nothing compared to what he could do with his *thoughts*. He ran an experimental hand down her body, and though she clenched her teeth, sick with worry, the terrible feeling didn't follow.

"You're thinking about him," he suddenly accused her, and he slapped her again so hard, she saw stars. She *had* been thinking about Hale. How much she wanted to be with him. How, if she got out of this mess, she would make it work between them. How it didn't matter what anyone thought. She wanted a future with Hale and hoped he felt the same.

And then she felt it coming, that awful snaky sensation, like being overcome by a dark sexual twine. She moaned in fear and blanked her mind to it, thinking only of Hale, and baby Declan, and the love she felt for her sister, who'd fallen victim to this madman. The throbbing sexual netting seemed to lessen, and she squeezed herself tightly, fighting him off.

"Fuck!" Charlie yelled in frustration. "You can't get away from me!"

But something must be working, or he wouldn't be so upset. She bore down inside her mind and thought about Hale some more, recalling the hard line of his jaw and the surprise of his smile, the long, dark lashes over steely gray eyes, the male scent that was uniquely his, which she'd smelled in his bedroom.

The bellow that rose from Charlie's chest made Savvy's eyes fly open. She was shaking uncontrollably now. Hypothermia.

He glared at her with consuming fury. "You want him? Your sister's husband? You want him?"

"Yes," she said, fighting to keep her voice from trembling. "I want him. Not you."

He ripped at his hair, clearly overcome with her defiance.

Then her phone started ringing from inside her messenger bag, and she recognized Hale's ring tone. With a screech of fury that made her worry the last shreds of his sanity might be fleeing, he grabbed up the bag and yanked out her still ringing phone, holding it up for her to see.

"Lover boy," he snapped when the ringing finally stopped. "He's been trying to reach you."

Savvy tried to keep her relief from her face. He knew she was missing.

"Well, maybe it's time we let him know where you are. . . ."

Her relief turned to instant fear for Hale's safety as Charlie scrolled to her most recent call, then began composing a message on her keyboard. He looked up when he was finished. "You texted him that you're at Bankruptcy Bluff. You want him. Let's bring him here!"

Hale was pacing the kitchen floor, with Victoria standing by, looking unhappy. "You told Savvy that you found a gun in Kristina's dress bag, and she said she would be right over," he reiterated.

"I've told you and told you. Yes. That's what happened."

"You didn't call me. You called Savannah."

"I'm sorry! It scared me."

Hale didn't completely believe her, but he didn't have time to dig deeper into Victoria's strange choices. When Savannah had called him earlier, he'd been certain she was in her car. He hadn't known where she was headed, but now knew she was supposed to come here. What happened to her? God, he wished he'd talked to her when she'd called. She was probably going to tell him about the gun. Since then, he'd phoned her cell over and over again, but she hadn't answered even once.

His fear was rising with each passing minute. Was this Charlie's work? He decided he would call the TCSD. If the reason she hadn't phoned back was something easily explained, like maybe there was some problem with her phone, so be it.

He was reaching for the phone he was recharging on the kitchen counter when it *blooped,* alerting him that he had a text. He snatched it up and saw in relief that the text was from Savannah.

At the bluff. Hurry.

Immediately he texted back: **Where's Charlie? Did u see him?**

Followed him here.

"Goddamnit," Hale muttered, half out of relief, half out of fear.

Quickly, he texted back: **Wait for me. Don't do anything.**

"Jesus." He stuffed the phone in his pocket and ran for the door.

"What did she say?" Victoria asked, staring after him with wide, scared eyes.

"She's okay. I know where she is. Just stay with Declan. I'll be back soon."

Charlie waved the cell phone at Savannah and chuckled. "Lover boy's coming to save his lady fair. How does it feel to steal your sister's husband? That your thing?"

Savannah quaked all over. The small smile that curved Charlie's hard lips was evil in its intent.

Hale, please don't come. Call Lang. Don't come on your own.

Hale backed the TrailBlazer out of the garage, his brain churning. Something wrong there. Why had she decided to go to Bancroft Bluff instead of the house? Some new clue that had turned her back to the scene of the Donatellas' murders?

He'd gone straight back rather than run into Victoria's Toyota, which was parked in the turnaround. Now he stood on the brakes, thinking. He threw the car into park and jumped out, running forward to the stretch of concrete driveway near the garage, seeing something on the ground.

Blood. A spray of it.

Whose? Savannah's?

Hale jumped back in his SUV. Deception Bay and Bancroft Bluff were twenty minutes away without traffic.

He grabbed his phone and put in a call to the TCSD. "This is Hale St. Cloud," he bit out when a female operator answered for the station. "I need to speak to Langdon Stone or Detective Clausen." He couldn't remember Clausen's first name.

"If this is an emergency, call nine-one-one," the voice responded.

"I need to speak to one of the detectives," he said, wondering if maybe he should call 9-1-1.

But a few moments later a male voice said, "Mr. St. Cloud, this is Detective Clausen. How can I help you?"

"Just got a text from Savannah. She asked me to come to Bancroft Bluff. I'm on my way, but as I left my house, I saw some blood on the concrete driveway. Savannah was supposed to be at my house, but she didn't show. . . ."

"You think something happened to her?" Clausen asked quickly.

"I don't know." He was relieved that the detective was taking him seriously.

"I'll run up there and see what's happening. Was thinking of going there, anyway. We got a homeless man that can't seem to stay away from one of your houses, Mr. St. Cloud."

Maybe the detective wasn't taking him as seriously as he'd thought. "I'll be there in fifteen minutes," Hale said, if the slowpoke in front of him would get his bucket of bolts off the road.

"Give me your cell number. I'll call you," Clausen said. Hale gave it to him, but Clausen hung up before Hale could ask him for his in return.

Savannah tested the bonds on her left arm; they seemed a tad looser than those on her right, and this was on the side away from Charlie. She had to free herself. Had to find a way to warn Hale. "You look into their souls before they die," she said, seeking to get him talking again. He'd gone silent, lost in some world of his own.

"Shhh . . ." He said then, "Bitch. I won't play her game, but she won't give up."

It took Savvy a moment to realize he wasn't talking about her. She was so cold, it was hard to think.

But now his attention returned to her. "It's like the best sex ever, and then it's so much more."

"That's why you killed them? To look into their souls?" She had several fingers almost free.

"I killed my mother first," he admitted. "Mary. On the island. I put the knife right here." He pressed on his own chest, just beneath the breastbone. "And then I slid it up, underneath the ribs." His voice was almost reverent.

Two fingers were free. "You killed the Donatellas with a gun."

"It was what we had." And then he dug into her messenger bag and pulled out her gun. He'd obviously stashed it there while she was unconscious. He held it loosely in his hand. "Did you know your sister had a gun, too?" Savvy wouldn't respond as she thought of the one Victoria had found. "Kristina had to hide it," he explained, "or she would have been aiding and abetting. She was standing right there." He pointed toward the front window, and a light flashed through the crack in the drapes. "He's here . . . ," he said gleefully.

As he turned around, Savvy tried to shake the rope from her left wrist. She needed her hand free. She needed to warn Hale. She needed *out*. She was screaming inside but finally she wrenched her left hand free of the bindings.

Quickly, she reached around to her right wrist, tugging on the stubborn rope. *Please, please!*

Charlie threw open the door, and Savannah screamed with everything she had.

Bang!

The sound of the point-blank shot stunned Savannah. She ripped at the rope on her right hand. Yanking and pulling. Cold tears on her face.

Charlie stumbled backward as a body hit him hard. They rolled on the floor as Savannah twisted upward, pulling at the ropes that were wrapped around her ankles and in one long loop around the granite top. She half jumped, half fell off the island, and her muscles locked up. She was too cold. Too frozen.

In horror she watched as Charlie disentangled himself from the pile of arms and legs, covered in blood.

Fred Clausen lay on the floor, gazing blankly toward the ceiling, and Charlie hunkered over him, staring hard into the man's eyes, as if the secrets of the universe lay there.

Savannah broke and ran stiffly for the back door.

Hale made the turn into the housing development, aware how dark and forlorn all the empty houses seemed. There was no light in the area apart from the brilliant moonlight that had broken through a few drifting clouds.

Clausen hadn't phoned him back, and since Hale couldn't call him, he didn't know if the detective had shown up yet.

But as soon as he got around the first curve, he saw the black-and-yellow TCSD vehicle.

And right beside it, Savannah's rental.

"Okay . . . ," he said aloud, assessing the situation.

A dark figure ran across the road in front of him, disappearing into bushes on the far side of the Donatella house. Immediately, Hale was on alert. He looked around the vehicle. His tools were in the back.

Pulling to a stop in front of the Pembertons', he got out, feeling a brisk, cold wind numb his face. He went to the back of the Trail-Blazer, opened the hatch. The light came on, and he felt completely exposed. Quickly, he snapped open the toolbox and grabbed a wrench. Then he shut the hatch and remote-locked the car.

Where was Savannah?

She ran along the headland, the rim of which was a jagged edge of crumbling dirt. Her bare feet ran over sharp sticks and gravel buried in the dirt, and she was certain they were bleeding.

Hale was walking into a trap. She had to draw Charlie away. If he caught her, he would kill her. He would find her and drag her back to the house and rape her and shove a knife into her chest.

And he would watch her soul depart. He would feed off it.

She heard him stumbling after her. It was dark. Neither one of them could see.

Faintly, her ears picked up the sound of an approaching engine. *Oh, no! Hale.*

She slowed down, listening for her pursuer, but he was turning back. Heading to meet Hale!

She waited, breathing hard, shaking all over.

And suddenly he was right in front of her, reaching for her.

Automatically, she stepped backward, into air.

He grabbed for her arm, and she slipped down, her body scraping against the edge of the headland, loose sand and dirt spinning downward toward the sea.

"Shit," Charlie gritted, looking behind himself.

There was a light from a car. Hale's car.

Savvy yanked her arm free and clung to a twisting root sticking out the side of the headland. Cold, naked, and scared, she was too vulnerable to fight. All she could do was scream. "Hale! Look out! Hale!"

And then Charlie was gone, and she was hanging on the root, her arms weakening, her lower limbs feeling like lead.

He heard Savannah scream his name.

Immediately he ran in that direction, then saw the dark figure streak into the Donatella house through the open front door. Was that where she was? He ran after the figure, the wrench tight in his right hand.

Inside the house, he heard the strike of a match, and he raised the wrench, intent on crushing in Charlie's skull. But the man who'd tossed the match onto the newspapers and wood and debris in the hearth looked wrong somehow, and he hesitated.

"Jesus loves me, this I know," he sang in a trembling voice.

"Where's Savannah?" Hale demanded.

The man cocked his head, concentrating. Then his attention went to the licking flames, and he warmed his palms. "My house is all boarded up," he said. "The Donatellas won't mind."

"What?" Hale had been looking around the room, searching for a sign of Savannah, but his attention snapped back.

"We need a fire."

The sound of a cry. Over the crackling and spitting flames. Hale turned back toward the door. "Savvy?" he called.

Something to his right. A flicker in the corner of his eye. Hale ducked automatically and felt a knife slice through the sleeve of his jacket and pierce his skin. He whipped around with the wrench, connecting with flesh. His attacker yowled and stabbed at him again. Hale caught a glimpse of the blade in the moonlight and grabbed for the man's arm.

He was shocked to see the man had a gun in his other hand and he was raising it to Hale's face.

Bang!

Savannah heard the shot and cried out in fear. She scrabbled for a hold in the dirt. Failed. Her fingers frantically pawed at the headland until she connected with something hard in the sandy muck. A boulder. Buried far enough back to offer some stability. A handhold. Another one.

Carefully, she dragged her body up over the boulder to the headland, her limbs violently shaking. She got a knee atop the ground and cried out in relief. Then she was staggering forward. Safe from falling.

There were three figures inside the house; she could see them through a window. Hale was alive! Thank God!

But three . . . ? Had Clausen somehow survived?

She stumbled forward, her knees giving out, her brain unable to command her legs.

There was smoke coming from the chimney. More smoke inside the house.

She found her way to the back door, aware that she had no weapon, that she was as vulnerable as she could ever be.

In the red light from the fire, she saw Hale and Charlie at a standoff. Charlie had a palm up to the bright flames, as if warding them off, and he held a knife in his other hand. Hale held a wrench. Her gun was nowhere to be seen, but at least the shot hadn't hit Hale.

And there, standing near Clausen's body, unbelievably, was Mickey. She'd thought the warbling of "Jesus Loves Me" had been in her head.

"Hale," she whispered through a raw throat.

Hale glanced up just as Charlie charged him, running at him with the knife. Hale moved back, but Mickey, by accident or design, tripped Charlie, sending him sprawling face-first into the fire.

The wail that rose to the heavens was inhuman and caused Savannah to grab the island granite countertop to keep from collapsing.

Hale jumped forward toward Savannah. Mickey moved at the same moment, accidentally blocking him.

Savvy said, "Watch him! Watch him!" as Charlie writhed and screamed on the floor. His movement tangled up Mickey's feet. The homeless man went down, grabbing at Hale, who managed to stay upright.

The smell of cooked flesh permeated the air, making Savannah gag. Where was the knife?

Then Hale was there, holding on to her. "Savannah," he said in a voice that broke.

"I'm okay."

He stripped off his jacket. "You're freezing."

"Detective," Mickey said weakly. They both looked over.

Charlie had dragged himself to Clausen and was pulling his gun free of its holster, still sobbing.

Hale lunged to the right, taking Savannah with him.

Bang. Bang. Bang!

The rapid-fire shots were aimed where they'd been standing. Glass shattered on the microwave oven behind them. Hale covered her with his body.

And then there was silence.

Hale lifted his head and looked over. Mickey was lying on the floor, his arms crossed over his chest. Clausen's body was beside him, his holster empty.

There was no sign of Charlie.

Hale started to go after him, but Savvy said, "No. He has Clausen's gun. He can't get far. . . ."

She lifted a trembling arm to him, and he sank down beside her. "My God, Savannah," he said.

She wanted to say, "I love you," but it came out as a trembling "Thank you for finding me."

And he did what she'd been dreaming about for days. He leaned down and kissed her. She wound her fingers in his dark hair and kissed him back, hard. *We have to go,* she thought. *Before Charlie comes back.*

"Come on," Hale said, as if reading her thoughts, helping her to her feet and guiding her arms into the sleeves of his jacket.

She clung to him and looked down at Mickey, feeling a weight on her heart at the sight of Clausen's dead body and Mickey's still form, while Hale reached into his pocket for his cell phone to call the cavalry.

"Nine-one-one, what is the nature of your emergency?" the dispatcher's tinny voice sounded from Hale's cell.

Before he could respond, Mickey drew a breath and sang lustily, "Jesus loves me! This I know, cuz the Bible tells me so. . . ."

Three days later Savannah sat curled on Hale's den couch, snuggling her baby boy to her breast. Hale was seated beside her, and they were both sober and quiet. The memorial service had been at the venue Astrid Carmichael had suggested, and it had been a solemn and poignant affair. Savannah had taken baby Declan with her while Hale addressed the crowd with kind words about Kristina, which made Savvy tear up and feel sorry for her sister all over again. She'd been one of Charlie's most tortured victims.

And Charlie was a ghost. She could scarcely credit it. In the wounded state he'd been in? With those terrible burns on the side of his face? How had he slipped through the sheriff department's net? Someone had to have given him help and shelter.

Meanwhile, Lang and Sheriff O'Halloran and everyone else in the department were angry and determined to find the psychotic monster who'd taken out one of their own. Savannah hadn't been back to work since Charlie/Declan Jr./Henry had kidnapped her and killed Clausen, but she'd seen Lang and she knew his dark mood reflected everyone's feelings. The memorial service for Fred Clausen was scheduled for the following week.

Lang had also told Savannah that the DNA test had come back from the blood sample on the knife Catherine had given her. Savvy hadn't taken the news to Catherine yet, mainly because there wasn't much to say, anyway. Only one type of blood was discovered, and it belonged to a female, so it was probably Mary Rutledge Beeman's. For now, an exhumation of the body was on hold, but when Charlie/Henry/Declan Jr. was caught, they might need to search for corroborating evidence, naming him the killer.

Hale turned to look at Savannah. "How're we doing?" he asked.

"We're okay," she said.

Then they both gazed down into baby Declan's sleeping face. She pressed a kiss to his clean little brow and said a prayer for Kristina.

The Toyota bumped along the highway, causing Charlie, who lay burned and broken in the passenger seat of Victoria Phelan's car, to moan involuntarily. They were traversing along the top of the state, toward I-5, which would take them north into Washington State.

"Where should we go?" Victoria said, fretting. "Canada? They'll be looking for you."

He closed his eyes, shutting her out. It was lucky she was so easy to control. He'd lost some of his powers. A lot of them, actually. He thought back to how easily he'd manipulated her into hiding Kristina's gun and calling Savannah, how much she'd been panting for him, how she would have done anything to have him, and now she was questioning him . . . ? Well, it just plain hurt, almost worse than his injuries.

"We gotta go east, across Washington. Maybe to Idaho," he told her.

"Y'think?"

"Yes," he said through his teeth.

Victoria had hidden him the past few days, bringing salve and bandages and food to the motel room she'd rented after Hale St. Cloud had let her go. The timing was perfect. No one paid any attention to her after she handed over the gun she'd "found," the one he'd given her to hide. Luckily, she'd gotten the money from her broken contract, and they were set for a while. But he was going to have to get rid of her soon. She was a liability. Didn't they all become one eventually?

Killing her would help. Just thinking of how he'd felt while looking into that dying detective's eyes . . . It helped ease the pain of his burns and the deep fury he felt over losing Savannah Dunbar. What a clusterfuck. That homeless dude showing up.

He sent his mind back to the dying detective . . . the dark hole that opened up to the other side for just a nanosecond. His blood heated at the memory, and his spirits lifted a teeny bit. Good Time Charlie wasn't completely dead.

And then the voice in his head, scratching against his skull like fingernails on a blackboard: *I'm coming for you.*

"You're a *dead* woman!" he snarled aloud, his patience with the bitch completely shattered.

"What?" Victoria turned wide eyes his way.

"Watch the road," he snapped. "I didn't mean you."

And then the voice came back with a surprising message: *Not a woman, big brother. See you in the next life.*

Charlie thought that over long and hard. No wonder she could play the game so well! *She* was a *he.*

"What's so funny?" Victoria asked.

Charlie hadn't even realized he was chuckling until she spoke, ruining one of the only moments he'd had without pain since the fire had burned him. Now he shuddered violently. He'd never liked fires. He'd sensed from a very early age that it was the method that he would die by.

"Shut up," he said to Victoria. Then to the voice, which he could feel was still waiting, *In the next life, then* . . .

Ravinia walked along the road, south, toward California. Sometimes she accepted rides; sometimes she just walked because she wanted to. The weather was holding for the moment, though rain was in the forecast.

She was south of Tillamook, and it was growing dark. She wasn't far from a place to stay, but she would rather keep going. As if hearing her, a car pulled up beside her, but it was two men, who looked at her lasciviously. She looked into their hearts, but she didn't need to. She'd already determined she wouldn't catch a ride with them.

"Ah, c'mon, honey," the one in the passenger seat said as the car pulled to a complete stop and he stepped a foot out.

Ravinia fingered her knife, but she felt a wraith move up beside her, maybe even through her. On her sudden intake of breath, the man backed up, jumped in the car, slammed the door, and the vehicle tore away.

She looked from the car to her left. A wolf stood beside her, its yellow eyes watching the departing vehicle.

Ravinia felt her pulse slow down and her awareness heighten. She looked into the wolf's heart and sensed its fiercely protective nature.

"Friend or foe?" she asked in a whisper, but it just turned away and padded back to the woods. As Ravinia continued toward the orange neon sign of the motel about a mile ahead, she caught sight of the wolf's gray shadow flickering in and out between the trees, tracking her progress.